Sword's Call
Illustrated Edition
Book One
The King's Riders Series

SWORD'S CALL

ILLUSTRATED EDITION

BOOK ONE
OF
THE KING'S RIDERS

C.A. SZAREK

Paper Dragon Publishing

Other Books by C.A. Szarek

Highland Oath (Book One)

Highland Essence (Book Two)

Highland Skies (Book Three)

<u>Crossing Forces—Romantic Suspense</u>

Collision Force (Book One)

Cole in Her Stocking (A Crossing Forces Christmas)—*FREE read!*

Chance Collision (Book Two)

Calculated Collision (Book Three)

Collision Control (Book Four)

Weekend Collision (A Crossing Forces HEA Story)—*FREE read!*

Superior Collision (Book Five)

Incendiary Collision (Book Six)—*Coming soon!*

<u>The Giovanni—Romantic Suspense</u>

King of Hearts (Book One)—*Also in Audio*

Queen of Diamonds (Book Two)—*Coming Soon!*

THE NORTH

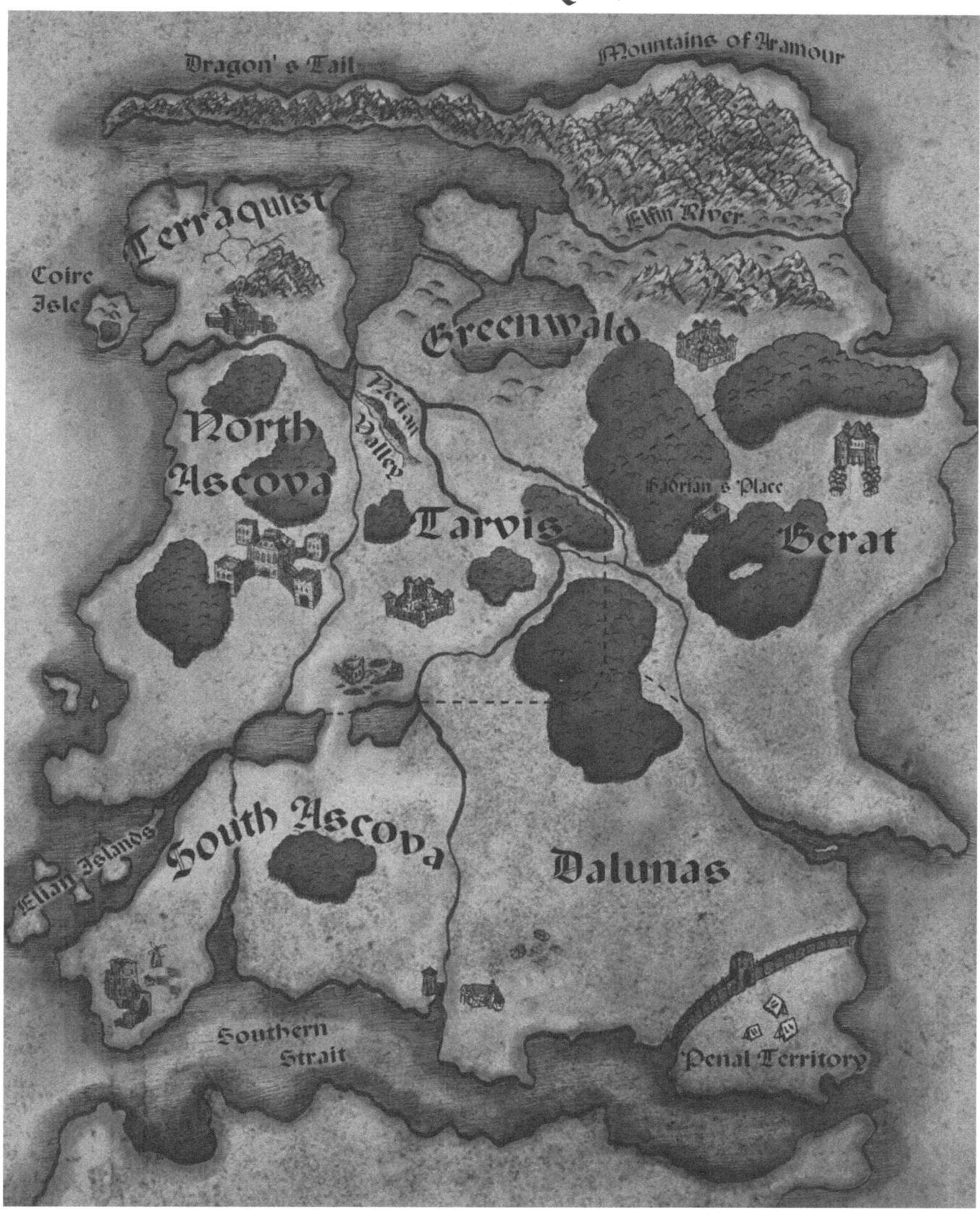

DEDICATION

For anyone who has ever believed in me. You have all made this possible.
And you know who you are.

Acknowledgements

This story always was, and always will be very close to my heart—for many reasons. I met Jorrin and Cera when I was a teen, so I've known them for a really long time, and I can't adequately express how exciting it is to share their story—and the world of the King's Riders with others.

There are so many people who have helped me along this journey of chasing my dream!

To my critique partners, Michelle, Clover, Jen, Gina: Y'all rock! Thanx for helping me make this book what it is! (AWESOME, of course!)

Susie and Kim, thanx for telling me I'm a good writer when I disagreed!

Amee, Jo-Anna ('eh Jo), Alanna, Kerry, Toni, Michelle—you girls are a so fantastic I can't even put it into words!

JoAnna (y'all Jo), Thanx for buying my book the day we met—LOL! A friend for life! *wink* Thanx for always being there for me!

To all my FB and Twitter friends who are staunch supporters, promo masters and just all-around made of awesome! Without you, I couldn't do this!

Chapter One

HEART POUNDING AND fists clenched, Cera sat in the *Dragon's Lair's* darkest corner. By choice, the candle on the table was unlit. The bowl of stew half eaten, food the last thing on her mind.

The door to the tavern swung open. Her white wolf growled low and deep beside her.

Cera glanced up, squinting in the sudden flood of sunlight. As the thick panel slammed shut and her eyes adjusted to the renewed murkiness, she took in the newest arrival.

Then she focused on Trikser. She couldn't have him going for anyone's throat. "Shhh, Trik, it's all right." She ran a hand through his fur, smoothing his hackles along the length of his spine.

The big wolf looked up and licked her hand.

One corner of her mouth lifted and she bit back a sigh.

The only reason the owner even let him in was because no one else was allowed to enter the *Dragon's Lair* if she was inside without him.

No one according to Trikser, that was. He'd almost taken the hand off the last guy who'd tried.

"What'll ya have?" Marshek barked, revealing his instant dislike of the newcomer.

She locked eyes on the bartender. Then she took a closer look at the man sitting in front of him.

His pointed ears betrayed his heritage, but his height suggested he was not of pure blood.

Marshek was known to be tolerant of elves, but hated half-breeds.

Cera could imagine what the grumpy, middle-aged tavern owner was thinking, and it wasn't friendly. She stood, Trikser also immediately rising, awaiting her move.

The white wolf was her bondmate, and had been since he was young.

Relax, she thought-sent.

Trik sat, but his body was tight, tense. He didn't otherwise respond to her mental order.

She moved to the bar, her wolf following. He moved in a slight crawl, slinking close to the floor. His belly probably touched the filthy wood planks.

Cera made a face, but forced a breath.

Detached control. Show them you don't care about anything.

She was just in time to hear the half-elfin man's order when she slid onto the stool next to him. His voice was clear and deep.

Marshek filled a mug with ale and started to put the jug in its place on the shelf.

"Wait, Mar," she said with a wave of her hand, "I'll have some of that, too."

With a curt nod, the older man poured her some, too. She brought it to her lips, glancing at the stranger. His coal black hair brushed the collar of his hooded gray cape, giving him a rather unkempt look, but rugged rather than messy.

Cera couldn't see the hue of his eyes from her seat, but his high cheekbones made his profile appealing, his sleek tapered ears adding to the attraction. His powerful jawline was clean shaven, an oddity in these parts. He was young, likely not much older than her, and had the stunning beauty of the elves. She could tell he was aware of her perusal.

His chest heaved, and he finally looked her way.

Blue.

His eyes were a deep, sapphire blue.

Her heart missed a beat, but she ignored it.

The man said nothing—not that she'd expected him to.

She set her stein down and swallowed against the liquor burning its way along her throat to her belly. Warmth exploded and her tongue got heavy. Cera bit back a grimace. How could anyone drink the stuff?

"Rotten, dirty half-breeds," Marshek mumbled under his breath, shoving a wet rag along the top of the weathered bar, but he wasn't carefully cleaning it.

The half-elf slammed his mug down, his brows tight and jaw clenched.

Some of the other rustics in the bar shared the bartender's sentiment, and before she could blink, a man named Herik had seized the stranger by the shoulders.

The half-elf cursed and tried unsuccessfully to slip out of the bigger man's grip, his hand missing the grab for the hilt of his sword.

"For the Blessed Spirit's sake," she muttered, scrambling to her feet. She drew the dagger from her belt pouch, but kept it hidden under her cloak.

There was going to be trouble.

She loathed trouble.

The problem was, lately it seemed to follow her.

Cera shouldn't get involved; should let the man handle the situation on his own, but somehow she couldn't hold her tongue. She'd do what she could, no matter how little that might be.

She was familiar with the rough men in the tavern. They all lived locally in the slums—Lower Greenwald. The mixed-blooded man's life would truly be in peril if she didn't step in.

Herik pulled him off the stool and held him from behind.

Another man readied himself to inflict violence.

He struggled against the hold, but they'd pulled his arms behind his back, pinning him.

Helpless. Dammit.

"C'mon, Gordo, this one's not worth it," she said to the tall, but portly dirty blond man—the ringleader of the rustics. *Dirty* was more than the color of his hair.

She was grateful that Trikser's way of slinking to the bar had raised little notice. They still didn't seem to see him, even though she could sense him bristling at her side. Cera sent him a mental command to wait, but he'd react to real trouble without her instructions.

"I bet his point-ears he is," Gordo growled, and many of the others nodded agreement. "They would look good above my fireplace."

"I don't think they would, Gordo." She pulled her dagger into view. Darting forward, she pressed the tip into the throat of the man that had seized the stranger.

"This is none of your concern." The bartender glared.

"It is if you want Herik, here, to live," Cera bit back. She sank the tip of her dagger further into the flesh of the man's throat.

Herik sucked in a sharp gulp of air. The scent of his foul breath roiled what little of the stew there was in her stomach.

No wonder the half-elf looked a bit green; the apple of his throat bobbed as if he'd swallowed several times. He probably needed to retch.

He should aim for Herik's filthy boots.

Gordo wrenched her arm to her back, twisting her wrist.

White hot pain jolted up her arm. Cera winced and her dagger clattered to the floor.

A snarl erupted as Trikser leapt up in a lightning flash of white, landing on the man's arm. Gordo screamed and dropped to the floor of the tavern. His hand and forearm hung from an odd angle, even as he tried to cradle it against him.

Blood spurted, spraying Trikser's white coat.

Cera scowled and snatched her fallen weapon, assuming a more defensive stance. She gritted her teeth. She felt the weight of the half-elf's gaze, but she had to stop her bond before he killed Gordo. "Trikser, no! Just hold him there," she commanded.

The wolf obeyed, holding Gordo to the ground, teeth bared and lightly covering the man's throat.

The rustic swallowed continually, face as white a sheet, and sweat dotting his wide forehead.

"Anyone else?" She sheathed her dagger and drew her sword. Her grip tightened as it began to glow, its pale aura tangible as the weapon's magic spread across the tavern, seeking, searching.

Her sword had been forged in magic and as the glow intensified, it drew on her own and surrounded Cera with its brightening radiance.

The half-elf blinked several times, his handsome face contorted. He shifted his feet, tugging against Herik's hold, as if that was all the resistance he could offer.

Her stomach dipped.

Could he feel the sword's magic? Did he possess any himself?

Elves, by nature, were born with magic, and even though he appeared to be half-human, he might have some. If he did, no matter the nature of it, he'd know the sword was magic, and *that* was the last thing she needed.

She brandished her weapon at each of the men, no one made a move.

The brutes in the bar, Marshek included, stood shaking and wide-eyed, sweat pouring down their rough-hewn faces. Her sword didn't find much magic in the tavern, but it was succeeding in leaving great fear in the wake of its probing.

Silence reigned until the half-elf stomped on Herik's foot. The man scrambled to maintain his hold, but the half-elf spun and punched him in the jaw, jumping over as he fell to the floor. He shook his hand as if his knuckles smarted and cursed, but it wasn't a word she understood.

He lunged for Cera, grabbing her hand and tugging.

She jolted, but didn't pull away as he made a dash to the door, dragging her along.

Why was he helping her get away?

No, don't question it.

Cera shoved her still-glowing sword beneath her cloak and called for her bondmate. Together they left the dark tavern.

Leaping up, she landed hard in Ash's saddle, her thighs smarting. Her black stallion shifted to absorb her weight, and let out a whinnying protest she'd apologize for later.

The half-elf stared, standing next to a dappled horse tied to the public posts. He reached for his horse's reins, but wasn't in a hurry.

"Are you coming?" She frowned. "It won't take them long to recover and come after us."

Still, he made no move.

"C'mon, you idiot."

The dark man dismounted, his movements tense and jerky. The bitch had been in Greenwald for a fortnight and his shades—mages in his service—hadn't sensed her until she'd been involved in a scuffle in a rundown tavern.

He stomped in the dirt, emitting a low growl. His stallion shifted and hoofed the dirt, but Varthan ignored him.

How could the she-dog have still been in town?

She'd been hiding out in the open, and *no one* had seen her.

Now he had to enter a disreputable establishment to receive a report from an overpaid, inadequate moron.

The *Dragon's Lair* was dim, the air rank. He ignored the turn of his stomach as the heavy odor of sweaty bodies hit his nose. There weren't many inside, as it was not quite midday, but they'd come and the place would stink even more.

He weaved his way to the table in the darkest corner.

"Lord Varthan." The imbecile bowed.

Varthan sneered and took a seat. "What progress have you made?" he snarled, waving the bar wench away.

"None, my lord. She is gone."

He threw his leather riding gloves on the table. "And *why* is this?"

"All we know is she left in a hurry, with an elf half-breed. My men pursued as soon as they realized it was her. Her beast ripped my man's arm off." Svender's words were hurried, the apple of his throat jumping.

Varthan drew a dagger. His companion's eyes widened, giving him some silent satisfaction. "I don't care about that. I need the bitch, and I need her now."

Svender's shoulders shook as he sputtered a response.

He drove the dagger into the man's jugular, shredding Svender's throat. Backed up as the body collapsed onto the table, head landing with a *thud* on the top.

Grabbing a dirty scrap of linen that posed as a napkin, Varthan wiped the blood off his jeweled dirk. "I'm sick of excuses."

Some of Svender's low class filthy blood marred his favorite riding gloves. He cursed and threw them to the planked floor, kicking the pair away.

Useless.

Why was he in this position? He stared at Svender's body. He should feel something other than numbness, but he did not.

The fault of the large blond man's death did not lie with Varthan, despite the fact that his dagger had taken the man's life.

King Nathal had betrayed him. And that bastard Falor Ryhan. If the Duke of Greenwald would've kept his mouth shut, Varthan would be in his own castle on his own lands.

Well, Falor couldn't speak against him again, could he?

Oh, how he wished the man would've begged for his life. He hadn't even given Varthan that satisfaction. Too bad he'd died so quickly. And that sweet daughter of his . . . She'd been as lovely as her mother, both with tresses of red flame. He'd had them both naked beneath him before he'd ended their lives.

The mother had begged him to spare the daughter. In return, of course, she'd received the gift of seeing her daughter perish before her eyes. It was really a shame he'd not kept the little virgin around. He could've taught her how to please a man, but it'd been good anyway. He liked it when they fought, and she'd been a screamer. Memories danced into his head, causing a slow smile.

Varthan met the bartender's beady eyes, but the older man looked away, busying himself at his scarred counter. There were no Knights of Greenwald, no Provost or his Marshals alive to report the *murder* to; although he was in the slums, so a killing at a tavern was often left for the barkeep to tidy up.

At any rate, not my concern.

He didn't linger, meeting two of his shades at the tavern door.

"My lord?" Dagonet queried.

"Gather the best," he barked.

The younger one, Lucan, blanched.

"Yes, milord." Dagonet inclined his head.

"Meet me at the ruins in an hour."

"My lord?"

Varthan scowled. *How dare he question me?*

"Just *do* it. I am going after her myself."

The boy gave a curt nod, and both rushed off.

He'd take the elite of his shades, and perhaps when they caught the girl and her companion, they'd relieve the population of the half-breed.

Varthan should've listened to the old adage about getting things done right by doing them oneself. Perhaps if he had, he wouldn't have lost the Ryhan magic sword, and the little bitch would be in the dungeons of her own castle right now.

Then he'd be using the weapon to raise his army and take over the king's throne.

Chapter Two

"WHERE ARE WE going?" Jorrin asked when they were farther south—a safe enough distance from Greenwald Main to slow their exhausting pace.

His companion's eyes went wide and her lips parted.

Surprised.

His magic tingled.

"We?" Her mouth tightened, her brow furrowed.

For the first time he took her in; she'd lowered the hood of her gray cloak. Dark auburn hair, curly and past her shoulders, big gray eyes, high cheekbones, and full lips—all features that added to her beauty. She was slender and tall, and he enjoyed her show of temper.

His heart stuttered, but he didn't focus on it. This woman of his father's race was lovely. Different from the graceful elfin maidens he was used to, but not in a negative way.

"I'm going to Castle Lenore, in Tarvis. I don't know where you're going," she said.

"With you."

She smirked. "I don't think so."

"Well, I do. Or have you forgotten about the men we had to outrun? Did you help me for nothing? It pains me to admit it, but you did save me—"

"I don't care that you're grateful. I already have a partner." She gestured to the white wolf and glanced away from him. "Besides, I only saved you because—" When she turned back to him, she faltered, guarded.

His magic surged. The girl was hiding something. She must have powerful mind shields his empathic magic couldn't penetrate without a deep probe. He got nothing else from her. "Why'd you help me then? I could've handled it."

She laughed out loud. "Yeah. Sure. You were doing so well. Sorry to have interfered. Good day." She kicked her horse after inclining her head. The stallion cantered away, the wolf running close behind.

His dappled mare, Grayna, jerked her head in surprise and Jorrin cursed. "Hey. Wait!"

The girl's fear flickered through a faltering mask of confidence.

Why?

And how much of it had to do with that magic sword?

She'd probably stolen it.

No. Jorrin shook his head. She wasn't a thief. Something told him she was highborn and trying hard to hide it.

He dug his heels into Grayna's flanks, and his mare bolted forward. Her muscles rippled under his thighs and he leaned into her, gripping the reins tighter.

When they caught up, the girl yanked her horse to a stop and whirled on him, dagger half drawn.

His mare neighed in protest as he pulled her up short.

Jorrin stared as his would-be companion's chest quaked as if she couldn't catch her breath.

With a sigh, she sheathed her weapon. "Oh, it's only you." She squared her shoulders, but her voice trembled. "Don't you know when you're not wanted? Go away."

"I'm not going anywhere." He crossed his arms.

"Well then, stay here. Just don't follow me. Blessed Spirit, can't you take a hint?" She cast her eyes upward.

The white wolf growled, and Jorrin shifted in his saddle, swallowing a gulp at the bared fangs.

"Trik, it's all right." She glanced at the wolf. The beast loosened its stance, but Jorrin didn't relax. "We just have to convince our *friend* to find another road."

His powers tingled. They were bonded; he felt the magic between them as a tethered rope. *Interesting.* Since when did a highborn *female* need an animal bond? It was permanent, not a casual thing. The protection of a devoted beast was handy, but if one party perished, the other would soon follow. The risk wasn't worth it. "Last time I checked, the roads were free to travel. That's one thing the lord has yet to tax."

"They are. Just not with me. Once again, you are *not* welcome." She looked him in the eye, her steel gaze haughty.

She's definitely noble.

Jorrin scowled. "Listen, *you* are the one who sat next to me. *You* are the one who saved my hide . . . and when I want to repay you, you won't let me."

"That's right. Now get lost, I have a castle to get to, and it'll be a better journey without you."

"Why? What are you afraid of?"

Her eyes widened and Jorrin couldn't look away.

She shook her head, opening her mouth as if it would help force the words out. Her hands appeared to tighten on her reins. "Nothing. You just don't need to be involved." She turned away and kneed her horse.

Once again, the magic he sent her way was shut down, rolling between them. Could she see or sense it? Her body and expression gave no indication.

The magic sword wasn't visible, but it was there, its powers throbbing.

Jorrin had to look away.

Was the sword what'd rejected the magic feels he'd put out?

He tried to probe with his senses to no avail. Forced a breath and turned back to the beautiful girl. "What if I am going to Tarvis, too?"

She relented with a groan. "Then I suppose this is the road to take."

He smiled and their eyes locked.

The girl shifted in her saddle, her cheeks crimson.

His smile slid into a grin, but he said nothing; his heart gave an odd *thud* like earlier. Why the blush? And why did it please him so much?

"Just stay out of my way," she muttered and kicked her horse.

Jorrin followed silently, glancing at her profile when their horses where abreast, their pace comfortable. Besides the fact she was obviously running from something, he knew nothing about this girl, not even her name. Instinct told him she wouldn't appreciate him pushing her.

Slipping into the memory of the sword back in the tavern, he felt his magical senses prickle again. He'd had to concentrate very hard to ignore the magic then, and focus on the men who'd wanted him dead.

His body had heated all over with the efforts to overlook it. His limbs had actually ached and shaken. He'd been frozen in place.

What broke its hold?

The sword and its glowing aura—the girl had been surrounded by it, too—had sensed his magic, even called to it. He hadn't sensed menace from the weapon, more a probing for magic which stopped when it found his.

What does that mean?

For what seemed the thousandth time, he wished he'd studied harder to hone his magical abilities.

And the girl . . . what magic did she have?

Humans were not known to naturally possess magic as commonly as elves were, but some were more prone to it than others. Some human mages matched elfin ones.

She could thought-send—he'd sensed it when she'd spoken to the wolf in the tavern.

It wasn't often someone could unconsciously shut out his empathic powers. What was this girl about?

Their eyes met and held.

"What?" Curiosity was etched in her expression.

"I don't even know your name."

Silence descended once more, but then she sighed. "Maybe that's for the better."

He shook his head. "I don't think so. Maybe it'll be easier if I go first?" When he saw her slight nod, so slight it was almost imperceptible, he continued, "Jorrin Aldern, of Aramour." He inclined his head, extended his hand, and gave a small bow from the saddle. "And my loyal steed is Grayna."

The girl laughed. The sound was even more glorious than her smile.

Jorrin grinned.

"Ceralda Ryhan, *formerly* of Greenwald." She bowed the same way he had, and then froze in her saddle, her eyes as wide as saucers. "But all my friends call me Cera." Her added words were rushed, shaky.

He cocked his head to the side, trying to read her again. Why the sudden shift in her mood? His magic told him nothing, but her smile was forced and she seemed ready to bolt.

"My stallion is Ash, and my bond, Trikser." She finished evenly, and he admired her ability to compose herself.

His curiosity about her slid into obsession. Narrowing his eyes, he stared. "So, he is bonded to you?"

"Yes, since he was a cub."

"Dragons bond to elves or even humans. They say they're fated to their bondmates. They're always exactly the same age, down to the day, and have to find each other. If the dragon doesn't find their bondmate, they can die, or so I've heard."

"Dragons?" she asked, head cocked to one side.

"Aye. There are many in the mountains of Aramour."

"I've never seen a dragon."

"I've only seen them from afar, but they are majestic nonetheless."

"I can imagine." Cera smiled, and he ignored how his stomach jumped. "Just what did you do in Aramour?"

"I grew up. I left to look for my father . . . he disappeared when I was wee, but in the last few turns, I have been . . . an occasional mercenary of sorts . . . I suppose."

"Your father disappeared? I'm sorry."

Why did she have to zero in on that?

He made a dismissive gesture with his hand. "I'll find him." His heart sped, unwanted emotion hitting him in a wave. Jorrin shut down his magic and straightened.

"A mercenary?" Her expression was thoughtful.

He nodded. Mercenary was a loose accuracy, really. He'd taken a few jobs where he'd been one of several guards to escort haughty highborn ladies to market in the Provinces he'd visited, but he'd still been a hired sword, and he knew how to use it.

However, *the Dragon's Lair* incident certainly didn't speak highly of his prowess. Those damned morons had taken him completely by surprise, and Jorrin's sword had stayed sheathed under his cloak.

A *female* saved him.

How embarrassing was that?

"And I can track, so I've picked up some gold doing that. What about you?"

She shook her head. "I'm just a girl."

For the first time, his magic gained emotion from her. Sadness and regret rolled off her in waves. He wanted to reach for her, comfort her in some way, but instinct kept his hands on his reins, to himself.

Cera said nothing more, and he didn't press.

Jorrin would get her to open up to him in time.

She cleared her throat. "There's a small town about twenty miles from here. We can get a bite to eat, and perhaps find an inn."

And then what? He left unsaid, but the thought was palpable between them.

Dragon's Tail
Mountains of Aramour
Elfin River
Terraquist
Greenwald
North Ascova
Netian Valley
Hadrian's Place
Tarvis
Berat
South Ascova
Dalunas
Southern Strait
Penal Territory

Varthan growled, slamming his fist on the table. The young shade jumped, but even that didn't give him any satisfaction. Lucan could tell him nothing he didn't already know. It'd been a waste of time to leave Greenwald without a more definitive plan.

He'd been content in Castle Ryhan for the last two months, since he'd seized it with his best shades and killed the Ryhans. He'd been running the Province as he saw fit.

It was a dump really; the castle much smaller than his own former lavish home on lands in Terraquist—stolen by the damned king when he'd been stripped of his title of archduke.

The only comfort had been killing every last wretch that was loyal to the *former* Duke of Greenwald.

Oh, and bedding every maid he'd left alive. His shades had enjoyed themselves as well.

But no one would tell him where the duke's eldest daughter was.

No matter what forms of persuasion he'd used—fist, weapon, or magic—not one of the blasted servants would confess her location.

On the other hand, it was a relief to discover she lived, because he'd first thought he'd killed all the Ryhans.

Varthan needed the little bitch, because the day he'd killed Falor Ryhan, Lucan had warned him against touching Ryhan's sword—*his* sword—because of a deadly spell.

Before he'd lost the damned thing because of that steward. Though the man had paid with his life, his death gave him no satisfaction.

Pity, really.

Killing something—someone—usually made him feel better.

His youngest and most powerful shade, was certain only a true Ryhan could touch the weapon without coming to harm.

The eldest daughter would help him break the spell.

Then Varthan would have his revenge on King Nathal. He'd look into the king's crystal blue eyes as he ran him through with Falor's magic sword.

I can't wait.

They'd already lost almost two full days because of the rain.

"We'll go to Tarvis," he said more to himself than to Lucan or the other surrounding shades. "The bitch has family there, and we'll reach them before she does."

His companions nodded, and the oldest, Athas, went to settle the bill. The other two, Markus and Dagonet, left the inn to ready the horses.

At least they could sense his mood and didn't question him.

All his shades had different gifts, which two elf wizards longtime in his employ honed and grew in his secret compound, until they were ready to use their magic at his behest.

Most of the boys had come to him as children. He'd clothed them, raised them and provided for them. They were all indebted to him.

Varthan was their god.

Though the name fit, he hadn't chosen to call the boy-mages *shades*. They'd earned the moniker from the king's knights for all their escapes from the king's *justice*. Not even one of his shades was in the penal territory in Dalunas, the Southeastern-most Province of the continent.

Moving their compound was an irritant he'd had to endure at least once a turn for the last several. Expensive, but they'd yet to be discovered.

Before the king's betrayal, they hadn't been tied to *him*, either.

He scowled at Lucan, who stood at his side shaking. Varthan resisted the urge to strike the boy, proud of his self-control. "Let's go."

The boy nodded and fell into step after him as he rose from the table and headed out of the putrid, shabby inn.

He made a face. Castle Lenore had better have more comfortable beds than the one he'd slept in the previous night. A backache always put him in a sour mood.

They left the small village late, in the pouring rain. Cera covered her head with the hood of her cloak. Jorrin should have enough sense to do the same. She cursed as the rain pelted down on them.

So much for a warm bed in a cozy inn.

Would they get into a fight in every tavern they entered?

Jorrin had drawn his sword, prepared to fight, but she'd grabbed his hand and urged him to run, as they had from Marshek's tavern. Taking the time for a real fight wasn't worth the risk. Someone had seen her magic sword again. She could've hugged the half-elf for not asking questions.

Should she be concerned or relieved that he'd been a mercenary?

If he was skilled with his sword it could be handy, but she should've never let him accompany her. Hired swords usually weren't the most reputable of people, either.

She stared at him for a moment, dismissing any worries. Cera was in no danger from Jorrin. Not physically, anyway. Getting lost in his sapphire eyes was another matter entirely. Her heart missed a beat.

Why the *hell* had she told him where she was headed? For that matter, why had she told him her real last name on the road the day they'd met?

Thank the Blessed Spirit he'd not recognized it.

She cursed. It was too dangerous to involve anyone else, even a handsome stranger. If anything, this most recent bar scuffle proved that.

He'd tried to blend in; he'd pulled up the hood of his cape. Jorrin had been antagonized into action. The men who'd pushed them had to be Varthan's hired thugs. Maybe their descriptions were already out, and the thugs had been trying to confirm their identities.

If Cera kept drawing the sword, the bastard would have an easily laid trail to find them. No telling how far his *eyes* could see.

She glanced over her shoulder. No one was following them yet, but they hadn't much time. She looked for Trikser and slumped with relief when she spotted him. Matted wet fur could be dried, but her bondmate couldn't be replaced.

Nor would she survive if she lost him—literally. The magic that bonded them was permanent, and both their lives depended on each other. In turn, if she died, so would her wolf.

The village was the fourth they'd visited since Cera had saved Jorrin's hide in Lower Greenwald. They were in Berat now, but wouldn't be able to ride all night.

With the mounting rain, mud was everywhere, splattered a foot high on the stone buildings. Large puddles widened the unpaved road and made for an even rougher ride.

The harder they rode, the more they risked a slip or fall injury. She wasn't willing to chance Ash breaking a leg, and he no doubt would feel the same about his dappled horse.

There look to be a few caves over there. We should check them out. It took her a moment to discern Jorrin's voice was in her head, not in her ears.

It was the first time he'd thought-sent to her. How did he know she had the ability?

They hadn't taken a moment to discuss magic, but he obviously had some. Not all humans could send and receive thoughts, so he must've sensed her speaking mentally to Trik.

Great. She had no desire for a little magic talk. Had to protect the sword at all costs—even her life. She needed to get to Uncle Everett and Aunt Em, and get word to the king.

Let's go for it, Cera responded with a thought-send, pushing away the dread closing in on her.

They rode into the cave's wide mouth, its size admitting their horses with ease.

She shivered against the dank air, but it would work for the night. At least the ground looked dry. No place to tie the horses, but they were far enough inside; that worry wasn't necessary. Ash wouldn't wander far anyway.

They could start a fire, get warm and dry. Even bed down around it.

She spotted a grouping of stones that'd be adequate for a fire ring, and chose a spot where she'd curl up with Trik. She heard Jorrin's boots hit the dirt.

He faced away from her, staring silently into the darkness behind them. He must be probing magically.

Smart. The last thing they needed was to disturb some wild animal.

Cera shot a glance at Trik. Her wolf was close, not reacting to anything, so they were probably all right, but Jorrin's caution couldn't hurt.

Leaving him to it, she dismounted, and took off her wet cloak. She loosened the straps around the stallion's middle, then yanked the saddle off, dropping it with a thud.

She wiped him down, getting Ash as dry as she could before covering him with a warm blanket from her pack. She grabbed her rolled sleeping furs, gathering them up in her arms and fighting a shiver.

Jorrin said nothing, and when Cera glanced in his direction, he was similarly tending Grayna.

"You can thought-send." Why the hell had she opened with that? Didn't she want to avoid magic?

With another quake, she pulled her furs close around her shoulders.

Trikser shook water off his coat and lay down against her. His warmth was welcome, but he was still wet, his fur soaking her already damp breeches.

Her teeth chattered, and she buried her hands in his fur.

He wiggled closer and licked her arm.

"So can you." One dark eyebrow raised, Jorrin followed her lead with his own furs.

"I learned to thought-send before I bonded. I have some magic, but it's limited."

Why was she being so honest? What was it about this man?

She frowned.

"I have magic, too. It's not limited. I suppose training comes with the heritage." He gestured to his tapered ears. "Magic comes in handy at times. Like this."

Sparks ignited from the damp air as Jorrin seemed to focus on a piece of wood lying between them.

Cera smiled in thanks at the fire's birth.

He went for something that looked like kindling from his pack and threw it into the flames. The blaze flared and briefly glowed blue.

Was that stuff magic, too? Would it make the fire last longer?

He said nothing as he settled across from her, the warmth between them.

Trikser wiggled closer to her and the fire, resting his large head on her lap. She scratched between his ears, but Cera couldn't tear her eyes away from Jorrin.

Which of his parents is elfin?

She'd seen half-breeds before, even met a few, but not one that favored the beautiful graceful elves so much. His long tapered ears were elegant, making her want to run her fingers along them.

Where is that coming from?

Cera shook herself, but continued to watch him.

Jorrin had a calming effect on her. She liked how the movement of the fire reflected over the smooth planes of his handsome face, the pleasant glow making him even more striking. Her eyes drifted to his mouth. Full lips in repose.

What would it be like to kiss him?

She cursed herself as her heart raced, and she forced her gaze away.

He didn't seem to notice.

She tried to convince herself it was a relief.

"Maybe we should get some sleep." Cera yawned.

He nodded. "I guess we're safe in here, but I'll stay up for a bit, take the first watch."

Thunder boomed and Ash neighed. Grayna echoed the stallion's nervousness and pawed the dirt.

After gently pushing her bondmate off her lap, she rose and went to her mount, running her hand down his muzzle and whispering. She made sure both horses were as secured as they could be and repeated her reassurance to Jorrin's dappled mare.

"Thanks." He smiled, inclining his head. "Good night." He snuggled his furs around his shoulders like she had, and scooted to lean against the cave wall. "We'll switch in a few hours. Get some sleep. I promise I will keep you safe."

Cera hesitated.

Should she let him assume such a responsibility while she slept?

She didn't even know him.

Jorrin tagging after her for a few days didn't count, but instinct told her he wouldn't hurt her. He'd never even tried to touch her.

Besides, Trik was here, too. Her wolf wouldn't let any harm come to her.

Two protectors?

Another huge yawn made the decision for her.

"Good night," she said softly.

Trikser yawned, too.

She patted his head and gathered her furs closer with a shudder as she lay down. Her bond-mate licked her face and cuddled against her back. Cera smiled and tucked her sword into her. She spared another glance at Jorrin, but he wasn't looking in her direction.

'I promise I will keep you safe,' echoed in her mind.

A vow, but why?

She chided herself for letting his sincerity get to her.

Jorrin Aldern, the half-elfin man from Aramour, was dangerous.

Cera trembled and blamed it on the chill in the cave.

Chapter Three

A VERY PANTED AS he looked over his shoulder. No one followed him, right?

He shook his head. Paranoia could *not* take him over, but knowing he'd gotten away cleanly didn't comfort him.

Mother . . . Father . . . No. Stop it. They'll be fine.

Pressing his knees into Valor's sides, he felt the white gelding bolt forward and leaned into him, gripping the reins until his knuckles whitened.

He had to find Cera.

His mother's urgent words echoed in his mind as a list of instructions he didn't have a choice but to follow.

It meant survival.

His cousin's family had already been wiped out.

Avery shivered, and it had little to do with the cold rain pelting down. A spell *surrounded* him, keeping his cape, horse and few belongings artificially dry and warm.

If only his task was as simple.

He'd ride all day and night if he had to.

Cera would be along the forested road, according *to his* mother's vision, but he had yet to discern any clue to her location. Hopefully, she was warm and dry.

Searching as best he could, given Valor's speed, Avery sent out magical feels, probing for her, but sensed nothing.

Was she cloaked in some kind of spell?

Probably not, because Varthan's shades could find her more easily, the more magic surrounding her, and his cousin was smart. She'd know that.

His heart tripped. Cera *had* to be all right. She was one of the strongest people he knew. Avery clenched his jaw. *Where* the hell was his cousin?

"I'm sorry about Ash," Cera told Jorrin as they sat in front of a small, cozy fire. Their horses were tied nearby, both covered with warm blankets. "I mean, I didn't remember your horse was a mare, or I would have reined him in . . ."

Earlier that day, his companion's stallion had gotten a bit too close to Grayna for her comfort and she'd tossed him on his arse in a mud puddle. Then the traitor had taken off down the road, leaving him on the ground without even a backward glance. Jorrin's new breeches now sported a tear in the soft leather, and his rump was sore.

Cera and Ash had helped him get Grayna back. Just one more way that she'd had to save him, after she'd gotten over her fit of giggles, of course.

Would she constantly be saving him? He didn't want her to think he wasn't a man. "It's all right." Jorrin made a dismissive gesture.

She tucked a long strand of her dark auburn hair behind her ear, and he tried not to stare. As aggravating as she could be, she was beautiful.

He took a bite of the dried meat she'd shared from her belt pouch. They'd have to hunt soon. He'd gotten a rabbit the day before, but that meat was gone.

At least they'd been able to wash up and fill their water skins from a clean stream.

Cera leaned on her wolf and shared meat with the beast as she ate.

How could anyone get close to her and keep his hands?

Jorrin had contemplated kissing her more than a few times, but it had to be an impossible feat. He chuckled. At least her bondmate hadn't attacked him . . . yet.

"What's so funny?" She sipped from her leather canteen.

"Nothing . . ."

She quirked an eyebrow. "Well, I am glad you amuse yourself, oh great one."

He held in a smile, because it'd anger her all the more. He'd learned quickly that she liked things to go her way, and was a great deal more than just *put out* if they didn't.

They'd been on the road for a sevenday, and though she hadn't said anything to the effect, it was apparent they were taking a long route to Tarvis, heading west through the Province of Berat, instead of the road due south, which was a straight shot.

With their pace, it'd be a few more days until they were half-way.

"You're right," Cera said.

Jorrin hadn't built walls in his mind, and now that they'd spent so much time together, they were becoming attuned to each other. As a result, she could sometimes pick up his thoughts, though because her magic was not empathic in nature, it was rare. However, it proved they had an emotional connection.

"Only when you think loudly," she added, smiling as he constructed his walls. "Sorry." She grimaced. "I hate when it happens to me."

"No problem," he said. Staring into her gray eyes, he asked, "Can I ask why we're making this journey harder than it has to be?"

"Sure, you can *ask*."

That meant she wasn't going to tell him anything more than she deemed necessary.

"I just want to stay out of trouble, is all," Cera said.

His instincts flared. *There's more to it than that.*

Cocking his head to the side, he chose his words carefully, "Surely, with a wolf bondmate, magical abilities, and a magic sword, you'd have no need to worry."

The avoidance of magic had been a chasm between them all sevenday.

Cera's eyes widened. "I don't know much about it."

She was lying to him; Jorrin didn't need magic to know that. Their eyes locked, and her cheeks flushed pink.

Should I push her? No. For now he'd let it drop.

Without breaking their eye contact, he nodded.

She swallowed. "There's another small town we should reach by tomorrow. This is the last night we'll have to sleep outside, provided a respectable inn is available. I suggest you wear your hood." She gestured toward his ears, taking a bite of meat and gathering her furs over her shoulders.

Jorrin ignored her implications, and concentrated to make the fire rise and heat. He met her eyes when he was done and shrugged, flashing a half-smile.

Cera said nothing, but her eyes bored into him.

He shot to his feet, chiding himself for being hyperaware of the way she was looking at him. "I'll be right back." He needed to relieve himself before they sought sleep, and he'd already told her she could sleep first. Besides, he needed a distraction.

She nodded, and he disappeared into the nearby woods.

Jorrin heard Cera holler, and his heart dropped to his stomach. He fastened his belt with shaky fingers and unsheathed his sword before jogging back to their small camp. He cursed himself for leaving her alone, even if it was only for a few moments, but Trikser was there, her bondmate would protect her. He told himself to breathe.

She's fine. She has to be.

He burst into the clearing just as she yelled again, and it took him a moment to discern that she was neither in pain, nor in trouble.

Cera was embracing a caped figure.

Who the hell is that? Holding Cera?

Jealousy flared, but he scolded himself and relaxed the hold on his sword as he made his way to the two humans.

The white wolf was wagging his tail, and Jorrin's step faltered. He lowered his sword, frowning.

"Avery, what are you doing here?" Cera's voice was breathless.

Apparently *Avery* was quite exhausted; he didn't answer. He leaned on the white gelding he'd ridden in on, then keeled over.

Jorrin shoved his sword in its scabbard just in time to catch the other man under the arms as he passed out.

He didn't miss the whisper, "Thank the Blessed Spirit I found you."

Cera thanked him and chewed at her bottom lip. She remained frozen and very pale, fists clenched at her shapely sides.

He got nothing but confusion and worry from her through his magic, and her sword was nowhere in sight.

After laying the tall lanky stranger down on his own furs, Jorrin covered him and turned back to her. "Who is he?"

She'd followed him back to the fire, looking lost. When her knees buckled and she landed hard on her bedding, he rushed to sit beside her and took her hand.

Cera didn't pull away.

"My cousin . . . Avery . . . Avery Lenore."

Her cousin's name jolted him. "Lenore? As in *Castle* Lenore?"

She nodded, her eyes finally focusing on his face.

"You want to tell me what you are running from?" he whispered.

She gave another slight nod and he bit back a gasp.

He couldn't look away.

Then her expression hardened.

She shut him out *again*.

"It's a long story . . ." Cera glanced away.

Jorrin caressed her chin, slowly guiding her face back to his, and making her meet his eyes. "I have all night." He couldn't let her win this round. Needed to show her he was there for her.

Whatever she was hiding, seeing her cousin had shaken her and made her secret too much to bear. He tried to catch her thoughts, but her mind was still closed. He could sense nothing more than vague feelings, and a strong underlying defiance. Couldn't tell if the defiance was meant for him alone, but it was foremost in her mind.

His brow heated and dampened from magical effort, so he took a breath and released his concentration.

Cera's beautiful gray eyes were still locked onto his.

Jorrin ran two fingers from her temple to her cheek, allowing himself to forget their conversation and give in to his desire to kiss her. Leaning down, he brushed her lips with his. The touch was sweet and left him wanting more. He pulled her closer, cradling her head, and covered her mouth.

Cera's lips moved tentatively against his, so he pushed harder, making her open for him and deepening the kiss. Her sweet essence washed over him as their tongues dueled, and she returned his kiss fully, fervently.

His magic tingled; her mind was open to him, but he concentrated on the kiss instead of invading her thoughts.

Blessed Spirit, she tastes good.

Desire flooded Jorrin and his manhood stirred.

More.

He kissed her harder, swallowing a half-moan as Cera put her hands on his shoulders. He tried to tug her against his chest, but she broke away, pushing at him and standing on trembling legs.

"No," she whispered, "I have to see to Valor." She lunged for the white horse's reins, her back to him, but she hadn't moved so fast he'd missed the heavy-lidded gray eyes, pink cheeks and kiss-swollen lips.

Biting back a groan, Jorrin ordered his arousal to soften, and chanted at himself not to push her.

She unstrapped the saddle on the gelding, but her whole body shook.

He couldn't get even an inkling of emotion off her; Cera's mind was totally shut down. Consciously. Jorrin shoved his hand through his hair, cursing himself to hell and back.

He shouldn't have kissed her.

Now she'd pull away from him even more.

Was her one-word statement denying his kiss, or just asserting she wouldn't reveal her secrets?

Despite the fact she'd kissed him back, her rejection burned through his chest. He rubbed the spot, wincing.

He needed to find out what was going on. Jorrin moved behind her, covering her hand with his on the horse's back.

She shivered and her shoulders stiffened.

"Cera, you don't always have to be so strong, you know."

She whirled on him, yanking her hand from under his. "Yes. I do." Cera hauled the heavy saddle from the gelding and threw it on the ground next to the other two. When she covered him with a blanket, her movements were still jerky.

Jorrin stood and watched her lead Valor to Grayna and Ash and tie him up.

She tossed a bundle of sleeping furs at him, and pure reflex made his arms rise to catch it.

"Those are Avery's. Use them for the night, since he has yours." Her chest heaved; he tried not to stare at her jerkin-covered breasts. "We'll talk in the morning, when I know why my cousin's here."

He didn't miss the tremors still gripping her tall slender frame even as she curled into a ball deep in her furs. He wanted to hold her, comfort her, but his gut said she wouldn't let him, even if he *hadn't* kissed her.

The white wolf curled around her, making his idea further dissolve.

Doesn't matter anyway.

It was obvious Cera didn't want to get closer to *him*.

The fire crackled and he glanced at it, then let his eyes skim over their small camp. They were secluded, but safety was an illusion.

How could her cousin have even found them?

All he could see of the other man as he lay wrapped in Jorrin's furs was a mop of curly red hair that shone in the dim light of the fire.

He needed to reenergize the fire to carry him through the end of his watch.

Cera was right about one thing, they needed to learn why her cousin had come to them. What the hell did it all mean?

Jorrin was sick of being in the dark, especially about the sword.

I can help if she'll let me.

Since she'd saved his hide in the tavern, he hadn't pushed her. At least she'd told him their destination. His empathic magic revealed a little about her, but it wasn't enough.

Well, that would come to an end first thing in the morning.

He'd respected her privacy because she'd been so shaken by the appearance of her cousin, but no more. Jorrin ignored the voice that chimed in; his kiss had jarred her, too.

He grabbed a handful of his magically-infused kindling to keep the fire hot and strong. He watched the familiar blue glow as he threw it into the flames until it faded away. The fire rose, warming his hands and face as he leaned against a nearby tree, sword on his lap.

Jorrin wouldn't have been able to sleep anyway. He could kick himself for kissing Cera. Even though she'd responded, the rejection smarted.

Blessed Spirit, she was sweet.

Innocent.

His gaze drifted upward, focusing on the stars as he cursed himself some more. Often on lonely nights when he was too restless to sleep, he named constellations until he drifted off, but this night, that wouldn't have helped, even if he had been trying to get some rest.

Cera.

He'd only known her a sevenday, but from the moment he'd met her, it was obvious there was something about her. She was in his dreams as he lay beside her every night since they'd left Greenwald.

Dreams where he did much more than just kiss her.

Jorrin shook his head. He was doomed.

She'd saved his hide. He'd known better than to enter the tavern—a human tavern—without covering his head.

Stubborn idiot.

In the mountains of Aramour, humans were the minority. He'd spent his childhood there, leaving for the first time to search for his father. Jorrin had been unfamiliar with the prejudices of the human world.

His mother had warned him of those who'd reject his mixed blood, but a part of him wouldn't hide his heritage. He wasn't ashamed of where he'd come from, or who he was. Hiding his pointed ears hurt his pride more than admitting he was half-elfin ever would.

Jorrin's parents loved each other, and his mother always told him he was the best of both worlds. And though he hadn't spent much time with his father's kind outside of his mountain home, sometimes he felt like he belonged more in their world than in the one he'd grown up in.

Maybe his elfin blood was the reason Cera had pulled away from his kiss. She'd never treated him differently because of it, but maybe she couldn't stomach being *more* than just friends with someone who was not *all* human.

He cursed and shook his head.

Just forget it. Focus. Pay attention. Keep her safe.

How was he going to get through the night?

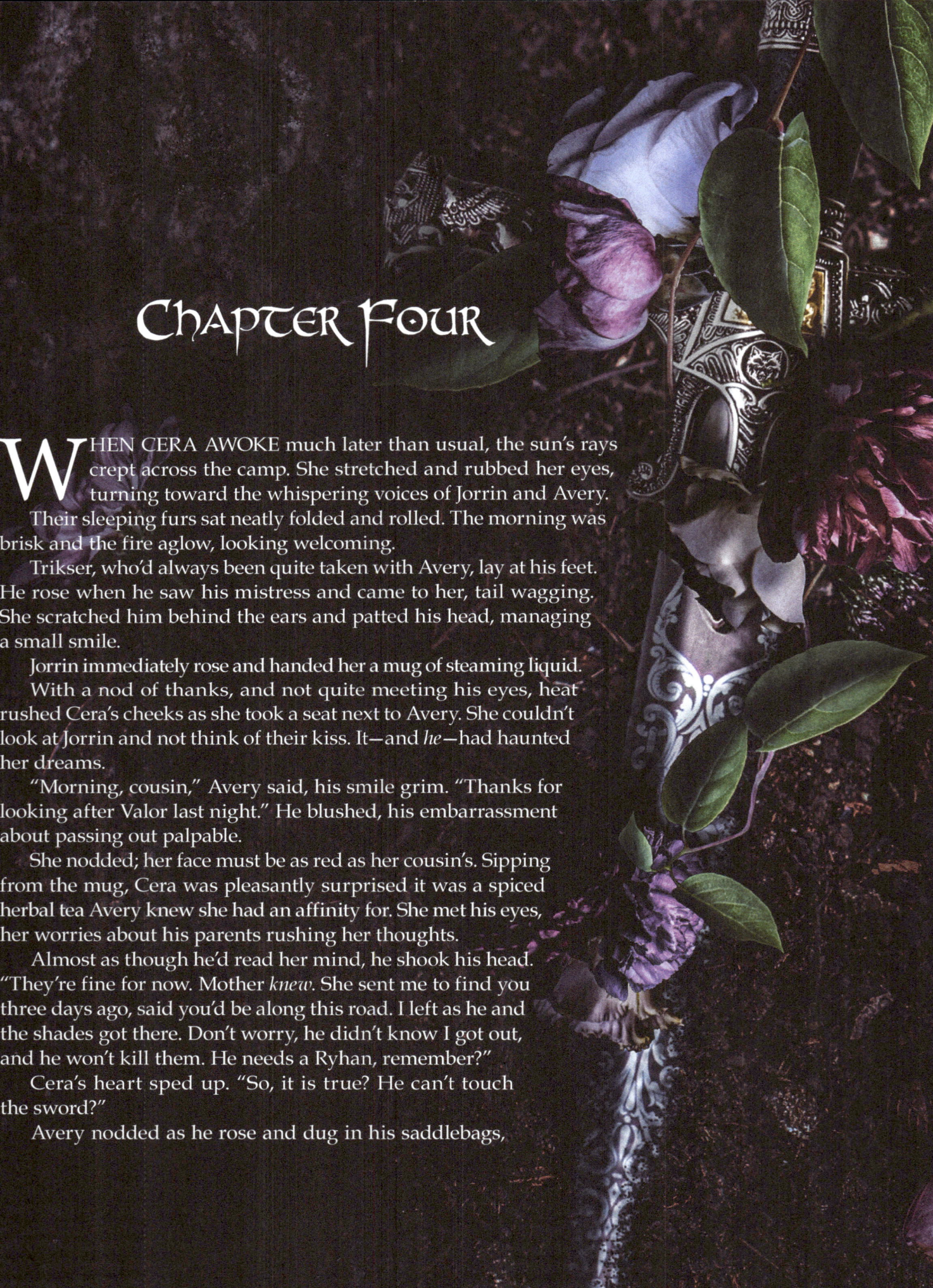

Chapter Four

WHEN CERA AWOKE much later than usual, the sun's rays crept across the camp. She stretched and rubbed her eyes, turning toward the whispering voices of Jorrin and Avery. Their sleeping furs sat neatly folded and rolled. The morning was brisk and the fire aglow, looking welcoming.

Trikser, who'd always been quite taken with Avery, lay at his feet. He rose when he saw his mistress and came to her, tail wagging. She scratched him behind the ears and patted his head, managing a small smile.

Jorrin immediately rose and handed her a mug of steaming liquid.

With a nod of thanks, and not quite meeting his eyes, heat rushed Cera's cheeks as she took a seat next to Avery. She couldn't look at Jorrin and not think of their kiss. It—and *he*—had haunted her dreams.

"Morning, cousin," Avery said, his smile grim. "Thanks for looking after Valor last night." He blushed, his embarrassment about passing out palpable.

She nodded; her face must be as red as her cousin's. Sipping from the mug, Cera was pleasantly surprised it was a spiced herbal tea Avery knew she had an affinity for. She met his eyes, her worries about his parents rushing her thoughts.

Almost as though he'd read her mind, he shook his head. "They're fine for now. Mother *knew*. She sent me to find you three days ago, said you'd be along this road. I left as he and the shades got there. Don't worry, he didn't know I got out, and he won't kill them. He needs a Ryhan, remember?"

Cera's heart sped up. "So, it is true? He can't touch the sword?"

Avery nodded as he rose and dug in his saddlebags,

then handed her a small scroll. "She told me to give this to you. It's all you ever need to know about it. Uncle Falor wrote it himself."

She took the parchment with shaking hands, eyes blurring at the first mention of her father's name. She recognized her father's hand before the paper went fuzzy. "He killed them."

Her cousin's mouth was a hard line, his own eyes welling up. "Aunt Ev, Uncle Falor, little Kait . . . Mother knew when it happened. It's not adequate, but I'm . . . I'm sorry, Cera." Avery threw his arm around her shoulders.

She buried her face against his neck and let him hold her as tears flowed.

Trikser whined and paced.

Cera sent him reassurance, but it didn't work. He pawed at her boots. Their minds were linked, and he didn't understand her fluctuating emotions. She'd had to run as soon as she'd heard about her family.

She'd barely processed it, let alone taken time to grieve.

Sorrow threatened to swallow her whole as Avery rubbed her back, squeezing her against his thin chest, but she had to pull herself together. They didn't have time for this. Besides, she was upsetting her bondmate. Cera pulled away gently, pressing a kiss to her cousin's cheek and wiping her tears away. "Me, too." She rested a hand on Trik's mane until he calmed.

"Hold it. *What* are you talking about?" Jorrin's sharp tone took her attention.

"You didn't tell him?" she exclaimed.

"No. I was waiting for you . . ." With an impatient wave of his hand, Avery glared.

"Never mind about that. Just tell me what's going on, and I suggest you start with that sword."

At the mention of her weapon, Cera rose to retrieve it. She unsheathed it and laid it on her lap, turning it over and over.

Jorrin's eyes were locked onto her weapon, his face drawn; pallid. Brow knitted, he looked a bit green. He swallowed hard, as if he might retch. The sword's magic must be bothering him.

She stopped flipping it, whispering an apology as she gathered the courage she needed to tell him everything.

He tore his eyes away, glancing at her cousin.

Avery nodded. "I feel it, Jorrin. I always have. Cera will explain."

After taking a breath, she sent thoughts of love to her wolf when he whined and leaned into her leg. She set a hand on his head and borrowed some strength from him. Needed it. "This sword was my great-great-grandfather's. On my father's side . . ." She forced words out.

"Who just happened to meet our great-great-grandfather, on our mothers' side," Avery said, "but that's another story. Our mothers are . . . were . . . twins." He looked down, as what he'd said washed over him.

Cera couldn't focus on her cousin's sorrow. Not if she was expected to get through this. "There's a family legend about how he received it, and I don't know how much relevance it has now, but maybe you should hear it anyway."

Jorrin's eyes were glued to her.

She cleared her throat. "His name was Montilagro. Montilagro Ryhan. He was known as Monty. Grandfa Monty wasn't the type of man content with farming at the old cottage . . ."

"We weren't nobles then . . ." Avery said.

Cera threw him a glare. Heat rose in her cheeks. She hadn't told Jorrin she came from a noble family and truthfully, she wished she hadn't been highborn.

Maybe then, her family wouldn't be dead.

"Monty decided to leave home and go adventuring. So, he asked his father for a loan to buy a reliable steed . . ."

"Evidently, he'd previously owned a nag . . ." Avery interrupted again with a grin.

She tried to ignore her cousin, but when Jorrin laughed, she found herself smiling a little. "Do you want to finish the story?"

He grinned even more. "No, no. You're doing so well." Avery gestured with his hand.

"Then by all means, *let* me." Cera paused, but her cousin didn't cut in. "Monty bought his steed, and rode all over the countryside looking for adventure, thinking himself the proper knight. Well, one day Grandfa Monty got his wish. He happened upon a carriage being robbed by bandits. He had no proper sword, but took on four bandits with a dagger and his bare hands. He overcame them. Got a bit wounded, but overall in one piece. Unfortunately, the carriage driver and footman were killed, but Grandfa Monty was what he always wanted to be . . . a hero."

"Get to the good part." Avery's gray eyes danced.

She glared again before looking back at Jorrin. "The courtier he thought he'd rescued turned out to be the princess and one of her ladies-in-waiting."

"And the king was so grateful that he rewarded old Monty with the title of duke, gave him lands and the gift of the magic sword," Avery finished, a triumphant look on his face.

Cera rolled her eyes. Since he'd been long dead by the time they'd both been born, they hadn't even known the man.

"Your great-great-grandfather was a duke?" Jorrin asked.

"Of course, how do you think she'd be the heir to Greenwald if he hadn't been?"

"Avery!" She scrambled to her feet, face hot. She couldn't meet Jorrin's eyes.

"What?" Her cousin shrugged. Gray eyes wide, his expression shouted he had no idea what he'd just revealed to Jorrin.

And he doesn't have a clue.

Cera threw her hands up and stomped away, leaving the camp and the warmth of the fire, leaning on a tree with her back to the two men.

Trikser wuffed, sending her puzzled thoughts at her change in mood yet again.

"Cera," Jorrin called.

She didn't acknowledge him.

Why did it please her that he'd come after her?

Her heart cantered.

"Why didn't you tell me?" His tone was soft and held none of the accusation she deserved.

She'd put *his* life in danger, after all.

"'Last time I checked, the roads were free to travel. That's one thing the lord has yet to tax,'" Cera bit at him. "I think it went something like that."

"Ouch." He winced.

Although it wasn't the reason she hadn't told him; it was convenient, wasn't it?

He rested a hand on her shoulder. "That's your anger talking."

The warmth of his touch seeped into her through leather and linen. Her cheeks heated even more, and her stomach fluttered. "You're right. I didn't tell you because I was running." Their eyes locked. Cera sucked in a breath. "I hid in the Lower Greenwald slums for a fortnight. That bartender, the one who initiated the fight . . . I was staying in his extra room. And don't get any ideas, I wasn't sleeping with him."

His jaw clenched, dark brows drawn tight. "*Friend* of yours?"

"No. He had a slight fancy for my mother in turns past; I just used it to my advantage. I knew of his prejudice against . . . those of mixed blood. That's why I sat next to you at the bar."

Jorrin's face paled, his shoulders tight, expression hard . . . like she'd slapped him or something.

She pushed off the tree. "I didn't mean anything bad by that, and you know it. If I felt the same way, I could have let Gordo kill you."

And I never would've let you kiss me.

Her body heated, but she planted her fists at her sides instead of reaching for him like she wanted to.

His expression didn't soften, but his blue eyes were intense.

Cera couldn't look away.

"I'm sorry, Cera. Though I've no idea what I said." Avery's voice snapped her back into her own skin. He'd made his way over to them from their campsite.

Sucking in a breath, she swallowed and tore her eyes away from Jorrin. She met her cousin's bewildered expression.

His gray eyes were wide, his cheeks pink. Her cousin had no idea why he'd upset her.

My fault.

She'd been totally lost to Jorrin. Unaware of her surroundings in the wooded area.

Dangerous.

Cera forced a smile. "I'm not upset . . . don't worry about it." She hugged him.

Jorrin's eyes burned her and when she met his gaze, she seared all over again.

What's he thinking?

"I don't think the tale about how your sword came to your family is the whole story," Jorrin said, his normal tone belying those sapphire orbs.

She and Avery exchanged a glance.

"I guess not," her cousin whispered.

Dread settled over Cera as they headed back to the campsite and the warm fire. How could she tell Jorrin the whole story?

He should've let her ditch him on the main road outside of Greenwald, but he had a right to know what he'd gotten himself into.

Her chest ached.

Would Jorrin leave her?

She cleared her throat, wringing her hands on her lap and fighting for air. "I suppose this story is just about as exciting as the family legend, but this one doesn't have a happy ending."

Talking about it didn't hurt as much as she'd thought it would, but it wasn't easy by any means. Cera swallowed back some tears, she took another breath.

"As you might imagine, the sword was passed down from Monty to his son, then to my grandfather, and to my father some turns ago.

"My father, Lord Falor Ryhan, the Duke of Greenwald, uncovered a plot to kill King Nathal. Unfortunately, an archduke was behind it. The king was quite close to the man and more than anything, was hurt by the betrayal of a friend. I guess that was the reason King Nathal didn't order the man put to death, though he should have. Instead, he banished him from the continent and stripped him of his lands and title.

"My father wielded his sword to protect the king. Varthan knew right away the sword wasn't *just* a weapon. My father was a trained mage, so the sword's magic was amplified, and the arch-duke was greedy enough to covet it."

"What kind of magic does the sword have?" Jorrin asked.

"It was always able to sense the presence of magic, but my father added a spell allowing it to sense the nature of magic, and ward against its being used for evil. As long as the spell holds, and anyone of my father's blood remains alive, he can't touch it. No one not of my father's line can. I don't want to find out what'd happen to anyone who tried."

Because of his magic, her father had been a warrior and a noble. He could do almost anything; move things with his mind, control fire and water, make nearly any spell work. Even though it was not his main gift, Falor Ryhan had also possessed some healing magic. He'd been gentle and loving.

Her mother had always said it was her father's healing powers that'd shaped him. He'd been a good man. Her father's smiling face danced into her mind. Jorrin's eyes wavered, and a droplet of liquid hit her hand.

Damn tears.

Cera lifted a hand, discovering her cheeks were soaked. She wiped her face, only to find Jorrin staring at her. Her stomach flipped, but she forced words out of her mouth. "He packed it away, to send to Tarvis, to my Aunt Emeralda, Avery's mother. The sword never made it.

"The former archduke is consumed by his greed and desire to hold the throne of King Nathal. He's convinced the sword will assist him. He and his shades, who are boy mages under his control, attacked Castle Ryhan shortly after midnight on the full moon two months ago.

"He killed my father. He beat and tortured my mother and sister, *raped* them both, one of those still loyal to Ryhans told me. Thank the Blessed Spirit my father didn't have to see that. My sister, Kacheralda, little Kait, was only fourteen. He killed her in front of our mother. Made her watch and then killed my mother, too." Her voice wavered as the words caused the reality to wash over her.

They're really gone . . .

Swallowing a sob, she trembled so hard her teeth rattled. Cera let Avery take her hand, but she got no comfort from the squeeze he gave.

Trikser whined and crawled into her lap. His heavy body was something she needed. She moved the sword and buried her free hand in the thick fur, fighting the urge to hide her face against his snowy coat.

Jorrin's expression was pinched, as if he could feel her pain. His warm sapphire eyes bored into her, comforted her, though they were not touching.

She wanted to push away from her bondmate and cousin and bury herself against Jorrin's chest. Would he hold her?

Drawing strength from her companion for the last sevenday, Cera sucked the hundredth breath of the last ten minutes.

Just continue.

"He took over Greenwald. Sent his shades all over the Province and killed those who were too loyal to the Duke of Greenwald to leave alive. I . . . I was not at home when it happened. I was returning from Spring Training with the King's Riders. I joined the messenger service when I was fifteen. We were training new recruits, and I was chosen to help teach archery and sword fighting.

"Our steward Michal, a man who'd served our family since my father was a boy, got two other servants out and met me on the road with the sword, wrapped in linens. They'd stolen it while Varthan slept, and they knew they had to get it to me. I went straight to the *Dragon's Lair*, Marshek's tavern. Varthan didn't know where I was. When he realized the sword was gone, the bastard killed Michal, and the two who had brought it to me. Michal's son, Venton, managed to remain undiscovered, and brought me information for the first sevenday I stayed in Lower Greenwald.

"Varthan knew all was not lost if he could find me. Only a Ryhan could handle the sword, and he hadn't killed them all. I'm sure Venton was tortured when he was discovered, but he didn't tell him my location. Varthan killed him as well. By now, he knows I'm gone from Greenwald. There's no way word of the scuffle when I met you hasn't reached him . . . the fact that he also went to Tarvis proves he's guessed my next move.

"He's killed my family, my friends, and now he has my aunt and uncle because of this stupid sword, a stupid piece of metal. And I wasn't there. If I'd been there the day he killed them, maybe they wouldn't be dead. I wasn't there." Her tears were hot on her cheeks.

"Cousin, I think you put too much stock in your skill." Avery's voice was quiet and he squeezed her hand again. "Do you really think you could have changed anything?"

Cera should've been hurt by the words, but she was numb. "I should've been there," she protested, but her energy was suddenly gone.

"No, then you'd be dead, too," Jorrin said.

"Maybe that would be for the better. Then he'd still be puzzling over how to use the damned thing." She cast the weapon to the ground.

Trikser wuffed softly and left her lap to inspect it.

Jorrin knelt in front of her. He cupped her face and forced her to meet his eyes. "No . . . if you were dead, he'd find some other way to override the spell. There is *always* more powerful magic. And if he hadn't killed you, you'd probably be wishing you were dead now. No, Ceralda Ryhan, too many people value you." He drew her into his arms.

Cera buried her face against him. She wrapped her arms around his waist and felt him pull her even closer. She closed her eyes as she inhaled the pleasant mixture of his clean scent and leather.

Fighting tears, she swallowed against the lump in her throat, but quickly lost the battle when Jorrin started making comforting circles up and down her back, rubbing with just the right amount of pressure.

The first sob slipped out, then the second, but he only held her and let her cry as her body shook against him.

Dragon's Tail
Mountains of Aramour
Terraquist
Elfin River
Greenwald
Netian Valley
North Ascova
Tarvis
Hadrian's Place
Berat
South Ascova
Islands
Dalunas
Southern Strait
Penal Territory

"What I don't understand," Jorrin remarked sometime later, "is why the king didn't do anything to prevent this. Why didn't he send the army to Greenwald?"

"Ah . . . I have an answer for you," Avery said as he groomed Valor. "Varthan may not have magic of his own, but his shades are the most powerful human mages on the continent. Believe it or not, some work for him willingly. He knows they have a gift and offers them training. In return, they're indebted to him for a time, but they usually stay in his service out of some demented sense of honor. It's rumored he has them trained by even more powerful mages than they are . . . elfin mages. Many other shades though . . . they never had a choice. For them, there's nothing else. No other way to be."

Jorrin shook his head. It disgusted him to think any of his mother's race would assist a madman like Varthan.

"It's the darkness that makes them stay." Cera's voice was quiet. "They can't break away. Dark magic makes them hungry . . ."

Avery nodded.

Jorrin looked from one to the other. The family resemblance was obvious. They had the same gray eyes. Avery's hair was several shades lighter than Cera's red, and it curled more than his cousin's.

Avery was young. He'd confessed he was a few months shy of his eighteenth birthday, and he was tall—almost Jorrin's own six feet three inches. Although he was somewhat lanky, he probably had girls all over Tarvis flocking after him.

"What does obsession with dark magic have to do with the siege on Greenwald?" Jorrin asked.

"The power of his mages has everything to do with it. Varthan isn't stupid. Wouldn't life be simpler if he was?" Avery mused. "Unfortunately, evil people are often intelligent, and Varthan is no exception." When Jorrin smirked, he continued. "Magic is stronger when performed in a group, correct?"

"Well, yeah." Jorrin sighed. *Spit it out, kid.*

"The night of the siege, Varthan got all his shades together and cast a large shield, a bubble if you will, over the capital city, over the castle . . . everything."

"Over all of Terraquist? Couldn't King Nathal's own mages do anything about it?" Jorrin asked.

"They could cast inside, but anything they threw at the bubble bounced back."

"They got zapped with their own magic?" he gasped.

"Yes, but it was gone the next day. Investigation yielded nothing. Perhaps they thought a powerful mage was experimenting and it was a side effect." The boy frowned, shaking his head. "Then they got word of what happened. The king was frantic.

"They left Terraquist that very evening, the king himself leading his best knights and their men, along with his most powerful mages. But when they got to Greenwald, Varthan and his mages cast the bubble spell again, but this time it was to keep something out. A few of King Nathal's mages were injured when they tried to dismantle the shield at Terraquist, but they tried to get in anyway . . . nothing worked."

Cera shot a glance to her cousin. "But I was in Greenwald then . . . how?"

"The wall was virtually invisible, and even though you didn't know it, you *did* pass through it. And when Varthan fled to go after you, he let it fall. He also left in secret, before the king and his men entered Greenwald, and then Castle Ryhan. Mother sent me to find you, so I don't know what happened after I left."

"But how were we able to pass through?" Jorrin asked.

Why hadn't his magical senses picked anything up? He'd always been able to tell when there was magic around him.

Always.

How the hell had he missed something as large—and as serious—as a spell covering a whole Province?

"The shield over Terraquist was designed to keep something *in.* I'm sure people entered the city when it was up, but they couldn't get back out. The shield over Greenwald was made to keep something *out,* which is why you were able to leave. If you'd tried to return to the Province, you wouldn't have been able to. Movement through the shields differed because of the nature of each spell."

"Aunt Em saw all this?" Cera asked.

"Actually—" Avery blushed to the tips of his ears, making his face match his hair. "I figured out the nature of the shields, but yes, Mother saw everything."

She nodded and chewed her bottom lip. "You really don't fear for their safety?"

"Not right now. Father will hold the castle with his personal guard. There are no stronger men in the entire Province. Mother saw Varthan coming. She sent me to find you because she needs you to come to Tarvis. Varthan is using them to draw you and the sword."

"Bait. And since he wants her to come, he definitely won't set up a shield to keep her out," Jorrin said.

Avery nodded. "Varthan's still planning to kill the king and take over. If he succeeded, he'd kill the remaining Dukes of the Provinces, my father included, and possibly their heirs." He pointed to his chest, then to Cera. "And though he needs you to handle the sword now, I'm sure as soon as he disposes of the spell, he'll dispose of you." He winced.

Cera nodded, her eyes misty, and Jorrin's stomach jumped.

He couldn't abide her tears.

"I'm pretty sure—and Mother agrees with me—in order to break the spell on the sword, Varthan's mages need you to be *holding it* when they attempt the counter spell. I'd hoped we could try to break the spell ourselves. Unfortunately, I have no idea what would do it. I've looked in many spell books—even ancient texts, researching—but I've come up with nothing. I don't think anything I could write would work, either, since I don't know what Uncle Falor's spell contained." Avery's shoulders slumped and he sighed.

"What do we do now?" Jorrin whispered.

"We go to Tarvis, that's what. Wasn't that always the plan?" Cera made a fist, her chest rising with her deep breath.

He reached for her hand and smiled when she didn't pull away.

CHAPTER FIVE

THEY LEFT AT sunrise, following Cera's original route.
Avery had argued that if they turned off the westerly road and continued due south, they could make Tarvis in four days, even with stopping for the night.

She'd pointed out that Varthan might've sent shades out to find them, and if they were to turn onto the main road, they'd be intercepted. And although Varthan was expecting her to arrive at Castle Lenore, if they were caught, they'd lose any element of surprise they had.

Jorrin had listened to them both, leaning toward Cera's plan, because she was right about needing any advantage they could muster. He'd said nothing, and hid a smile from time to time during their bickering.

"I made it in three days," Avery had muttered, just loud enough for both of them to hear as they were tacking their horses and preparing to move out.

"Yes, you may have; but you rode seventy-two hours straight, strapped to your horse so you wouldn't fall off," Cera had barked.

Jorrin had ducked behind Grayna and reached for his saddle pack to hide his amusement.

"My way was clear and safer." Avery had crossed his arms over his chest.

"Not with shades after us. Discussion over, Avery. We go the way I say, or we don't go at all." She'd glared, making a cutting gesture with her hand.

"Don't be ridiculous, Cera. We *have* to go!"

"Exactly. So shut up and get on your horse." Her expression had declared an end to the argument as she mounted Ash. He whinnied and Trikser wuffed.

Jorrin had felt her sudden remorse at being rough, and had seen her caress the stallion's neck before they tore off to the road.

He'd sighed—then and now.

It's gonna be a long day.

They caught up quickly, but Cera rode at least ten feet ahead, nudging Ash faster if either of them got too close.

He chuckled and Avery threw him a black look. "So . . . how long do you think she'll stay mad at you?"

The younger man echoed his sigh. "One time, when we were little, I put a frog down the back of Kait's shirt when we were swimming. She screamed, went under and swallowed some water. Coughed and coughed, but she was all right. Cera beat me up, got me in trouble, and then didn't talk to me for a whole sevenday."

Jorrin laughed. "Somehow, I can believe that about her."

Avery gave a small smile and glanced around.

"Don't worry about Cera, anyway. Her pride was only a little hurt at the thought of you challenging her prowess, I think," he said.

Her cousin shot him a sharp look. "Prowess? She's *my* cousin. I know her a bit better than you do. After all, you've only known her for a sevenday."

"A sevenday is a long time to get to know someone, sometimes." He shifted in his saddle, looking away. Without waiting for an answer, he gave his heels to Grayna's sides.

The mare bolted forward and soon she and Ash were abreast.

Trikser barked a protest at being nudged over by the bigger animal, but neither horse, nor people paid any attention.

"Hi, there," Jorrin ventured, giving her a onceover.

She was brooding; her emotions positively reeked of it; his magic tingled. Cera glanced in his direction and their eyes locked.

His heart pounded, his voice caught in his throat. She was absolutely *stunning*. All thought fled as she flashed a half-smile and Jorrin tried not to stare at her full lips. Tried not to remember them moving beneath his.

"Hi, there," she responded in the same light tone.

"What were you thinking about?" He swallowed a cringe at the crack in his voice.

She cocked her head to one side. "Varthan, mostly . . . Aunt Em and Uncle Everett . . . what we're going to do when we get to Tarvis . . . the list is a circle that doesn't end."

"Those are very dark thoughts. Too dark, in fact, for such a lovely day."

Cera harrumphed.

"Just trying to lighten your mood. Did it work?"

"Not really."

"Still angry with Avery?"

"Avery? No, I wasn't mad at my cousin. I was . . . annoyed."

"Annoyed? Sheesh . . . I hope you never are *annoyed* at me like that."

She giggled, and he grinned. Jorrin had succeeded in lightening her mood, and her laugh made his heart stutter.

"I'm not annoyed with him—anymore, at any rate."

"Did you hear that, Avery?" he called. He glanced over his shoulder.

Cera's cousin was riding closer to them, within hearing distance.

"Yes. Thank the Blessed Spirit," Avery said with exaggerated relief, allowing them all a small laugh.

Trikser made a barking-growling noise Cera had never heard before.

She glanced over from the banter with Jorrin and Avery in time to see him fly away like an arrow—disappearing into the woods edging the entire length of the road.

They exchanged quick looks, then Cera turned Ash off the road.

"Can you call him?" Jorrin asked.

She paused. "I suppose I could shout." She tried not to roll her eyes.

"I meant with your mind."

"I can't. My abilities are limited by distance. Besides, I've never seen him do this before. He seemed pretty hyped about something. He probably wouldn't respond right away, even if he did hear me."

"But he's your bondmate."

"Yes, and sometimes things work as such," Cera snapped, then frowned. "Look, I don't have time—"

"I could teach you," Jorrin said.

"Teach me what?"

"I could teach you to expand your abilities. Even to see through his eyes, as if you were riding beside him while he ran. I've done it before, but your influence is too strong for it to work if I tried now. There are spells, as well as simple techniques to widen and deepen your magic—your bond with him. I could also show you how to understand him better."

Intrigue washed over her, distracting her from the task at hand. "Like words?"

"Not that advanced. It's possible, but not with a wolf, I don't think."

She loved Trikser, and though she considered herself rather skilled at communication with him, she'd love to learn more. When they'd bonded, her teacher hadn't been the most adept mage. Karolyna had been bonded to Trikser's mother, though, and had taught Cera all she knew.

"That's all well and good, cousin, but don't you think we should find him now?" Avery cocked his head to one side, and gestured toward the woods with his dagger.

Jorrin drew his sword and Cera reached for her own dagger with a nod.

"Back, beast, *back* I say," someone shouted as they struggled through the underbrush.

She kicked Ash harder, ignoring Jorrin's shout to wait. She had to stop Trikser from being hurt, or even killed. She followed the continuing shouts, yanking her horse to a halt when they'd come to a small clearing.

Straight ahead was a bedraggled cabin with smoke drifting from the chimney. A ragged horse, its ribs showing, was tied to a post outside. The old nag gave a curious whinny, which Ash returned.

Cera swung her leg over the saddle, sliding down his side in a hurried and improper dismount. She listened hard, not seeing the owner of the shouting voice, nor did she see her wolf.

There was a small barn to the left, perched at the edge of the woods. It was in better shape than the cabin.

"Cera . . . what . . . ?" Avery asked from his seat on Valor.

Jorrin dismounted beside her at the same moment, and she shushed them both.

"Did you hear the shouting?" she asked.

"Aye," Jorrin whispered. "It was over there, I think." He pointed into the woods to the right of the clearing.

"Stop," the voice shouted again. "Bring that back, you scoundrel! Thief!"

Then something she didn't understand, but they were likely curse words, if the inflection was any indication.

Trikser ran out into the clearing, something clutched between his strong jaws. His tail wagged wildly, and she received playful thoughts from him.

The owner of the item and voice didn't follow her bondmate.

Cera stared as he skidded to a stop at her feet. "Trikser, what . . . ?" She shot a look at her cousin when he gasped and jumped down from his white gelding.

"Look at that!"

She exchanged a glance with Jorrin, and then followed Avery's gaze to see what Trikser had dropped at her feet.

Her wolf was very proud of himself and gave a small wuff as she bent to retrieve it. She absently scratched his ear as she tried to determine what she'd picked up. Trikser leaned into her hand, sitting heavily on his hindquarters.

The piece was about a foot long, and looked like a refined stick. It was light and flexible.

Avery bristled when she shook it, then bent its end. "Cera, *don't*. Do you know what that is?" He snatched the stick from her hand.

"It's a wand," Jorrin said matter-of-factly.

"Yes," her cousin breathed, "but I've never seen one this . . . this . . . well crafted." He looked up from the wand as if reluctant, gray eyes full of wonder.

The shouting in the woods became louder, but Cera couldn't understand the words.

Cursing? What the heck language is that? Wait. At least one word was something Jorrin had said at *the Dragon's Lair.*

"That's because it's an elf wizard's wand." He looked toward the wooded area with wide eyes, his full lips parted.

"Really?" Avery asked, turning the wand over. Green sparks flew when he bent it. He jumped back, yanking his hand away, almost dropping it.

She snorted. "I thought you said not to do that."

"Never mind that. Don't you think we should find its owner?" Jorrin gestured. He glanced at her bond, but Trik only wagged his tail.

"Why?" her cousin asked. "If it's an elf's wand, shouldn't we keep it? I mean, I don't know of any elves around here, do you?" He went on before either of them could answer. "I mean, whoever Trikser took it from probably stole it."

Jorrin cocked his head toward the voice that was still shouting. "Since I'm the only one with expertise in that area, I can assure you the cursing from the woods over there—and it *is* cursing—is

Aramourian. Last time I checked, most beings who speak it with the correct accent—again, as he *is*—would have to be elfin."

"Oh . . ." Avery muttered, crestfallen. He'd always been intrigued with magical items, and probably would've given almost anything to keep the wand.

Cera covered a smile and turned to her wolf. "Trik, what have I told you about stealing things?" He rose, wagging his tail so hard his rear end wiggled. She probed his mind, but he seemed to have acquired selective comprehension. She threw her hands up and sighed. "Take us to the wand's owner."

She ignored Jorrin's laugh as Trikser dove into the woods to the right of the clearing. Cera followed at a jog, the two men on her heels. She gaped as her bondmate came to a stop in front of a wizened figure.

Jorrin had been right about the wand's owner. He was an elf, no taller than a ten or eleven-turn-old human child, and his face was flushed several shades of red. His bushy white brows were tight and low.

She was no empath, but irritation rolled off him in waves. She could feel the magic.

The elf's clothing was as shaggy as his bushy white beard. His brown tunic hung off of his thin shoulders, his dark breeches oversized and baggy with a belt tightly wrapped around his reedy waist. There was a ragged black triangular hat in the fallen leaves near his left foot.

He glared up at them and yanked with all his might, attempting to free his right foot. A dark green vine-like plant Cera had never seen before encircled his ankle.

The more he pulled, the tighter it got, creeping up his bony calf, well on its way to his knee. "About time." His accent was thick, although his earlier shouts in her dialect had been clear.

Trikser wuffed at her feet, stepping forward, then backing up. He looked up at her.

"You," the elf shouted, pointing at her wolf.

Trikser only wagged his tail.

She gasped, looking from the elf to her bondmate and back. She had to order herself not to step in front of Trik to protect him.

A reversal of their usual roles for sure.

The elf shook an angry finger at him. It was quite a long finger for his small wrinkled hand.

Cera cocked her head to the side, studying him. His tapered ears were longer than Jorrin's, and his wild white hair partially concealed their tips. Somehow, he was still beautiful. Delicate.

Narrowing his eyes, he scowled at her wolf.

Trikser wagged his tail, taking a step toward him again.

Was he thought-sending to him?

"Don't give me that. They'd have come anyway." The elf gestured to his caught foot. "You left me helpless to my strangleweed." He sighed, rolling his eyes to the tree canopy and muttering something in Aramourian. Then he glanced at Cera's cousin. "Lord Lenore, may I?" He gestured to the pliable wooden stick.

Her cousin gaped and gave the wand to its owner with shaky hands.

She shot him a look and mouthed, "Do you know him?"

Avery shrugged and shook his head.

"*Reverserio*," the old elf commanded, waving his wand over the weeds. "Ah, much better."

The strangleweed unraveled and straightened, bouncing up and appearing perfectly harmless.

He stepped forward, then lost his balance. Shaking his head, he looked at Jorrin. "Master Aldern, will you assist me?"

The apple of Jorrin's throat bobbed, but he gave a hasty nod, stepping forward to grasp the elf by his arm.

Cera wanted to demand an explanation, but couldn't find her voice. She followed the others out to the clearing. Glared as Trikser ran ahead.

What's going on?

The elf tugged free of Jorrin's hold when they reached the front of the cabin. The little man nodded thanks and jammed the pointed hat onto his head. He limped a few steps and shook his leg. "Hate strangleweed. Hate it worse when my own traps turn on me . . . mangy mutt's fault, it is . . ." He threw a glare at Cera's bond. "Leg won't be right for days . . . too old for this . . ." he reverted to the other language after a moment.

"I don't think he meant any harm." Jorrin's blue eyes were wide.

She wished she could understand the almost musical language. Even the cursing sounded pretty.

The elf shot a look at Jorrin and laughed.

Exchanging puzzled glances with her cousin and Jorrin, Cera stared at the diminutive figure.

"I knew you spoke my mountain language. I miss them, how are they?" The longing in his voice made her sad. They were a long way from Aramour.

"The mountains?" Jorrin asked.

"Aye, of course."

"Same as always?" He shrugged, a dark brow raised.

"Ha. I should have figured you wouldn't have known . . . *mages* . . ."

"But . . . aren't you a mage?" Avery asked.

"Wizard, my lad, old-fashioned wizard . . . if you see a wand, you have a wizard."

"There's a difference?" her cousin asked, frowning.

"Much. No offense, since all three of you have the tendency, but there's something wrong with a person who works magic without a wand."

Avery did indeed look insulted, so Cera rested her hand on his arm to temper a response. She glanced at Jorrin, who was still studying the wizard as if something bothered him about the old elf.

Is something wrong?

"No offense taken," she said, tearing her eyes away.

The elf wizard gave a curt nod and grumbled something under his breath.

When he turned toward the cabin, it was obvious he wanted them to follow.

The bony-looking horse tied to a post near the front door whinnied as they passed.

The elf shot him a sharp look. "Don't talk to me like that."

Jorrin's magical senses screamed. What kind of spell did the wizard have on the horse?

As they entered the cabin, it actually screeched. The whole place was saturated in magic. Colors and shapes whirled around him, making him feel like he was spinning in a circle. His ears ached, temples throbbed. His body hummed and his fingertips tingled.

Too much.

He planted his feet so he wouldn't keel over, dragging in labored breaths. Squeezing his eyes shut, he concentrated on shutting off his senses one by one. Slowly everything muted, the colors dimmed and he could function, but his head still protested.

"Shut up," the wizard snapped. He was brandishing his wand threateningly in the air.

Cera's bondmate rushed inside and flopped down on a rug in front of the fireplace, like he belonged there. When Trikser noticed Jorrin looking his way, he wagged his tail.

What the hell? That's a first.

The wizard gave a small smile and pointed his wand into the hearth. *"Firos."*

A warm, friendly fire sparked to life. The spellword was much the same as the one he used to start a fire with his own magic, but after what the wizard had said about mages, he wasn't going to point it out.

"Come, come," the elf beckoned.

They were huddled not far from the doorway. Jorrin and Avery took a step forward, but Cera did not.

"I shan't bite you, Lady Ryhan, have a seat." He gestured to three comfortable looking chairs that were rather large compared to the stool he was perched on, not far from Trikser and the fireplace.

"How do you know our names?" Cera demanded, throwing a glance at Jorrin.

He shrugged and looked at Avery, who just shook his head. Much the same as when they'd been in the woods with the elf.

"I know your name, my dear, and that of young Lord Lenore, from him." The wizard pointed to Trikser, who wuffed to reassure his mistress. "Animals have always been my gift. Young Master Aldern, on the other hand, I've been waiting for."

"What?" Jorrin sputtered. "Just *who* are you?" He'd dreamt someone was calling him—for months.

When the wizard said he'd been waiting for him, Jorrin's magical senses tingled, warming his arms and legs, making his fingertips quiver. He shook his hands out as everything clicked into place.

The wizard had been calling him . . . that'd been the reason he'd had no real objection to Cera's travel route. He'd *had* to journey this way, to this cabin, to this wizard.

There was something *familiar* about him.

"Well, I'm glad you finally asked," he said with a laugh and a wry smile. "My name is Hadrian Rowlin, and I know your parents."

Jorrin's heart thundered. Shock rolled over him, and he stifled a gasp. He locked his gaze on the wizard, ignoring curious looks he could feel from Avery and Cera. *"You're* Hadrian . . . Mother spoke of you often. She thinks you dead . . ."

"Your mother was always beautiful, yet she never had much faith in wizards, or magic, for that matter." The elf chuckled and waved his wand.

Four goblets materialized and settled into each of their hands as if they had reached for them.

He focused on the old elf's face. Intelligent pale blue eyes, so pale they were almost clear, stared out from under the brim of the hat.

"You should have finished your training, lad," Hadrian admonished with a shake of his wand in Jorrin's direction. "Your powers are greater than you know."

He ignored the comment and muttered thanks for the drink.

Cera and Avery did the same.

"Where's my father? You left to find him . . ."

"Aye, you were just a babe. He and your mother were my dearest friends. I owed it to her to find him." He shook his head. "But I never did." His sorrow hit Jorrin's magic, making him wince.

"But you left *to* find him, and you never returned. Mother *mourned* you."

Sorrow shifted to regret, and Jorrin's heart ached for the elf wizard. Although he'd likely never admit it, Hadrian was lonely and sad. He had no desire to talk about Jorrin's father, but felt it was necessary.

The rush of emotion was more than he normally felt from someone he didn't know well, but the wizard's mind was open. And he was aware of the information Jorrin had just absorbed from him.

"I searched and searched for him . . . not far from *here* is where I sensed him last. There's a small village nearby, on the outskirts of Berat, but you know that." Hadrian glanced at Cera. "I decided to settle here temporarily, in hopes he'd return. I meant to go back to the mountains, to Aramour, but I had nothing to lose by staying here. I had nothing there . . . I'd lost my lifemate, my child was gone . . ."

"But you had *us*. You *promised* my mother. You could've sent word . . ." Jorrin clenched his fists so tightly his knuckles smarted.

"The pain was too great. My gift is animals. I can heal, as well as understand them, and the villagers often call upon me. I was fortunate to have found a place that does not mind our kind. I settled here, trying to forget what I had lost, trying to forget Aramour. The battle was more than I could deal with, and I was wrong to promise your mother I could find him. He had to run, you know. Did she tell you that?"

"Yes." Jorrin's whisper was bitter.

"I looked for him, Jorrin, using magic and tracking alike. Whenever I sniffed him out, the trail went cold. He was just *gone*. When I got here, I felt a sort of finality about it, and I knew until he *wanted* to be found, he'd not be, by friend *or* enemy. His powers were as great as my own." He chuckled. "When I train someone, I do my job well, even if they are not born an elf."

"You were his closest friend." Jorrin swallowed hard. "He always promised to come back when it was safe. Mother said he held me for hours before he left. That *used* to comfort me . . ."

"He left to protect you," Hadrian said.

"I would rather he stayed, so I could know my father."

"You might've been killed. With him gone, his family would be left alone; protected."

"Aye, well he entrusted that to *you*, his closest friend, but even *you* left."

"She made me promise to find him, you know that," the wizard snapped. His fists clenched and his blue eyes flashed.

Jorrin had hit a nerve, but he didn't feel guilty. He leaned forward, glaring.

Cera laid her hand on his arm to keep him in his seat, and he glanced at her—half-grateful, half-annoyed.

He didn't take a moment to revel in her touch. "Something you've struggled with?"

"I see you have talent as an empath," Hadrian said.

Jorrin nodded.

"He was a great empath, you know. Quite a strange natural trait in a human mage. And may I say, you favor him, in height and coloring. Of course, your mother's ears and eyes may give you away. Yet, that doesn't seem to bother the lovely lass here."

Cera blushed scarlet, yanking her hand from his forearm.

He let her reaction go, his stomach fluttering. Wanted to save her embarrassment, but wished he could reach for her. Their kiss danced into his mind, but Jorrin pushed it away.

Not now.

He cleared his throat and met the wizard's eyes. "So, why were you waiting for me?"

"Because *you* have to find your father. He will be needed."

"He's not dead?" Jorrin held his breath for the elf's answer.

"I never said he was dead. I just said *I* couldn't find him."

"I left Aramour against my mother's wishes to find him, Hadrian. It's been three turns . . . I have yet to come across the smallest clue to his whereabouts. How can *I* find him, and why will he be needed?"

"Only you, his son, can find him. He'll be needed, of course, to help *her* cause." The wizard pointed to Cera with his wand.

"*What?*" Cera, Jorrin, and Avery exclaimed at the same time.

Chapter Six

"BUT WE HAVE to get to Tarvis *now*. We can't wait," Cera argued for what seemed the thousandth time. She looked at Avery, who was nodding. At least her cousin agreed. "The more time we waste, the more damage Varthan will do. We *have* to go now."

"I'm afraid it would do you no good," Hadrian's tone was quiet, but firm. "The lad's father is your only hope."

Jorrin sighed, his chest heavy, shoulders slumped. How was he supposed to find a man he'd been looking for since he'd left home three full turns earlier? He hadn't run into *any* signs. Hadrian was master of magic, and *he* couldn't find him . . . so how was he, a half-trained mage, supposed to?

When he'd left Aramour, finding his father had been the original plan, but his search for months had proved fruitless, the task near impossible. He'd refused to crawl home, proving his mother right, so he'd focused on living. Moved around from place to place, feeling for magic, continuing to half-search, but finding nothing. He hadn't exactly given up, but his search had fallen into the background.

He had to eat, so he picked up coin any way he could; tracking, and selling himself as mercenary a time or two. Jorrin had even lowered himself to performing magic tricks in busy parts of the cities he'd been to, though that was only when he had been especially desperate. He wasn't proud of it, and definitely wouldn't admit it aloud.

Of course he wanted to find his father; that fact had never changed, but never in a million turns did he think Cera would play a part in the search.

Time was everything right now; he had to agree with her about that.

Gray eyes wide, her desperation poured from her, making his magic ache.

The last thing Jorrin wanted to do was hurt her. "I don't know what to do," he admitted.

She deflated, and his heart skipped when her eyes welled with tears.

"Cera . . . don't . . ."

"Wait a moment . . ." Avery broke in. Three pairs of eyes looked at him expectantly, "Hadrian, do you have spell books?"

"Of course, but why?"

Avery's expression was sober and serious, more so than Jorrin had ever seen him. "In some reading I've done in the past, I've come across some spells that allow wide geographical scrying. Maybe we can leave a message tuned to Jorrin's father that only *he* can see." He sounded so grown up, Jorrin saw him in a new light.

"Hmmm, that may be possible, but it'll take some time. I know a few spells, but you're right to want to look in a book. There're many variations. Maybe we can find something more powerful than I'm familiar with. Or fashion our own?"

Crafting an original spell that would work was tricky. The words, tone, rhythm all had to line up to form a powerful incantation. Could the wizard and the boy do it?

Blessed Spirit, give us something.

Hadrian rose from his stool and went over to a large bookcase in the corner of the room. He muttered in Aramourian, but he spoke too low for Jorrin to catch what he'd said. He moved his hands back and forth, squinting to gain a better view.

Just like the rest of the small cabin, the books were full of magic, too. They came forward of their own accord, one by one so Hadrian could examine the titles. If it was not the book he was looking for, it would return itself to the shelf in order, and as if it had not been disturbed.

"One of the reasons I failed when I tried was because I didn't have anything that belonged to Braedon." Hadrian returned to his stool, three thick tomes on his lap. The spell books looked old.

He blinked away sudden emotion at the first mention of his father's name. "It should work then, this time." Without another word, Jorrin went outside to where their horses were tied.

Grayna neighed, so he took a moment to caress her nose, whispering to her and dropping a kiss on her wide forehead. She lifted her head and lipped his cheek, making him smile. With one last pat to her neck, he went to his saddlebag.

He only had one thing that'd belonged to his father. His mother had given it to him when he was a little boy, and it'd comforted him many a time when he didn't understand why his father had left.

His fingertips bumped the cool metal. "Got it," he whispered.

Jorrin stared at the belt buckle, his heart pounding. It was meant to be decorative, with a fire-breathing dragon etched into it. He ran his thumb over it, feeling the smooth embossed edges. He kissed the buckle and sent a small prayer to the Blessed Spirit.

Avery had to be correct, the scrying *would* work.

When he returned to the dwelling, he tossed the buckle to Hadrian.

The wizard hastily caught it, then smiled. "I remember when your mother bought this for him."

Jorrin just nodded, his voice caught in his throat.

Avery sat at a wooden table he hadn't noticed before, already poring over one of the spell books, the other two stacked beside it. Concentration on his task was complete.

Had Cera's cousin even noticed that he'd come back inside?

"This is going to take a while," Hadrian remarked, gesturing to Avery. "He'll need my help. He caught me up on the goings on of that evil man and his shades. Magically speaking, there is much to do." Then the elf smiled very gently at Cera. "Not to worry, Lady Ryhan, we'll be as speedy as we can."

Time was slipping through her fingers.

No one was listening to her.

She needed to get to Tarvis.

Cera needed to save what was left of her family, and she *needed* to defeat Varthan. "Time is what we don't have." Her voice came out cracked, weak. Barely containing her threatening sob. Her throat ached.

"Cera, we need to try," her cousin urged, not looking up from his task.

She sighed, her body limp, but her chest heavy. Avery was supposed to be on her side . . . they were *his* parents, after all. She hadn't moved from the seat the wizard had first invited her into.

Jorrin laid a hand on her shoulder, squeezing gently.

Cera refused to acknowledge how his comfort made her heart skip, how welcome it was. How she wanted more. When he'd held her by the fire that morning, she'd never felt so safe, despite the fact she'd been crying like a weakling.

Trikser whined and rose from the hearth rug, sitting at her feet and looking at her, amber eyes warm, concerned. He rested his large head on her lap.

She placed a hand between his ears, but it was an automatic response. "It'd better work," she whispered.

"It *will* work, cousin." Avery looked up from the old tome. His gray eyes bored into hers. "I'm as worried as you for my parents, but my mother wouldn't have sent me away if she thought she couldn't handle things, believe me. She can scry for us, too. Mother will know what we're doing."

Cera shrugged. What did it really matter? She didn't have a choice but to wait. "Your father had better be *good*," she told Jorrin.

One corner of his mouth lifted, but he didn't respond.

Hadrian chuckled. "I trained him . . ." the old elf winked, his blue eyes sparkling.

She managed a small smile, leaning into Jorrin as he gave her another comforting squeeze. She didn't want to resist his touch, she wanted more of it.

"This is going to take me some time, and I need to concentrate." Avery took a deep breath. "I *will* find what I am looking for, Cera, I promise. And we'll find your father, Jorrin."

She grudgingly admired her cousin's determination.

Jorrin whispered thanks.

"In the meantime, I'm rather low on supplies . . ." The elf grimaced, glancing around the room. "It's a bit late to go into the village . . . can either of you hunt?"

Dragon' s Tail
Mountains of Aramour
Terraquist
Elfin River
Loire Isle
Greenwald
North Ascova
Netian Valley
Hadrian' s Place
Tarvis
Berat
South Ascova
Islands
Dalunas
Southern Strait
Penal Territory

"I'm good with a bow, if you have one. Mine's in Greenwald," Cera said.

"I can fix that," Hadrian said, "if you'd be willing to catch supper."

"Of course. Are you up for it, Jorrin?"

"Aye."

Her heart thundered. She'd be alone with him again. She stared into his blue eyes.

He didn't look away, either, making her shift on the chair.

"Well, then, let's get your bow," the wizard said.

Reluctantly, she tore her gaze away from Jorrin and gave Hadrian her attention.

He raised his wand and began to recite a spell. It was Aramourian, but it was obviously a couplet, the words had flow and sounded as if they rhymed.

The wand began to glow green, and he moved it back and forth several times. His chanting became louder and he closed his eyes. The green glow brightened, slowly moving outward from Hadrian's wand to surround his arm, creeping up until it encircled his whole body like an aura.

A moment later, a bow and a quiver full of arrows appeared, hovering in the air.

Cera gasped.

It was her *own* bow, a gift from Captain Moray, leader of the King's Riders. She'd received it upon achieving the rank of Senior Rider. She'd had to leave it at Marshek's tavern in the room where she'd been staying. Mourned its loss, too. Never expected to see it again. Tears blurred her vision.

"Well, go on, I can't hold it up forever," Hadrian said.

"How did you . . . ?" Her voice trembled as she rose from the chair and grabbed her prize. Cera took the quiver, slung it over her shoulder, holding the bow with one hand, and landing heavily on the cushioned seat. She'd always loved the bow. She caressed the smooth wood from top to bottom, fingering the grip and hugging it to her chest.

King Nathal himself had bid his weapons crafter to make it for her, and it was the finest bow she'd ever owned. It was short, but performed like a longbow and had the smoothest pull she'd ever used. She'd loved it from the first time she'd shot an arrow from it.

"I'm a wizard, that's how." Hadrian winked.

"Thank you, Hadrian. I mean it—thank you. This means so much to me." Cera planted a kiss on the old elf's cheek. His face reddened, and she giggled.

Jorrin chuckled.

"Get outta here and get me some dinner, then," he barked.

They hurried out, Jorrin holding the door open for Trikser. They exchanged a grin and burst out laughing.

She heard Hadrian ask Avery just what he thought he was looking at and her cousin's answering laugh as Jorrin shut the panel.

"Here lad, eat." Hadrian set the full bowl of hearty deer stew on the table in front of Avery.

The redhead didn't even look up from the dusty old tome.

They'd been able to down a white-tailed deer.

The wizard was overjoyed he'd not been required to make the kill himself. He'd explained, due to his gift of understanding animals, hunting was very graphic for him. He could hear and feel the animal's pain. Though it was always for sustenance, Hadrian couldn't bear it. He always bought meat from the nearby village market.

"This is delicious." Jorrin spooned the biggest mouthful he could manage.

The thick venison stew reminded him of home, and his mother's cooking. If he closed his eyes, he'd relive a memory of his mother in the kitchen of his childhood home, stirring a large kettle as it simmered over the fire of the largest hearth. His heart gave a painful twinge.

I miss you, Mother.

"It is. Hadrian, thank you. Avery, you really do need to eat. You rode hard from Tarvis, and the dried meat I had wasn't enough," Cera said over her own bowl.

"I'm busy." He still pored over the old book. Didn't even spare her a glance. "I have to find it. I have to find the right one."

"Geesh, no wonder you're so skinny," Hadrian exclaimed, shaking his head. "Don't be foolish, lad."

Avery still didn't look up from the book.

"The dedication is appreciated, but you need to eat, or you won't be able to do a damn thing with whatever you see in there," Jorrin said.

"Come on, cousin," Cera encouraged. "It's getting cold."

He looked up and relented when he saw the inviting bowl of food. "All right, but I'm going to make it quick. I may be getting somewhere. Maybe."

"Oh yeah?" Jorrin asked.

Nodding between mouthfuls, Avery shoveled food into his mouth.

Jorrin quirked a half-smile. Was he even pausing to chew?

The younger man would choke at his current pace.

"Slow down and taste your food," his cousin admonished. Had she read his mind? "You're going to choke to death, then where will we be?" She quirked an auburn eyebrow.

He looked from one cousin to the other, waiting for Cera to smile.

She's serious.

Avery made a face at her, but his next spoonful wasn't at the same top speed.

"You said you almost have it?" Jorrin prodded.

The younger man turned the page in the dusty tome and pointed. He did not, however, put down his bowl or stop eating.

Jorrin was glad the stew had most of Avery's attention. He didn't want the redhead to forego his own needs.

His father would arrive in good time; he had confidence in Avery and Hadrian. Exactly what role he'd play at this point, Jorrin hadn't a clue, but he'd assist in any way he could.

He just wished he could assure Cera everything would be all right, and they'd make it to Tarvis in time. They'd stop Varthan, especially with his father's help.

"There are a few possibilities here, and one here." Avery pointed to both pages of the open book.

Jorrin sighed. He couldn't see the spells from his seat, and the gestures were slight, as if he was standing over Avery's shoulder.

"There's nothing much to see, anyway, at this point."

His expression must have betrayed his thought. He grimaced. "Sorry."

"I need to find the right combination, and that's the problem. The options are not so bad, individually, but I can't seem to find one that has *all* I need the spell to be able to do," Cera's cousin continued, as if he'd not spoken.

"Combining spells can be done. We just have to get the tempo right," Hadrian said, snapping his fingers and waving his wand. His empty bowl promptly disappeared, as did his fork.

Cera paused her meal, pretty gray eyes wide.

The old wizard shrugged. "What? It's the easiest way to do the dishes."

Jorrin laughed.

Avery didn't even look up. The spell book had sucked him back in again.

Had he even seen Hadrian's *cleaning*?

"But where does it go?" She leaned forward in the chair.

"In the cupboard, of course, where dishes belong." The elf inclined his head, blue eyes twinkling.

Brow knitted, she cocked her head to one side. "But . . . is it . . . clean?"

Jorrin chuckled again, and she glanced at him but it was as if absently. He didn't need his empathic magic to feel her disbelief and wonder. Her facial expressions were so vivid and readable.

"Of course. I wouldn't be much of a maid, if it weren't, now would I?" Hadrian asked, straight-faced.

"And the fork?"

"Clean also, in its proper place, the drawer."

She looked at her empty bowl, then at the wizard. "Gonna do mine?"

"I shall. I wouldn't want to leave any dirty bowls out. Draws bugs."

She blinked at Hadrian's joke and Jorrin bit back a laugh. "This is commonplace to you?" Cera met his gaze.

"For most elfin households, yes. It's all right, Cera, really."

"Can we get back to the issues at hand?" Avery snapped.

He glanced at her cousin. With his attention on the book, it was a surprise he'd followed the conversation.

Hadrian cleared his throat. "Aye, certainly, but as I said before, combining spells shouldn't be a problem. Saves the energy needed to write your own and make it work. Show me what you're referring to." He stood beside Avery at the table, studying the book.

Standing, the wizard was as tall as Cera's cousin sitting.

"Hmmm . . . that could work." His lips moved slightly as he read. Hadrian turned to an earlier page. "This one's better." He tapped the tome.

"But how . . . ?" Avery's face reddened.

The wizard laid a slender hand on his arm. "I'll show you."

Jorrin's admiration of Hadrian shot up a degree. With that much kindness, there was no doubt he was a great teacher.

"Cera," he said after several more moments of watching the wizard and the younger man. "We're going to be in the way here."

"Where should we go?" She looked around the small room pointedly.

"Well, I could show you what we talked about before, how to see through Trikser's eyes."

"Really? Now?"

"Yes, but let's go outside. There's more room, and we won't be in the way."

Privacy, too.

He'd be alone with her.

She nodded and glanced at the white wolf. He was lying in front of the hearth again, licking the bowl clean from his own portion of venison. He'd earned it, because he'd flushed the doe from the woods to allow his mistress a clean shot. Cera had told him that Trikser was used to hunting that way with her, and he obviously loved his reward.

Watching her with the bow was intriguing. She was skilled and graceful, even on horseback. Never missed a shot, either. It'd been hard to remember she was highborn.

"Trikser." Her smile was brilliant when the wolf looked at her, tail wagging. "Want to go outside?"

Jorrin's heart quickened.

Her bondmate rose to all fours and headed for the door before either of them. When they didn't come immediately, he glanced over his shoulder.

"See? He understands me." She threw him a smug look and crossed her arms over her breasts.

Jorrin chuckled and shrugged.

They slipped out the door, leaving Hadrian and Avery deep in discussion. Neither seemed to notice that they'd left.

"All right, then, elf-boy. Show me what you got."

He laughed and had to restrain himself from kissing the look off her face.

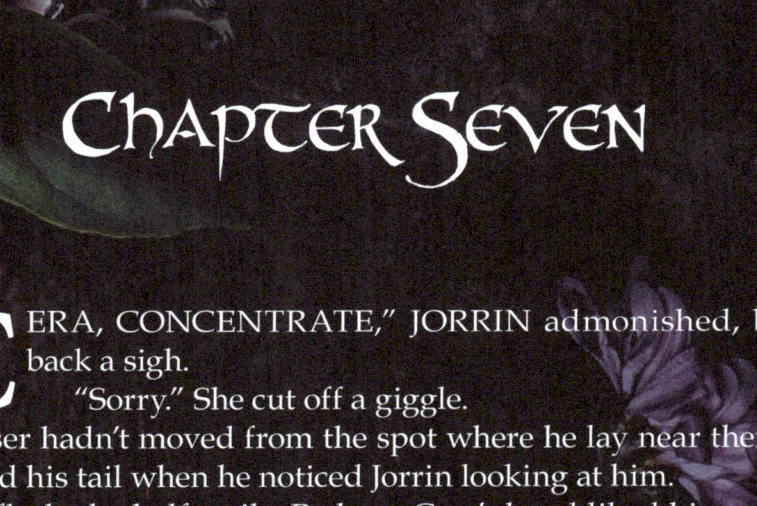

Chapter Seven

"Cera, concentrate," Jorrin admonished, biting back a sigh.

"Sorry." She cut off a giggle.

Trikser hadn't moved from the spot where he lay near them. He thumped his tail when he noticed Jorrin looking at him.

He flashed a half-smile. Perhaps Cera's bond liked him now, or was that just a dose of wishful thinking? "What happened anyway?"

"My nose tickled." She wrinkled the object of discussion.

"Wait. When?"

"A moment ago. Why?"

"Because there was a fly on *Trikser's* nose." He paused. "I think you did it."

"I did?" Her pretty gray eyes widened and her face lit up.

Jorrin's stomach fluttered, and he fought the urge to fidget.

"Did you hear that, Trik?"

The wolf caught the excitement in her tone and rose, coming forward to lick her face.

His breath caught when their eyes met. He'd not seen her so lighthearted since they set out to Tarvis, and it was a welcome change; especially with her earlier urging to continue the journey. He laughed. "Calm down."

"But it's a start," she protested

"Precisely, a *start*." He tried hard to keep a straight face. She was adorable, and he ached to tug her into his arms and kiss her again. "Let's try again."

Cera sighed, resting a hand on each knee and sitting straighter. She nodded.

"Now, like I told you, open your mind to Trikser's. Explain what you're attempting, and tell him to relax."

Her nose wiggled again, and Jorrin could almost see the question forming in her mind. He probably would've been able to pick it up if she hadn't built walls to keep him out. Now that she knew he was an empath, her walls were even stronger.

"What is it?"

"If he has to relax, how can this work in a tense situation?"

"When you become more familiar with joining your mind with . . . or into his, neither of you will need to relax to do it. Concentrating will also become a lot easier. You'll just be able to slip in, almost without a thought. He won't fight you even now since you're bonded, but he'll become more accustomed to having you there, sharing his mind space with you."

"Ah, understood." She took another breath, and her breasts rose and fell in her jerkin.

He tried not to stare there.

"Well, I'm ready to try again, then."

"Go ahead."

Cera let her eyes slip closed. She explained to her wolf what she was trying to do.

He didn't send any thoughts in return, but she felt him loosen and become more open to her. Trikser understood completely.

Minutes passed—or was it hours?

She slipped further into concentration, reaching for the magic that bonded them. Tried to see it as a rope, thick and woven tightly, something Jorrin had suggested. She pictured wrapping it around her waist, around her wolf's torso, and saw herself stepping *into* him.

Cera felt almost divided then, as if she was sitting beside herself. Unsettling, but she excluded it as a distraction. Delving further into his mind, she kept her thoughts in the *now*.

There was no past . . . there was no ability to think of what was to come.

To Trikser, there was only *Cera*.

She truly understood how he was bonded to her. He would always look to her, but at the same time, she was something he would *always* protect. Loyal to the end, he would never question or betray her. He wasn't capable of it.

They *belonged* to each other.

She loved him, as her bondmate, and as one who would always be her friend.

Always be at her side.

This experience was already making her appreciate Trikser more than she ever could have before. She wanted to go farther; she wanted to learn more from him.

Cera saw Jorrin looking calmly at her. Then. . . she saw herself, sitting legs crossed, hands on her knees, and . . . eyes *closed*?

The vision was different somehow. The coloring of everything was off, but her sight had never been so clear, so sharp.

What's happening?

Trik sent an answer to her mental question.

She felt the concept of *'together'* from him. The wolf was telling her they were together, as he understood it. Closer than normal. Sharing mind-space, as Jorrin has put it.

It wasn't a word from her bondmate, but the idea was clearer than the pictures and emotions he usually thought-sent when they communicated.

Her heart sped up. She saw the ground and the woods, but her own eyes were closed . . .

I actually did it! Excitement took over, concentration slipped away.

She had to blink several times to clear and focus her eyes when she'd opened them. Pulling away from Trikser was more tangible than when she'd finally joined her mind with his.

"What?" Jorrin leaned forward.

"I . . . I think . . . I think I did it." Cera smiled and looked at her bondmate.

Trik wagged his tail, so she reached for him, gazing into his amber eyes and scratching his ears. He lay across her lap, stretching and rolling his body into her.

She giggled and rubbed his belly, despite the fact he was too heavy, pushing her against the hard ground.

He wagged his tail harder, making her laugh.

"Tell me about it," Jorrin encouraged.

"I pictured our magic as a rope and wrapped it around us. I stepped into him, making us one. I concentrated and I saw you; but then I also saw me. My eyes were closed, and I felt like I was sitting beside myself. It was . . . unsettling, at first; but then Trik told me we were together. Then I saw into the woods, he moved his head. . . he turned, right?"

He grinned. "Yes, he did. You *did* do it."

"His eyesight is so sharp. It was a wonder to see." Their gazes locked and held. Air ruffled her hair, causing gooseflesh to rise on her neck as a breeze kicked up.

Trikser made a noise in his throat, but she ignored him.

Jorrin looked so wild and beautiful with the wind in his dark hair, his high cheekbones flushed with color to the tips of his slender tapered ears. Her heart skipped as his blue eyes darkened and she read intense heat there.

Last night he'd been in her dreams.

Try as she might, Cera could no longer deny how attracted she was to him. She'd liked that kiss he'd stolen, what seemed ages ago.

Will he kiss me again?

Heat crept up and burned her cheeks. The way he was looking at her made her lose her trail of thought, and her worries.

"Tell Trikser to move."

"What?" But she already sent the mental command.

Her bond slipped off her lap with little encouragement. He'd caught sight of a rabbit and took off after it.

Jorrin grabbed her hand and tugged.

She fell onto him, moving into instead of away, ignoring mental cautions that this wasn't a good idea; despite her dreams, her admitted attraction.

Their lips met in heated rush. Cera's arms shot around his neck and she pressed closer. His body was hard against hers, and a tremor shot down her spine.

Her breasts pressed into his chest as he pinned her against him. Jorrin shoved his tongue into her mouth and groaned.

She clung to him, moving her mouth under his.

When she touched her tongue to his, he moaned, and his hands shot down to cup her bottom.

Cera wiggled in his arms as an unfamiliar warmth enveloped her like an embrace. His erection pressed into her hip, and she clutched his tunic with both hands.

When he kissed her harder, her head spun.

She felt his urgency and confusion rushed her. She whimpered, fighting the sensation of his warmth, his strength as he squeezed her against him.

Her desire for more.

Her desire for him.

I can't lose control.

Yanking back, she panted against him.

Jorrin's chest rubbed her breasts as they both struggled for air. "What's wrong?" he croaked.

"I'm sorry," Cera breathed. Struggling with the protests of her body, she scooted off his lap, gently slipping from his arms.

Hurt flashed through his sapphire eyes, but she didn't focus on it.

She *couldn't*.

"Did I hurt you?" he asked, dark brows furrowed.

"No." She shook her head. "It's not that."

"Cera, I—"

"I can't do this." Her insides clenched, shrieking against her words. The hot and cold warred, as if her whole form couldn't decide whether to give in to desire or rejection. Neither side would relent, spinning her mind into even more chaos.

Jorrin's expression fell, and her heart thundered.

Cera could feel his pain.

They already had a bond she couldn't deny.

Biting her lip was the only thing that held back the threatening tears. She didn't want to hurt him.

She . . . cared about him. More than she should.

It's too dangerous.

Avery appeared in the cabin doorway and shouted for them. "I found it. I really found it!" Oblivious to what had just happened, her cousin pumped his arm, smiling brilliantly.

Sweat beaded Avery's brow and slid down his temple on the way to his cheek, only to be replaced with more when he wiped it away. He had to put forth a substantial magical effort to keep up with Hadrian and Jorrin.

His limbs stung as if they were on fire. A slow burn started to take his muscles over. Ignoring what was starting to feel like pain, he leaned forward, bracing his hands on his knees. He wasn't used to casting where it required such energy, but they needed him to endure a while longer.

Finding the spell hadn't been enough.

Its complexity required their combined magic to strengthen it.

They needed it to go as far as it possibly could. There was no way of knowing where Jorrin's father was. Hopefully, he was on the northern continent.

He'd discovered a way to prevent them from having to cast continually, because it wouldn't be possible to pour unending magic into it. Even a wizard with the skills of Hadrian would tire after a few hours.

So they cast small centers of energy in various locations, so the signal would bounce off and go even farther. The reverberation should keep the signal clear, but Avery had never tried it before.

That was his main contribution to the spell. He'd gotten the idea from the bubbles Varthan's shades had cast over the Provinces.

Hadrian had told him he would've never thought of such a thing. The praise had made him flush.

The spell itself, and the bounce points, would fizzle out in about a sevenday, and they planned to recast if Braedon didn't show up by then.

His cousin had fervently expressed her dismay if they had to cast the call again. It meant the journey to Tarvis would be delayed even more.

He'd tried to assure Cera his mother and father would be fine for a bit longer. Her tears had about killed him. He'd never seen his cousin cry so much.

Avery understood she was grieving *her* parents and younger sister—who wouldn't—but she'd *always* been the strong one. He'd always admired her, looked up to her, and even wanted to be like her.

To see weakness in her scared him more than he cared to admit.

He didn't want to lose his parents like she'd lost hers, but would never say that aloud, of course. His heart ached, and it had little to do with the magical energy he was exerting. He saw his mother's smiling face in his head and forced a breath.

Emeralda was well trained, and had much greater abilities than he himself. His mother would have to handle protecting the entire Province. She'd struggle if Varthan had a great number of shades, but he didn't want to think about that. Couldn't give in to heartache or worry.

He wasn't there, so his mother *had* to handle things.

His father was one of the greatest men he knew.

Their family's personal guard was made up of brave, honorable men who would protect Castle Lenore and the Province of Tarvis to the death.

Surely, both his parents would be fine.

Avery believed it with all his heart.

Braedon opened his eyes. His magical senses had to be fooling him. He heard, or *felt* a call . . . no, it couldn't be . . . it'd been turns. *Couldn't* be real.

It had to be due to his recent dreams . . . dreams of a home he'd fled some twenty odd turns ago. His beloved lifemate—as the elves called spouses—and the infant son he'd left in the mountains of Aramour.

Dreams he dreaded more than welcomed. He cherished the memories, but they were rather like a double-edged sword—reminders of what he lost, what he'd had to leave behind.

His body ached for the touches of Vanora's slender elfin hands to be real again. She'd not caressed him, embraced him in turns, but her touch was as vivid in his mind as the night they'd first joined.

He'd not taken another since he had left, his heart would always be with his son's mother.

Braedon sighed.

And what about Jorrin?

He hoped his son had grown up to become an honorable man, and had honed the magic he was born with. Just as the elfin wizards and mages, he'd sensed magic present in his small son not long after his birth. He prayed to the Blessed Spirit Jorrin had embraced it, and wasn't ashamed of his human father.

A human father he didn't know.

It'd almost killed him to leave, but it was necessary to ensure his family's survival. They would've come to Aramour for him and killed his wife and child. If he wasn't there, they'd leave the peaceful elfin community alone, and they had; Braedon had been in hiding all these turns.

He'd been running the entire time he'd been gone, but for the past several turns, he'd not been pursued. Whether it was because he'd managed to cover his trail with magical spells, or they'd given up the search, he'd never figured out.

He looked around the crowded, noisy tavern and shook his head. He'd not been in the small village very long—only two days—and he didn't plan on staying.

Running was ingrained, and though he didn't sense anyone after him, he couldn't change his ways. So Braedon would move on, to the next town or village, as always.

He set down the empty mug. Didn't need another. Perhaps the drink had made him feel the magic call. But . . . there it was again.

Right?

Cocking his head, Braedon listened harder, squinting to concentrate. He blocked out the din in the bar. His body hummed and heated as he called upon his magic. He sent out magic feels and tried to ascertain if it was real, or if he was going crazy.

"Shall I get you a refill?" The pleasant, normally-welcome voice of the young barmaid broke into his thoughts, destroying his concentration.

He listened for a moment before looking up at her, but it was gone. "Drat," Braedon muttered. *Almost had it.*

"What was that?" Big brown eyes looked at him expectantly. She'd told him her name was Lilia, and she'd been flirting since he'd ventured into the place.

When he'd rented a room upstairs and paid, she'd offered to join him. He was flattered and told her so, but declined gently. Would continue to do so if she persisted.

"Oh, sorry, it's nothing. Nay, I need nothing more, thank you. I'll be heading out in the morning."

"That's a shame." Lilia lifted his empty mug and put it on the tray. Leaning in more than necessary, she flaunted her ample bosom in her low-cut bodice. She grinned, flashing dimples.

He found himself smiling back.

She *was* a beauty.

"She's a lucky woman, your wife." Without another word, she went toward the bar, setting her tray down.

His wife's smile danced into his mind. Blessed Spirit, he missed Vanora.

What's gotten into you lately?

Braedon wasn't prone to dwelling on his memories, or former desires. For the most part he was able to distract himself. There *had* to be a reason his family haunted his mind after all this time.

He sucked in a breath and mounted the stairs leading to his rented room. It was on the corridor with the larger suites—nicer linens and bigger beds.

The tavern's working girls stayed there. He'd heard many a moan of passion from neighboring quarters, and heavy foot traffic during the previous night. Booted feet and enthusiastically closed doors.

Braeden had no doubt Lilia had placed him here in hopes of being his bedmate for the duration of his stay.

Poor lass.

He didn't have many things, but there was no harm in preparing his belongings for his journey in the morning.

He'd leave early, before the bar got busy.

Hopefully, Lilia would forgive him for leaving.

He chuckled.

Chapter Eight

THEY ARRIVED IN Tarvis faster than Lucan had thought possible, but as they entered Tarvis Main, it was obvious their arrival had been foreseen. Someone had evacuated all the townspeople, even from the slums.

Lord Varthan would be angry.

Lucan stifled a wince.

His master chuckled, and he jumped in his saddle.

Dagonet caught his gaze and stared for a moment, but the older shade said nothing.

"Dagonet, Markus, Athas, each of you take a direction and scout the city. Take notice of anyone or anything that may pose a threat to us and dispose of it. Lucan stays with me. Report back at city center in two hours."

"Yes, milord," the eldest of the four, Athas said, inclining his head and turning his black stallion south.

Dagonet went east, and Markus west, leaving Lord Varthan and Lucan to the north.

"What do you see?" his master barked.

The blood drained from his face under the weight of Lord Varthan's stare.

"Well? Tell me where magic is, boy."

Lucan shifted in his saddle as the lord growled, but he wouldn't delay his master's demands. He closed his eyes, searching for magic. He gripped the pommel of his saddle for balance, able to probe great distances, taking mental notice when the source of magic was significant. He passed over his fellow shades, seeing them riding, their magical auras glowing with the different colors of their strengths.

Searching toward the castle—the center of the normally busy Province—he saw the sign announcing Castle Lenore.

is magical senses surged, jerking him in his saddle.

A great source detected his magic and immediately shut him out. He couldn't probe further. Something wasn't right. He'd been shut out?

Unheard of.

He tried again, asserting more energy, but was once again rejected. Lucan's temples throbbed. It wasn't often he had to work so hard with magic. He squared his shoulders, narrowing the scope of his energy, concentrating solely on breaching the magic inside the castle.

Body thrumming, his head pounded. His chest ached with the effort to breathe normally, and he ignored the burning in his lungs as he pushed one more powerful surge of magic against the spell.

He was, yet again, shut out.

I'm getting nowhere.

The protection spell was very powerful, thick with control. Whoever had put it in place had a great deal of skill. It'd take an amazing amount of power to breach it, and only if he and the other three shades cast together. Lucan wiped the sweat from his brow and forced a few deep breaths. How could he tell his master?

He'd seen firsthand that anyone could outlive their usefulness to the man, and it scared him to death. He wanted out. But how could that ever be possible?

Lord Varthan never had him far from his side.

He'd do his best *always* to be useful to him.

"The city is deserted, my lord," Lucan said.

"I can see that," his master snapped.

"There is only one place I sense magic. In the castle."

"It won't be a problem," the tall man said. Statement, not question.

His heart's galloped in his small chest. "My lord . . ." Lucan winced.

"Go on."

Swallowing hard, he forced himself to sit still. His knuckles were white from his tight grip on the reins. "Whoever it is . . . is very powerful. There's a very complicated protection spell cast over the castle. My probing could not penetrate it."

Lord Varthan laughed, long and hard.

Lucan froze as he unwittingly met his master's dark eyes.

"It looks like the bitch's family is playing for keeps."

He gulped and a tremor shimmied down his spine. He didn't answer his master.

The other three shades met them in front of Castle Lenore, exactly as instructed.

"What did you find?" Lord Varthan barked.

Athas sneered at Lucan before bowing to their master from his saddle. "I did not come across so much as a dog, milord. They cleaned out the whole Province—Main, Upper and Lower to the south." He inclined his head and looked at his two younger companions.

Lucan felt the disdain Athas sent his way, but he couldn't retaliate. The shade was older and bigger, and would clobber him even if he'd had the guts to try anything. His magic was much more powerful than Athas', so he took quiet victory in that.

"Even the inns, no smoke in the chimneys to the west," Markus said, but failed to bow.

Lord Varthan will smack him for sure.

"I also did not encounter anyone, or feel anything, my lord." Dagonet inclined his head as Markus should have.

The lord scanned their group, but this time Lucan was not a part of his master's all-encompassing gaze. He cleared his throat. "Lucan, brief them on the shield."

Nodding, he closed his eyes and broadcast his memory into the minds of Athas, Markus and Dagonet. Showing them was easier than telling them, and they'd be able to judge the power of the spell if they experienced his recollection of it.

All three of the older boys looked at him, astonishment written in their expressions. They'd comprehended the complexity of the spell over the castle.

"That is a great deal of power," Dagonet mused.

"It will not be a problem," Lord Varthan said, but his tone called for the shade's opinion.

"No, my lord," Dagonet said. "It'll take effort and strategy to break through it, but I don't see that it's impossible."

Lucan looked the shade up and down. The older boy was almost as powerful as him. What would it take for their master to consider him as invaluable as Lord Varthan currently saw Lucan? He was envious that Dagonet could get away from their master as he saw fit.

"Athas, did you see a proper inn?" Lord Varthan glanced away from Lucan and Dagonet.

"Yes, deserted, of course, but not far from here."

"Lead the way." Their master kicked his horse.

"Milord?" Dagonet inquired.

"We will need to rest before you take the spell down," he growled.

The older boy gave a curt nod.

Lucan urged his horse to follow, remaining silent, ensuring he was between Dagonet and their master so Athas couldn't have open access to him.

No shade other than Dagonet actually questioned Lord Varthan and escaped punishment.

He glanced over his shoulder to find the older boy's hazel eyes steadily regarding him.

Lucan looked away, shifting in his saddle. He was relieved their master was allowing them to rest. Although, he'd not gotten anywhere when he'd probed for magic, exhaustion from the energy he'd expended was paramount. Their master was well aware magic was stronger if a body was rested.

Lord Varthan had pressed them hard to get to Tarvis, and they all could use a hearty meal and a real bed.

Not that Lucan ever complained, but he'd be happy to lay his head on a real pillow. It'd been quite a while. Hopefully his master would let him have his own room. Or at least a room away from Athas.

"There will be no people there, milord," Athas said.

"Less coin to pay for the room." Lord Varthan gave a humorless laugh.

Markus and Athas exchanged a nervous glance and Lucan gulped.

Dagonet was the only one that seemed unbothered, but that just made Lucan shift in his saddle even more.

Dragon's Tail

Mountains of Aramour

Terraquist

Elfin River

Greenwald

Median Valley

North Ascova

Hadrian's Place

Tarvis

Berat

South Ascova

Dalunas

Islands

Southern Strait

Penal Territory

Braedon rode hard.

He was worried he was asking too much of Roan, for his stallion was rather elderly. He *had* to get there. Patting the horse named for his color, he urged him to greater speed.

If he pushed his mount, he risked taking longer; the old stallion wouldn't survive injury, but he didn't want to stop. He was a good hard three days' ride away from the center of the call's location.

"I'm sorry, lad, but we've a call to answer. It's important, I promise." He leaned closer to Roan's neck to ease his horse.

The stallion was dear to him. His horse was two turns older than his son, and had accompanied him when he'd fled Aramour. Roan was the only sense of home that remained with Braedon every day.

When he'd left his family, he'd honestly believed he would never see them again. His heart beat faster. He'd see his son, after all these turns.

He kicked himself for questioning the call for two days. Dreams had continued to haunt him, so he'd blamed it on that. Meditating to clear his mind, he'd seen it.

Like a slap in the face. And Braedon was an idiot.

Very clearly . . . three magical auras . . . *calling to him.*

The first was familiar. Hadrian, his mentor and very old friend. The second had a magical trail not so different from his own. Jorrin *had* to be at the center of the call. He wasn't familiar with the third, but the call was being simulcast, so it couldn't be hostile magic.

The desperation was palpable.

What in the Blessed Spirit's Name could be wrong?

He needed to get there now.

The call hadn't come from Aramour. It was from somewhere due east—near Berat, the best he could figure.

Why aren't they in Aramour?

He hadn't been that far east in turns. Braedon had learned how to mask his trail with more skill than Hadrian had ever been able to teach him. The first one had covered his trail for almost two turns. Then they'd found him again, but hadn't caught him. He'd improvised even more with his magic afterward, learning to devise even more powerful masking spells. Otherwise, he wouldn't have survived.

Braedon had tried to cast an answer to let them know he was on his way, but the magic was closed, a signal only. The call was surrounded in a protection spell that carried the signature of the first presence. Hadrian had left considerable power in it, not even friendly magic could enter.

Generally if magic was closed, it was so dark magic couldn't intercept the energy or harm the sender. Nature of the spell mattered not.

Is Hadrian afraid of dark magic?

The situation had to be dire, because his old friend was usually not afraid to open cast.

Why had they left Aramour? Was Vanora with them? Was she all right?

Is Jorrin?

His heart thundered in time with Roan's hoof beats.

What the hell is going on?

CHAPTER NINE

JORRIN WAS WAITING. Blessed Spirit, he was *sick* of it. Four days since they'd simulcast the spell to call his father.

Braedon hadn't turned up.

Hadrian assured him Braedon would sense it; that he'd come to find them, but how could they be sure? It was less than three days before they'd have to recast. He'd have to dig deep to muster the energy. Getting over the initial disappointment was hard enough.

Avery had also been disappointed. Each morning with no sign of Jorrin's father, Cera's cousin withered even more.

She wasn't taking the waiting any better, but at least Jorrin hadn't had to witness any more tears. He didn't want to think about her tears. Didn't want to remember what it was like to hold her, and *definitely* banished the memory of her kiss. Especially the last one.

Damn, he'd botched things with her.

He'd not tried to kiss her again. Nor had they discussed it. Both were striving for normal. And although he ached every time he looked at her, he was dealing with it . . . pretending he'd not drowned against her sweet lips, felt her luscious body against his, and melted into her gorgeous gray eyes.

Liar.

Jorrin couldn't get her out of his head. Or his dreams.

With a heavy sigh, he dropped Hadrian's axe. He'd been helping the elf wizard by halving firewood logs. Bigger and stronger than the elf, he could accomplish twice what the wizard could in about half the time.

He smiled to himself, remembering Cera's shock that Hadrian didn't have some magic spell to do it for him.

"He's got something for *everything* else," she'd remarked, eyes wide.

The redheaded beauty had laughed out loud when the elf had told her that magic for chopping wood just wasn't practical.

"But it is for doing dishes?" she'd asked.

Jorrin laughed like he had earlier. Obviously, she'd no idea Hadrian was pulling her leg.

"Almost done?" Her sweet voice pulled him from his memory.

He looked up, meeting her gaze.

She smiled and his sense of gloom dissipated.

"I guess so." He surveyed the neat stack of firewood he'd made for the elf wizard. "This should last him quite some time, so I can probably stop."

Cera looked him up and down. "You look hot. Want some water?"

He was suddenly hot all right, but it had little to do with his chopping wood. Heat crept up his neck. He ordered his body not to respond any further to that stare of hers. "Nah, I'm all right." Jorrin swallowed, glancing over his work again, desperate for a distraction.

She hadn't acknowledged his dismissal. She disappeared into the cabin.

"Here you go." She handed over a large mug of iced spice tea. "It's not water, though. Avery fixed it, it's my favorite."

"Then you drink it." He shook his head and attempted to hand the mug back to her.

Cera put her palm up. "No, it's for you. C'mon, Avery would be upset."

He studied her for a moment and his stomach fluttered.

She's reaching out to me? Maybe *normal* wasn't so bad if she'd talk to him, spend time with him. Had she made the drink?

She was being awfully insistent with him.

"Well, Lady Ryhan, you shouldn't be serving me, a lowly half-elf. It should be the other way around."

She wrinkled her nose and stuck her tongue out.

Jorrin laughed. "That was very *unladylike*."

"It was?" Cera giggled. "Then I shan't do it again." Her tone and manner were haughty. "Well?"

"Well what?"

"Weren't you going to serve me?" She bowed gracefully.

Somehow, it looked wrong since she was clad in breeches, and not the long skirts a lady would normally wear, but then again, she wasn't like any highborn lady he'd ever met.

He chuckled and gestured to a log big enough for a seat, not far from the chopping block. "By all means, my lady, have a seat."

She sat on the log, overacting, but still graceful. "Not the best accommodations for a lady of my rank, I have to mention," she said in the same haughty tone, and then looked away.

Their eyes met after a moment and they both laughed.

His heart ached. Jorrin wanted more with her. He pushed the thought away, clinging to what they had at the moment. Not nearly enough, but it would have to do.

For now.

The banter was a welcome diversion from the seriousness of their situation. Before he'd met Cera, life had held a simplicity he'd been missing lately. On the other hand, his purpose had been lacking. Which did he prefer more? No purpose at all, or one that affected the very lives of people—people he was starting to care a great deal about?

Nothing he'd asked for, but a role that could fulfill his greatest desires and his greatest fears at the same time.

"Thank the Blessed Spirit you're not really like that." Jorrin ignored his trail of thought.

It's for the better.

She rolled her eyes. "I wouldn't be able to stand myself. Though I know many a *lady* who really is."

"I wouldn't like you half as much as I do."

Her cheeks reddened, but she locked her gaze with his.

Jorrin's heart missed a beat. He cleared his throat. "Actually, I care about you . . . a great deal." It was more than that, but if he told her, Cera would shove him away. And he already wasn't fond of being at arms' length. Besides, he wanted to gauge her reaction to his lesser confession.

Her eyes widened and her blush deepened. "Oh," she whispered.

Oh.

Oh?

She said oh?

He blinked. His head reeled and his chest burned, heart tearing in two.

They stared at each other.

He put his hand to his forehead and turned away. Jorrin shook his head, and when he glanced back at her, she stood, hesitated, then took a step toward him.

"Jorrin, I . . . I'm . . ."

Hadrian appeared in his home's doorway. "Braedon's coming!"

The interruption was like Avery's the other night, when she'd put the first dent in his heart. Now the organ pounded for a different reason.

His father was coming?

Cera looked at the wizard, then back at him.

Jorrin swallowed, torn. Ordering himself to get it together, he smiled at Hadrian and walked past her without another word.

She looked down, and his magic stung as he caught her rush of pain, but he ignored his answering guilt.

She'd just crushed *him* after all.

Why did *she* feel bad?

"Did you hear what I said, lass?" Hadrian stared at Cera.

Jorrin ignored both the elf and Trikser, who'd rushed past him on his way to his mistress. He headed to the cabin, stepping inside and refusing to meet Avery's gray eyes as he slipped into a seat at Hadrian's table.

"Something wrong?" the younger man asked, the brilliant smile on his face falling off a bit.

"No," he mumbled. "My father's coming?"

"Aye, let me show you," Hadrian said.

He forced another smile and ignored Avery's curious expression. He couldn't meet Cera's eyes as she came to the small table as well.

Braedon turned off the road, plunging into the woods. They'd slowed from their grueling pace of the past several hours. His old stallion's energy had returned, but Roan was still breathing heavier than he liked.

"Almost there, my friend." He rubbed the horse's neck.

The center of the call radiated just ahead. It was so strong it made his magical senses leap, causing him to squint. Not a light exactly, but it had the bright trail of the same three auras he'd sensed when he'd first realized what it was. The spell was fading, no longer at the height of its power; he could feel it wane.

He was glad he'd not answered the call when it had been first cast. Coming this close would have certainly knocked him off Roan. Smiling at the image in his head, he ducked as his stallion went under the low hanging branch of a tree. Maybe he would get knocked off his horse, yet.

"Are you upset with me?" Braedon asked with a low chuckle.

They came to a clearing. He sighed when he saw the small cabin, which looked as tired as he felt. Smoke drifted from the undersized chimney, so someone had to be home, but he could see little proof of that outside.

Roan gave a whinny that was answered by the rapid clopping of hooves and an aggressive snort. A nervous stallion.

Braedon looked in the direction of the din and saw three horses. One black, another white and the last dappled several shades of gray. They were tied along a small fence at the opposite end of the clearing, and it even looked decrepit.

Which horse was the stallion was a mystery at that distance, but if all three horses pulled away at the same time, the rotted posts would pull the fence right out of the ground.

Good thing they wanted to stay put. None were saddled, and a small barn stood to the left of them at the edge of the woods. It was in better shape than the cabin.

Another horse's whinny took his attention. A very skinny animal, grayish in color, small in stature, was tied to another post in front of the cabin. The poor wretch had to be older than Roan, and looked like it hadn't eaten in months.

Who would treat an animal that way? Surely not Hadrian, for his old friend and wizard's strongest magic was related to animals. If the horse was the elf's, it couldn't possibly be as bad as it looked from his position.

He walked Roan into the clearing slowly, instinct making him keep his guard up. Deep down, he doubted he was being led into a trap, but from what he'd known over the turns, one could *never* be too cautious.

A wolf came flying toward him out of nowhere, fangs bared and growling, hackles standing on end.

Braedon discarded the idea of drawing his sword and attempted to steady Roan. The horse's muscles rippled under his thighs as his stallion pranced.

The snow-colored beast lunged, and he shifted his weight to maintain his seat. The wolf wasn't making contact; it was only pushing them back, trying to keep him out of the clearing.

Braedon was about to say a spell to force it away from them, when a young woman with curly dark red hair appeared in front of the cabin. He didn't focus on her. He couldn't allow the distraction; he wanted the wolf away from his horse.

"Trikser, *no!*" She raised her hand, beckoning. "Stop."

He stared as the thing obeyed; it moved to her, tail plastered between its legs.

Sitting beside her, it looked like a peaceful puppy, not the vicious animal he'd just seen before him. Magic flowed between them.

Ah, they're bonded.

He'd seen the likes of it before, of course, but not in some time. Smart move, though. Had he a daughter, he'd approve of such a pairing. The lass would have a ferocious protector for life.

Bonded animals always gained the benefit of living much longer than their normal lifespan. The wolf would survive as long as the girl did. Unfortunately, if one party died, the other usually did not last long, no matter which of the two perished.

Three more figures appeared behind her, the last almost tumbling out of the cabin's door. The last took Braedon's attention immediately.

The last was Jorrin.

My son.

He wouldn't have noticed if the king himself had been one of the others. Tears sprung to his eyes. He blinked to clear his vision.

The smallest of the four figures took a step toward him. "Well, are you going to get down from there, or do we have to drag you?" Hadrian demanded, hands on his hips, his head cocked up at him. "I'm short, remember? C'mon, you're hurting my neck."

Braedon chuckled. "Not even a hello, old friend, after all these turns?" He dismounted, and his boots hit with a *thud*, sending jolts of ice up his calves to his knees. He hadn't been on his feet in hours that felt like days, and fought the urge to shake his legs out.

Hadrian grinned, his crystal blue eyes sparkling. "Of course, where are my manners?" The elf wizard embraced him, not quite coming up to Braedon's chest.

They both smiled, then shook hands as they stood back to survey each other.

"You look good. The same, really," Hadrian remarked, his approval apparent.

"As do you."

"No, I'm old."

Braedon laughed.

The elf's answering grin was impish.

He looked around, his gaze settling on Jorrin. He was eager to greet his son.

The lad wasn't far from the doorway of the cabin, looking like he wanted to run, his mouth a line, complexion pale. His shoulders were tight, but it didn't keep Braedon from spotting Vanora's beauty all over his son, down to his tapered ears. His heart raced.

So tall.

Tall and dark-haired like him, but he knew without looking Jorrin had his mother's sapphire eyes. He needed to greet him, hug him. Speak to him.

Braedon, my friend, he's going to need some time. He heard Hadrian's voice in his head, and the comment left his chest aching.

He shot the elf wizard a glance. Disappointment crashed over him in waves, emotion making his magic throb.

Jorrin radiated bitterness, and he winced.

Braedon couldn't blame the lad, but it didn't lessen the pain of rejection. His son couldn't understand everything, but then again, he had no idea what Jorrin knew about his past.

All in good time.

He tried to smile, but only succeeded in his lad shrinking away, moving back into the shadow of the doorway.

"Thank you for coming." The redheaded lass spoke for the first time, taking Braedon's attention. "I'm sorry about my bondmate. You weren't hurt?"

"Nay, I wasn't hurt. I'm sorry I didn't get here sooner."

Cera looked the tall man over. Was he old enough to be Jorrin's father? He didn't look much over forty turns—if that—but his contribution to Jorrin's looks was obvious.

They had the same coal black hair and high cheekbones, which she had first assumed to be an elfin trait. Like Jorrin, Braedon was handsome—gorgeous actually. They shared the same height and broad shoulders; trim waist and muscular build, though the elder had a little more bulk.

She almost gasped when her gaze met his.

Instead of the sapphire orbs Jorrin had, Braedon's were amber, and she'd never seen amber eyes on a person.

Captivating.

Jorrin's father and Hadrian were speaking in Aramourian, but one look at his elderly stallion worried her too much to wonder what they were saying. "Avery, can you see to his horse? He needs tending."

"Yes, of course, the poor lad needs a drink." Her cousin stepped forward.

"No, no . . . I'll do it," Braedon protested.

Cera shook her head. "I'm sure you're tired from your journey, and my cousin doesn't mind."

"Not at all." Avery nodded and took the stallion's reins from the man's hand.

"Don't argue with her, you won't win." The elf winked and flashed a smile. He was teasing her, something she was still getting used to.

Heat rushed her cheeks. She prayed she wasn't bright red.

Braedon relented, and let her cousin lead the horse toward Ash, Valor and Grayna. There was a spot for him on the end of the fence, and grain and water in Hadrian's small barn.

"We have a lot to talk about," Jorrin said. He stepped away from the cabin door, but he didn't come close enough to really join them.

She glanced at him and bit her bottom lip, stopping herself from reaching for him.

He hadn't talked to her much; she'd screwed things up so badly. Pulling away from him, then hurting his feelings by the woodpile. Her intended bribe of the spiced tea had failed miserably. She'd crushed him twice, when all she really wanted to do was fall into him, savor and return his kiss, admit she cared about him, too.

More than *cared* about him?

Since Hadrian had confirmed Braedon was on his way, Jorrin had seemed to sink further into himself. Did it really have to do with the advent of his father? How much of it was her fault?

Cera *had* to defeat Varthan and save her family. Getting closer to Jorrin was too dangerous. Not just for her heart.

The ex-archduke was a bastard. He had powerful magic at his disposal. His shades had the ability to retrieve information deeply blocked and buried in someone's mind. So, if she was caught, no matter how she tried to protect him, she'd be unable to.

She couldn't risk caring for him any more than she already did, but as much as she'd hurt him by pulling away, she stabbed her own heart, too.

She wanted him.

To be close to him, be in his arms. Kissing him, touching him. Damn, the man could kiss. Only two times, and Cera was already addicted.

She'd had a hard time paying attention to the scrying spell Hadrian had used to show them Braedon's progress on the road. Normally, she would've been fascinated by it.

He didn't use a map, like traditional scrying did, but opened a small window, a bubble, showing a picture of where Braedon actually was. The spell was centered on the belt buckle that had belonged to Jorrin's father, in the same way traditional scrying depended upon a personal belonging of the person that was being sought.

Avery, of course, had been amazed and wanted to learn the skill immediately. The wizard had told them one only needed a flat surface to make it work, and it didn't matter what the surface was. An easy spell, anyone could master it. Her cousin hadn't wasted any time. He'd started to practice right away.

Sighing, she let her thoughts sink back to the man she was still trying to convince herself she couldn't have.

Jorrin stood next to Hadrian as the elf spoke to their new arrival, his shoulders slumped, not meeting his father's eyes.

Denying him in her own head was a failure. Thinking of him made her smile, no matter what. Her heart never behaved normally when they were in the same room, especially if he was flashing that smile of his. Her stomach rolled, and her cheeks were always hot.

The feeling was more than physical attraction.

But as much as that made her heart skip, she dreaded it. Opening herself up to him? Letting him know the real Cera? She'd already let him see her cry. That was something not even Avery had seen very often.

But as much as that made her heart skip, she dreaded it. Opening herself up to him? Letting him know the real Cera? She'd already let him see her cry. That was something not even Avery had seen very often.

Immediate family had been everything to her; she'd shut down when she'd lost them. A connection like that was too much of a risk. Letting Jorrin in was different than the love she'd had for her parents and Kait.

She hadn't shared her feelings with anyone. In many ways, Cera was afraid to take that step. If she voiced what she was feeling, she'd have to face it. It was easier to deal with if her lips were sealed, but hurting him made her heart ache.

How much longer could she get away with not coming clean?

He was part empath, after all, so he'd be able to pick up thoughts and emotions without prying. How much did he already know? Wild, unstable emotions were hard to hide, no matter how strong the walls she tried to maintain in her mind.

"Aye, I assumed you called me for a reason." Jorrin's father's voice was steady and even, his accent revealing he was a man from the far north, though it wasn't as thick as Hadrian's. It was like Jorrin's, or even a tad softer, depending on the words he was saying.

"Yes, we do have a great deal to discuss." Cera's words repeated the only statement Jorrin had made since his father rode into the clearing. Forcing herself to speak lessened the throbbing in her head. At least a little bit.

She glanced at her object of desire, but he was studying his boots. Her stomach fluttered, and she clenched her fists at her sides instead of reaching for his hand like she wanted to.

He'd probably push her away, anyway. Her eyes smarted and she swallowed against the lump in her throat.

"Let's go inside then," the elf said, gesturing to his small home.

She nodded, meeting Hadrian's eyes before looking at Jorrin's father. He offered a small smile, which she returned.

Braedon's appearance meant returning to her original plans and dark thoughts.

Hadrian had said Jorrin's father was her only hope.

Cera was going to see about that.

Jorrin kicked himself. He was acting like a spoiled child. His father had been at Hadrian's cabin for two whole days. Two days of briefing, planning various strategies, approaches, and strong magic . . . but not two days of catching up on lost time and getting to know the man he'd left his childhood home to find.

Since reaching adulthood, he'd not had ill feelings toward his father. Selfish childhood desires were in the past. The bitterness at Braedon's physical appearance was a shock. Fear and hurt had hit him, made him want to recede into the shadows. He was that abandoned little boy all over again, and afraid if he said anything to Braedon, he would've regretted it.

So, he'd remained silent, letting Hadrian and his father catch up happily, which had only irritated him even more. Cera and Avery liked his charming father, too. They'd talked, laughed and eaten, all at ease with each other, as if they had known one another forever.

He cursed, shaking his head. Why couldn't he have loosened up then?

Jorrin had been quiet, unlike himself, staying in the corner near the fireplace, even sitting on the hearth next to the white wolf.

Every time he'd looked at him, Trikser had just thumped his tail and met his eyes.

Ironic.

He might've been amused at another time.

All the words he'd wanted to say to his father had dissolved on his tongue. Even now, he was brooding outside Hadrian's cabin at the edge of the woods, his hand buried in Grayna's mane.

She hoofed the ground and bumped his other hand with her nose until he caressed her.

He smiled and rested his forehead on her wider one, discarding the urge to throw his arms around her neck like a child. He hadn't spent time with his horse since before he'd met up with Cera, and he missed it tremendously. The mare always calmed him.

"When are you going to give me a chance to talk to you? I've waited for two days, and I don't want to wait any longer to talk to my son."

Jorrin jumped. He'd not heard his father approach. "Two days? What about twenty turns?" He didn't bother looking over his shoulder.

"I deserve that, but then again, you don't know the whole story. Hadrian shared with me what he told you, what your mother told you, and let's face it, it wasn't much." Though Braedon spoke calmly, he sensed hurt his father wasn't trying to hide.

He should let it go, be grateful his father was with them, but a part of him wouldn't let it happen. "What's there to know? You left, and we were forced to cope without you." He didn't bother to hide his emotions, either.

Highly trained, highly skilled empath, so why not give him the onslaught? Emotions could tell his father how he was feeling much more than any words he could form.

"But you did. You and your mother were *always* survivors," Braedon said, his tone irritatingly patient. "That's how I knew you two would be all right. And you were." He sucked in a breath, betraying some of the calm in his voice. "Did she tell you I had to leave? They were after me. They would've killed both of you. The two I love, not *loved*, more than anything else in this world."

"Who is '*they*'? I'm always hearing about *they*, but no one can, or will, tell me about *them*. So *how* am I supposed to understand why my father was *forced* to go away from me?" Jorrin whirled on his father, looking him in the eye for the first time since he'd arrived at Hadrian's.

"They have another time and place. We have important things to do for your lovely Lady Ryhan. You understand that. I hope you won't hate me forever. I promise I'll tell you everything you ever wanted to know about me and why I had to leave, but not now." Braedon paused, sighing. "I didn't want to go, Jorrin. I love you. I love your mother, too. I never have, and never *will*, love another woman."

"I have nothing more to say to you." Assurances of love from the man meant nothing. He had to have information to accept any of his father's justifications.

Braedon closed his eyes, pain radiating from him. Sorrow and regret hit Jorrin's empathic senses in waves, making his head throb.

Damn him.

Damn the magic he'd inherited from him, too.

Neither of them spoke.

Jorrin turned back to Grayna.

Braedon retreated, the door to the cabin opening and closing with a small *thud* that resounded in his temples.

He closed his eyes and buried his face against his dappled mare. "That went well."

"Jorrin?"

He winced. Hadn't heard Cera's approach, either.

Why won't everyone just leave me alone?

He'd not spoken to her since she'd answered his confession with the one word that cut him deeper than any ballad of rejection ever could have. He was as frustrated with her as he was with Braedon.

What was he supposed to say to her? He was tired of her *not* wanting him.

"What is it, Cera?" Jorrin whirled on her like he had on his father.

Her eyes widened and her face flushed. "I . . . I just . . . " Her voice wobbled. Then she clenched a fist, and her mouth set in a firm line. "Never mind. Talk to me when you're not an idiot."

His heart sank. *No. This isn't how I want things.*

As she turned away, his hand shot forward. Touching her sent an electric charge up his arm and he stared at his fingers enclosing her slender wrist. Her skin was soft and he wanted to explore her more, pull her into his arms and kiss her, beg her to be with him. "Cera, I'm sorry."

She shook her head and yanked away.

He released her and tried to cup her face, but she backed away, squeezing her eyes shut, tears shining on her cheeks.

Jorrin was an arse.

A total arse.

He couldn't stand to see her cry, yet he was here, causing her tears when she already had so much to deal with? "I'm sorry," he repeated, but she still wouldn't look at him.

Cera shook her head once more, rushing away as Braedon had, slamming the cabin door.

Great, now everyone would know what an idiot he was. Just what he deserved, right?

Jorrin's vision blurred.

Crying? *Are you really crying?*

As he belittled himself for not being much of a man, he took a few steps backward and leaned heavily on Grayna.

She whinnied, but the notion didn't give him any comfort.

What the hell was he supposed to do now?

Chapter Ten

CERA SAT AT Hadrian's small table, not really a part of the conversation. The past day and a half had been a whirlwind, she was locked in some sort of haze she couldn't escape.

Braedon and Hadrian were deep in discussion, a map of Tarvis laid out before them. They were pointing and nodding, but she couldn't recall a word.

She couldn't clear her mind, couldn't focus on the task at hand. And she needed desperately to do so. Guilt crept up from the pit of her stomach.

A door closed, jarring her as Avery entered the small cabin. His face was flushed, he looked flustered, but he said nothing as he took a seat at the table next to Hadrian.

She remained silent while her cousin jumped right into the talks. More guilt assaulted her.

Avery agreed to something almost immediately.

Then three sets of eyes turned, staring.

Had Hadrian addressed her? Why hadn't she heard him the first time?

"Wouldn't you agree, lass?" The wizard's crystal eyes assessed.

Cera shifted in her seat and exchanged a glance with her cousin.

Avery's head was cocked, his eyes wide. His jaw rippled, as if he was angry about something. Was he mad at her?

"What was the question?" Her cheeks burned.

Hadrian smiled.

Stop looking at me like I'm five turns old.

Braedon sat across from her, gazing with what could only be considered fatherly concern.

She shifted in her seat again, then screamed at herself to sit still. *What is wrong with me?*

"I was trying to decide the best manner to enter the Province. Avery thinks from the Southgate, farthest from the castle. Although, indeed it may be safer, it would be the most ground to cover." Hadrian tapped Tarvis Southgate on the map for effect, and Cera focused on it.

The parchment looked old and fragile, which was akin to how she felt.

She gulped and wanted to cringe. "Avery thinks it's best?"

"As do I," Braedon said.

Her gaze shot to his amber eyes, and suddenly she was unable to look away. Though a different color, they were the exact same shape of Jorrin's. Her heart raced, starting an unpleasant throb in her chest. She wanted to rub the spot, but didn't. She chided herself to calm down, clasping her hands tight on her lap.

The haze started to consume her again, and Cera had to concentrate to clear her head enough to answer the three people who were expecting her input.

This was her quest, after all.

"I'll agree with what you think is best," she whispered.

Sympathy and fatherly concern consumed Braedon's expression again, and tears sprang to her eyes.

She needed *out*. "Excuse me, I need some air." Jumping up, she shoved the chair away from the table so hard it toppled. Cera winced as it clattered to the floor. She fled, not pausing to pick it up, already sobbing before she hit the door.

Trikser shot out the doorway behind her just in time to miss the slam she hadn't meant to cause.

What could she do? Where she could go?

It wasn't like she could grab Ash and Trikser and leave. She needed every person in that cabin, and they knew it, too. She even needed the person who was absent from the cabin, the person who was causing Cera's fog.

Hadrian's small barn was the only refuge she could find. As she threw herself into a pile of hay, her bondmate came along, lying down flush to her body.

Trikser's mind was quiet, but he wrapped her in feelings of love that only made her cry harder.

She buried her face in his furry warmth, sinking her hands into his white mane.

He whined and licked her ear, but she didn't take any comfort.

Jorrin hadn't spoken to her in two days, since she'd tried to check on him and he'd ended up crushing her, but he hadn't *really* conversed with her since before that, when she'd hurt his feelings by the woodpile.

The back and forth was killing her.

Cera hurt him, he hurt her. His confession hadn't been a surprise, but hearing the words had jarred her. Pushed one word from her lips that he'd taken the wrong way . . . but had he? She didn't know what to say to him anyway. Admitting she cared about him was just too hard.

Coward.

Going outside after Braedon's dejected reentry of Hadrian's cabin, she'd only wanted to make sure Jorrin was all right. Talk to him; maybe even try to explain something of her feelings, if she could've mustered the courage.

What did she get instead?

Disaster.

And more hurt. Now he wouldn't even look at her.

Was her mission really the only thing keeping her away from Jorrin?

Getting close to people had always been a struggle. She was highborn. Female, so there were even more specific things that were expected of her. Childhood had consisted of that knowledge being drilled into her. She'd grow up, marry a nobleman, and bear children. It was the cycle of those with land and titles.

Cera respected duty and what was required of her. For the most part she'd never even questioned it. Her parents had expected her understanding, while not inhibiting who she was. She'd been lucky in that.

Then again, she didn't fit the mold of the highborn heiress, duke's daughter.

She'd always been a tomboy, climbing trees and playing with wooden swords as a child, even challenging the boys to countless duels. She won most of the time, too. It'd gotten so they would even refuse to spar with her until she'd pulled rank, and they'd have to.

One corner of her mouth lifted at the memory.

She'd learned to ride younger than most girls, and rarely worn dresses. Her father had never discouraged her, and her mother had teased she should've been born a boy.

Kait had been the dainty one.

Cera crushed her eyes shut. Her sister had been as girly as she wasn't. Always wanting a new gown, a new hairstyle, fascinated by pretty, shiny things. Jewels, brooches and hair ornaments. Her younger sister had never even worn a pair of breeches. Kait had always asked for lavish, flowing and embroidered gowns. The more shimmery the fabric, the better.

Their seven turn age difference was obstacle enough to seeing eye-to-eye with her little sister, but she'd still adored her, despite their diverse interests. The older Kait got, the more they'd really talked.

Varthan had stolen that from her, the bastard.

She'd never see her sister into adulthood, never be a true friend to her.

Tears scalded her cheeks and she burrowed into her wolf, wrapping her arms around his neck and holding him tight.

Cera cried over her family. She cried over Jorrin, and she cried because she'd never taken the time to grieve.

Trik whined again, but cuddled closer while memories sucked her in.

Her mother had protested when she'd wanted to join the King's Riders. Everalda had thought it was past time she stopped acting like a boy. She'd be fifteen that summer, and they'd have to start thinking of marriage matches. Her future.

Falor had disagreed, stating she was a better rider and archer than most boys her age, and his wife had acquiesced. Never completely with everything, but her mother had still been proud of her.

Cera hadn't been at all bothered that girls were in the minority of the King's Riders ranks. However, many girls followed in her footsteps. Something she would always be proud of. She'd made friends that were more like sisters.

Ansley and Aimil.

Blessed Spirit, no one knew where she was. They were probably all frantic, including her captain and the king. Were people looking for her? Or did they assume her dead like her family?

Her parents' smiling faces danced into her head, and her chest burned.

She'd never stop missing them.

There'd always been plenty of hugs and kisses from Everalda and Falor to their daughters. In a world that wasn't so prone to open affection, she was grateful she'd been raised by parents who had shown their love. Her parents had loved each other very much, and she'd always prayed for a love like theirs when she was ready to marry.

However, letting someone in, letting someone get that close to her heart petrified her.

Cera was in love with Jorrin.

She didn't want to love him.

She couldn't have him.

There were too many obstacles. Not including the bad timing for the whole dratted thing. And she had too much pride to go pining after him. She'd reached out to him, and Jorrin had pushed her away. A voice whispered that *she'd* pushed him away two times, pulled away from his kiss, but she ignored it.

He'd hurt her and love wasn't supposed to hurt. Besides, what if he didn't love her? Jorrin had said he *cared* about her. That wasn't a declaration of love.

I'll get through this. I have to.

She'd go with her cousin, the wizard and Braedon to Tarvis and defeat Varthan. Save the rest of her family. Protect the sword.

Then she'd return to Greenwald and forget about Jorrin.

My only choice.

Young Avery's stare was locked on the door Cera had slammed moments before. "Blessed Spirit, *damn* him." He pounded his fist down on the table. "She's *crying*, dammit. She *doesn't* cry."

Braedon exchanged a look with Hadrian.

His old friend's pale blue eyes were wide.

What the hell was either of them supposed to say? He shook his head, as shocked as Hadrian looked. Braedon righted Cera's chair, sighing as he slid back onto his seat and glancing at the lord.

The lad's gray eyes flashed. From what he knew of Avery Lenore, this outburst was uncharacteristic. He was radiating dark emotions mixed with love for his cousin. "I'm going to rip him to pieces," Avery promised.

Braedon opened his mouth to speak, but Hadrian beat him to it.

The wizard placed his slight hand over Avery's forearm. "It's not our place, lad. They need to work it out." The elf nodded for effect, his voice steady and calm.

Cera's cousin frowned.

"Aye, and they'd better do it fast, because we need everyone's head in this plan," Braedon said. He'd been struggling the last few days not to act on his son's behalf, but what could he do, really? Muting his empathic magic had failed, and he couldn't help but notice the lass' torment. His head was at a constant ache. At least now the pain wasn't as sharp as it had been moments earlier when she'd been sitting at the table with them.

Dragon's Tail
Mountains of Aramour
Terraquist
Elfin River
Greenwald
Netian Valley
North Ascova
Tarvis
Hadrian's Place
Berat
Islands
South Ascova
Dalunas
Southern Strait
Penal Territory

He'd tried to project calming thoughts to her, but her mind was closed as tight as a vise; however vocal at the same time. She probably had no idea her magic was amplifying her feelings; broadcasting them.

Hadrian should be grateful his gift is animals.

Much, much simpler than people.

Although he hadn't known the young woman long, he admired her strength and determination. Speaking with her was easy and enjoyable. She was quite the match for his son. They looked good together, too.

If Jorrin and Cera could overcome their problems to accomplish their very serious task, the rest could be allowed to fall into place.

He had no idea what'd happened between them, but neither lass, nor his lad, had any idea how to react to each other. Braedon wanted to half-throttle Jorrin and half-hug him. The same could be said about her. His magic told him she rarely let people get close. It was obvious she was so with her cousin, but the lad was blood family. His gut told him her wariness around others wasn't only because of her situation.

She'd never taken the time to grieve her family. Cera had survived their loss, but only just. Keeping her guard up because of the sword made sense, but she needed to learn to rely on those who cared for her.

He considered himself in that category and Hadrian also cared for her. Braedon didn't need empathic magic to feel Jorrin was in love with her.

The cabin's door handle rattled.

His son was on the other side.

Jorrin sighed as he reached for the cabin door. He needed to go inside, although cowardice inched up from his gut. He took a deep breath.

Moments earlier, Cera's cousin had found him wallowing by Hadrian's woodpile and confronted him. Jorrin had admitted he had feelings for her.

Avery had reminded him his parents' lives' were in jeopardy, and his cousin didn't need any more stress. *Be a man* was the theme of the little talk, though he hadn't called him out that directly. He hadn't even mustered a biting retort, because the younger man was right.

He needed to fix things with Cera.

They were to depart for Tarvis the next day, and they *all* needed to be strong for her cause. The lives of Avery's parents were not the only ones at stake.

So far he hadn't played any major role in the planning. Jorrin did of course, possess magic that'd be necessary, but his father's and Hadrian's would be the most pertinent. But he'd have to be a contributing party, and not just because he was in love with Cera.

If Varthan's ultimate plan was to succeed, a great number of people of all races would die. The former archduke was nothing but a murderer, an exploiter, and he had to be stopped.

However, at the moment he'd rather face the evil man than look into the gray eyes that'd held so much pain the last time they'd interacted.

He'd hurt her, and it was unnecessary. Just as unnecessary as the words he'd shared with his father. It didn't matter that she'd pushed him away.

He loved her.

What was he supposed to do? Jorrin needed to act like a grown up, for one thing.

Which would be worse, admitting to Cera he'd been an arse, or telling Braedon he was wrong? Aye, Varthan seemed like a more welcome opponent than either the man who had given him life or the girl he'd inadvertently given his heart to.

Jorrin took a deep breath and opened the door, squeezing his eyes shut.

Get hold of yourself. Are you five turns old?

He shook himself and took a step inside the cabin, then two more. Glancing toward the table, he saw Avery, Hadrian and Braedon.

No Cera.

The conversation was companionable. Both Braedon and Hadrian acknowledged him with a nod, so he slid onto an empty chair.

Avery didn't look at him, but he didn't blame Cera's cousin, considering how they'd left things.

She was nowhere in sight, but he didn't want to ask where she was.

"She rushed outside several minutes ago," the younger man said, as if he had read his mind. Avery still wouldn't meet his eyes. His jaw was clenched, and both of his fists balled up, resting on the edge of the table.

Jorrin was compelled to look at his father.

Braedon made an almost imperceptible nod.

Avery was angry enough to strike him? Though unspoken, that was Braedon's message.

He liked Cera's cousin, and had never seen a show of temper from the redhead, not even during his argument with her about their journey. Would the lord try to fight him?

Hadrian looked like he was trying not to smile.

What the hell is there to smile about?

Avery being angry enough to beat him into mulch certainly wasn't funny.

Jorrin needed to go find Cera. They had a hard day ahead of them, and they couldn't achieve a damned thing in the state they were in. With a nod to his father, he scrambled to his feet.

Braedon tipped his head in return.

How was he instantly able to communicate nonverbally with the man? He was glad his father wasn't shutting him out after their argument, but how could he tell him that? He'd follow. Let his father lead.

Braedon loved him.

Despite his unwillingness to acknowledge it during their argument, his father had spoken the truth. Jorrin believed the words, but he could also feel the man's emotions.

Love and openness. Desire to be close to his son. Could Jorrin do the same—feel the same—for his father?

He'd also been honest when he told him at the right time Jorrin would know all he needed to about his father's past.

He didn't have to like the waiting, but it would have to do for now. Besides, it wasn't time for Braedon, it was time for Cera.

Chapter Eleven

CERA BREATHED IN time with the footsteps coming into the small barn. She panted with the effort. Even before she saw his tall, lean form, she *knew* it was Jorrin.

She didn't want to see him. Had just decided to forget him. No need for sapphire eyes, tapered ears and coal black hair to change her mind.

Strength was needed to start out for Tarvis in the morning. She needed to grasp it with both hands.

It was just past twilight, so they barely had enough time to get a good night's sleep. She didn't have time for him or the bundle of emotions he stirred in her every time he looked at her.

Their eyes locked and she rose to her feet, ready to demand he leave her alone.

Trikser sensed tension—even though no words had been spoken—and started to growl deep in his throat. He leapt to his feet, landing in front of her.

Jorrin froze in the doorway.

"Trik, it's all right . . . shhh . . ." Cera whispered, smoothing his hackles.

He calmed, but she'd have to get him out of the barn.

She didn't know what would transpire with Jorrin, and wild emotions lent to difficult communication with her bondmate. Trikser would protect her from him as long as he perceived Jorrin a threat. "Go outside." She sent her wolf a picture of the clearing in her thoughts.

He whined.

"I'll be fine."

His ears plastered to his head, tail between his legs, he made a slow exit. Trikser paused to look over his shoulder from the doorway, his amber eyes glowing like an aura.

She nodded for him to go, feeling his reluctance through their bond. Cera reinforced her order with another thought-send.

The sliding wooden door to the small barn squealed as Jorrin yanked it shut. Magic lit up the place, as glowing orbs in each corner flared to life.

Her heart sped up and she tried to turn away, but wasn't quick enough.

He grabbed her arm.

"I don't want to do this, Jorrin." Her voice shook.

Damn.

Tears were already threatening.

"Why do you always resist what you feel?" He locked his gaze with hers and backed her against the wall, arms on either side, pinning her against it so she couldn't move away.

So she had to look at him.

So she couldn't run away.

Cera gulped. "What do you mean?"

He was so angry, jaw clenched, broad shoulders tight as he leaned into her. She didn't like to be cornered by him, but it wasn't out of fear. Jorrin would never hurt her.

She broke their eye contact, but couldn't make it last. She took a deep breath and met his eyes, feeling almost compelled to face him. Was he trying to probe her thoughts?

"You and me. We have to do something about it."

This time avoidance wouldn't work.

Jorrin wouldn't release her until she was honest with him.

Cera averted her gaze again, but for the second time couldn't evade his stare for very long. She tried not to decipher his expression or the mixed emotions raging there.

"Why won't you let me be there for you? I told you before; you don't have to be the strong one all the time. I can support you. I can protect you. I want to. You need to let me." He shook his head, but didn't release her.

What could she say? She closed her eyes. She'd have to admit, out loud, how she felt about him. Open herself to him, risk her heart with him. Could she risk *him* with Varthan? She had to be strong, had to be determined to go after Varthan; no one else could.

Hadrian had even said she was the only one who could do it.

How could she possibly handle it if she had to worry about someone else? Faltering could get him killed. Knowing Varthan, it would get Jorrin killed and she couldn't live with that, ever.

She loved him.

"Cera, look at me," Jorrin ordered. "Look at me and tell me you don't feel for me what I feel for you. Lie to me."

Cera couldn't take it anymore . . . being this close to him . . . hurting him.

Reach for him, you idiot. Tell him how you feel.

Words wouldn't come. Her arms didn't encircle him. She couldn't make her feet push her into his chest, where she wanted to be. Her vision blurred and hot tears fell down her cheeks. She closed her eyes again. She wanted to sink into the smallest corner and disappear.

Why is this so hard?

Why couldn't she just look Jorrin in the eye and tell him she loved him?

"Dammit. Just tell me what you're thinking." *Since you won't let me sense it,* was implied. He slammed the wall with the palm of his hand.

Cera flinched, but he still didn't move away from her.

"Don't sink into yourself. Let me in." His tone weakened. Jorrin was begging.

Again, she was cutting him deeply. Her heart ached and she chided herself for her cowardice. *Say. Something.*

But her voice was gone, tears coursed down her cheeks. Nothing but silence remained for minutes that felt like hours.

Jorrin sucked in a breath, his shoulders slumped, blue eyes misty. "Fine. If you can convince me I mean nothing to you I'll drop it. I promise I'll never bring it up again. Tell me you don't love me, and I'll leave. You can go to Tarvis with my father, Hadrian and Avery. I can't take this anymore."

What's happening?

This was supposed to be it; now was time to lay it all on the line. He'd gone after *her*. Why wasn't she cooperating?

Cera was shutting him out again and her tears were killing him.

Jorrin's magic throbbed with her pain, her worry, but her mind was still closed to him. She'd never accept him. Never let him love her. He had to stop it all.

He needed to let her go.

Maybe she didn't care about him after all. Maybe his instincts had been wrong, but his mind and heart rejected that because it just hurt too much.

Even standing there with her eyes closed and tears running down her cheeks, her beauty stunned him, the waves of her dark red hair floating loose around her shoulders. Her high cheekbones flushed with color and wet with tears, her kissable lips begging for him.

He stared, heart pounding, aching and wanting.

Why couldn't he have her?

Cera's chest rose and fell as she took a deep breath. She leaned into him, reaching up to press her lips to his.

His emotions surged.

What's happening?

She wouldn't talk to him, but she'd kiss him?

Don't question it, idiot.

Jorrin wrapped his arms around her, holding her to his chest. She snaked her arms around his neck and nestled closer. A tremor shot down his spine, and she shook in his arms.

On a groan, he fused their mouths, cupping the back of her neck. Sensing her opening for him in a way she hadn't in their previous kisses, he groaned when she pushed her tongue into his mouth.

Melding, mating, dancing, Cera kissed him hard, he could feel her desperation with his lips and his magic. Her mind was open as she slipped to passion, and he fought for control as he fell into desire for her, her emotions mixing with his and amplifying feelings.

His magic throbbed along with his erection.

He *needed* her.

Needed inside her.

She pushed even closer, flattening her full breasts into his chest, and Jorrin shoved her against the wall, deepening their kiss even more. He swallowed her moan as they were melded, chest to breasts, hips to hips.

He ground against her. Cera rocked right back, and he was about to lose it. It took all his self-control not rip her breeches down and take her. Urging her away from the wall, he mapped her back with his hands, cupping her bottom and lifting her, pulling her against his arousal.

She moaned into his mouth.

They fell onto the pile of hay in a tangle of limbs, Cera landing on top of him.

Jorrin tugged her down and she kissed him again, her mouth searing his. She explored and plundered as much as he did. He drew her onto his chest, burying his hands in the red curls flowing down her back.

She straddled him, their bodies touching in all the right places, but they had far too many clothes on. The pressure of her rocking on him was exquisite torture, but not nearly enough.

He kissed her harder as she caressed his face. Fingers fumbling, he ripped at the ties on her jerkin.

Cera helped him, wiggling out of the worn leather. It fell to the planked wooden floor next to the pile of hay. She gasped when he cupped her breasts through the soft fabric of her white linen tunic.

Jorrin teased her nipples to hard peaks, but that wasn't enough either. Needed her in his hands, in his mouth.

She froze at the first brush of his fingers across the soft skin of her bare stomach.

Their eyes locked, making his magic ache with the intensity of the emotion between them. They both panted, and he had to resist pulling her down for another kiss.

Her hair was pleasantly mussed; gray eyes heavy-lidded, cheeks rosy red and her lips swollen from their kisses.

She swallowed and trembled.

He could feel her nerves. His stomach fluttered.

She's never done this before.

It made sense she was a virgin. A noble, duke's daughter, the heir to a Province.

He'd even tasted the innocence in their first kiss, which seemed ages ago. Yet, after the ferocity of her kiss when he'd taught her to deepen her bond with Trikser, it hadn't crossed Jorrin's mind again. Not to mention her fervency now, her un-shy touches, the way she rubbed her body against his. Undulating in his lap, shoving her hips against his.

She wanted him. As much as he wanted her. Nervousness aside, she was willing to give him her innocence.

His heart flipped, but he wasn't taking her for the first time on a pile of hay in a barn. "Cera, we don't have to—"

Cera leaned down and pressed her mouth to his before he could finish his statement.

Ordering himself to calm down, and *slow* down, Jorrin made the kiss tender and languorous, trying to show her the love he'd yet to tell her he had for her. He wrapped his arms around her, reveling in how it felt to hold her. Good. Right. *Perfect.*

When the kiss ended, he rested his forehead against hers, flashing a smile.

She promptly broke into a sob, clinging to him. Not the reaction he'd expected, but he couldn't let her go. As he nestled her closer, she snuggled into his chest, lying down with him on the hay. She wrapped her arms around him, burying her face against his neck.

He rested his cheek against her soft hair, inhaling the sweet floral scent. "Cera?" he whispered when she quieted. Jorrin's heart fluttered when she met his eyes, her cheeks stained, expression desperate. "What's wrong?" Gently, he cupped her face and thumbed away her tears. Would she pull away from him again, even though she was letting him hold her? His magic told him she was still in turmoil; he didn't want to push her.

"I love you," Cera whispered. She squeezed her eyes shut and tightened her grip around him as if she dreaded his response.

Jorrin's heart tripped over itself.

What did she just say?

He grinned so hard his face hurt. He'd remember this moment, always. "I know."

She gasped. "You know?"

He nodded.

"You know?" Her voice went up an octave.

Jorrin bit his lip to keep from laughing. His magic tingled as he felt the rise of her ire. He blinked twice, fighting for a straight face.

"Do you have *any* idea how *hard* that was for me?" Cera poked him in the chest, glaring.

"Ow. That really hurt." He batted her hand away. "All right, all right . . . don't look at me like that, I was playing."

Her gaze bore into his.

He took a breath and framed her face again, pressing a quick kiss to her mouth. "I love you, too, Ceralda Ryhan," he whispered against her lips.

She shoved her tongue into his mouth, deepening the kiss.

Jorrin trembled as he *felt* her love through his magic. It washed over him like waves of pleasure, threatening to snap his control all over again. He wanted to slip inside her and lose himself in her sweet body.

Cera was *his.*

I love you, he thought-sent, letting her feel his longing and desire for her.

Her hands tugged his tunic out of his breeches and he let her, tilting his hips to assist her. Soon it was over his head and off. Cera's teasing touch caressed his bare skin, tracing each line of his chest and abdomen, setting him on fire from the inside out. His erection threatened to punch through his breeches, he was so hard.

He brought her knuckles to his mouth and lavished kisses over them.

"What's wrong?" she whispered, gorgeous eyes wide.

"I love when you touch me, but you're killing me."

"But—"

"I'm not taking your innocence on a pile of hay."

Blushing scarlet, Cera averted her eyes. "How did you know?"

Jorrin guided her face again to his and smiled. "I'm honored, you know. That you would pick me."

"I love you."

He kissed her. Couldn't seem to stop. "I love you, too."

"Then why—"

"Not here. Not tonight, but I do want you. I need you more than I need to breathe."

She nodded, her cheeks an even more adorable shade of red. *I want you, too.* The words of her thought-send tickled his mind, because his silly love wasn't brave enough to voice them.

His magic absorbed her longing, her desire, and Jorrin suppressed a groan. His erection didn't have a problem with their location, but his sense of honor did. "Come here." He closed his eyes and drew her to his bare chest.

Cera sighed and buried her face against his neck, tightening her arm across him as they settled into the hay pile.

Telling her he loved her lifted a huge weight. The fact she loved him, and had actually told him, was the sweetening on top of it all.

"What do we do now?" she whispered.

Magic warmed his body as fear of what was to come started to creep in on them. It was in her expression as he met her gray eyes.

Jorrin squeezed her against him. Refused to let anything ruin this moment for them. "Nothing's changed, love. First and foremost, we still have a job to do. We'll figure out the rest along the way, I guess." He liked the sound of the endearment, and the smile she flashed him.

"Thank you, Jorrin."

"What for?"

Cera kissed him in answer.

They'd face Varthan and Tarvis in the morning when they didn't have a choice. Tonight was his to savor with the woman he loved. Jorrin deepened the kiss and pulled her closer.

Chapter Twelve

LORD VARTHAN CURSED as he threw Lucan to the ground. "Do it again."

Dagonet stepped forward, obviously intending to help him to his feet, but their master's glare stopped him cold.

Lucan bowed his head as he scrambled upright. "We all need to put magical force in. Equally." His voice was just above a whisper, and he took a breath, trying to banish the shaking.

"Then. Do it. Now," Lord Varthan commanded.

Athas opened his mouth, but one look from their master changed his mind. He sneered at Lucan.

Dagonet bowed to appease their master, and Lord Varthan's chest heaved with a breath. "We shall try again, my lord," the shade said, his sharp hazel eyes on the older man.

The lord growled, but nodded brusquely and clenched his fists at his sides.

Leave it to Dagonet to use magic on Lord Varthan and not get caught. He'd used a small spell; Lucan had sensed it, and their master had calmed. He was envious of the older boy's confidence, but shifting moods was one of Dagonet's gifts. Since Lord Varthan was aware of that, why didn't he ever suspect Dagonet would use magic on him? Perhaps their master was too arrogant to realize any shade would have the courage to do so.

Resisting the urge to incline his head to Dagonet for his attempted assistance, Lucan reminded himself the older boy wasn't really an ally. He was the most polite and reserved of the shades, but none of them could be trusted. Growing up at the shade compound had shown him that, if nothing else.

He took a deep breath and glanced around at the other three shades.

Athas sneered again and Markus looked indifferent, his sky blue eyes studying the castle. Dagonet was looking at Lucan, expression curious.

Lucan ignored Athas and made eye contact with Dagonet.

The four of them joined hands, and Lord Varthan took a step back, crossing his arms over his broad chest.

Lucan averted his eyes and sighed. How many bruises would he have before this was over? The lord always singled him out in his rage. He'd barely escaped broken bones so far. He had the healing shade to thank for that. There were many times he sensed the presence of magic when he was being abused. His master had none.

He cast at the protection spell, feeling his body warm as he called upon his magic. He didn't really want to break through it, but he pushed that feeling away, lest the others sense it. Athas would jump at the chance to see him disciplined by Lord Varthan.

The sooner they broke through the spell, the better. They'd been trying for three days, and the effort was exhausting.

Lucan felt the other shades put forth their magical energies, and sweat beaded his brow as they were all met with resistance. His body heated even more, his limbs started to glow.

Dagonet was also glowing brightly beside him.

Their master lifted a hand to shield his eyes.

She's getting weaker.

With regret, Lucan pushed further, adding more power and feeling the other shades join him. Closing his eyes, he concentrated harder. He thought of nothing but the spell collapsing, picturing a bubble popping in his mind. The image helped him focus his power surge.

The resistance faltered; it wouldn't be long now.

He shoved energy against the center of the spell as hard as he could. His whole body was radiant, alight, and sweat poured down his face on its way to his collar.

Triumph from the other shades rushed him as they recognized weakness in the spell.

Just breathe. One deep puff of air, then another.

They won. The spell collapsed.

Lucan dropped Dagonet's hand before his regret was too obvious.

It's no victory.

Athas informed their master that it was done.

Biting his bottom lip, Lucan tried to stand taller. The next step was even worse. Horrible.

All my fault.

"Well done. Mount up. Be ready for anything." Lord Varthan swung himself up onto his black stallion.

Lucan grimaced. Any expression of praise from the master was few and far between, but he was rarely proud of his accomplishments anyway.

"Swords will be waiting for us," the lord said.

The other three shades nodded collectively and unsheathed their weapons.

Lucan shuddered. He would be the cause of people being killed.

Again.

Guilt made his eyes smart and he swallowed back tears. He was too old to cry. His gut was hard, like he'd eaten rocks, but his stomach roiled. He fought the urge to lose his breakfast, gripping his horse's reins as he planted his rear end on the saddle. His master was always going around killing people.

"Lucan, stay close to me," Lord Varthan growled, drawing his own sword.

They didn't meet resistance until they were well inside the castle's gates.

Lord Varthan sneered at Lord Everett Lenore.

The duke led his men himself.

Lucan shuddered as his master let out a malicious laugh. He did a quick head count. Lord Lenore had twelve men with him. No doubt the knights would totally underestimate the shades. He gulped.

"Kill them all, except Lenore," Lord Varthan barked.

The three shades gave curt nods and attacked.

His master pulled his horse up against the inner wall on the right side of the courtyard, and Lucan stayed tight behind him, as usual. He laughed again as they both saw Markus lift a man by his neck with his mind, using his magic to paralyze him and then running him through with his sword.

Tears threatened, and Lucan panted to keep them at bay.

"Varthan, I *will* kill you!" Lord Everett Lenore ran toward them, sword drawn.

"Lucan." His master's voice was deceptively calm.

Lucan lifted a hand, saying a spellword silently.

The Duke of Tarvis flew backwards, landing hard on his rear end, legs flying up. The lord was unhurt, but his eyes were wide, and he seemed frozen for a moment, making no move to scramble up.

"You've always been pathetic, Lenore," Lord Varthan snarled.

"You're a dead man, Varthan," the duke retorted, finally righting himself.

His master gave another hearty laugh and jumped down from his horse, pointing his sword.

A tremor started down Lucan's spine, radiating across his back until his whole body shook; even his teeth rattled. He struggled for breath. He couldn't watch his master kill the duke. Not three feet from him.

Helpless. All my magic and I can do nothing.

Lucan swallowed a whimper.

"Come at me, Lenore. I'll show you who's a dead man. Lucan, stay where you are." Lord Varthan didn't spare him a glance, which was fine with him. "Stay out of the fight."

"Yes, sir," he croaked, grasping the reins of the lord's stallion.

Everett growled as he charged Varthan. He'd kill the bastard. His wife had told him the former archduke and his shades would get into the castle, but he'd change that. Emeralda's visions were rarely wrong, but he couldn't allow himself to consider that.

Around him, he could hear his men screaming and dying. The vile din steeled him to kill Varthan himself.

His niece shouldn't have to endure the job. It wasn't right for one so young, let alone a lady.

He'd never had so much rage toward a person in all his turns, no matter what war or battle he had been involved in. His body shook as he slammed his sword into the evil bastard's, and Everett fought to stay upright. His blood boiled and he snarled.

I will defeat him.

His skill was equal to Varthan's, but the man wouldn't fight fair. They'd been lads together, trained together. He might've even considered them more than mere acquaintances at one time, but not for a great number of turns.

The man was pure evil.

Everett had known it even before Varthan had boldly stormed Greenwald and killed his wife's twin and her husband—the best friend he'd ever had in his life. Not to mention his youngest niece.

There had been rumors at court surrounding Varthan for turns. Horrid rumors of kidnapping, murder, rape. More than half of the King's Court suspected he'd killed all three of his wives. Varthan would do anything for power. He'd been bold enough to make an attempt on King Nathal's life. Had the man not had so many ties to powerful magic, he'd have been dead a long time ago.

The way Varthan was stalking him told Everett he was being toyed with. The bastard didn't desire to fight him.

He rushed him and was effortlessly blocked. Everett cursed. "This is not a game. Come at me, you bastard."

The traitor laughed. "We do this on my terms, Lenore, not yours."

The nonchalant tone made his ire rise even more.

"Shall I kill him, Master?" one of the shades asked, his tone almost sweet as he appeared at Varthan's side. "I mean, I'm finished with the rest."

"No, Athas," Varthan said. "He's mine."

The shade nodded, his expression crestfallen.

Everett looked at Varthan, and then at the boy…young man actually, he was probably nineteen or a few turns older. The shade had to be Varthan's son. They were wearing the same arrogant expression and had the same hair and eyes, same wide jaw, same nose. Even their stance was the same. The lad looked like a younger version of the former archduke.

A moment later, the other two shades flanked the one at Varthan's side. "It's finished." The fair-haired boy to left remarked, sounding bored.

Everett reared backward as a slow smile spread across Varthan's lips. His knees weakened; his stomach roiled. Grief threatened to overtake him, but he couldn't afford it. He straightened his spine and gripped his sword tighter.

Varthan made no move toward him, so he spared a glance around the courtyard.

His personal guard had been decimated. Their bodies lay bloody and broken all over. They'd not only been his men, but his friends. Most of them had been in his service for turns, some even as boys. He'd knighted some of them himself.

Shouting a battle cry, Everett charged Varthan again. With the clang of metal on metal that jarred his body, he sent a silent prayer to the Blessed Spirit he could win his fight. He needed to win, for his wife, his son, and his niece.

His Province, his King.

Varthan laughed as he plunged his sword into Everett's side.

He collapsed, panting from the white hot pain burning through him. Sweat dripped down from his brow and his whole body shook. He couldn't move. Breathing was painful. "Even if I die, you won't win this. There will be others." Everett clenched his jaw.

The former archduke laughed like the maniac he was. "You'll die when I say you will. Dagonet, heal him." He gestured to a tall brown-haired young man who looked dimly familiar.

Where had he seen the boy before? He looked to be around his own son's age.

Everett tried to scramble away as the shade approached him, but calm washed over him. *Everything will be all right.*

What had he been doing?

His side . . . hurt. Pressing a hand where the pain was, he shifted. His mail was ripped, torn tunic sticking through it. Both were covered in . . . blood.

What happened?

"I will not hurt you," the young man told him, kneeling at his side.

Jolting, then wincing from the pain, everything came back to him, and Everett gasped. "Get away from me."

"I'm going to heal you." The boy's voice was low, even.

Everett felt compelled to look into his warm hazel eyes. There was no possible way this boy was evil. Why was he in Varthan's service?

Healing was an unusual trait for a shade. Even healers in the cities who charged gold for their magic and services were usually of a gentle disposition.

This boy was no evil warrior.

Dagonet, as Varthan had called him, laid his hands over Everett's wound and closed his eyes. A very hot sharp pain bit and he cried out as the flesh came back together. Then the pain was gone. The healing shade's face was pale and he was covered in sweat. The bright glow of his hands was fading now. He trembled and put his knee to the ground to steady himself, sucking in a gulp of air.

Had the situation been different, Everett might have apologized for draining the boy's energy. He looked down at his side. No sign of a wound. The flesh was sealed, not even a scar.

The only proof of injury was his bloodied ruined chainmail and overtunic. He locked eyes to the boy's; once again feeling compelled to do so.

I'm sorry I can't make it last, but you'll get out of this alive, I promise you.

It took him a moment to discern the voice was in his head, not aloud. The healing shade had thought-sent to him?

Dagonet helped him to his feet, his eyes flickering with emotion he masked before he'd turned away.

Where the hell have I seen this boy before?

Emeralda was the only one who ever thought-sent to him, and it was odd, jarring, to hear a male voice in his mind. Everett had no magic, so he'd never managed to learn how to communicate mentally, despite his wife's efforts to teach him.

"Seize him," Varthan barked.

The other two shades snatched him by each arm. Pain bit back, radiating into his shoulders and neck, they were holding him so tightly.

Dagonet gave him an apologetic look and punched him in the jaw.

Everett's head tipped backward as the blackness enveloped his vision. He slipped into the darkness.

Chapter Thirteen

T HE JOURNEY TO Tarvis was a hard ride, taking only a day and a half. They'd stopped once, but just for a few hours in the middle of the night. Exhaustion threatened to overtake them all, but they were steeled to be strong for one another.

They hadn't spoken much, every one of them overcome with the darkness Cera had been dealing with for sevenday after sevenday.

Braedon led most of the time, and when they'd stopped in a small clearing to rest, they'd taken turns on watch, Avery starting off.

She couldn't sleep, so she didn't try. The closer they got to Tarvis, the more twisted her stomach got, so she'd kept her cousin company. Barely said a word to him, but neither of them needed to talk.

He'd finally given up and went to sleep for his hour, switching out with Jorrin.

Cera had ignored his admonition to try to close her eyes and stayed with her love, cuddling close in his arms and wishing he was holding her under different circumstances. *Naked* in her rooms at Castle Ryhan would've been good.

At any rate, she wouldn't have minded the distraction, despite their location. She loved Jorrin, and wanted to give herself to him. *He* was the one so concerned about propriety.

They'd made it through the Tarvis Southgate unchallenged. Focusing on her surroundings, she fought a gasp as she surveyed her cousin's Province. Varthan and his scum hadn't been there even a fortnight, yet the place looked desolate. On the other hand, it was evident her aunt and uncle had been able to evacuate the people, so innocents wouldn't be harmed or killed.

Jorrin sat high on Grayna, his sapphire eyes as wide as saucers as he looked around.

Braedon was next, on Roan, his expression intense. No telling what he was thinking. Planning their next move, likely. Strategy seemed to be what he was best at.

Avery, on his white gelding Valor, just looked exhausted. Complexion pale, dark circles under his eyes. He looked how she felt.

Cera couldn't read anything in his expression, but he was probably glad to be home.

Hadrian rode the skinny nag he'd spoken to so harshly the day they'd met. As slight as his weight must be, it was a wonder the horse could support him. He was a tough old one though, and hadn't complained once on their rough journey to Tarvis.

Winthrop was a regal sounding name for such a non-regal looking animal, but it wasn't his fault he was old. He'd lived a long life and surely hadn't always looked as forlorn as he did now. The wizard had a great affection for him, so that was all that mattered. Her own Ash was much more than just her mount.

"They know we're here," Braedon said, drawing her attention.

Avery glanced at Jorrin's father. "Are you sure? I don't feel *anything*."

"I think they knew from the first moment we entered the Province," Hadrian said.

"They won't intercept us then? I would've thought shades would meet us at the gate if they knew," Jorrin said.

Cera shuddered. How could Varthan and his shades know they'd arrived? Was that a preview to the power and magic at the former archduke's command? She tightened her hold on Ash's reins.

They'd arrived; no going back now.

"They know our destination, and Varthan loves a challenge." She straightened her back and growled.

Trikser let out a low snarl of his own in response.

She calmed him mentally, but he remained bristled at her side, closer to Ash than the stallion was comfortable with. He let out a low whinny. A pat to his neck calmed him some, but he hoofed the dirt.

"All right, so what now?" Her cousin slumped in his saddle. "Do we march right home? Or make him wait on us?"

Cera shrugged and looked at Braedon. Since they'd left Hadrian's holding, she'd been constantly deferring to Jorrin's father. It was an adjustment, because she'd always been the one in control—even in the ranks of the King's Riders—but she needed a break from decision making. Needed time to gather her strength to do what needed to be done. It was *real* now, they were here and she had to face Varthan.

She had to kill Varthan. *Had* to be strong enough.

Braedon's support helped in a different way than her other companions. Jorrin's father hadn't even paused since arriving at Hadrian's. The problem had been presented, and he'd immediately been willing to take everything on.

She'd never be able to make it up to him.

"Is there someplace where we could regroup?" Braedon asked. He addressed her cousin, the one most familiar with the area. "If we don't get some rest, we'll be of no use to anyone. Plus, we need some element of surprise. He may know we're here, but he doesn't know what our plans are."

Avery shrugged. "Where can we? If he knows we're here, *how* can we hide?"

"Perhaps a masking spell?" Hadrian said.

Braedon nodded. "That's my plan. Have a place in mind? I have a spell that's nearly magic proof."

Cera stifled a yawn. Some sleep and reaffirming of plans would delay things.

Perfectly acceptable at the moment.

In the morning she wouldn't have a choice. A tremor slid down her spine, and she shifted in her saddle. "How about that place by the lake where we used to play as children?" She met Avery's eyes. "It's close enough to the castle, and very old . . . very forgotten."

"That could work." Her cousin nodded thoughtfully.

"Let's go then. When can we cast the cover for our trail?" Jorrin said.

"Leave it to me." Braedon turned Roan to follow Ash and Valor. "I have a simple spell that I've used often." He smiled and closed his eyes. Taking a deep breath, he chanted aloud:

*"Let our scene remain unseen by
those whose means would bring
us harm."*

"That's it?" Avery whispered. He looked around, as if expecting some sort of visible magical response.

"It works," Jorrin's father said, "So don't knock it. Everything is as it should be. They won't be able to see us, or what direction we go. We're under their shields, so to speak. It's not complicated, but it's virtually undetectable. We just disappeared to magical senses, even strong ones."

Cera's cousin threw an astonished look in Jorrin's direction, but her love just shrugged.

She shared his sentiment. The spell wasn't as musical as some she'd heard, but it had rhythm, even without rhyming words. As long as it worked, she didn't care about the rest. She closed her eyes for a moment, memories of the lake and happy childhood times filling her mind. Her sister's laughter was palpable. Tears stung her eyes.

Kait is gone. She'd never hear her carefree giggles again.

Tightening her grip on Ash's reins, she squeezed until her knuckles whitened.

I will kill Varthan.

She'd kill him for all he had taken from her.

Won't be much longer now.

"Dark thoughts again, love?" Jorrin whispered, making her jump in her saddle. "Sorry, didn't mean to startle you."

"It's all right," Cera said. "We're almost there." She glanced over his profile, relieved by his distraction. A jumble of emotions hit her, grief over her sister, flipping to love as she looked at Jorrin, both adding to her determination.

Since he'd cornered her in the barn and what was left unsaid no longer was just that, there'd been a constant ease between them. It was in their interactions, conversations, and everything else.

Except, she wanted him so badly Cera shook with it. Every time he kissed her, she melted into a puddle, only to be left unfulfilled. Beyond kisses and touches, he'd done nothing more, even when she'd urged him on. She wasn't going to beg, and Jorrin promised when the time was right, they'd be together. Besides, they didn't have privacy, or time.

Dragon' s Tail
Mountains of Aramour
Terraquist
Elfin River
Greenwald
Netian Valley
North Ascova
Hadrian' s Place
Tarvis
Berat
South Ascova
Dalunas
Southern Strait
Penal Territory

Her worries about a romantic relationship diverting her course had been unfounded. She'd protect what she held dear. Her family view and its importance increased by one. Well, it was more like three, because she couldn't help but think of Hadrian and Braedon as family as well.

"Well?" Jorrin persisted.

"No dark thoughts. Just fears and plans."

He nodded and reached for her hand. She entwined their fingers, and he gave a squeeze. "It'll be all right, love." He dropped a kiss on her hand.

"We're here," Avery said.

The ruins were more lost and forgotten than Cera remembered. She forced a breath, staving off the hopelessness the place exuded.

The remnants of the old castle were to the right; the decrepit stone wall that once offered protection no longer wholly surrounding it. Sections were still standing, but most of it was rubble, in much worse condition than the picture in her mind from childhood.

The lake lay to the left, as large and sprawling as always. She remembered days of playing and fun the three children had shared. Since reaching adulthood, she'd never been able to feel that free of responsibility, but more than anything, she wished she could feel *safe* again.

When was the last time she'd felt truly secure?

Jorrin squeezed her hand again, and she shot him a grateful look.

The few times in his arms had made her feel warm and safe, she supposed. She was thankful for him in so many ways.

They dismounted at the same time and started exploring the area, mapping a perimeter before coming together at the center of what used to be the castle's main courtyard. Avery was the only one not with the rest of them.

"How long can we stay here undetected?" Jorrin asked his father.

Cera studied the two men. Since they'd settled things, Jorrin had admitted he'd found it easier to speak to his father, but wasn't completely over being in the dark regarding Braedon's past. He'd also told her he needed to let it go for now and focus on ridding their world of Varthan. She smiled.

What would she have done if Jorrin hadn't come into her life?

"My spell will hold. They won't be able to see us. Trust me. I know how to remain unseen." Braedon's amber eyes were serious as he regarded his son.

"So, there's not a certain time limit?" Jorrin asked.

"I don't think so . . ."

"You never stayed put long enough to find out, though," Hadrian said.

"But I wouldn't take our safety for granted, no matter what magic we have," Cera said.

All three males nodded.

Jorrin threw his arm over her shoulders and she leaned into him, needing his warmth and comfort.

Avery appeared at what used to be the doorway of the castle, but it was half gone, as was most of the front supporting wall. "We can sleep in here. This wall has crumbled, but there's still a great deal of roof, so we should be covered."

"Provided the ceiling doesn't cave in on us," Jorrin said.

Avery shook his head. "I probed it, and my magic says it's stable."

"I've stayed in worse." Braedon shrugged.

Jorrin glanced at his father, disbelief written in his expression.

Braedon and Hadrian laughed.

Cera grinned.

They broke their little meeting, leading their mounts inside the perimeter of the dilapidated stone wall.

She grabbed her pack and furs from Ash's saddle and patted his neck, then unsaddled her horse and rubbed him down. When she'd finish tending him, she patted his rump and left him on his own to graze, but her stallion wouldn't go far.

Jorrin strode to her and took her hand without a word, dropping a kiss on her cheek. She smiled and pressed into the arm around her shoulders as they headed back to his father.

Braedon gazed at them, wearing soft smile.

"I would like a bath," she said.

"The water will be cold," Avery warned, striding over.

"I don't care. I want to feel clean."

"I'll see if I can snag a rabbit or some other small game. Meat for a meal would make us all feel better. Then I'd like to wash up in a bit, myself. I'm sure everyone would," Braedon said.

The others murmured agreement.

"I'll start a fire," Hadrian said from the doorway of the castle's ruins. "The hearth isn't what it used to be, but it should be fine for us." His expression was wry. "Nothing much to burn down, anyway."

Braedon chuckled.

Jorrin exchanged a glance with his father and smirked.

"I'm going to see if I can communicate with my mother," Avery said. "Will it interfere with your masking spell?" he asked Braedon.

Cera's heart ached with worry over her Aunt Em, but she ignored it. *Soon. Just be strong.*

"Hadrian can show you how your spell won't interfere with mine," Braedon told her cousin.

Avery nodded and disappeared into the ruins.

"I guess I'll go with you," Jorrin said to his father.

"Fine by me."

"I'll go then," she told father and son. "See you in a bit." Cera trotted off to dig in her saddle bags for clothes and soap.

Trikser was on her heels, and she threw him a grin as she bundled breeches and a clean tunic in one of the soft linen drying sheets Hadrian had given her.

She clutched the pudgy roll close, shivering at the thought of the water. It'd be chillier than the air, but feeling clean was going to be worth it.

Chapter Fourteen

CERA QUICKLY BATHED in frigid water.

Trikser lay on the shore, wagging his tail whenever she caught his eye.

Need to hurry before I freeze solid. She shivered and glanced over her shoulder when she heard a noise in the woods, paranoid that someone would see her naked in the lake.

Someone being Braedon or Hadrian, really. Avery wouldn't bother her, and Jorrin . . . well, she'd love to have courage to be naked with him. One kiss and she was a goner, so it wouldn't take much to get over insecurities.

She grinned and shook her head. Needed to stop fantasizing.

Her bondmate was a great guard. He'd alert her to anyone's presence. Trikser was still relaxed, his head resting on his paws.

She rubbed soap into her hair. *Clean* would make her feel better.

When her hair was adequately scrubbed, she dipped her head under the water. Shuddering, Cera wrung her hair with her hands, trembling as water droplets hit her shoulders and back. Her teeth chattered.

She finished washing and sped to the shore.

Need to get warm.

She wrapped herself in one of the two bathing sheets Hadrian had given her, rubbing her body vigorously, and grateful for the elf's thoughtfulness. She reached for her clean clothes, fighting the tremor that shot down her spine as she donned undergarments and jumped into fresh breeches.

Yanking the tunic over her head, Cera banished the last chilled quiver and was lacing the front of her jerkin when Jorrin called her name.

He waved as he approached the shore of the lake.

When he pressed a kiss to her cheek, she shivered for a different reason.

Trikser did a long body stretch, groaning. He sneezed, causing them both to laugh. When he came closer, he wagged his tail at Jorrin.

Cera smiled and patted her bondmate's head, letting her love take her hand and interlace their fingers. "Hunting trip successful?"

"Yes. Two large rabbits. Hadrian's cooking them. Braedon's handy to hunt with. He uses magic."

"Really?"

"Yes, he taught me a thing or two." Jorrin winked.

She laughed and he tugged her into his arms. Cera sighed into his chest. Her heart quickened against his, and she wanted to bury herself in his arms. Never leave. "Want to take a bath?"

"Is that a hint that I need one?"

"No, I didn't mean it like that." She averted her eyes, her cheeks burning.

"I was teasing you, love."

She mock-glared.

He lowered his head and brushed his lips against hers. The quick touch wasn't nearly enough. She wanted to melt into him, but it wasn't the time. If Jorrin claimed her lips properly, it'd only leave her aching for him.

She wished they had true privacy. She wanted to sleep in his arms like the night in Hadrian's barn. Wanted to be warm and safe, and *be* with Jorrin. Cera wanted to give herself to him. "I have soap." Rushing her words, she swallowed.

"All right, all right, I'll bathe." He held up his hands.

Cera kissed him.

Jorrin hauled her back to him, sinking his hands in her wet hair.

She moaned into his mouth when he deepened the kiss. Warmth settled low in her belly, and she forgot all about the freezing water as the rest of her form seared. Wrapping her arms around him, she kissed him until her knees weakened.

He held her up, pinned to his chest, and she ended the kiss, pushing her face in his neck and panting.

So much for not letting myself get swept away by him.

Especially since she'd started it.

I love you, Jorrin thought-sent.

Cera lifted her head and met his heavy-lidded sapphire eyes. "Good." She slipped from his arms and handed him soap and the other drying linen.

He made an attempt to grab her, but she eluded him, laughing.

"We have Hadrian to thank for the bathing sheets."

Jorrin nodded, gripping his tunic and lifting it.

At the first sight of bare, defined abs, heat crept up her neck. Her cheeks seared, because she couldn't look away. Her feet were frozen in place.

One dark brow shot up, but wickedness flashed across his blue gaze when he tossed his shirt to the loamy ground.

Leave. Leave now.

Her feet would not obey.

Still looking at her, Jorrin bent over and started to unlace his boots.

She tried not to stare at him, but her eyes traveled up and down his body. Her fingers needed to follow suit; needed to touch him. Cera hadn't had nearly enough the night they'd spent in Hadrian's barn.

His chest was beautiful—broad, yet lean, leading to a trim waist, displaying prominent abdominal muscles. Nearly hairless, with only a small path of dark curls beneath his navel disappearing into his breeches. His well-defined muscles rippled even with the slightest movement as he undressed.

Jorrin's strong arms begged for her hands.

She'd never seen him fully naked, but if she stood there much longer, she'd get the chance.

He met her eyes, hands on his open breeches. "I had no idea my love was a voyeur." He laughed, his eyes daring her. The slight breeze shifted his dark hair, hiding one of his tapered ears for a moment. Color lit his high cheekbones, a teasing smile curved his full mouth.

Cera panted, struggling for breath as longing settled over her. Her body trembled, need throbbing low.

Stay or go?

She wasn't naïve enough not to recognize physical desire just because she'd never been with a man.

Cera wanted Jorrin, and he wanted her just as badly.

If she stayed on the shore, maybe he wouldn't tell her it wasn't time like he had in Hadrian's barn. The look in his eyes scorched her as much as one of his kisses.

"I love you," she whispered. She cleared her throat. "Well . . . I'll go. Give you some privacy. I'll call you when the meal is ready if you're not back by then."

She jogged away, Trikser on her heels.

Coward.

Jorrin chuckled and shook his head as he watched her go. She hadn't given him the chance to assure her he didn't want or need privacy from her.

Cera wanted him. She'd made no attempt to hide her desire, her passion for him.

Even if he didn't have empathic magic, the look on her face would have made him hard as a rock—which happened to be his current state of discomfort.

His blood was singing, and he'd only kissed her once. He wished he could've taken the time to make love to her, but the shore of a lake wasn't any better than a hay pile in Hadrian's barn.

It'd killed him when he'd had to stop her exploring hands the few times he'd held her. Chiding himself to stop kissing her before he got swept away was becoming too-normal—and left him burning for her.

He shed the rest of his clothing and shivered as he stepped into the frigid water. At least the lake would cool his ardor—maybe.

When Jorrin rejoined everyone at the ruins, entering what used to be the castle, Avery was speaking in serious hushed tones, so he quickened his step.

Am I missing something important?

The younger man had drawn a diagram of what had to be Castle Lenore in the dirt at his feet; Braedon and Hadrian were studying it.

Avery was gesturing to various points on his map and shaking his head. His face was white as a sheet.

"What's wrong?" Jorrin asked.

"My mother's locked in her rooms. She doesn't know where my father is. She can't cast, they have some sort of spell on her . . . or her rooms. It took them three days to break her protection shield and get in. Varthan was very, very angry. He killed our family's entire personal guard." The younger man's tone broke; Cera's cousin fought a sob.

Jorrin glanced at his father as Braedon rested a comforting hand on Avery's forearm.

Braedon paled, his expression pained.

He was suddenly glad he was not as much of an empath as his father.

"I'll kill him." Cera joined them by Hadrian's fire. She had her magic sword clutched in her hand and her cheeks were tear-stained.

Trikser was right behind her, but he was wary, tail between his legs.

Jorrin turned away from the sword so it couldn't affect him, but he could already feel the tug of its magic. He blocked it as best he could.

"They were good men. I've known most of them since childhood." Avery had tears in his eyes. "I know their families . . ."

"Your mother wasn't put in any danger speaking with you?" Jorrin asked, trying to take his attention from the murdered men. His heart ached for Cera's cousin and his father, who was effected by what they all were feeling.

"No, she said the shade who guards her is all brawn, the weakest in magic, from what she can tell. She thinks his name is Athas. She said there are only four, and he's not at her door at all times. They must have confidence on the spell over her rooms."

"Four? That's all?" Jorrin asked.

"Yes. They work together. The one the bastard keeps at his side is the real danger. She said he's very young, but very powerful. Varthan thinks he's the key to breaking the spell on the sword."

"I *will* kill him," Cera repeated.

She was so wrong about that.

He would handle it, but now was no time to argue with her. Jorrin grabbed her wrist and tugged her down onto a large log that had been dragged inside to act as a bench. He threw an arm around her shoulders as soon as they were seated, but she was taut against him. "Cera, relax. It's all right," he whispered in her ear and kissed her cheek.

Trikser whimpered, but lay at their feet.

She glanced at Jorrin, the ghost of a smile playing at her lips as she stood the sword against the dead wood. "Thanks," she whispered, but her expression was distant.

Trikser pawed at her boots.

Jorrin absently put his hand out and stroked the wolf's head, freezing and staring at the soft white fur under his fingertips. He made eye contact with Trikser for a split second, but turned away. He wasn't making a challenge for dominance, and wanted Trik to know that, but Cera's bondmate licked his hand and wagged his tail. He bit back a gasp.

Cera looked at Trikser, then at Jorrin and smiled. She relaxed against him, resting her head on his shoulder.

"Wow," he whispered.

"He says he's accepted you, lad," Hadrian said, smiling.

Braedon also wore a soft smile.

The interruption was a mood lifter for them all.

Jorrin took a breath and scratched Trikser's ear until the big wolf leaned into his leg. "That's great. We can really be a team, now."

Cera grinned, patting his thigh and giving her bond a good scratch behind his other ear. *You'll spoil him to death now,* she thought-sent.

He grinned.

Trikser had rarely growled at him lately, and he'd wagged his tail in his direction quite a bit. Acceptance was good. He could get closer to them both. She'd have Trikser for life; they might as well like each other.

"But what else did your mother say, Avery?" Jorrin asked.

"Varthan didn't kill my father, she'd feel it if he was gone; but she's afraid he's been injured. She can only sense him some of the time, but admitted it could be the spell."

"He can't get off on me watching Uncle Everett die if he's already killed him, so I agree with Aunt Em. He'll use them both to get the sword. And he won't try to kill her until he decides whether or not he can use her magic to his advantage." Cera took a breath.

Jorrin squeezed her against his side, wincing as her fears and grief hit his magic. He wanted to hold her and kiss her and shield her from all this.

Avery nodded. "She thinks so, too. That's why she was untouched and left in her rooms. He didn't even try to beat her, which surprised me. Knowing his infamous temper and since it took so long for them to gain access to the castle."

"The king should've been alerted by now," Braedon remarked.

"You think?" Jorrin glanced at his father.

"A whole Province deserted? I should think so," Hadrian said.

"Yes, I already told Cera and Jorrin my father sent word the same day I left to find her."

"Don't you think there should be an army arriving then? We were at Hadrian's almost a fortnight . . ." Cera mused.

"Well, now King Nathal has definitive proof of Varthan's actions," Braedon said. "One would think he has enough evidence to have him put to death for all the murders he's committed alone. Not to mention his . . . other crimes." His father shot a look at his love.

Rape was unsaid.

"King Nathal won't have to kill Varthan," Cera said. "I'm going to run him through." She thrust her sword forward, her jaw locked, full lips a hard line.

The sword's magic swirled, making Jorrin's head spin. He blinked.

"Lass, have you ever taken a life?" Hadrian's tone was gentle. The look on her face was all the answer the elf needed. "I thought not. Let Braedon and me handle Varthan."

"You don't need blood on your hands, dearheart," Braedon added in the same gentle tone.

"I'll kill him," she vowed, brandishing a fist. "I *will* kill him. He killed my family."

Braedon and Hadrian exchanged a look, but said nothing more on the matter.

"My mother said Varthan rarely leaves the great hall. All the servants he didn't kill are forced to wait on him and his shades hand and foot. I'm sure he's taken liberties with the girls as if they were willing bar wenches." Avery growled.

The young lord's family probably cared deeply for and took great care of all those who served Castle Lenore. Cera had told him the same was true of those in service to Castle Ryhan and Greenwald. She and Avery were some of the most unusual nobles he'd ever met.

"I have to admit the numbers are much more equal than I'd imagined," Jorrin mused as Avery pointed out the various locations on his diagram in the dirt.

"They are highly trained shades and malicious," Hadrian admonished. "They have no conscience. They'll kill you with a spell before you can even prepare yourself for it, lad."

"Plus they are trained with the sword as well," Cera said. "Varthan loves to make them well-rounded, dutiful little minions."

"Mother is sure the youngest is the true threat, but she noticed he cowers even when Varthan isn't directly addressing him," Avery said.

"That may work to our advantage." Hadrian scratched his bearded chin.

"Blessed Spirit knows what kind of things he's witnessed at Varthan's hands," Cera said. "He gets them any way he can. As soon as someone senses their potential, he buys, kidnaps, kills their parents—whatever it takes. Even if this boy is young, there's no telling how long Varthan's had him. Turns, if he's one of the elite. Maybe from infancy."

"We can't let Varthan use him to break the spell. Especially if he's as powerful as my mother senses."

"Then we take him out first," Braedon said.

"I agree," Hadrian said. "Stun him and get him away from Varthan."

The breath Cera must've been holding erupted from her lungs. She relaxed against Jorrin when the elf referenced stunning the boy. Her eyes were wide, she gnawed her bottom lip.

His magic only told him she was apprehensive, but he didn't miss the look Braedon shot her. What had his father caught that his powers hadn't?

"My lady, a tender heart does not have a place here. Fear is one thing, but it doesn't mean the lad would hesitate to kill you."

"I know." She looked down. "I know we're all putting our lives at risk. There's nothing I can do to adequately thank you, but I don't want anyone else to die, except Varthan."

"I don't plan on it, lass." Hadrian grinned, making a fist.

"Me either," Jorrin said.

"I'm not going to die," Avery put in.

"I feel the same way," Braedon said, grinning.

Cera looked at each of them, then at her bondmate, who was wagging his tail. A small smile bloomed on her lips. In seconds, it became a grin that made Jorrin's heart stutter.

"Now that we're all decided on that, what else did you learn, lad?" Hadrian rubbed his hands together.

Avery continued to brief them.

Cera stood. "I'll take first watch." She squared her shoulders and re-sheathed the magic sword at her waist.

Their eyes locked, and Jorrin discarded any ideas of going with her. He didn't need his powers to tell she needed to be alone. Nodding, he kissed her knuckles before she slipped away, Trikser on her heels.

He caught Braedon's much too-knowing smile. At least his father had had the tact not to remind her of the highly effective protection spell he and Hadrian had erected, in addition to the masking spell still around their perimeter.

They'd be more than fine for the night.

Old habits die hard, my son, Braedon thought-sent.

One corner of Jorrin's mouth shot up.

Avery quickly piped up that he'd also take his turn at being on watch.

Braedon chuckled.

Staring in the direction she'd gone off to, Jorrin smiled to himself. He'd take watch, too. Anything to make her feel more secure.

CHAPTER FIFTEEN

"J ORRIN?" CERA CALLED. She watched her step as she walked along the crumbling stone wall in the darkness. It was late and true to his word, he was on watch. She'd been unable to shut down her racing mind enough to sleep. The new information haunted her.

Her aunt was unharmed, which was a relief, but worry for her uncle and grief for the dozen men of his personal guard were eating her alive.

I'm responsible.

She'd known most of them. She tried not to remember their names or think of the times they'd guarded Avery, Kait, and her when they'd played outside the safety of Castle Lenore's walls.

"You're supposed to be asleep," he admonished, hopping down to the ground. He'd been perched on the wall.

Cera gave the section a onceover. How had it been sturdy enough to hold his weight? "I couldn't sleep." She flashed a smile and shrugged.

Jorrin returned her smile, opening his arms.

She moved in quickly and sighed as she leaned against him, closing her eyes. His heart beat against hers, grounding her.

He rubbed her back, and she sank into him, smiling when he tucked her head under his chin.

Trikser appeared around the corner of the wall, wuffing and running to her. His thoughts were a scold.

She pulled away from Jorrin and knelt, throwing her arms around her wolf. "Sorry, Trik. I didn't mean to leave you behind." She dropped a kiss on his furry head and gave him a pat.

He wagged his tail and lay down, accepting her apology.

Turning back to the man she loved, Cera rested against his broad chest. "Sorry." She felt the rumble of his laugh.

"I'll always be jealous of him."

"Really?" She pulled back to study his face. Seeing the tease for what it was, she couldn't help herself. She pressed her lips to his.

He took control, plunging his tongue into her mouth, devouring more than exploring.

She opened for him, rubbing her tongue against his. The fire started where their mouths were fused. Heat consumed her body, making her breasts heavy before settling into her lower belly, burning its way between her legs. She clutched his shoulders to stay upright, pressing closer as her thighs trembled.

Cera was lost.

Her heart pounded, and a shiver made its way down her spine when she felt the hard length trapped between them. The pulsing at her core increased in response.

She needed Jorrin's arms around her. Needed him beside her, always. And right now, she needed him *inside* her. Urgency won out over nerves about virginity. Her body was already leading her; she was more than willing to follow. If she could just convince him, they could make love, right here, right now.

The dangers of their situation were gone. She had no worries; no actions had to be taken right now.

There was only this man and what she felt for him.

Jorrin kissed her hungrily, overwhelmingly, but she was right there with him, anticipating where it would take them next.

Cera clutched his arms and rocked her pelvis into his. He pressed right back, and she moaned.

He ripped his mouth from hers, panting hard. "Hey . . . how can I watch for the shades when you do that to me?" His voice was thick, much deeper than normal.

Her breathing was ragged as she gathered her voice. "I needed you for a moment."

"Oh. Only a moment?" He arched a dark brow and playfully attempted to push her away, but she held on tight.

"No. Not a moment. Forever."

Blessed Spirit, it's true.

She never wanted to be parted from Jorrin. Her whole form relived a head-to-toe flush.

"Good, because you couldn't get rid of me if you tried. I love you."

Cera closed her eyes. The words washed over her, and she tilted her head, shivering when he kissed her throat. "I love you, too. And I want you." Her cheeks blazed.

"Love . . ." His face was pained.

"Don't tell me no. I want this. I want you. I don't care where we are, as long as I'm with you."

Jorrin groaned, shaking his head. "Your first time is a big deal."

"It'd only be a big deal if it wasn't you."

Something passed through his sapphire eyes, visible even in the dimness. "You'll only be with me," he ordered, glaring.

She grinned and kissed him. *That's what I want. To be with you*, she thought-sent as his mouth moved over hers. She melted into him as their tongues dueled.

His fingers tugged her jerkin, and she let him undo the ties, loosening and opening it. Separating their mouths for only a moment to slip free of the leather, she rushed back into his chest.

Jorrin wrapped his arms around her waist, and lifted Cera to the section of the wall he'd been perched on. He moved her tunic and pressed a kiss to her belly.

She rested her hands on his shoulders and quivered.

"This has to go," he breathed, pulling on her shirt.

Laughing, Cera gripped his face. "Don't rip it, my other one's a mess."

He grinned as she raised her arms and let him take the tunic off her. He let it drift to the ground as she crossed her arms over her breasts.

Stepping between her legs, Jorrin kissed her gently. "Don't hide from me, love. I want to see you, I want to taste you."

Embarrassment flushed to her toes, but she didn't look away from his eyes. She unfastened her breastbands and slipped it off, shivering as the air greeted her nipples.

He enclosed her in his embrace. "Are you cold?"

"No." Cera kissed him again, burying her hands in his hair.

Jorrin devastated her mouth, making her want more as she thrummed for him. When he cupped her breasts and spread a trail of hot wet kisses down her neck, she cried out, clutching him as close as she could.

She tugged his tunic out of his breeches, running her hands up and down his back. "Off," she ordered.

He stepped back and ripped his shirt off, tossing it next to hers. Jorrin rushed back to her before she could say a word, but she gasped when his bare skin brushed hers.

Warm. Safe.

Mine.

"Blessed Spirit, love. You're going to kill me," he breathed into her neck, his chest moving against hers.

Nipples tingling, Cera rubbed into him, needing more. She wanted to lie with him, have him on top of her.

Inside her.

"Where are you furs?" She traced her fingertip up and down the length of his tapered ear.

He shuddered and met her eyes. "Not far."

"I want you now, Jorrin."

She yelped as he scooped her up, and she nipped at his chin when he laughed. She scrambled for a grab around his neck.

"I won't drop you, love."

Trikser stared as Jorrin arranged their sleeping furs into the most comfortable bed he could muster.

Her wolf's thoughts were a mixture of curiosity and understanding. He could feel Cera's pleasure, but didn't know how to react to it. He knew she wasn't being harmed, but he stayed nearby, watching.

Jorrin kept whispering reassurances she didn't need to hear, but it made her love him more.

"Uh, love, can you make him . . . go somewhere?" He knelt on the furs, raising his hand for her to come to him.

"Thought you liked voyeurs," Cera teased.

He chuckled, but shook his head and tugged her down with him.

She landed sprawled on his chest, their legs entwined.

"Not of the canine variety," he muttered against her lips.

Cera looked over her shoulder, smiling at her bondmate, her heart for the past seven turns, then glanced back at Jorrin—her new love. She wanted them both with her forever.

Trik, I love you, but go. I promise I'm safe with Jorrin. She wrapped the thought-send in feelings for him, and showed him a picture of where their horses were tied.

His amber stare bored into her for a moment, then Trik swished his tail and took off at a run, without a backward glance.

She giggled. In his own way, Trik understood. He'd accepted Jorrin as her mate.

"That's better," Jorrin whispered.

"I love him, you know." She looked down at him, nestling closer and loving the feel of his hot bare skin on hers.

"I know. He's a part of you, I understand." He ran his hands over her shoulders, caressing her back.

She warmed and wiggled.

He groaned and pulled her closer still. His erection pressed into her hip through too many layers of leather.

"I want you to be a part of me, too."

Jorrin grinned and flipped them, landing in the cradle of her body.

Cera wrapped her arms and legs around him.

He seared her mouth with another kiss as his hands worked her belt, then jerked on the ties of her breeches. She lifted her hips, helping him pull them down and off. Boots and undergarments soon followed, the soft furs tickling her naked bottom.

Jorrin pulled back, staring until nerves made her shiver. He said nothing, and she fought the urge to cover herself, wishing she had four hands.

"Jorrin," she whispered, voice shaking.

"I've never seen anything so beautiful in my life." The apple of his throat bobbed.

Cera averted her eyes, but he gently cupped her face and made her meet his gaze.

"I love you . . . so much it makes me ache."

She smiled and slipped her arms around his neck, pulling him down for another kiss. When they parted, she nibbled his earlobe.

He trembled against her, his chest brushing her nipples.

"You have breeches to remove, my love," she said into his ear.

Jorrin nodded and made quick work of the rest of his clothing. He put his knees into the fur beside her.

It was her turn to gasp. *Gorgeous* didn't begin to describe him. Her eyes darted all over, Cera didn't know what to look at first. His chest never ceased to amaze her. His thighs were thick with muscle, and she couldn't wait to feel their legs entwined.

Her gaze honed in on the trail of dark hair that led to the proud erection jutting at her, and she bit back a gulp. He was larger than she'd imagined, but he wouldn't hurt her. She shifted on the blankets and opened her arms. "Come to me, Jorrin."

"I'd better, because I'm going to be in trouble if you keep looking at me like that." He settled over her, kissing her into oblivion as soon as his chest touched her breasts.

She moaned into his mouth at the glorious skin-on-skin feel. His hips pressed her down, his erection resting against her sex, searing her throbbing core.

Her stomach fluttered and she wriggled under him, but his kisses didn't stop. Jorrin dragged his mouth downward, nibbling and licking his way to her collarbone, his stubble tickling as he cupped and kneaded her.

Cera wanted more. She writhed, shoving her hips upward. Her blood simmered, on its way to a rolling boil.

Though he made a noise in his throat against her, he didn't stop his ministrations.

She whimpered when his hot mouth enclosed her nipple. He suckled and traced his tongue around it, then did the same to the other.

More.

She needed more. He was trying to kill her.

Jorrin laughed, the vibration shooting a tremor down her spine. "You're not very patient, my love."

Cera moaned, thrashing under him.

"We're just getting started. I have to make sure you're ready, so I don't hurt you."

"I'm ready."

She jolted when his hand shot between her legs, parting her tender folds.

He closed his eyes and took a breath. "You're wet . . . Blessed Spirit." He teased the bundle of nerves at the top of her sex.

Cera cried out and lurched. What was he doing to her? Pleasure rolled over her, so she lifted her hips again.

Spreading her thighs with his hands, Jorrin leaned down, scattering kisses over her belly, continuing to where his hands were making her feel so good.

Whatever he was doing, she didn't want him to stop.

When he kissed her inner thigh, she whispered his name.

Jorrin lavished wet kisses on the other as well, massaging her core with his thumb. His rough face only excited her more.

She gasped at the first swipe of his tongue up the length of her center, and when his fingertip probed her. Then he did it again, and all thought fled. Cera threw her head back, tugging at his hair.

He sucked her into his mouth, teasing her with his rapidly-moving tongue.

She lifted, twisted, shifted and moved back and forth until he grabbed her hips with both hands to hold her still. Her muscles tightened, her thighs shook, as a wave of intensity rolled over her and she panted, calling his name over and over.

"Relax love, let it come." He pressed a kiss into the soft part of her belly as his fingers moved over her sensitive nub and slid partway inside.

She didn't get a chance to ask him what he meant. The wall of sensation broke, making her inner muscles contract and release continually, her hips rise of their own accord. Ecstasy hit like a pile of bricks crumbling on top of her. Her spine stiffened; her sex pulsed. Cera panted and blinked to clear her vision, moaning Jorrin's name.

He was in her arms in seconds, kissing her deeply, his tongue melded to hers. She tasted herself and shivered, then ground her pelvis against his.

Pulling away gently, he captured her gaze with his. "Are you ready?" His thick whisper was strained.

Cera nodded, wrapping her arms around him. Her body was languid from what he'd done to her, but she wasn't done. Still wanted him.

"I'll go slow, and we'll stop if it hurts, all right?" Positioning himself at her sex, he pushed forward gradually.

She gasped as he stretched her, and she gripped his arms.

He groaned, closing his eyes and throwing his head back. Jorrin steadied her, holding her hips with both hands. One last push, and he filled her completely.

Sharp pain took all her attention. She cried out, tears stinging her eyes.

Jorrin froze. "Look at me, Cera."

She met his intense blue eyes and swallowed hard.

He frowned. Sweat was beading his forehead. "I'm sorry." Leaning back, he started to pull out of her, but she whimpered a protest and wrapped her legs around his waist.

Lifting her bottom, Cera rubbed against him. The movement made them both moan.

I still want you, Jorrin, she thought-sent.

He nodded, sucking in an audible breath. Bringing himself body gently against her, he propelled forward.

She bit her lip and moved with him, rocking in a gentle sway as they found a rhythm. Pain slid to discomfort, but she still didn't want to stop. His thrusts were tentative at first; hurt faded, pleasure jolting her every time he moved. Cera tilted her hips to take him deeper; needed him closer. She ran her fingers up and down his back, exploring.

Jorrin picked up speed.

She followed the curve of his rear end, grabbing him with both hands as her body demanded a more frantic pace. Met him thrust for thrust, moving under him, with him, against him as he pumped in and out.

Wrapping around him, she trembled at the approach of climax. She flattened her breasts into his chest and whimpered, straining against him.

He took her mouth, pushing his tongue in time with his hips.

Desperate. Wanton. Perfect.

Physical feelings entwined with magic and emotion; made every sensation too much. Pleasure smacked into Cera.

They stiffened at the same time. He grunted into their kiss, then tore his mouth away, panting her name and burying his face against her neck. Her whole body shook beneath his and he thrust forward again.

She struggled for breath and coherent thought as Jorrin's release shot into her, a warm wet rush making her belly tingle.

He collapsed on top of her, and she held him hard and fast, not ready for them to be parted. His mind was open, but his thoughts chaotic, a mixture of pleasure and love. The magic-enhanced sensations were tangible; she felt their bond strengthen. She'd never been so close to another person.

Cera shivered, a pleasant aftershock of passion moving over her as he trailed kisses along her jaw line before pressing his mouth to hers.

The kiss was tender, heated and languorous all at once, making her already boneless form melt even more.

"Blessed Spirit, I love you," Jorrin whispered against her lips, resting his forehead against hers.

Cera caressed his stubbled cheeks. "I love you, too."

He slipped from her core and rolled to his back, taking her with him.

She snuggled close, sighing as she rested her head on his chest. His heart was slowing from its frantic pace beneath her cheek.

Jorrin ran his fingers through her long loose curls, stroking her back and following the curve of her hip and bottom.

She felt truly soothed for the first time in a long time. "Thank you." Cera kissed his right pectoral.

He caressed her face. "What for, love?"

"Making it special."

He smiled. "It was special for me, too."

She scooted up to kiss him.

They didn't speak for some time, but the silence was companionable. Jorrin's hands didn't stop their comforting touches, and Cera melted into him, swallowing back a yawn.

"Why don't you try to sleep, love?" He pressed a kiss to her forehead. "I'll hold you."

She met his eyes, smiling softly. Didn't want reality to close in on them again. It was too soon. "All right, but we should get dressed."

They made quick work of their clothes, the pleasant ache between her legs begging her to change her mind; stay naked and make love to him again. But as soon as Jorrin nestled her close, wrapping them both in sleeping furs, Cera couldn't keep her eyes open.

"Sleep, love," he ordered, placing a kiss to the crown of her head. "I'll watch over you."

With his assurance, she drifted off, trying not to dread what was to come.

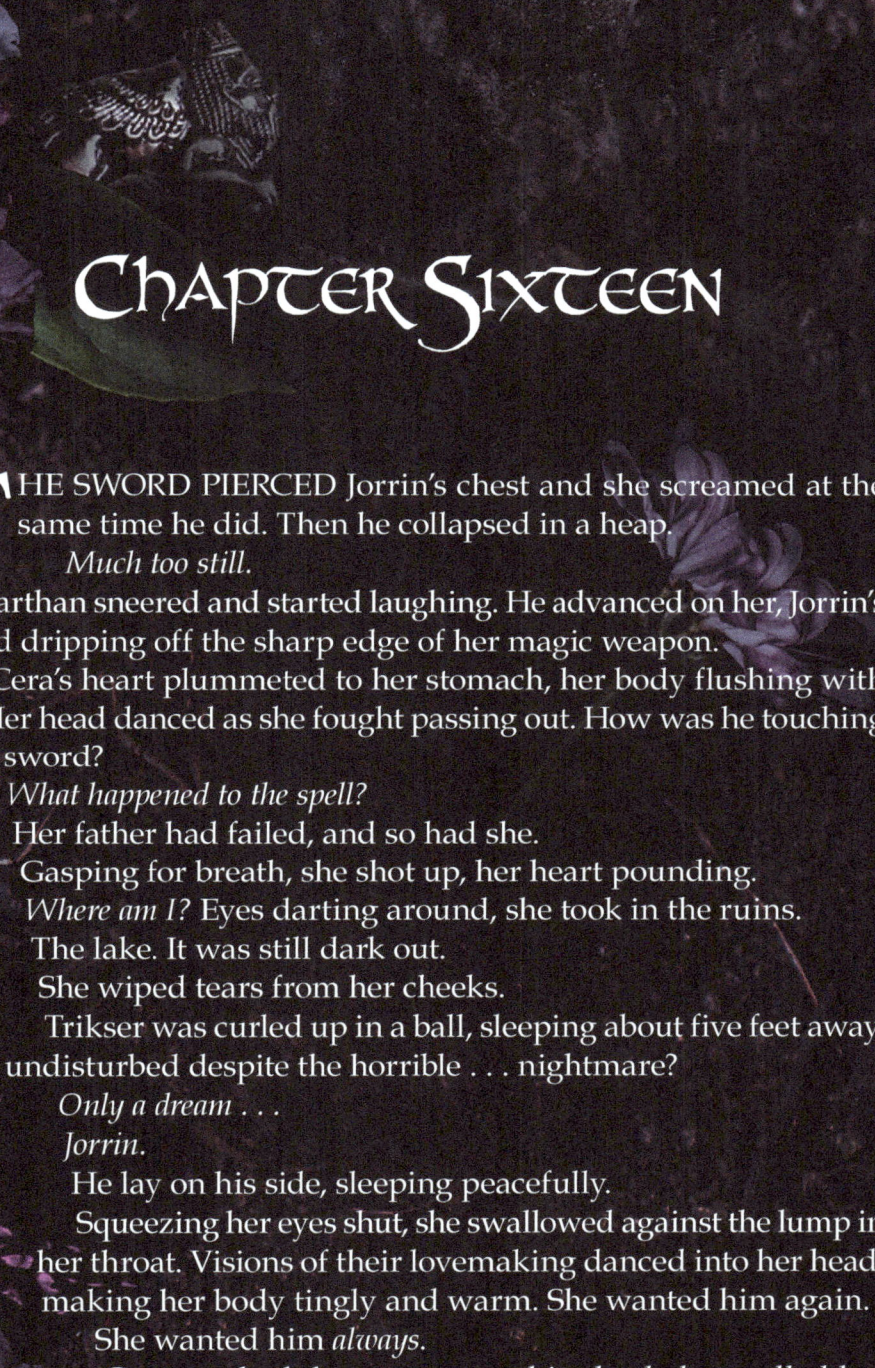

Chapter Sixteen

T HE SWORD PIERCED Jorrin's chest and she screamed at the same time he did. Then he collapsed in a heap.

Much too still.

Varthan sneered and started laughing. He advanced on her, Jorrin's blood dripping off the sharp edge of her magic weapon.

Cera's heart plummeted to her stomach, her body flushing with it. Her head danced as she fought passing out. How was he touching the sword?

What happened to the spell?

Her father had failed, and so had she.

Gasping for breath, she shot up, her heart pounding.

Where am I? Eyes darting around, she took in the ruins.

The lake. It was still dark out.

She wiped tears from her cheeks.

Trikser was curled up in a ball, sleeping about five feet away, undisturbed despite the horrible . . . nightmare?

Only a dream . . .

Jorrin.

He lay on his side, sleeping peacefully.

Squeezing her eyes shut, she swallowed against the lump in her throat. Visions of their lovemaking danced into her head, making her body tingly and warm. She wanted him again.

She wanted him *always.*

Cera reached down to caress his cheek, but pulled her hand back before making contact with his stubble.

It's better not to wake him.

She watched him, heartbeat increasing steadily. Wanted to curl back up against his chest, feel his arms around her, but couldn't.

Now she knew what she had to do.

Cera had to prevent her nightmare from becoming reality at all costs.

Her stomach jumped as she glanced at the castle's ruins. She couldn't endanger the lives of Avery, Braedon, or Hadrian, either. Avery was blood kin, but the elf wizard and Jorrin's father were a part of her family as well.

Trik made a noise in his sleep and her eyes darted to him. Her bond. Her life was his life. They were entwined. If he died, she would. If she got him killed by Varthan or the shades, her life was forfeit anyway. If she left him and got herself killed, at least he wouldn't have to see her die. His death would be peaceful. Perhaps Hadrian could even ease it. Was it fair to endanger him?

Jorrin shifted against her.

Cera froze, waiting to see if he'd wake. When his breathing settled back into a deep rhythm, she leaned down and placed a gentle kiss on his lips, her heart aching.

He smiled in his sleep, but didn't stir otherwise.

Love for him washed over her, tears welled. She'd given herself to him because she'd wanted to, because she loved him. She didn't regret it; at least he'd have her memory if Varthan killed her.

Taking a deep breath, she donned her boots and cloak as quietly as possible, then covered him with the furs and stepped away.

She consciously built walls in her mind. She'd have to block everything out. Every feeling, every thought, would be a sharpened edge, a weapon to pierce her with. Cera would have to be stronger than she was even capable of.

I don't have a choice.

"Lass, have you ever taken a life?" Hadrian's words teased her memory, but she banished them, sucking in a breath and making a fist.

She'd do what she had to do.

If she went now, she could—would—take Varthan by surprise and run him through with the weapon he coveted. Her friends and the love of her life wouldn't be in peril if they weren't with her.

Trikser opened his amber eyes as soon as she scooted from Jorrin's side. He rose alert, shoulders tense.

Cera cursed. She should've known he'd understand something was very wrong. Her thoughts and feelings were disturbed and she'd blocked everything and everyone from her mind—including her bondmate.

How was she going leave him? He'd follow without any command.

Her wolf whined as she reached for him, but his stance didn't relax.

She knelt and threw her arms around his neck.

He was stiff against her, whimpering.

"It's all right, Trik. It's something I have to do." Cera pulled back to look at him, meeting his eyes.

He wiggled his tail a bit, but still looked ready to strike.

"I need you to stay here," she commanded as calmly and evenly as she could.

Trikser started to growl.

She gasped. Her bond had *never* growled at her before.

What the hell am I going to do?

"Dammit."

Trikser growled more deeply.

He'd never disobeyed before either, but she'd never tried to ditch him to run *into* danger. Would he bite her if it was to keep her safe?

Cera forced a breath. "Trikser. You will stay here. You will protect Jorrin." She gestured to her sleeping lover, but her wolf lowered his head as if she was prey, his amber eyes boring into her.

What can I do?

She couldn't lie to him. Even with her mind partially blocked, her wolf could sense dishonesty. It was like a smell, palpable to him, just as he could sense fear. She sighed when he whined and pawed her hand. "You can't come with me."

She'd have to stun him, but it wouldn't work if he had any warning. Guilt crept up from the pit of her stomach.

Avery had taught her the small spell not even a sevenday ago. It wouldn't hurt her wolf, but that didn't quell her reluctance to use it. The spell wasn't long-term. It'd give her just enough time to get away. Her cousin said it would knock someone out for a half-hour at most.

Leaning into him, Cera dropped a kiss on his furry head.

Trikser relaxed his stance and licked her cheek.

She whispered she loved him as well as thought-sent it, wrapping him in warm emotions. She clamped her eyes shut, scrambling to her feet. It was the only way her determination wouldn't collapse entirely.

Extending her arm as Avery instructed, she clearly said the spellwords. Her tone was hushed, but her resolve remained firm.

Her wolf yelped and collapsed in a heap, unconscious.

She knelt and caressed his head; whispered an apology, blinking away tears. Cera jogged away from Trikser and Jorrin, soothing Ash when he started hoofing the ground and jerking his head up and down as she rushed to saddle him. She rubbed his nose, resting her forehead against his, sucking in great gulps of air as shivers crept down her spine. "I have to do this, Ash."

He bumped her hand with his soft muzzle when she broke their contact.

She patted him one last time and mounted, shuddering; the motion had little to do with the chilly night air. Tucking her magic sword against her, she made sure it was hidden under her cloak. Her fingers searched frantically for her dirk, even though she knew it was there.

"I'm sorry, Jorrin," Cera whispered, nudging Ash away from the other horses, "but I can't let you die, too."

She leaned low, brushing his mane with her cheek as Ash covered the ground at a run. She steeled herself as best she could, pushing away the voice that called her a fool. Ignoring the one that piped up, demanding, *go back.*

I'm doing what I have to do.

Right?

Arriving at her destination came too soon. She still cursed and declared herself a coward. Cera jumped off her stallion, the ground jarring her body. Her eyes roved for Trikser, but her stomach somersaulted when the memory hit her.

I left him behind.

The sun would be up soon, and she'd have to sneak into the castle before anyone was awake. A vision of marching right into the great hall and attacking Varthan danced into her head, but she disregarded it. She had to protect the sword from him. Turn herself in, in return for her aunt and uncle? She wouldn't give him the sword, though.

No matter how she got into Castle Lenore, she'd have to be stealthy. Why hadn't she learned how to communicate with her aunt as Avery had? Aunt Em could've helped.

She headed into the stables, entering the smallest building—where most of the ponies were kept. Several animals were inside; leaving her horse there should go unnoticed.

Encountering no one, Cera hid Ash in the stall farthest away from the entrance. She slipped out of her cloak, laying it over the saddle and whispering reassurances to her stallion.

She froze in place when noise greeted her ears. Flattening herself against the wall, she paused, cocking her head to one side.

Who's awake at this hour?

Muffled cries—female—had Cera narrowing her eyes.

"Ow. I can't believe you bit me, you bitch."

A smack of flesh on flesh, and the girl screamed.

Cera moved out of the stall just as his laughter started. Why the hell had she left Trikser behind? She crept along the line of stalls just as the fair-haired young man threw the girl onto a pile of hay. He had to be a shade, and what he intended with her was obvious.

She recognized her. Her name was Neomi, and she was a maid of her Aunt Em's. Was a few turns younger, but they'd played together as children any time she'd been in Tarvis.

Bile rose as the shade roughly began to fondle and kiss Neomi.

The maid was doing a valiant job of resisting, and she almost got a good knee into his groin. He slid his hips away from her, but then slammed his pelvis into Neomi's.

Cera winced.

Neomi pounded him on the back with tight fists until he pinned her arms to the hay pile. She whimpered and struggled, but got nowhere.

She'd have to move fast. Cera yearned to slip her sword—or dirk—into his back, but Avery's stunning spell would work better . . . allow her to save the girl and remain unseen. The spellwords were a harsh whisper and she pushed all her power behind them, clenching tight fists at her sides.

The shade stood, then whirled toward her, his light-blue eyes wide as he collapsed in a heap.

Growling, Cera kicked him.

Hope he hit his head.

Probably around eight and ten, he was younger than she'd first estimated. Pale, unmarred skin; he was handsome.

Irritating.

Plus he'd seen her, and that wasn't part of her plan.

She scowled.

"Lady Ryhan?" Neomi's whisper was tremulous, fat tears rolling down her cheeks. Her dress was ripped, and she shook from head to foot.

The bruising already visible on her wrists and right cheek from the boy's slap made Cera's blood boil, though the maid appeared otherwise unharmed.

Neomi hadn't moved from the hay stack, so she put her hand out.

"Is he dead?" she asked as Cera pulled her to her feet.

"No, just stunned. I'm hoping it'll last a while." She should kill the shade, but didn't want to traumatize Neomi any more than she already was. A little voice pointed out that Braedon and Hadrian had spoken the truth, she had no blood on her hands so far.

Neomi threw herself into Cera's arms, almost knocking her over. When the maid started to sob, she was too surprised to do anything other than hold the shorter girl. Patting her back, she whispered reassurances.

"Lady Em said you would come." She swiped at her wet cheeks with a shaky hand. "Thank you for saving me from Markus."

Cera met big brown eyes, smoothing her disheveled blonde hair as the girl seemed to take a deep breath. "Why're you here? Aunt Em said she'd evacuated everyone."

"I wouldn't leave Lady Em. She's been better to me than the woman who bore me. Several of us stayed. Greta and Jarina have already been raped by Markus and Athas." Her voice broke on a sob.

Rape was not a fair tradeoff for loyalty, and neither was getting killed. She had no doubt her aunt and uncle felt the same.

"I'll kill them all. Have they touched you before now?" Cera demanded.

The girl's eyes were wide when their gazes collided, and Neomi shook her head vehemently. "No. Markus said he was tired of Greta."

"What about the other two shades? Do they have a penchant for rape?"

"You know there are four?" Her eyes widened even further.

She nodded, making a fist.

"The third is called Dagonet and he's very quiet, but cunning. He doesn't seem to be as cruel as Markus or Athas. And no, he's not laid a hand on any of us."

"And the fourth?"

"A child. He can't be more than twelve or three and ten turns old. It doesn't seem like he could hurt a fly, but the lord keeps him at his side at all times. Milord is awful to the boy. Throws him around and beats him. Lady Em said his magic is a threat, but I haven't been able to get into her rooms for two days."

A child?

Cera's stomach plummeted.

Kait.

She couldn't kill a child, no matter what Braedon cautioned, but why did the boy remain so loyal to Varthan if he was so abused? She cursed colorfully and Neomi shot her a sharp look. "Sorry. I know I don't sound much like a lady."

The maid grinned. "Lady Ryhan, you and I are not strangers."

She smiled sheepishly. "So I was never good at being a lady," she demurred. "But stop with the *Lady Ryhan* nonsense. It's always been Cera to you."

Neomi blushed and nodded. "Where are your companions? Your wolf? And where is Lord Avery? Lady Em mentioned others."

"I'm alone," she said in a tone the girl would not question. "Where's Varthan?"

The maid looked down and trembled, paling. Appeared to struggle for breath. "He rarely leaves the great hall. Except to bed a maid. He's tried to make us all whores. Neysa goes to him willingly. She said it's to protect us all." Neomi made a tight fist, but didn't stop trembling.

"You're not a whore if it's not your choice. Did that bastard touch you?" Cera shivered. She didn't know Neysa well, except that she was a dark-haired beauty from the wild tribal lands of the Southern Continent. Although older than either of them, she shouldn't have had to give herself to Varthan for *any* reason, even an honorable one.

Cera would geld the bastard when she was done running him through. Or maybe before...so she could see his eyes when his tender parts hit the floor.

"Not really," Neomi whispered. "Not for lack of desire on his part. Fondled me a bit the first day. He lined us up, all the younger ones, ripped the tops of our dresses down and touched us .

. ." she shuddered, and so did Cera. "'*Sampling the merchandise,*' he said. Markus took Greta that night." Tears coursed down the maid's cheeks again, and her heart ached.

Resting her hands on her upper arms, she gave a slight squeeze. "I *will* kill them all."

"Lord Everett tried to defend us. Lord Varthan fought him."

"Is my uncle all right?" Cera held her breath for the answer.

"He was stabbed in the side, but Dagonet healed him. Lord Varthan said he needed him in one piece for now. He just beats him unconscious every time he comes to."

"Blessed Spirit." She digested the new information. *One of the shades can heal?* "They're in the great hall now?"

"Yes, but Markus doesn't take long . . . so Athas might be here soon . . . for his turn with me . . ." Neomi gulped.

"I need to get into the castle undetected."

"Follow me," the maid said without hesitation.

Dammit, if the other shade would be checking on his companion, Cera's element of surprise was ruined.

Markus had seen her.

When he woke up he'd have more than just a headache. He'd tell Varthan she was there. The smartest thing to do was stash her sword somewhere safe.

Separating herself from her weapon—willingly—made her shake from head to toe, but it was the best way to keep it out of his hands.

Keep it protected. Especially if she got caught. Her heart sped up.

Actually, Cera had to be caught . . . but without her weapon. It was the only way she could have a sense of control over Varthan. How far it would get her was unknown, but it was better if *she* made the decision.

Making a fist, she gave birth to a new plan. It *had* to work. She'd barter herself for her family.

She grabbed Neomi's wrist, and they halted, molding themselves against the outside wall of the stable. Cera closed her eyes and concentrated. She uttered the words of Braedon's masking spell and prayed to the Blessed Spirit that it worked.

They went into the kitchens through the servants' entrance, hidden from open view, encountering no one—not even another servant.

What to do now? She drummed her fingers against the wall.

"Something wrong, milady?" Neomi whispered.

Everything. "Not really," Cera lied, shaking her head and schooling her expression. "I need a place to hide my sword. Varthan *cannot* gain access to it. Do you know a place where it'll be safe?"

"He never ventures into the kitchens."

"Show me the least-used room."

The maid led her to a small smoke room at the far end of the vast kitchens of Castle Lenore. They slipped inside. The place was empty. Fresh rushes lay on the floor; she could smell them, but the shelving that lined all four of the walls held nothing.

Neomi flashed a smile when their gazes met.

How could she be so calm? Cera needed to absorb her strength; the girl obviously had faith in her, and she'd have to live up to it.

Intimidating.

"There's a false wall," Neomi whispered.

She shot her a look. "Show me."

The girl went to the far wall, feeling around for something, both hands spread.

Cera watched until she heard a *click.* Behind an empty shelf, a narrow door opened, sinking into the wall. She helped Neomi move the shelf just enough to slip past her into the small space no bigger than a closet, and so dark she couldn't see her hand.

She shuddered and didn't ask how Neomi knew about the hidden space. Undoing her belt, she slid the scabbard off, squeezing the sword's hilt as if it could lend her its magic. She sent a prayer to the Blessed Spirit she was doing the right thing as she laid it on the floor.

"Lady Ryhan?"

"Cera, remember?" she chided.

As she stepped out, Neomi depressed the, button to close the door and they replaced the shelf in front of it. "Cera, then. You'll need a sword."

"Yes, but it's not like I can sneak into the armory." She'd already taken too much time.

Why couldn't Jorrin be at her side? He had a sword. He'd promised to protect her, and he would've honored it.

Cera would probably never see him again.

Palms damp, her heart thundered. She swallowed against a lump in her throat.

No self-doubt.

"Why not?" the maid asked.

"You won't have to go to the armory," a male voice drawled.

They both jumped.

Drawing her dirk, she shoved Neomi behind her.

"Relax, Lady Ryhan." Amusement rippled through his words, and Cera scowled.

"Gamel?" Neomi gasped. She stepped around Cera as the youth slid into the small smoke room. He had a sword in his hand.

"Gamel?" She echoed, looking the boy up and down. He was the son of her uncle's head steward, and she'd not seen him in several turns.

He was tall and leanly built, and his brown hair was as curly as Avery's. Even in the dimness of the room, she could see his deep blue eyes dance. His handsome face wore a playful grin.

Taking a breath, she gave a slight smile, sheathing her dagger.

"I thought you were dead," the maid breathed, throwing her arms around his neck and squeezing him tightly.

The boy blushed scarlet, and Cera's smile widened to a grin.

"I know my way around this place better than anyone. I got you this, Lady Ryhan. Lady Lenore said you'd need it." Gamel handed her the sword.

When Neomi went to step away, the boy shot an arm around her slim waist and pinned her to his side.

Cera averted her gaze when he kissed the maid's cheek. Neomi grinned up at him, and her heart ached for Jorrin. She slipped the new scabbard onto her belt, banishing all thoughts of her half-elfin love. He was supposed to be locked safe from her thoughts. "You've seen Aunt Em?"

"I've been slinking around, watching since they got here. I can get into her rooms."

"Then take Neomi there and stay out of sight. Markus will be angry I thwarted his attempts with her. She cannot show herself until this is over."

She gasped. "No, Cera. I want to help." The maid grabbed her hand.

"You've already helped, and I'll not further risk your lives." Cera ignored Neomi's frown and looked at the boy. How old was he now? Sixteen? Seventeen? Not so much older than Avery, but Gamel's age didn't matter. His eyes named him a soldier, and she needed that. "Get her to my aunt and both of you stay there. She can protect you."

He nodded. "I've already gotten Greta and Jarina there. The bastards don't seem to want the older ones, so we've all agreed. We'll protect the shades' targets. Lord Varthan is content as long as he has Neysa, food on the table and someone to beat."

"Is my uncle still in the great hall?"

"Yes. From what I can tell, he's all right. Mostly unconscious." Gamel made a face.

"What is it?" Cera asked.

"Lord Varthan beats on him until he passes out, then one of the shades heals him. Over and over." She growled. "Neomi told me."

"I can get us to Lady Lenore's rooms quickly. You should come, too." His eyes clouded with concern.

"No, I have to get to the great hall, but I can cover you with a masking spell."

"No." Gamel made a cutting gesture with his hand. "No magic. I've been moving around in the shadows and secret passageways the whole time he's been here. Never detected once, but the youngest shade—his magic is stronger than I've ever known. He'll sense me if I'm spell-covered. Even Lady Em agrees."

Did that mean they hadn't made it into the kitchens undetected? "When's the last time you talked to my aunt?" she asked.

"She woke me several hours ago. She knows you're here."

"Good. Take Neomi and go. Tell her the sword is safe," Cera ordered.

"Where are your companions? Where is your bondmate?" he asked, looking around as if it'd just occurred to him.

"I am alone."

His gaze showed concern, but he said nothing. He kissed Neomi's hand, arm still around her shoulders. "We'll go."

The maid gave a muted protest, but allowed the boy to drag her out of the smoke room.

Cera sighed and leaned against the wall. Had she made the right choice? She shook her head, straightening and reaching deep inside for her anger.

She drew the sword Gamel had given her, testing it, tossing it from hand to hand before making a few slashes in the air.

Perfect weight and size for her.

She silently thanked the boy and her aunt. She took a deep breath and re-sheathed her new weapon.

It's time.

Jorrin awoke to someone tugging at him. Or perhaps it was *something*. Yawning, he opened his eyes, stretching his back and his arms.

The sun crested the horizon, but the sky wasn't very bright just yet.

When teeth brushed his ankle, he bolted upright, wide awake. Cera's damn wolf had bitten him.

"Blessed Spirit, Trikser!" Scrambling backward in the furs, he tore at the pant leg of his breeches so he could see his ankle. He exhaled when he saw only an angry welt. He'd expected blood. Jorrin rubbed the spot; no doubt it'd leave a large bruise. He glared at the wolf. What the hell was wrong with him?

Trikser knew he was awake now. The wolf barreled into him, knocking him over.

Fighting for breath, he sat up, shaking from the wolf's muscular body slamming against his chest. "What the . . . ?" he muttered, standing on wobbly legs and brushing himself off.

Trikser bounded away from him, whining and whimpering.

Cera was nowhere in sight.

She was probably just inside, but Jorrin needed to find her and see what was wrong with her bondmate. Stomping into his boots, he rolled up Cera's furs. He smiled when her sweet scent clinging to the soft covers tickled his nose. Too bad she'd not woken him when she'd risen. He could've taken her again.

Flashes of her beneath him, her taste, her touch, and them moving together danced into his mind and Jorrin shook himself. She'd been passionate, sweet, brave, and innocent, all rolled into one. He'd never had such an experience. Such a responsive lover. Couldn't wait to have her again. His manhood stirred and he tugged on his breeches.

Not now.

He needed to prepare mentally for the day's battle.

Trikser darted back and forth, his movements more frantic with each pass in front of the ruins of the old castle. Then the wolf skidded to a halt, kicking up dirt. Sitting back on his haunches, Cera's bondmate threw his head back and began to howl.

Jorrin gaped. He'd never heard Trikser howl before, but the wolfsong bled desperation.

Hadrian ran from within the ruins, Braedon on his heels. The elf wizard's face was as white as a sheet.

Jorrin's heart stopped. Even before the wizard laid his hands on the wolf's white mane, he *knew*.

Avery exited the decrepit castle as well, dashing to where their mounts were tied together.

"No. She didn't . . ." he whispered. His father made it to his side just as his knees buckled and he tumbled to the ground.

Her cousin's face was devoid of color. Avery panted to stave off panic, but Jorrin ignored the emotions as they rolled over his magic. "Ash is gone." The lord bent at the waist, hands on his knees and sucking in air.

"No," Jorrin repeated. His lungs deflated. Every breath stabbed.

"Why would she leave Trikser?" Avery demanded. His hands clenched into tight fists, his knuckles white.

Hadrian was still speaking to the wolf, trying to calm Cera's bondmate. No one else was better equipped to communicate with the beast, but it didn't make Jorrin feel any better.

Why would she be so reckless?

"To your feet, son," Braedon ordered, tugging on his elbow. His father had recovered from his own shock; his features were set, expression determined.

Dragon's Tail
Mountains of Aramour
Elfin River
Terraquist
oirc
sle
Greenwald
Netian Valley
North Ascova
Tarvis
Hadrian's Place
Berat
South Ascova
Dalunas
Southern Strait
Penal Territory

"Trikser said she knocked him out with a spell. She's got an hour or two lead on us," Hadrian said, rejoining the group.

Avery covered his face with his hand, but Cera using the magic he'd taught her wasn't his fault.

"Then we must hurry," Braedon's tone was firm.

Avery and Hadrian rushed to their horses.

Jorrin's face was hot. His fists clenched and unclenched at his sides. He forced a breath, then another, his chest aching. How could she have just *left*? Especially after last night. She'd given herself to him. He'd made love to her. *Showed* her how much he loved her. Was it her sick way of saying goodbye? His eyes smarted and he swallowed the sudden lump in this throat.

All the way to Tarvis, Cera had been determined, but had finally seemed to accept that it wasn't weak to work as a team, to let them help her.

Had it been lies?

No. What happened?

"Father?"

Braedon startled. When the man glanced at him, his amber eyes were wide. It was the first time Jorrin called him that since they'd been reunited. "Aye, son?" His father clasped his forearm.

"She'd better hope Varthan doesn't kill her. When we catch up, I just might," Jorrin choked out.

Chapter Seventeen

L UCAN BLINKED. HE sensed something, but then it was gone. He looked around the great hall, but nothing was out of the ordinary. Lord Varthan was still dozing in Lord Everett's intricately-carved chair at the head table on the raised dais.

Dagonet was watching, as he always did.

Athas and Markus were gone.

Markus had dragged that poor maid off somewhere because their master had barked to shut her up. Ironically, it'd saved her life for now.

No telling where Athas was, but he'd take a turn with the girl as well. Before the two had left, they'd argued over who deserved her virginity. Markus had already stolen that from Greta and Athas from the other girl.

Lucan trembled.

Why their master hadn't retired to the bedchamber he'd been occupying since they'd gotten there was a mystery. He hadn't seen Neysa lately, either. She'd been the lord's bedmate willingly, so at least Lord Varthan hadn't beaten her, but Lucan still felt horrible for the girl. His master was rough in *everything* he did.

All four of the girls were unmarried and the one, he thought her name was Jarina, couldn't be much older than him. Tears pricked his eyes, but he blinked them away.

He wanted out, away from Lord Varthan and all the killing, beating and raping, but how could he get away from the master without being killed?

Lucan cocked his head to the side and listened harder. He'd felt a hint of magic, but then it was gone. *Nothing.* Just like the day the unidentified group had entered the Province through the Southgate. They were there and then they weren't. He winced.

Lord Varthan had been so angry Lucan hadn't been able to see through whatever spell had been cast.

All four shades had joined together to try to find the invaders, to no avail.

How could a spell be undetectable to him? It'd never happened before. He'd *always* been able to sense magic, and to interpret it.

It was his gift.

Unfortunately, his *gift* was also his curse, and *why* Lord Varthan rarely let him out of his sight.

Glancing at Dagonet, he tried to gauge whether the other shade had noticed anything. The older boy usually had keen senses, but at the moment didn't seem to be bothered by anything.

Lord Varthan hadn't stirred from his nap, so Lucan would hold his tongue. Perhaps he'd been wrong. However, he wouldn't tell his master until he knew something definite. The lord would beat him for uncertainties.

He felt Dagonet's hazel gaze on him. Flinching, he chided himself.

Dagonet isn't Athas.

His heart fluttered anyway.

"Lucan, come here." The shade whispered, but it was an order nonetheless.

Dagonet glanced at the boy as he jumped. Lucan had felt something, though he'd said nothing. Concentrating, he sucked in a breath. *Nothing*. What had Lucan sensed?

Once again, the lad's abilities astonished him. Made him more determined than ever to get Lucan out of this alive. And Lord Lenore. His promise to the duke would ring true. Hopefully King Nathal's reinforcements would arrive sooner than later.

Lord Varthan expected Lady Ryhan, but he wasn't so sure about that. He hadn't seen the lady in turns. Would she even remember him?

If so, his mission was in jeopardy.

Although he'd spent a great deal of time with her father in Greenwald; Lady Ryhan, a few turns older than his nineteen, had already joined the King's Riders and had been living in Terraquist.

No matter what, she needed to stay away. Probably had no idea the king was prepared to kill Varthan and save her family—avenge the ones they'd lost.

Under no circumstances could the bastard get his hands on the sword. With his abilities, Lucan had more than a fair chance of actually breaking the spell Lord Falor Ryhan, Dagonet's former mentor, had placed on the awesome weapon.

The king and the Lords of the Provinces had debated for months whether or not to send someone in disguise to gather proof against Varthan. Finally, after the former archduke's betrayal had been made public and he'd been punished, it was decided Dagonet would go.

He'd been with Varthan for two months when Lord Falor Ryhan had been murdered. The king had wanted him out immediately, as had his father. They'd been worried about discovery, but Dagonet had vehemently refused.

Lord Falor had been like a second father.

Dagonet always been of a gentle nature—his healing magic had shaped him—but something inside him snapped when he'd been told Varthan had killed his mentor's wife and youngest daughter. Raped them. Rage—uncharacteristic in its intensity—had washed over him, blinding reason.

He hadn't given his father or his king a chance to pull him from his mission. He'd demanded retribution for the loss of the Ryhans. And it'd come to a head; he was about to get it.

It was probably a blessing the travesty had occurred while he was away on a recruiting mission for Varthan. He wouldn't have been able to endure the slaughter of his mentor and his family. He would've revealed himself that night, made an attempt on Varthan's life.

Dagonet had managed to maintain detached control all this time, and he couldn't throw it all away now. He'd love to be the one to thrust the sword into the evil man's heart, but the king had claimed that honor.

Lord Lenore was sprawled on his side sleeping, thankfully appearing to be in a somewhat peaceful slumber. Each time Varthan injured him, Dagonet healed what bruises he could; each time the man awoke, the bastard beat him senseless again.

He'd been ordered to leave the duke bruised and broken, but he'd heal Lord Lenore little by little, wishing he could put the duke into a state of unconsciousness to protect him. There was a way to force a deep sleep, but it was prone to produce long-term harm. Still, he did everything possible. So far, his 'master' hadn't noticed Lord Lenore didn't look quite so black and blue.

His heart was sick over the death of the lord's personal guard. He'd done what he could to end pain and suffering quickly, but Dagonet couldn't save any of them from Markus and Athas.

He'd dealt no death blows, only eased pain at the end.

Varthan had been distracted with Lord Lenore, and he'd been lucky to have escaped detection by the other two shades. To be caught would mean death, after slow torture. He couldn't allow the former archduke to discover his true identity.

Dagonet had to protect all those he cared about and conceal the king's plan.

Lucan jumped again.

He glanced at the 'master,' who was sleeping soundly in Lord Lenore's chair. He gestured the lad to come to him, instead of repeating a verbal command. Would Lucan obey?

Varthan was a notorious light sleeper, and if he awoke, Lucan would be punished.

"What do you sense?" He kept his voice low.

The boy's face flushed. "I . . . I don't know," Lucan sputtered.

"Come now, Lucan. I won't tell Varthan, you have my word," Dagonet said, his tone gentle. *Damn*, he'd forgotten to call Varthan 'lord'.

Had the lad noticed? Would he comment?

Lucan looked him up and down, visibly hesitating.

Even if he did succeed in getting him away from Varthan, how would Lucan ever be able to trust again? The boy was still a child. Much too young to have endured what he'd already been through.

"It's like the day I sensed them coming to Tarvis. They were there, and then they were gone. I felt the same tingle."

"A masking spell." Dagonet sighed. His gut told him who'd cast the spell. He murmured a curse. He bit back a cringe as he caught wide leaf-green eyes staring.

The lad's expression confirmed he'd caught the sigh, as well as reference to Varthan without his former honorific.

Double damn.

Lucan was sharp.

"Dagonet?"

"Aye?" His heart hammered and it ordered it to calm.

"Never mind." He shook his head.

"What is it, Lucan?"

Will he finally open up?

Lucan shook his head again, this time vigorously. "I think we have company. Even though I can't say for sure, I think someone's here."

What can I say?

He didn't like that the youngest shade was probably correct. Shifting on his feet, Dagonet averted his eyes from Lucan's much, much too insightful gaze.

The lad was evaluating him, his unusual crystal green eyes showing great maturity for their turns.

"Tristan . . ." Lucan whispered.

He planted his feet to stave off the stagger, fighting for composure. Lucan *knew.* Blood drained from his face, on its way it his feet. Tristan hesitantly met Lucan's eyes. No denying it, not with the reaction he'd just given. How had the boy known his real name?

Tristan had never seen Lucan before being accepted as one of Varthan's best.

"Your name isn't Dagonet." Lucan spoke so low that he had to strain his ears to hear.

He didn't want to harm Lucan, but just how far did the tremulous trust between them extend? His instincts shouted Tristan still needed to protect the lad. How much he could reveal safely to Lucan?

What will it take to get him to turn on Varthan?

He'd keep protecting him from the evil man as much as he could without being detected. "No, it's not," Tristan admitted finally, forcing a breath.

"Who are you?"

"Tristan Dagget." He prayed to the Blessed Spirit he could trust this lad.

"As in Lord Dagget of Berat?"

"He's my father. I'm the third son." Tristan latched onto Lucan's arm as the boy's knees buckled.

The youngest shade looked up at him. He'd no idea he'd lost his balance.

"Are you all right?"

"Just shocked. You could've been killed, you know. *Will be* if they find out." Lucan's green eyes were wide again, his dark hair mussed.

"I'm well aware of that. He has to be stopped, and I'll get you away from this." He made a vow to the boy.

The look on his young face told him he'd recognized it.

Good.

"How can I help?"

Tristan fought a gape.

He can't be serious . . .

"I'm not a betrayer. I . . . only want out. I've never been his, not truly."

"I've never thought ill of you, Lucan. I sensed your fear of him the first day."

"Thank you," the boy whispered.

Tristan smiled; wanted to drag Lucan into his arms. Had he even ever been hugged? Touched with a gentle hand instead of a kick or a punch? With the affection of an older brother, or a father? Even his mother? He'd not known him very long, but he could easily see the lad as a younger brother.

Lucan's eyes shone with unshed tears. He sniffled and wiped at his nose.

He said nothing, even a child had his pride.

Given what the boy had been through, he could probably fill a lake with tears and rightly so, but Lucan was stronger than he knew.

Tristan squeezed his shoulder gently and Lucan's mouth curved with a shy edge.

Even one smile from the lad's a start.

Chapter Eighteen

MARKUS GROWLED, RUBBING his throbbing head.

The bitch was here.

She'd kept him from his conquest.

Stomping his feet to try to stand resulted in almost toppling over. He cursed long and hard. Had to grip the side of the nearest stall to keep from falling back onto the pile of hay. The spot was supposed to have been where he bedded the pretty little maid. The ache in his loins had gone unsatisfied.

He'd kill that bitch, no matter what his master said. Maybe he'd have some fun with her first, though.

"What the hell happened to you?" Athas bit at him, striding into the barn. The other shade looked around. "You let her go?" His voice was full of venom.

Markus met his dark eyes, sneering. "Nay, you fool. I was stunned . . . by a *spell*. Don't you even sense it?"

"What? By who? What happened?"

"Ryhan is here." He kept his tone flat.

Athas's eyes widened. "We must tell Lord Varthan."

"I was on my way to do so."

Will my legs work?

His fellow shade would take great satisfaction at an appearance of weakness. Markus would pound the sneer off of his face. *Later.* "She took the girl with her."

"Before or after?" Athas asked, one eyebrow shooting up.

He growled again. Contemplated lying, but even though Athas wasn't so powerful in magic, he'd always been able to sense lies, his one talent that kept him close to their master. "Before." He made a tight fist when his companion laughed.

"Good. My turn will be the first."

Shaking his head, Markus forced a deep breath. "Let's go. We can discuss it later. We must not keep Master waiting on this news, I've no idea how long I was out," he admitted, grimacing.

Athas shot him a look that told him he wouldn't discuss anything later, but he didn't let it bother him. He already risked a throttling from Lord Varthan by allowing himself to be knocked out. He hadn't even sensed Lady Ryhan's presence in the stable until the magic was being thrown at him.

The master would be less than pleased. Perhaps he and Athas would even be forbidden from wenching.

"I wonder why she didn't kill you," Athas mused.

He could have no idea exactly what position Markus had been in when he'd been attacked, and he wasn't about to enlighten Athas. "To protect the girl, you fool."

"I suppose so . . ." He looked far too pensive for Markus' liking.

He'd flatten him with both fists as soon as he got the chance.

When they made it to the great hall, he spotted Lucan and Dagonet deep in conversation, their heads bent together and tone very low. He sneered, but was curious. Markus didn't trust either of them, but then again, he didn't trust Athas either.

Dagonet was much too quiet for his liking, and Lucan was far too jumpy. He admired all the power contained in the boy's small frame, but wasn't fond of his place—Lucan's closeness, to the man Markus admired most. It cut more even more, since Lucan didn't want the favored position.

They looked up at the same time, Dagonet meeting his eyes. The healer nodded politely, and Markus made himself echo it. He'd no real reason to dislike the other shade, he merely *did*.

Markus joined them, suppressing the urge to smack Lucan when he blanched. Athas was on his heels, so perhaps the reaction was due to the eldest shade, who had never quite concealed his contempt for the youngster.

"Ryhan is here," he said.

Dagonet's hazel eyes widened, but his instinct told him it was faked.

He'd examine that later. He needed to explain everything to the other two shades before they woke their master.

"What happened?" Dagonet said, but his voice was just above a whisper.

"She stunned me in the stable. I have no idea how long I was out."

"You were gone over an hour," Dagonet said.

Markus nodded. *Not as bad as I feared.* He exchanged a look with Athas, who said nothing. The older shade could've supplied that information, instead of jesting with him. *Idiot wretch.*

"I wonder why she left you alive," Dagonet mused.

Athas laughed. "I said the same thing."

"To protect the girl, I would assume. She took her away." Markus gritted his teeth, fists clenched.

"I see . . ." The healer cocked his head to one side.

Lucan had said nothing, so Markus glared at him. He took a small step closer to Dagonet.

Markus sneered. "What do you have to say?"

"N-n-nothing . . ." the boy stammered. "I sensed nothing."

Markus looked at Athas to see if he thought he'd lied.

"He speaks the truth," Athas said.

"I also felt nothing," Dagonet remarked.

"He won't like it," Markus whispered, gesturing to their master.

"You tell him," Athas ordered.

Markus grimaced and clenched his fists harder, until his knuckles whitened. He was going to pound Athas into the floor sooner than later. He sighed, acquiescing, but he'd never admit that to Athas.

Lord Varthan hadn't struck him in a long while. Would that continue, considering the news he had to present? Taking a step forward, he threw a glare over his shoulder as Athas snickered.

Dagonet gave him a small smile and though there was no menace in it, Markus glared at him, too.

"Lord Varthan."

The older man's eyes snapped open, Markus took a step backward.

"What is it?" the master demanded.

"Ryhan is here," he said, gulping. Had he just stuttered?

His master's brows tightened and he sat up taller in the chair. "Tell me what happened," Lord Varthan commanded.

"She caught me unaware in the stable." Heat crept up his neck. Had his master noticed?

"Unaware?"

"Yes, she stunned me with a spell and took the maid," Markus confessed, looking down.

"Why did she not kill you?"

He didn't get a chance to answer, but the master shot a glare at Athas's sudden outburst of laughter. The other shade cut it off immediately.

"Find her. Lucan stays with me. The rest of you go, now. Do not harm her and keep your hands to yourself." The lord gave him and Athas both meaningful looks. "We must *welcome* her to her family's home."

Cera heard voices and flattened herself against the wall. *Markus.* She remembered his harsh tones from the stable.

Her plan was still to turn herself in to be taken to Varthan, but she didn't have to go quietly. They didn't need to know it was on purpose. Inflicting a little damage to the bastards would be fun.

Bickering.

Markus was arguing with someone.

She rolled her eyes.

Taking a deep breath, she stepped out into the corridor in front of two shades. Cera raised her arm, guessing Markus would assume she'd try to stun him.

He was ready and screamed a spell that made a visible shield surrounding him and the other shade.

Might be handy to learn that one.

She took off running.

"Dammit," Markus shouted.

The pounding of boots echoed as the two shades gave chase. It didn't take them long to catch up to her and back her into a corner.

Cera brandished Gamel's sword.

Markus laughed and drew his own. "She's mine," he told the other shade, who gave a curt nod. She smirked.

He's mine. He just didn't know it yet.

"Don't hurt her. The master said unharmed." The dark haired shade leaned against the wall as if he was bored.

Was this Athas? Or the healing shade?

His statement gave her a moment's pause. Why would Varthan want her brought to him unharmed?

Cera gripped the sword tighter and shifted her stance. She smiled at Markus and put her palm out, beckoning. "Come at me, you bastard. Let me show you what it's like when a girl can defend herself."

He let out another hearty laugh, then lunged, and she gracefully deflected his charge. Markus turned his body, guarding himself well.

She didn't miss his eyes widening, though. Like most men facing a *lady*, he'd underestimated her.

It was to her advantage. She was good with a sword; she'd just have to prove it.

Stalking him, Cera came at him a few times. When she barely missed cutting him the second time, she cursed, but Markus was already reevaluating his strategy.

"She plays with you, Markus," the other shade said nonchalantly.

"Not for long." He didn't even spare his friend a glance. He growled and charged again.

She grinned; she had him.

Cera should just run him through, but she needed them to take her to Varthan. It was the only way her plan would work.

She laughed as her sword slashed through his shirt and upper arm, leaving a deep gash. She'd gotten a good piece of him.

Markus dropped his weapon and cursed, grabbing his arm. Blood seeped through his fingers and a starburst stain spread over his white tunic sleeve around his grip.

Staring, she waited to see what he would do. She didn't relax her posture.

He screamed a spellword, and Cera flew backward, the air forced out of her as she slid down the wall and landed in a heap on her rear end. Her chest ached as she struggled for breath. She cursed him to hell and back.

Markus prowled toward her, one fist raised. He was filled with rage, his expression menacing, but the other shade grabbed his forearm as he passed.

Scrambling to her feet, Cera lifted her sword, ready to defend herself again.

"No, Markus. Lord Varthan said unharmed."

"The bitch cut me!"

"Dagonet can heal you." He lifted his arm and muttered a spellword she didn't catch.

She cursed aloud as her sword went flying out of her hand, wincing as it clattered to the floor at the dark-haired man's feet.

He must be Athas, if he isn't the healer.

He bent to retrieve her sword, and Cera gasped.

Athas looked so much like the evil man he could be a younger version of Varthan. He shot her a look, but said nothing.

He has to be Varthan's son.

Did he know? If so, why had he said *'Lord Varthan'*, not *'Father'*?

Varthan had several children; sons and daughters from all three of his dead wives. Acquainted with none of them personally, she'd never heard he that had a child employed as a shade.

"You grab her, then. I'm too angry." Markus paced in front of her.

Cera did a double take.

His skin was luminescent, his hair looking windblown and an even lighter shade of his already pale blond. He was lit up from magic.

She ordered herself not to be fascinated. He was a bastard, her *enemy*. "Oh, does your arm hurt? It's a pity I didn't cut you lower. I would love to chop off something *smaller*," she drawled, smiling sweetly.

His face reddened, and he glowed even more brightly. Markus marched over to her, but the other shade stepped in front of her, holding his hand up.

"I'd let you slap her, but Master said *unharmed*. You can have a turn later. If he sees a mark on her, you know you'll regret it."

Markus growled and brandished a fist.

Cera grinned. He looked like a child about ready to stomp his foot. She didn't regret maiming him one bit. She could use his anger as a weapon against him, especially since it appeared to be linked to his magic.

He took a deep breath. Snatching his sword, he shoved it into its sheath, his free fist clenched at his side. The glow of his skin started to dim. "Take her other weapons, at least," Markus ordered.

She uttered a protest when Varthan's son searched her and stripped her of her dirk and bow; more of a groping than a patting down; the gleam in Athas's dark eyes told her he'd intended it, the *bastard*.

Unfazed by her low growl, he flashed a smile. It made him appear handsome and harmless— far from the truth.

Narrowing her eyes, Cera said nothing. Since he'd been the voice of reason thus far, there was no need to make him angry, or she *wouldn't* make it to Varthan unharmed.

Markus grabbed her right biceps, yanking her away from the wall, and she felt the tip of a sword in her back as the other shade fell in behind them.

If she had to wager a guess, she'd bet was being prodded with her own weapon.

"Get going," Markus barked.

Cera started down the corridor without further protest, biting back a smile. So far, things were going as planned. Could she hold onto the upper hand?

Chapter Nineteen

THE ELABORATE DOUBLE doors to the great hall of Castle Lenore opened.

A slow smile spread across his lips as Markus and Athas led the little Ryhan bitch into the vast room. He shot a look to where Lenore lay, but the man was still unconscious.

Varthan had time to play with her.

"We have her, my lord." Athas tossed a sword, dagger, a quiver full of arrows and a bow to the floor in a pile.

He'd been with him longer than any other shade. Too bad the boy couldn't understand or appreciate what that said about him; but then again, Athas had no idea he was Varthan's bastard son. It was a wonder, because he looked just like him. They had the same black hair and dark eyes, facial structure; they were the same height and build.

Shame Varthan couldn't claim him. He preferred Athas to any of his legitimate sons. The lot of them were pawns of the king, just as their mothers had been. He hadn't had much luck with wives either. Hadn't taken a fourth after killing each of the previous three.

He hadn't been named murderer by his wives' families or anyone in the King's Court, but he did hate to have to play the grieved widower. Quite a point in favor of sticking to whores.

Nodding at his son, Varthan glanced at the sword. Disappointment flooded him. It wasn't the magic sword. Glaring at the little bitch, he rose from Lenore's ornate chair. He looked the girl up and down.

Very attractive.

Her dark red hair was long and curly, and she was peering at him with lovely rage-filled gray eyes. She had high cheekbones and even though her mouth was currently an angry tight line, her lips were plump. Lady Ryhan had a nice curve to her hips, and long, long legs. Her leather jerkin didn't adequately hide her full breasts, either.

Perhaps I'll see if she's as sweet as her sister.

Tall, too. Both Athas and Markus were several inches over six feet, yet her head was above their shoulders.

She was struggling to keep her emotions in check, her body shaking, seething; her expression full of disgust at his perusal.

Oh, how I'll enjoy our time together.

Dagonet entered the great hall, distracting him.

Varthan glanced at him, and the boy nodded, striding to stand next to Lucan. He scowled. However, he couldn't allow anything to bother him; nothing mattered right now but his sword.

Cera gritted her teeth to keep from showing a reaction to the painful grips on her upper arms. She could feel Markus's rage to her right, his hold on her was much tighter than that of the other shade. This was what she'd wanted; the way it had to be.

I will endure.

Markus grinned and stepped in front of her. He nodded to Athas, who released her arm and took a step back.

Grimacing, she braced herself for anything.

The blond shade grabbed her face and slammed his lips into hers.

She made her mouth a firm hard line as he tightened his fingers on her face and tried to force his tongue inside.

Cera wished she could vomit on command.

When he squeezed her right breast and agony bit, she struggled.

Stomped on his foot.

Markus yelped and raised a hand to strike her.

"Enough," Varthan roared. "Seize her."

Though his eyes promised violence, Markus said nothing. His skin was glowing ever so slightly.

Both shades resumed their previous positions, holding her upright between them.

Cera didn't fight either.

"I will get you, bitch," Markus whispered in her ear.

Varthan didn't notice, or chose to ignore the shade.

She didn't react, but fantasized about how good it would feel to run him through. The slash on his arm wasn't enough.

Should've gutted him.

Varthan stood on the dais in front of the head table, wearing a sneer that cocked his mustache to an unnatural angle. "Where is the sword?"

"I lost it." Cera prayed her voice was steady.

Before she could even blink, the former archduke strode down and backhanded her.

She reeled, and both shades had to take a step back to keep them all on their feet.

"Impertinent bitch," he said in a low deadly tone, shoving his face in hers. "Athas?"

"She lies, milord."

"I could have surmised as much. Any other clues?" Sarcasm dripped from Varthan's voice.

The shade on her left flinched and shook his head, and his grip on her arm tightened.

She bit the inside of her mouth to stave off a wince. Her cheek smarted, her head pounded from the slap, but she banished tears.

"Lucan." Varthan gestured without looking, his gaze locked with hers.

"Then why bother asking him?" Cera drawled.

He slapped her again, harder than the first time.

Her head lolled back and she fought the blackness creeping in from the corners of her vision. She blinked, forcing her eyes to remain open. Both cheeks burned now.

She steeled herself and built the strongest walls in her mind she could. The next assault would be magical. Looking the boy over as he took a timid step forward, Cera could sense his hesitance, and offered a smile.

A smile? When he was about to attack her?

When his eyes widened and he averted them, she wanted to make him feel better. Wanted him to know she didn't blame him. Although she could tell he was powerful, she wasn't afraid of him.

Odd.

This shade was the greatest threat, even according to Aunt Em.

Have I finally lost it?

She should be shaking before him.

Varthan grabbed the boy's arm and yanked him forward. "Probe her mind. Tell me where the sword is."

"My sword is right there, where it was tossed when I was disarmed." Cera cringed at the look the former archduke shot her. She braced herself for another slap, but he didn't hit her.

"Yes, master," the boy answered, as if she'd not spoken.

Tristan bit down until his jaw ached as Varthan continued to pummel Lady Ryhan. He wanted to thought-send to her, but Markus would pick it up, especially standing so close.

Dragon's Tail
Mountains of Aramour
Elfin River
Terraquist
Greenwald
Netian Valley
North Ascova
Hadrian's Place
Berat
Tarvis
South Ascova
Dalunas
Southern Strait
Penal Territory

He wanted to pound the shade into the ground for the kiss and rough handling. Vowed, when all was revealed, he'd kill the wretch so Lady Ryhan wouldn't have to. Tristan had seen the rage in her eyes; had she had a weapon, Markus wouldn't be breathing right now.

Looking at Lucan, he prayed the boy would lie and get away with it if the youngest shade discovered where the sword was.

Athas could detect lies with his gift, but if Lucan could convince himself he was telling the truth, it'd be harder to detect. And Varthan would never suspect Lucan of lying to him.

She turned herself in.

There was no other explanation for Markus and Athas dragging Lady Ceralda Ryhan right to Varthan. What the hell was she playing at? Instinct told him everything she'd done was with a purpose, but what?

Where the hell is her wolf? Bondmates were *always* together.

Tristan hoped for the Blessed Spirit's sake he could maintain his cover and keep her alive. There was no way he could fail to act if Varthan actually tried to kill her. Or . . . rape her.

He'd flattened himself against the corridor wall and witnessed the tail end of her sword fight with Markus. Saw the girl slash Markus's arm, when she could've easily killed him.

Lady Ryhan fought like a man. Her weapon had not been the broadsword used by many a knight, but it'd been the perfect size for her, and she'd used it well, with practiced ability.

"I sense nothing, master," Lucan whispered.

He winced as Varthan backhanded the lad. Lucan sprawled to the ground before Tristan could even soften his fall.

"Nothing?" the bastard roared. "Get. Up. Now."

Lucan whimpered, earning a glare.

"Must you beat on a child?" Lady Ryhan asked, her tone equaling Varthan's.

She needed to stop goading him before he really hurt her. Tristan would be ordered to heal any damage inflicted, but if she kept her mouth shut, her silence would go a long way.

He had to admire the way she stood tall as Varthan towered over her and smacked her face for the third time, but her lack of reaction infuriated the man all the more.

"Tell me where the sword is. You only have yourself to blame for my rage against the boy."

Lady Ryhan laughed.

Tristan closed his eyes, sucking back a gasp as the evil man's hand slammed into her face for the fourth time.

She slumped, unconscious, in Markus and Athas' hold.

"Dagonet, make her wake up. Now," Varthan barked, without even looking in his direction.

Tristan hurried over, looking at the two shades. "You have to let her go." He could thought-send to her during healing, and it'd remain undetected by all but Lucan, disguised by his healing magic. Blocking his words was no problem either, but the lad wouldn't give him away to Varthan, even if he didn't hide his words.

He pulled Lady Ryhan into his arms gently, and laid her across his lap as he squatted down. Even unconscious, her beauty was stunning, and soon he'd rid of her of the bruises the *'master'* had inflicted.

Brushing a dark red curl from her forehead, he winced at Varthan's damage. Both high cheekbones were stained and swollen. Tristan cupped her face, concentrating on healing and willing her to awaken. His forehead beaded with sweat and his limbs tingled, but he didn't have to use as much effort as if she'd been cut. Closing wounds was more complicated; bruises never sapped as much of his strength.

His skin began to glow, and his hands warmed as his powers began to work.

As soon as she blinked gray eyes up at him, Tristan smiled.

He had to move quickly. *Stop intentionally angering him, he'll be more brutal because of it. I promise I will get you out of this.*

Her eyes widened, but she said nothing.

Good. He couldn't chance telling her more. He reluctantly relinquished her to Markus and Athas.

Lady Ryhan's gaze burned him.

Tristan wished he could explain everything. He'd have to hope she'd be sharp enough to catch on when it was time to make a move. Taking a moment, he healed the cut on Markus's arm.

The shade gave him a nod when it was done.

Then he forced a deep breath as dizziness threatened to overcome him. Rushing his magic always made his head reel. Tristan took a few more breaths, stepping away slowly.

"Ah, the shade who will help prolong my misery," Lady Ryhan drawled.

He was still struggling on his feet, and looked away from her jibe. The constant state of exhaustion lately was taking its toll on his body and his magic. Widening his stance, he crossed his arms over his chest, sweat dripping from the bridge of his nose. Tristan prayed he'd regain his strength in a moment as his pulse thundered in his temples. He should've taken his time with Markus's arm.

Or not healed the bastard at all.

Varthan let out a malicious laugh. "That's the beauty of it, *Lady Ryhan,*" he said, making her name and honorific a slur. "I can bring you to the brink of death, yet pull you back at a whim . . . *my* whim."

"Oh . . . you frighten me so." She arched one delicate eyebrow.

Tristan winced as the man's hand connected with her face yet again. Why hadn't she heeded him? Perhaps she *did* have a death wish.

Her lip split open and the lady winced. Blood trailed down her chin.

"You will be more than frightened," Varthan said, nose to nose with her, voice deadly. Promising horrid things.

Lady Ryhan shuddered. She grimaced at the smile that spread across the former archduke's thin lips.

The bastard was already getting off on her reaction. He liked it best when women fought him so he could bend them to his will.

Swallowing a growl, Tristan planted his feet and chided himself to calm down. He couldn't be discovered.

Varthan caressed her face, and she jerked away, but he gripped her chin and dragged her face back to his. "You are quite beautiful."

"Don't touch me," she ordered, shaky for the first time as her shoulders trembled. She locked her legs together.

Tristan's stomach churned. He wanted to kill Varthan on the spot.

Lady Ryhan spit in Varthan's face.

The *'master'* gave a scream of rage. Varthan punched her, closed-fist to her face.

His mentor's daughter and the two shades were thrown backward from the force of the bastard's violence. In a pile of limbs on the floor, *she* was the only one who didn't move.

Neither shade said anything; they just returned to their feet and began to brush themselves off.

Tristan rushed to her without an order from Varthan. Her neck was at a strange angle. He needed to heal her, *now*.

He couldn't heal the dead.

Not bothering to pull her into his arms, he knelt by her side.

Her face was covered in blood, nose broken.

Tristan looked up at Varthan, who gave a curt nod as he wiped her bloody spittle away with a silk handkerchief.

Good. Hope she got her blood in his eyes.

Laying both hands on her neck, his breath exited in a rush.

Not broken.

She'd be all right, but mending a broken nose wasn't much different than a broken bone. It'd take a great deal of energy.

Closing his eyes to concentrate, he paused, still a bit woozy. Sweat bathed Tristan's face and neck; his chest burned as he struggled to hold himself together enough to heal her. A jumble of emotions washed over him. It'd do no good for him to pass out as well.

Tristan sucked in more air, calling to his magic. The familiar warmth greeted his extremities as his healing-touch took over. Even without opening his eyes, he knew his skin was glowing brightly, increasing with his exertion.

Minutes felt like hours, but the cartilage of her nose moved back into place. At least Lady Ryhan wouldn't look like it'd been broken. Her beauty wouldn't be permanently marred. Little or no scarring was a benefit of the healing-touch.

He helped her sit up as she opened her eyes, and he wiped as much of the blood from her face as he could.

I'm sorry, Lady Ryhan thought-sent, meeting his eyes.

Her strong voice in Tristan's head took him off guard, but he didn't react as he pulled her to her feet.

Athas grabbed her by the arms and threw her into a chair Markus had removed from the dais. The other two shades had obviously not enjoyed being a buffer to their master's blows.

Tristan shot a look at Varthan, who said nothing about their decision.

"Tie her down," he barked.

"I'll do it," Tristan offered. He tied the best knots.

No one offered a comment, let alone an argument.

He could make it so her bindings could be easily exited and without being questioned, or the adjustment being noticed. Shooting Lucan a look, Tristan silently promised he'd heal the giant bruise that was already forming on the boy's face as soon as Varthan's back was turned.

The lad studied his small boots as he stood silently at the master's side, forlornly waiting for the next order.

I've made it so you can pull out of the rope when the time is right. Don't struggle against the bindings and it'll go unnoticed, Tristan told Lady Ryhan as he wrapped thick ropes around her slender wrists at the back of the ornate chair.

He'd taken a chance with the thought-send, but he needed her to sit still. One glance at Markus told him he'd gotten away with it for now.

Who are you?

Hiding his surprise at her response, Tristan met her eyes and gave a slight shake of his head. He couldn't risk answering her any other way.

Markus could be sharper than expected at times.

Even without another word, Lady Ryhan's expression told him she understood.

"Get away from her. She is secured," Varthan commanded.

Tristan didn't even look at the man as he obeyed.

Resting a hand on Lucan as Varthan took a step toward the girl, he took the opportunity to heal the boy.

When it was done Lucan looked up at him, thanks written on his young face. One corner of his mouth lifted.

They exchanged a nod.

Tristan's respect for Lucan went up a notch and he squeezed the lad's shoulder.

The other two shades flanked Lady Ryhan at Varthan's command, and he continued his inquisition.

Cera looked up at Varthan and gave a sneer of her own, saying nothing. She needed to keep her temper in check and guard her words. Should be grateful for the healer, but then again, it just meant she'd be in one conscious piece when the bastard killed her. A low laugh escaped her lips at the irony, and she looked away from her tormenter.

The healer was so familiar. When she'd looked into his eyes, a memory niggled and scooted away. Where'd she seen him before?

Even before he'd taken a chance with his thought-sends, she knew—simply *knew*—he wasn't evil.

Much more hid behind the words than what the healer had told her, but she couldn't guess the rest, it'd been carefully protected.

She'd watch him and decide what to do when she made her move.

"Where is the sword?" Varthan's tone brooked no argument.

Cera met his dark eyes. "Haven't we gone over this?" She tried to sound bored.

Varthan bristled and took a step toward her. "Where is the sword?"

Smiling, she shook her head. She didn't move as he slapped her.

"You *will* tell me what I want to know."

"Will I?" she asked in her sweetest tone.

He growled and slapped her again.

Her head reeled, and she could taste the metallic tinge of her own blood. Her lip must have split open again, but numbness spread slowly over her body. She didn't tremble or shake. Cera couldn't feel any pain.

Handy.

"Dagonet, wake Lenore," Varthan ordered.

It took every ounce of her willpower not to react to the fear that bubbled up. She'd seen her uncle in the corner when she'd been dragged into the great hall. Unconsciousness was better. He'd not had to endure watching Varthan's treatment of her. She'd have to dig deep to maintain composure. Uncle Everett wouldn't watch Varthan hit her in silence.

Cera couldn't watch the bastard hurt her uncle.

And he *would.*

Varthan would torture Uncle Everett until she disclosed the location of the sword.

Closing her eyes, she prayed to the Blessed Spirit for help and strength as the healer knelt beside her uncle. Jorrin's smiling face popped into her head. Along with her love, she saw his father, her cousin and the elf. If she concentrated, she could hear Trikser's whine.

Banishing thoughts of them, she clenched her jaw until it hurt.

If the Blessed Spirit was trying to tell her something, this time the heavenly being had missed Her mark. Cera had left them behind to protect them. She loved them all.

Varthan ranted and raved as he paced in front of her. Shuffling his feet, the evil man paid no attention to the healer following his orders. Spittle dribbled from the former archduke's mouth; he clenched his fists.

She looked away, her eyes glued to the healer and Uncle Everett.

The dark-haired shade helped her uncle to his feet, the move looked gentle. He leaned in for longer than necessary, but the movement was subtle.

Had he whispered something her uncle?

They both straightened.

Cera stared, trying to decipher the scene. What was the healer's game?

"Bring him over here. Now!"

"Coming, milord," the healer answered. Snatching Uncle Everett's arm, the healing shade dragged him closer.

Cera made eye contact with her handsome uncle and couldn't hold in her gasp.

He was a ragged mess. His hands were bound in front of him, his face covered in bruises. Dried blood was all over it, too, and his bottom lip was cut. The duke's overtunic and shirt were torn and bloody, as were his breeches, but he had no serious injuries, because of the healer's ministrations.

She swallowed back tears.

My fault!

Uncle Everett's tall frame was slumped, his shoulders caved in. Normally thick wavy golden brown hair, almost the exact shade of his eyes, now hung limp and tangled around his shoulders. He moved as if his whole body hurt, most likely, he was hiding how much pain he was actually in, but his curt nod shouted he didn't want her to worry about him.

It made sense the healing shade couldn't fix him entirely, it would anger Varthan and be obvious he was up to something, but it made Cera's heart ache.

Her uncle was a kind, decent, gentle man. Always wore an easy smile that lit up his handsome face. What if that was changed forever?

Cera bit her lip. She **couldn't** cry right now.

Varthan drew his sword and held it to her uncle's chest. He poked him a few times.

Her uncle didn't even flinch. For that, she was proud. "Get on with your games," Uncle Everett said calmly, his eyes locked onto hers.

"I was just discussing our situation with your lovely niece."

His smile made her shudder.

"You better not have touched her, you swine," Uncle Everett barked.

"He has done naught, Uncle," she answered, praying her voice didn't shake. She winced when Varthan slapped him.

"Markus, show him," Varthan growled.

The blond shade gave a curt nod and stepped away from her. Lifting his arm, Markus pointed and Cera's uncle's bindings fell away.

Uncle Everett's body lifted into the air and was held suspended, his arms and legs involuntarily spread apart.

"You will die for this, Varthan," her uncle shouted as Markus continued to hold him floating about ten feet off the floor.

Varthan laughed. "Where is the sword?"

"Tell him nothing, niece," her uncle ordered. "No matter what he does to me, tell him nothing."

She looked at the duke, and then back at Varthan. "Go to hell."

"Your uncle first," the man snarled.

A slow, evil smile spread across Markus's face.

Uncle Everett screamed and his body contorted in the air.

She fought tears. Cera had no intention of revealing where she'd hidden her sword, but how long she could watch Varthan and his shades torture her uncle?

Dagonet's words echoed in her mind; she didn't strain against her bindings, but it proved difficult to sit still.

"No matter what you do to me, she *will not* tell you what you want to know," her uncle breathed.

She gasped.

Uncle Everett was so strong.

The shade twisted his hand and her uncle screamed again. Markus' skin glowed even more brightly. The bastard enjoyed torture.

Swallowing a sob, Cera bit her tongue to keep from shouting for him to stop.

Markus's magic wouldn't hold up for long, would it? His brow was already beaded with sweat. Surely, he'd tire, wouldn't he?

Chapter Twenty

"WHERE IS SHE?" Jorrin demanded of no one in particular, as they neared the castle.

"I think she used my masking spell." Braedon pulled Roan to a halt next to Grayna.

Hadrian halted Winthrop next to them on his other side, looking at Jorrin then his father. "Then at least she'll be safe for a while."

Braedon nodded. "They cannot see through the spell."

"For how long?" Jorrin asked.

"We need to get out of sight." Avery's tone was desperate.

"Indeed," Braedon said.

"I suggest we follow Trikser." Hadrian gestured.

The wolf was sniffing low to the ground, onto an obvious trail. Very shortly, Trik led them to the smallest building of the stables.

Cera wasn't in the stable, but Ash was.

Trikser frantically searched, becoming more agitated as he sniffed each stall.

Jorrin cursed colorfully in Aramourian.

"Magic was used here," Hadrian said, looking at Braedon.

His father nodded agreement.

Avery and Jorrin exchanged a look.

"Let's hope it was Cera, and not someone else," Avery whispered.

"I agree." Jorrin's voice shook. He forced a breath, but couldn't get the image of Cera, as a lifeless body before Varthan out of his mind.

Braedon grimaced when he met his father's eyes.

He hadn't shielded his thought. "Sorry."

"It *will* be all right, son. Get a hold of yourself. We need you as much as Cera does."

Jorrin nodded. What else could he do?

"I can get us into the castle. My Lenore ancestors must've been a very suspicious people, because my home is riddled with secret passageways," Avery said.

"And you know them all?" Braedon asked.

"Most, if not all. Cera, Kait and I spent hours at a time exploring them when we were children. Cera even made a map at one time, though I have no need of it now."

"Let's go, then," Hadrian said.

"What about Trikser?" Jorrin asked.

All four men looked at the white wolf, who was still desperately sniffing around inside the small barn.

"As soon as he finds what he's scenting we should follow to see where he leads," the elf wizard said.

"Aye, I agree," Braedon said. "He can tell us exactly where she went."

"And then we can get inside, hidden," Avery said.

When Trikser led them to the servants' entrance of the kitchens, Hadrian took control of the white wolf. Trikser whimpered, but the wizard was able to make him understand they needed to remain hidden.

"This will take us directly behind the great hall," Avery whispered as they entered a secret door off the main hearth in the kitchens.

Slipping in was much easier than he'd anticipated, but Jorrin's worry over Cera ate at his stomach, stealing his thoughts. His heart was at a constant pound. He sucked in a breath, clutching the hilt of his sword until his knuckles whitened. He was still furious, and as the minutes ticked by, he grew more worried they would be too late.

Why would she take this on herself?

He'd promised her he'd protect her. Jorrin had never imagined that she'd take the ability to do so out of his hands.

What if she dies?

The thought hurt too much to fathom. Memories of her kiss, how she felt in his arms, wouldn't be enough to sustain him the rest of his life.

"This way." Avery gestured to the right when the corridor split into two separate tunnels.

The passageway was wide, but too dark to navigate. Hadrian lifted his wand, muttering a spellword Jorrin didn't catch. The wand came to life, the green glow illuminating the path before them.

"Stop." Avery's whisper was urgent.

"Look," Hadrian said, his tone also low.

They'd arrived in a small room. Light poured in through a large window that looked directly into the great hall.

Jorrin ducked with a curse.

"They can't see us," Avery said. He quickly explained it was as if they were looking through a window into the hall, but the view from the other side was a large mirror.

They'd be protected, unseen. The lord said he didn't know how or why it'd been installed there, but his mother's magic maintained the effect.

After watching for only a few moments, Jorrin's blood boiled. He gritted his teeth Cera got knocked to the ground, unconscious.

Only his father's firm hold on his forearm kept him from leaping to his feet and leaving the cover of their hiding place.

"He . . . healed her . . . ?" He breathed, exchanging a look with Avery, then his father.

"A healing shade?" Cera's cousin echoed.

Braedon's expression was just as stunned.

They watched the shade heal her and help her to her feet.

A low growl took his attention. Trikser bristled at his side, baring teeth. Hadrian's grip around his neck was tight, holding him in place, the elf wizard tiny against the large wolf.

When do we act? Jorrin demanded in a frantic thought-send to all three of his companions. *Let Trikser rip out his throat.*

No one answered.

The young dark-haired boy looked up, staring in their direction.

Braedon squeezed Jorrin's arm in warning.

The shade had sensed the thought-send.

Jorrin muttered a curse. He held his breath as they waited for the boy to sound an alarm. It never came. He exchanged a puzzled glance with his father. "I know he heard me."

"I agree."

Trikser's growling increased as Cera was shoved into a chair and bound.

"Hold," Hadrian whispered to the wolf.

Cera's bondmate stilled, but his whole body shook. How much longer could the elf wizard maintain control over him? Face bathed with sweat, the skin of the old elf shone bright red against his white beard. Although animals were his gift, he did have to expend magic to maintain the connection.

Trikser was fighting hard, ruled by his need to rescue his mistress. It wouldn't be long now before Hadrian was exhausted.

"Another thought-send . . ." Braedon whispered, looking at Jorrin.

"You sensed it?"

"The lad tying her to the chair . . ."

"Perhaps we have an ally we didn't know about," Avery whispered.

"I wouldn't count on anything," Jorrin said.

"I'm not." The lord shrugged. Moments later, Avery was spewing a litany of low curses as they heard Varthan's order to awaken his father.

"He slapped her again," Jorrin growled, looking at his father. "I *will* kill him."

"Relax," Braedon ordered. "You mustn't rush in there if you can't even maintain control over your emotions."

"He's hurting her . . ."

"My cousin is stronger than she looks, Jorrin."

"I agree. The lass can hold her own." Hadrian's voice was strained.

"I can't just sit here and watch this." He forced air into his lungs, fists clenched.

"Rushing in could get her killed," Braedon said.

"She should've never left on her own, dammit," Jorrin spat.

His father sighed, and Avery nodded fervently.

"At this point, that is immaterial," Hadrian said.

"The one who sensed the thought-send. He's the one. The smallest shade. You grab him, Jorrin. Hold the lad here, out of the way. The rest of us will attack. We'll free Cera and contain the other shades," Braedon said.

"Nay." Jorrin's tone was so vehement his father's eyebrows lifted. No one was going to talk him out of going in the great hall.

He *would* save Cera.

Braedon sighed again as their eyes locked.

Jorrin didn't give a damn if his father thought his emotions would inhibit him. Rescuing Cera was the *only* option.

"Fine. I'll grab the lad and contain him. The rest of you attack."

"That's better," he muttered.

Braedon looked like he'd add something, but then just shook his head.

"I shall not be able to control Trikser when we enter the hall." Hadrian swiped at the sweat on his bushy brow.

"Order him to stay by my side. I'll take him to Cera, free her and get her a weapon," Jorrin said.

Hadrian exchanged a look with Braedon, but nodded at Jorrin.

Jorrin narrowed his eyes and swallowed a growl. He didn't need his father's approval. He needed to get into the great hall.

"I want the one who has my father," Avery snarled.

"I'll stun the lad and quickly rejoin you," Braedon said.

Jorrin and Avery drew their swords in answer, and Hadrian broke his physical hold on Trikser, bringing his wand into view.

The four companions exchanged one last look and charged into the great hall.

Chapter Twenty~One

KING NATHAL WAS a big man. However, at the moment he'd never felt more insignificant as he sat upon his large white warhorse, Destroyer.

His army was still out of sight as he looked down upon the large Province of Tarvis, disguised by magic and geography. The foothills would keep them out of sight as long as they desired, but it didn't make him feel any better about the task he had to carry out.

On his right, Lord Dugald Dagget sat on an ash-gray stallion almost as large as Destroyer, the sun glinting off his embossed chest plate. He wore the colors of his Province, the dark brown breeches and bright green collar peeking out from his armor. The hues were also present in the Berat seal on his shield and saddle. His shoulder-length dark hair was mussed from the helm tucked under his arm instead of being worn. His hazel eyes were sharp as he surveyed the scene before them.

Nathal had always been fond of the Duke of Berat, but he missed Falor Ryhan. They'd grown up together, trained together, been made knights together. He looked to his left, the usual spot of Lord Everett Lenore, another boyhood comrade, and was once again reminded neither of his friends rode at his side.

One he had to rescue; the other he would never ride with again.

Not to mention the missing fourth of their boyhood tribe, the captain of his personal guard, Sir Murdoch Fraser. Gone on a mission to the penal colony of Dalunas. It couldn't be helped, but *damn*.

He had good men at his side, no doubt, but not the ones he desired.

Lord Paxton Gallard, the Lord of Ascova, rode on his left astride his dark bay gelding. His short black hair hidden by his helm, his armor was just as elaborate as Nathal's,

the etched scrollwork showcasing the talent of his head blacksmith. The man's work was sought out all over the continent. Rarely was it matched.

The deep red of North Ascova was woven in with the navy blue of South Ascova and present in Paxton's breeches and tunic, as well as his double-colored gauntlets. His naturally golden skin and dark eyes were typical of Ascovans, though he was a bit pale, owing both to age and their present circumstances. By donning both colors, the duke represented a unified front of his once-shattered Province.

Paxton, oldest of the three men, but also a man Nathal had long considered a good friend, also had his eyes glued on Tarvis below them.

"Do you think my Tristan was able to accomplish his goals, my liege?" Dugald asked, taking Nathal from thoughts of his companions and their vast histories together.

"Let us hope so." He nodded for effect. He hadn't received any word from the lad in more than a sevenday.

Dugald was worried about his youngest son, and admittedly, so was Nathal.

"Yes, or our children shall never see their wedding," Lord Gallard said. His youngest daughter, Aimil, had been betrothed to Tristan Dagget from the cradle.

Nathal could remember signing the agreement as though it was only yesterday. Both third born.

"My Aimil has had her heart set on him for quite some time," Paxton said with a small smile the king was able to mirror.

Arranged marriages were quite common, but it was much better when some love went along with the bond. King Nathal himself was not embarrassed to be widely known to adore his queen. "I hope we can get Tristan out of this alive so he will not disappoint his young bride." Young Lady Gallard was one of his Riders. Ranked Senior, like Cera, and one of his best archers, as well.

"I have faith in my son," Dugald said.

"Aye, Dugald, as do I—else I never would've allowed his undertaking of this task, no matter how close he was to Falor." He tried to smile.

Something flickered in Dugald's hazel eyes, but was soon gone. The tall duke was once again battle-ready, looking down at Tarvis along with his companions. He was a good man, adored by all five of his children.

Even though Nathal was not as close to either Paxton or Dugald as Falor and Everett, he could still rely on both dukes. Neither had hesitated when he'd called upon them. Both meant more to Nathal than merely their positions as leaders of two of his Provinces. They were good men, who loved their families and never failed to do what was right. And putting Varthan down was *more* than right.

Heavy hooves pounded toward them.

Nathal turned Destroyer, hand on the hilt of his sword, his two companions following suit. He didn't relax until he recognized the buckskin mare heading toward them at a speed that made his mount shift nervously. He felt the stallion's powerful muscles ripple under his fingertips as he patted his horse and whispered calming words. Another pang hit. Murdoch should've been riding toward them on a huge black stallion, long red hair flying.

"Your Majesty, my lords." Sir Leargan Tegran inclined his head when his mare had reached them.

One of Nathal's personal guard, Leargan was an adequate fill-in for his longtime friend. He was very fond of the dark-haired young man, who'd been raised in his castle's household as a ward, brought up destined for a knighthood—which the lad had achieved two turns ago.

He'd kept Leargan close since they'd left Terraquist. Rather un-king like, but Nathal had ranted about Murdoch's absence the day they had prepared to leave. His captain had been gone for most of the sevenday. Even if he'd sent his fastest messenger to retrieve him, Murdoch and his men couldn't have gotten back in time.

He'd had to leave without him.

Murdoch would hate missing this mission. He'd never been fond of Varthan, even before he'd betrayed Nathal.

"Leargan. What news have you?" Nathal asked.

"Myself and two others have checked the Province. It's as Lord Lenore's messenger reported. They've successfully evacuated the entire Province."

"Were you intercepted?" Paxton asked.

"No, milord." Leargan inclined his head to the Duke of Ascova.

"What did you see?" Dugald asked.

Leargan looked to the king for permission, and Nathal nodded. "We didn't travel beyond the gates of Castle Lenore, but from what we were able to see of the courtyard, Lord Lenore's guard did not survive." The knight's dark eyes widened, his young face flushed and he squared his mail-covered shoulders. Emotions flickered across his face.

The seal of Terraquist—a fierce lion surrounded by a bright blue shield painted on his chest plate—caught Nathal's eye. If the lion could have roared in agony, he would have.

Pure anguish threatened to overtake him. His stomach roiled, he sucked in air. He'd known each and every one of Everett's men. He'd trained them, shaped them, and even appointed at least two of the knights to Everett's personal guard. Like all his knights, he viewed them as his children. Their murders made Varthan's betrayal hurt all the more. "Bring my mages," Nathal ordered, his tone rough.

Leargan nodded curtly as their gazes locked. "Right away, your Majesty."

Paxton let out a litany of curses. "What of Everett himself?"

"We'll find out, Paxton, but instinct tells me if Varthan has Falor's daughter, Everett and Emeralda are alive." He made eye contact with his friend.

The lord's dark eyes went black, his naturally golden skin paling. "Let us hope Lady Ryhan is also alive."

"Oh, of that, I have no doubt." Nathal gave a small smile. Even as a small child, Ceralda Ryhan had been a spitfire. He was proud to have her as a member of his Riders. She had a wide variety of skills to her credit.

"There are no guarantees," Dugald said. "We never thought he'd go after Falor and his family."

He nodded reluctantly. "Aye, but I *can* guarantee Varthan will not live to see the gallows. He *will* be a casualty of this battle."

Both his companions nodded.

Nathal's grip on Destroyer's reins tightened. Although he couldn't see them, his knuckles were white inside his Terraquist-blue gauntlets. He forced himself to relax his grip and turned, once again, at the sound of approaching hoof beats.

Leargan led two other riders.

He was quick to recognize two of the four mages with them.

Rory Leodin, most powerful of the four, sat on a black stallion and inclined his head to the king and two lords. His strawberry blond hair shifted in the light breeze, his light green eyes keen with interest. Both the colors were a contrast to those of Terraquist blue that covered him from head to foot.

Between him and Leargan sat Edana, Rory's twin sister, and the only female mage in Nathal's entourage. She was a dainty little thing with bright red-orange hair and big, dark green eyes. She looked even smaller astride her huge red roan stallion, but Nathal had no concerns about her abilities as either a horse master or as a mage. The cape around her thin shoulders was also the bright blue of Terraquist, but her tunic and breeches were black, the color Nathal had most often seen her in.

The siblings were half-elfin, and had come to him seeking protection from some scum, most likely outlaws, trying to kill them just because of their heritage. That'd been ten long turns ago, when they were small children. He'd been happy to shelter them, and ended up keeping them in his service when their talents had been discovered. Fortunately, they'd agreed to stay in Terraquist. They were both valuable members of his army.

Edana had keen senses, even sharper than her brother's.

Nathal turned to her first to gauge her reaction of the scene below them. He made eye contact with her and she smiled, sitting taller in her saddle and tucking an errant strand of bright hair behind her long, tapered ear.

"I sense very little magic at work right now, my liege. However, there are very powerful magical beings inside the castle . . . not all bad."

"Tristan is there," Nathal said.

"No . . . it's not only Lord Dagget," she said, her face contorting. She glanced at her brother.

"I sense him, too," Rory said, and Edana's shoulders eased.

"Who?" Nathal asked, forcing his impatience away.

"An elf . . ." the siblings said at the same time.

Nathal exchanged glances with the two lords and met Edana's unusual emerald eyes, "Evil?"

"Nay." The word was rushed. "More . . . one like us." She looked at her brother, eyes wide. "Also a source of good magic . . ."

"And I sense an empath . . ." Rory added, cocking his head, confusion written in his expression. "He is not elfin."

The female twin nodded. "Both very powerful." She exchanged another look with her brother.

"Allies?" Dugald asked.

"They are not evil." Edana nodded.

"What of Lady Ryhan?" Paxton asked.

"I sense her, which means she's alive," Edana said. "I cannot tell you more than that. The Lenores are alive, including the heir. I see his magic as well."

"Shades?" Nathal asked.

"There are three . . . but . . ." She made a face, then closed her eyes, small chest rising and falling as she relaxed.

Her brother grabbed her arm and jostled her in the saddle. "Edana, no. He'll see you."

She blinked large eyes and stared. "But that's the thing," she whispered, as if she was speaking to herself. "He's not what he appears to be . . ."

"Tristan?" Nathal asked.

"Nay. Not the healer. The shade," she said, her voice sounding as if she didn't comprehend her own words.

Nathal sighed, but knew from experience Edana needed to work it out in her mind before she could present it to him.

"I'm not afraid he will sense me, brother. He's not evil."

"A shade who is not evil?" Paxton sputtered, disbelief in his tone and expression as he looked over the young half-elf.

"Aye. Rory?" She reached for her twin's hand.

Rory smiled and intertwined his fingers with hers.

Nathal had seen it dozens of times. They were going to probe. The young half-elfin mages had better not get caught. He had total confidence in their skill, but Varthan had the best of his collection with him. If a shade with sensitivity to equal Edana's was inside, she'd better be damned sure he was not evil.

He scratched his head. Paxton was right, a non-evil shade was laughable. Watching them, Nathal was glad Leargan had brought the twins, instead of Afton and Dagon. Though his other two mages were very skilled, Edana and Rory worked better cohesively.

Two sets of wide green eyes opened and refocused on their companions.

Although it was only minutes, Nathal released a sigh and sat taller in his saddle.

"We remain undetected," Rory said, expelling his breath. "I don't think he sensed us, but I agree with my sister. The shade is not evil."

"Did you gather any more information?"

"Yes, Majesty." Edana looked at her brother so he would continue.

"Lady Lenore is in her rooms. There's a spell suppressing her magic and locking her inside. I can break through it easily, even from here, but not without notice. She's not alone in the room, though I cannot be sure how many are with her. No magic is there. The rest of the magic is in the great hall, including the good magic." Each word was steadier as the male twin recovered from the probing.

"That's all we can sense from here," his sister finished, wiping sweat from her brow.

"The good magic is in the great hall?" Nathal asked. "Are they battling?"

"Nay. There's not much magical activity. The more the magic, the more of a beacon for me to see. That isn't the case now. I see magical auras, both good and evil. I sense no spells other than the one containing Lady Lenore and, as I'd mentioned, it is not very strong," Rory said.

"What of the sword?" Lord Gallard asked.

"It's not in the great hall."

"I see it elsewhere. I believe it is safe for now," Edana said.

Her brother shot her a sharp look.

Nathal shifted in his saddle. If Rory hadn't sensed something his sister had, it could be bad news. Especially regarding Falor's magic sword. "Do you know where it is?"

"Inside the castle." Her voice was emphatic.

"Nothing more specific?" Dugald asked.

"It's safe for now," she reiterated, saying nothing more.

Rory gave her a long look, and then smiled. "Then it is safe." He looked first at Nathal, then at the two dukes. "Trust my sister, my lords."

"You know I do. I trust you both. Implicitly. Thank you." Nathal inclined his head to his mages.

The twins nodded understanding at their dismissal. They headed back to the army camp, hidden in a clearing and surrounded by woods.

"What now, Majesty?" Leargan asked.

"We attack. I want to look that bastard in the eyes when I run him through," he growled.

The lad gave a brusque nod.

Nathal had forty-odd men with him, not including the men Dugald and Paxton had brought. Not even that number should be necessary to bring down Varthan and three, no two shades, if the twins' assessments were correct. However, he'd learned the hard way, never underestimate magic, so he could only pray his men and his four mages were enough. If he had his way, everyone save Varthan and his shades would make it back to their homes alive.

He couldn't blindly count on the other sources of good magic his half-elfin mages had sensed in the castle. Perhaps they had unknown allies, but he had to focus on solid facts.

When word of Falor's death had reached him, he'd named Lady Ceralda Ryhan the sole heir to Greenwald.

Immediately.

Publicly.

Nathal would *not* have any of the other lords squabbling for the territory, particularly taking the horror of Ascova from nearly twenty turns ago into consideration. Civil war had split the Province into two, North and South Ascova, though the Gallard family ruled over both peaceably now. Nathal's first battle as the king of the continent, he'd barely been out of boyhood.

Like Ascova had with the Gallards, Greenwald would remain in the Ryhan family, whether Cera decided to marry or not. It was his rightful place to find a match for her as her king— especially now, since she had no living male blood relative—but he wouldn't push her into anything she didn't want, after all she'd been through.

If Cera wanted to remain a Senior Rider, Nathal would send someone to hold Greenwald until she felt otherwise. Dugald's younger brother, Roald, would suffice.

As the second son, Roald Gallard held a castle in South Ascova, but it wouldn't take much convincing to move his large family to Greenwald. He could even raise his horses there. The duke's brother was widely known for his skills as a breeder. Destroyer came from fine Ascovan stock.

Nathal had contemplated appointing Everett as Cera's guardian, but she needed no guardian. One and twenty was an acceptable age for an unmarried lady still to have a guardian, but he knew her.

She was strong and independent, and she could run Greenwald on her own if she wished. Nathal would place someone to advise her at Greenwald and make sure Castle Ryhan was fully staffed. He wouldn't pressure her into much else.

No forcing her to court, or parading suitors in front of her. He owed Falor that much, at least. Perhaps he'd even lend her Leargan to lead her men-at-arms or personal guard. The young knight was more than capable, though he'd miss having him at his side.

Varthan's betrayal still stung every time he thought about it, but he'd never be a victim again. All the turns he'd disputed—quite publicly—the rumors floating around about brutalities, rapes, kidnappings, and murders at the hands of Varthan disgusted him.

Nathal had been a fool.

He'd never forgive himself; wouldn't blame Cera if she held him responsible for the death of her family . . . Falor . . . beautiful Evie, and their younger daughter.

Falor had worked to convince him of Varthan's black heart.

Nathal regretted not heeding his friend. He should've listened the first time the Duke of Greenwald had begged him to look more closely at Varthan's doings. If he had, maybe Falor wouldn't have taken it all on himself, ultimately causing the bastard to target his family.

When he'd been exposed and punished, Varthan had taken being stripped of his lands and title as a personal affront at Falor's hands. If Nathal had listened just three months prior to what Falor had been trying to convince him of, the duke and his family might still be alive.

Heart heavy, he sighed. It was too late now. Falor was gone and all the regret in the world wouldn't change it. So he had to take the next step to be rid of the problem. It was the only way he could make things up to Cera. And to the rest of her family, Blessed Spirit rest their souls.

"I'm sorry I believed you too late, my friend," Nathal whispered.

Perhaps Falor would hear and forgive him, wherever the afterlife had taken him.

"Did you say something, Majesty?" Leargan asked.

Nathal met his dark brown eyes, smiling when he saw the concern there. "Just feeling sorry for myself, lad."

One corner of his mouth lifted. "It won't be much longer now."

"Aye, I know it."

When they rejoined the small army, Nathal sent Leargan to ready the men so he could address them. Efforts would be coordinated. He'd split them into four groups; each guarded by a mage upon their approach, so they'd be protected by magic and take the castle by surprise.

He didn't expect real resistance until they made it inside. A magical assault worried him more than swordplay. Nathal had brought his most skilled mages.

They were ready for anything.

Chapter Twenty-Two

THE NOISE BEHIND Varthan distracted his latest tirade against her. With a growl, he drew his sword. "We have company." He nodded at his other two shades as they followed suit and drew their weapons. "Markus, keep Lenore where he is. This shouldn't take long. If it does, kill him."

Markus laughed, and Cera glared. She wanted to wipe the arrogant look off his face. Her heart leapt when she saw Jorrin, Avery, Hadrian and Trikser rush into the great hall. How had they gotten there?

No.

She shook her head. They shouldn't be here, this was *her* fight.

Where was Braedon?

Wait. She didn't see the little shade either.

Her mouth went dry when she heard Jorrin shout a battle cry that had to be Aramourian, because she couldn't interpret his bellow.

Varthan gave a maniacal laugh and turned toward her love.

Just like my dream.

The evil bastard advanced on Jorrin with a sword. He was primed to receive the blow, but Cera's mind rejected what she was about to see.

Trikser snarled beside him, waiting to strike.

"No!" She yanked away from the chair. The ropes fell to the ground with a shuffling sound. So she could trust Dagonet after all, but had probably just put him in danger, revealing her bindings were rigged.

"You," Markus yelled. He let his spell go; her uncle crumpled to the ground, lying much too still for her liking.

She couldn't focus on him.

Markus was furious. His body's bright glow with a red tinge, pale hair standing on end, looked far more angry than after she'd cut him in the corridor. He wasn't stalking over to her, but to Dagonet.

Her heart dropped, and she froze by the chair.

"You betrayed us, you filth." The fair-haired shade whipped his arm up almost too fast for Cera to see.

Dagonet was thrown backwards, hitting the dais with a resounding thud.

Markus drew his sword and rushed the healer.

He struggled to wobbly legs, drawing the sword at his waist. Blood trickled down his temple. He must've hit his head.

She felt a stab of guilt. Needed to get her sword and help Dagonet. He'd risked himself for her more than once.

"She cares for the filthy half-breed, milord," Athas shouted as he stalked toward her.

Cera sprang away, managing to grab the sword Gamel had given her from the floor.

Athas swore, and pointed his own at her. "I will cut you down, bitch."

Varthan didn't acknowledge Athas's shout, for he was fighting with Jorrin in earnest. Her lover was holding his own at the moment, anyway. He knew his way around a sword.

The evil ex-lord's lookalike was just as furious as Markus.

Cera steeled herself, turning toward him. She couldn't lose to him.

The shade would rely on physical strength rather than magic; she could sense Athas wasn't as strong in magic as the others, but he was big, almost as tall as Jorrin, and she had a feeling he was skilled with the sword he brandished at her.

A sword much bigger than her own.

Backing up, she made herself focus on her foe and not the other two battles going on.

Trikser would help Jorrin, and Avery or Hadrian could help the healer, if he needed it.

Cera risked a hasty glance over her shoulder when the clash of swords rang in her ears. Markus and Dagonet were locked together in battle. Dagonet struggled to maintain control, and she was hit with another pang of guilt.

Allowing the distraction was a mistake. She barely escaped Athas's first charge. She lost her footing and stumbled. Hit the ground and rolled away just in time to dodge his attempt to stomp her.

Someone screamed her name.

Her shoulder bumped into the chair she'd been bound to. Cera hurled the thing as hard as she could at the shade.

Athas grunted as he scooted away, but the chair grazed his side, taking him off-balance.

It was enough for her to get to her feet. She didn't have to do more. As she readied herself for her own strike, a flash of white crossed her vision.

Trikser threw himself into Athas.

She said nothing to her wolf as he pinned Athas to the floor and ripped out his throat.

Cera squeezed her eyes shut at the shocked, gurgling sound Athas made. Blood spurted everywhere. Her stomach roiled and she swallowed hard as life faded from Athas's dark eyes.

Trikser returned to her side and she pushed away revulsion at the sight of all the blood marring his muzzle and white coat. She couldn't touch him, but she sent thoughts of thanks and love for saving her life.

His response was equal parts love and reproach for leaving him behind. His amber gaze burned her as she promised her bondmate she'd never leave him to run into danger again.

"No!" Varthan's shout dripped raw emotion. "You've killed my son, you bitch."

She gasped, barely ready as he left Jorrin and rushed her.

Trik slid in front of her, baring teeth, but Jorrin leapt out of nowhere, intercepting the ex-archduke and slamming his sword into Varthan's.

Cera jumped back.

Her lover rushed him again and again, their swords locking as he pushed Varthan away from her.

She watched the fight, fascinated. She'd never seen Jorrin swordfight before, but he was good, *very good*. He was strong and graceful as he blocked and lunged with ease. So far, neither of them had drawn blood. If Jorrin could maintain his advantage, he could kill Varthan.

Even though she'd made the vow repeatedly to do the deed herself, it was a relief to think of someone else killing the evil man—even Jorrin.

Sucking in a breath, Cera surveyed the room.

Uncle Everett!

Avery already knelt next to his father, and they exchanged a glance as she rushed over. They both helped him into a sitting position.

Uncle Everett groaned and opened his eyes.

"Father, are you all right?" Avery asked.

The duke blinked his golden brown eyes into focus. "Avery?"

"Yes, Father, it's me."

"See to your Mother. I don't know if she's all right."

"She is, Father. Mother's safe in her rooms. And it's almost over."

Cera's heart raced, and she swallowed against the lump in her throat when her uncle looked at her and smiled.

"I'm proud of you, niece. You didn't tell him where the sword is."

"I'm sorry, Uncle Everett." She squeezed his hand. "I'm sorry about all this."

"Nonsense, child," he croaked.

"Father?" Avery exchanged a worried look with her.

"I'm all right, son." Her uncle let his eyes slip closed.

"The healer, Avery. He'll help." Her voice urgent, she looked at the young man fighting for his life.

"If he survives," Avery said.

Uncle Everett had slipped into unconsciousness.

Placing her hand on his neck, Cera sighed. "His pulse is strong, cousin. I think he's just asleep. He'll be fine."

He nodded. "Jorrin won't last forever, Varthan is strong. I'll see if I can help." Avery jumped to his feet and drew the sword he'd obviously only sheathed to check on his father.

Nodding, Cera watched the fight between Markus and Dagonet. She shot a glance to her uncle, begging silent forgiveness for leaving him.

Trikser growled.

Dagonet was struggling. Wavering on his feet, each sword strike was a bit wider and obviously weaker than the last.

Markus threw spell after spell at him, and the healer was barely able to block or deflect each with one of his own.

Cera rushed forward, her sword ready and waiting for an opening.

Trikser was on her heels, but she ordered him to wait for her word. Even fighting, Markus could kill her bondmate with magic.

Then her death would follow.

But Varthan gave a loud growl of frustration, and she glanced in his direction.

Hadrian, Avery and Jorrin were closing in on him.

She threw a look of regret to Dagonet. He'd have to hold his own. He'd understand her need to get to Varthan. "C'mon, Trik," she told her wolf. Her grip on the borrowed sword tightened.

Cera joined the circle around Varthan.

Chapter Twenty-Three

L UCAN STOPPED STRUGGLING against the big man who'd seized him, but he needed to get back into the great hall. His captor would have to understand he wanted to help. Why hadn't his magical senses warned him before very large strong arms had enclosed him from behind?

Suddenly he was free and he whirled, holding up his hand and flinging a spell to repel the man.

He was ready for his attack, yelling a spellword.

When their magic met between them it stalled, disappearing after bursting into a bright light that caused them both to squint.

Lucan looked up, glaring. "I have to get back." He extended his hands so he could strike if necessary.

"I don't think so, lad."

Why hadn't he stunned him? He gasped. "You don't understand. I need to help Tristan. If Markus finds out he's not really a shade, he'll kill him. And the girl. I have to help the girl."

His captor's brows drew together tightly, his stare intense.

Lucan's magical senses perked awake. This man believed him. This man was an empath and knew he was telling the truth. A very powerful empath stood before him.

"What's your name, lad?"

"Lucan." He looked him up and down.

He meant him no harm, but Lucan wanted to convince him he could be a help, not a hindrance. His open mind would show the empath he spoke the truth. How had he been able to grab him without a magical alert?

"I cast a masking spell."

"A masking spell that I cannot sense," he said, more to himself than to his captor.

"It took me turns to perfect it, and yes, it's usually totally safe from all magical detection," he said. "It is possible to shield your thoughts, lad."

"I know. I will as soon as I'm convinced you believe me. I need to get back and help. Markus becomes more powerful the angrier he gets; it's part of his magic. Athas can detect lies and knows many spells, even if he doesn't have the power I do, but he's excellent with a sword and he doesn't fight fair. The same is true of Lord Varthan. I have to help Tristan." Lucan took a breath. That was the most he'd spoken at once, probably ever.

"I believe you, lad."

"I need to go. Now."

"Braedon, you're needed!"

The northern accented shout took Lucan's attention from the tall man. He gasped when he saw the elf. His magical senses surged.

This elf was more powerful than the teachers at the shade compound.

His head throbbed with power; Lucan's hands tingled, his body starting to warm. Soon, his skin would glow if he didn't shut his magic down. Just probing the elf gave his own powers a jolt of energy, and the elf wasn't even all that close to him.

He wasn't very large.

Lucan, small for his age, was probably taller, but he didn't get more time to observe him, because he disappeared into the secret passageway, wild white hair flying about his form as he ran.

Braedon swore. He should've convinced Jorrin to take the lad, but his son wouldn't be deterred from joining Cera.

The shade was staring at him with the greenest eyes he'd ever seen.

A child indeed.

As soon as he'd closed his arms around him, he knew the lad wasn't evil. Lucan was possibly the most powerful being he'd ever encountered. The youngest shade's magical aura radiated bright light.

Did he even know what he was capable of?

Braedon had little doubt this small one could shatter the spell on Cera's sword without breaking a sweat. He gave him a long look. "I feel you speak the truth, but if somehow your magic is tricking me into believing a lie, you'll not be spared, despite your youth."

Lucan squared his shoulders and stood taller. "I'm not lying. I'll help you and I'll help Tristan. He promised to get me out of this, but I don't think he can do it alone."

He gave a curt nod and guided the child in front of him.

The moment they reentered the great hall, the lad screamed with rage and ran away from him.

The dark-haired healer was in a fight for his life, a fight full of magic and swords, with the fair-haired shade they'd seen torturing Cera's uncle.

He ran forward without a care for himself and shouted a spell so fast Braedon couldn't have understood the words if he'd tried.

The fair-haired shade flew into the air at break-neck speed, and then was hurled down, slamming to the floor so hard his head bounced.

Dead instantly.

Braedon winced.

The littlest shade was seething, shaking hard and gasping for breath.

He went to him and slipped his hands onto his shoulders to calm him.

Lucan said nothing. The lad had never killed before, no matter how long he'd been a shade. Large green eyes locked onto his, unshed tears shining, threatening to spill over. He trembled, but didn't push Braedon's hands away.

The healer dropped his sword and collapsed, exhausted, but mostly unharmed.

"You betraying little whelp. I will kill you," Varthan shouted.

The fact the evil man was surrounded by Cera, Avery, Jorrin, Hadrian and Trikser didn't seem to dim his anger.

Varthan brandished his sword, but made no move away from his would-be captors, eyeing the white wolf more than the others.

Hadrian cast a containment bubble, but the elf was tired, pale and panting. It wouldn't last long.

"No, *I* will kill *you*!" Lucan glared, shoving Braedon's hands away and rushing forward. He lifted his arm, hand already glowing. He slipped into a concentration.

Braedon took a step back, squinting against Lucan's magic.

Chanting, the lad shined more brightly with each passing second.

Everything happened at once.

Varthan leapt forward, crashing through Hadrian's bubble spell as the doors to the great hall were thrown open.

The elf wizard tumbled to his rear end, but cursed and climbed to his feet again, wiping his bushy brow and yanking his dark brown tunic straight.

Armed men, all holding swords at-the-ready, poured into the vast room.

Avery was knocked to the ground, shouting in pain and gripping his arm.

Varthan's blind strike had sliced his upper arm. Cera's cousin rolled out of the way of stomping feet and uttered a curse.

The former archduke whirled, his sword ready, looking about to see who would fight him next.

When everyone seemed too stunned to move, he continued his stalk toward the youngest shade.

"Varthan," someone shouted.

Cera's jaw dropped open when she saw King Nathal, his sword drawn and pointed at Varthan. He didn't have a helmet on; his tawny hair framed his face like a lion's mane. His pale blue eyes flashed; his large chest was covered in mail and armor, breeches the royal blue of Terraquist, and a shield on his arm. It depicted a roaring lion and a blue flag, the seal of the capital.

She couldn't move for a moment, but then chided herself for allowing a distraction and refocused on Varthan.

He was free of their circle now, but wouldn't go far.

The king's men encircled the room, and all exits were blocked.

But Varthan was obviously desperate and aware his own mortality was staring him in the face. He changed direction and charged Cera with an angry shout.

She was barely able to meet his strike. Her arms shook from the energy needed to block his sword, and she sensed Trikser's bristle from somewhere behind her. Her wolf's growl was low and steady, but she couldn't focus on him. Nor could her bondmate save her this time, because there was too much risk of harming her.

Varthan's body was too close. The evil bastard cursed as he pushed her back, sword locked against hers.

How much longer could Cera's arms hold him away from her body?

"You bitch. You've ruined everything. You've killed my son."

His physical strength bore down on her. Cera couldn't have spoken if she wanted to, panting with the effort to stay on her feet.

"Get away from her," the little shade bellowed, throwing his arm up and screaming a spell.

Varthan's body whipped up and away, his dark eyes wide, face paling as his arms and legs scrambled for purchase and only flapped in the air. His sword clattered to the tiled floor of the great hall.

Cera lurched backward, losing her footing and tumbling to the floor. She winced as her sword went flying and pain radiated in her rear end. She looked up at Varthan, suspended in the air much as her uncle had been; limbs involuntarily spread wide. She glanced at the boy.

The tiny shade wasn't fearful like when Varthan had ordered him to probe her mind. He wasn't weak, either. His clear green eyes flashed with pent-up rage.

The boy would kill Varthan if no one stopped him. He'd already taken one life.

Varthan needed to die, but not by the youngster's hand.

Jorrin rushed to her side and pulled her to her feet.

She flashed a smile of thanks and refocused on Varthan, whose face and body were contorted in pain. Cera didn't feel anything as she watched, her love at her side.

Everyone in the room had eyes transfixed on the glowing little shade and the former archduke; stunned into a silence that was probably partly because of the youth's strength, and partly because the bastard was being betrayed by one of his own.

"Lucan, no, not you!" The healer rushed forward, but it was too late.

The boy was concentrating so hard his figure was consumed by his glowing aura. He was a ball of light.

Many of the others put their hands up to cover their faces from the radiance, but Cera stared, unable to tear her eyes away.

Varthan's head was thrown back, his dark eyes popping out of his skull.

Several people, her included, winced at the resounding snap, followed by various cracking and popping sounds as the ex-lord's spine was crushed. Cera shuddered as the awful noises went on forever, every bone in his body pulverized.

He slumped and the boy dropped his arm. The evil man fell to the ground like a pile of rags. *Varthan's dead.*

It was too simple. There was no blood, no torture. Too good a death for him.

She half-wanted to grab her sword and run him through, ensuring he couldn't get up. It wasn't supposed to be so easy for him to die . . .

Relief warred with regret as tears threatened. Her knees buckled and Cera collapsed.

She was in Jorrin's arms in seconds, as hot tears streaked down her cheeks.

Why am I crying?

Trikser walked circles around the two of them, whimpering, but she couldn't comfort her wolf until she gathered her thoughts.

"It's over, love," Jorrin whispered, stroking her hair.

Words deserted her.

A child killed him. A child had done what she was supposed to do.

She looked into Jorrin's blue eyes, reading worry there.

Commotion in the hall brought her head around. Her aunt, uncle, and Avery were in a tight embrace, not far from them.

Neomi, hand-in-hand with Gamel, and two other young maids had also entered the great hall with a smattering of people.

It was a relieved chaos, knights and her uncle's servants everywhere.

Cera had to say something to Jorrin. She didn't like his tight expression. "I'm all right."

He nodded and helped her to her feet, wrapping her against his chest.

She held on, needing his physical strength to compose herself. Leaning up, she brushed her lips against his. Jorrin returned the soft kiss with one of his own. When she pulled away, he smiled and she suddenly felt much better. "Thanks," she whispered.

"Anytime." He released her.

Cera turned to her wolf, patting his head and sending him thoughts of love. She asserted she was fine to him, too. Giving him a scratch behind one ear, she told him he needed a bath.

Trik sat at Jorrin's side, and she admonished him to stay there as she surveyed the room.

She wiped the tears from her eyes as she caught sight of the littlest shade. Cera needed to say something to him. '*Lucan*,' the healer had called him.

Jorrin followed her gaze. "Go ahead, love."

Cera flashed a smile and nodded.

The little shade was standing with the healer and Braedon. Devastation dominated his expression, as it did Braedon's.

"Lucan," she called.

The greenest eyes she'd ever seen met her gaze, tears on his cheeks.

She gathered the boy into her arms without hesitation, pulling him close.

His surprise lasted for a second—then his arms snaked around her waist, and she squeezed him tighter. The boy's head didn't quite reach her shoulders.

"Thank you," she whispered into his soft dark hair, her breath causing movement that tickled her nose.

Lucan looked up and shook his head. The impact of what he'd done was hurting him.

Cera could feel it, even though she was no empath. She looked at Braedon. He, too, felt every-thing Lucan did.

The boy didn't know how to hide his anguish.

"Lucan, you saved us. *All* of us. You did what I couldn't. You saved Dagonet, and the rest of my family."

"Tristan . . ." he whispered, glancing at the healer.

"Tristan?" The name clicked. "Tristan Dagget," Cera breathed, releasing Lucan.

"I couldn't tell you, Lady Ryhan," the healer said, taking a step forward and holding out his hand.

She shook it and met his eyes. "I can't believe I didn't know you," she said more to herself than to him. She glanced at Braedon, who smiled and pulled Lucan to his side, throwing an arm around the boy's shoulders.

Lucan looked up at Jorrin's father and offered him a tremulous smile.

"With as much time as I spent in Greenwald and with your father, I'm surprised I was able to pull it off." Tristan grinned, his hazel eyes twinkling and lightening the serious expression on his handsome face.

Cera met and held his gaze.

They both thought of her father, and his expression was suddenly fraught with sadness.

"I miss him so much . . ." she whispered.

He squeezed his eyes shut for a moment, then nodded. "As do I. He was as much a father to me as my own . . ."

Braedon paled, his expression pained. The apple of this throat bobbed as he swallowed.

She flashed a smile. "Sorry, Braedon. It's a wonder you don't go hide in a cave."

Jorrin's father chuckled. "I have before, lass." He smiled, looking a great deal like Jorrin at that moment.

Her heart skipped. "Lord Tristan Dagget, this is Braedon Aldern," Cera said. "Braedon, Lord Tristan Dagget, son of the Duke of Berat, and a former ward of my father."

The two men murmured greetings and shook hands. They fell into comfortable conversation, Lucan shifting from foot to foot.

Braedon gave the boy a comforting squeeze against his side, and Cera suspected Jorrin just might have an adopted little brother when all was done. King Nathal wouldn't punish Lucan, but the boy would likely have nowhere to go. She'd take him back to Greenwald if Braedon or Tristan didn't claim him. She owed Lucan her life.

"Tristan." The Duke of Berat himself, Dugald Dagget strode over, his expression a mix of relief and pride. Same hazel eyes, rich brown hair, even lean muscular build, Tristan resembled the tall, thin man so much there was no mistaking their relationship.

"Speaking of my father . . . If you'll excuse me, Master Aldern, Lady Ryhan."

"Just Cera," she muttered.

Tristan nodded and flashed a smile. He grabbed Lucan's hand. "Come, Lucan. I want you to meet my father."

The boy blanched, but placed his hand in Tristan's.

She smiled encouragingly and glanced at Braedon.

Jorrin's father smiled at Lucan as well, fondness in his expression.

Cera didn't have to worry about the boy after all.

Chapter Twenty-Four

"HELLO," THE QUIET female voice pulled Jorrin from his thoughts.

He turned away from the scene of Cera and the little shade she held in her arms. He'd witnessed it with his own eyes, yet he was still stunned. The child had accomplished quite a feat.

A child had saved them all.

Looking down, Jorrin met a pair of emerald eyes.

She was a tiny little thing with bright hair and tapered ears slightly longer than his own, but instinct and magic alike told him she was half-elfin like him. Her black tunic, wide and mostly shapeless, fell to her slender knees, covering black breeches, but he could sense a slender waist beneath, see the outline of small, high breasts. A Terraquist blue cape covered her thin shoulders and stopped mid-calf. She might be small, but she exuded femininity. Beautiful and slight, just like a fully blooded elf maiden.

It was an oddity to meet someone like him away from Aramour, and he sensed her curiosity. Before he could answer, another appeared at her side.

Jorrin looked at the other half-elf trying not to be rude as he took in the tapered ears.

The man was almost as tall as him and his hair and eyes were the same hue as the girl's, but in lighter shades. Siblings. He was clad in Terraquist blue from head to foot, but the belt around his trim waist was thick and black. He was the opposite of his sister; tall, muscular and solid.

"Hello," he said, nodding to both of them. "Jorrin Aldern."

They appraised him silently. Hadn't they ever seen another half-elf?

"Rory Leodin." The other male finally reached to accept

his outstretched hand. His voice clear and deep, his accent was northern, but not Aramourian. "This is my sister, Edana."

"Nice to meet you both."

"He is your father?" the female asked without preamble, gesturing to Braedon, where he stood with Cera.

Jorrin glanced at his lover and father. He'd missed the healer and little shade leaving their company. "He is."

"He is an empath." Edana's eyes were wide, head cocked to one side.

"Yes, he is."

"Very odd," she whispered, more to herself than to her brother or Jorrin.

He hid sudden amusement, not wanting to offend her, and caught Rory's eye.

"My sister can be rather intense when she's trying to understand something," he said, a smile playing at his lips.

"I see." Jorrin smiled.

"Where's your mother?" Edana asked.

Jorrin met her emerald gaze, furrowing his brow. "At home. In Aramour."

Rory and Edana exchanged a glance.

His magic tingled. The siblings were saddened at the mention of his childhood home. Why?

"Jorrin," Hadrian called.

Two sets of green eyes widened as the elf approached, but neither said a word.

He greeted them warmly in Aramourian, but at their obvious confusion, Hadrian spared Jorrin a glance.

The siblings didn't understand Aramourian.

"Hadrian, this is Rory and Edana Leodin," Jorrin said. "They're two of King Nathal's mages." He guessed their role, though they hadn't said.

Rory confirmed with a nod.

"You don't speak Aramourian." Hadrian's surprise was evident. The siblings exchanged another sad glance and shook their heads collectively. "Twins?" the elf asked, quirking a smile.

"Yes, sir." Edana's tone was shaky.

Hadrian was a full head shorter than she, so Jorrin was further amused at her apparent nerves.

"We've never been to Aramour," Rory admitted.

His stomach clenched. *How awful.* Growing up, Aramour was home, nothing spectacular, but at least he'd belonged there. He couldn't imagine growing up in the human world. What horrible prejudices they must've dealt with. Yet, the king had accepted them. He had a new insight into King Nathal; admired him.

"Come, come, let me tell you all about Aramour," Hadrian told the twins.

Jorrin smiled as they sat, the wonder in their eyes making them seem like children. The elf held their rapt attention, for sure.

"Ceralda Ryhan, come here," a deep voice bellowed.

He looked over at the man who'd just been in his thoughts.

Without hesitation, Cera left his father's side and strode to the king, giving a small bow when she stopped in front of him.

Jorrin gaped, and room fell silent when King Nathal enclosed her in a rib-crunching embrace. Standing at his full height with her still in his arms, he lifted her off the ground. The king had to be six or seven inches over six feet, and just as broad.

A blond giant.

His love was held tight against the king's massive chest. His heart skipped a beat when she grinned.

The king said nothing as he released her, but their gazes locked.

Jorrin's magic tingled.

The king was feeling some pretty substantial sadness, although he smiled at Cera. "I'm so sorry about your family, lass." His deep voice carried across the large room and pinpointed just how far north he was from originally. His accent was reminiscent of Hadrian's. "I miss your father more than I can say." His voice was thick with grief.

Cera's face scrunched with the obvious effort not to cry, but she nodded. "It's over." Her gaze remained locked with King Nathal's.

Even as they spoke, some of his men were taking the bodies out of the great hall. Three bodies of evil men. The only consolation was that no others had been harmed this day.

"Aye, that it is. You must introduce me to your companions." The king smiled.

Jorrin had been aware she was acquainted with the king personally, but she'd never mentioned what seemed to be a relationship between them. How insignificant he must seem. He grimaced. Had he been fooling himself to think he was good enough for her?

His father's hand squeezed his forearm in comfort, and he turned to meet amber eyes. He hadn't heard his approach. Trying to smile, he couldn't fool his empathic father.

"She's not concerned with what you have, or don't have, my son." Braedon's tone was gentle. "She loves you."

"I know, Da," Jorrin said, calling his father something he'd never gotten the chance to as a child. "But I can't say the same for the king."

Braedon sighed and smiled.

Was it forced? Had his father just unconsciously confirmed his fear?

Jorrin's heart dropped to his stomach.

"It will all work out," Braedon said.

Nodding absently, he stared at Cera as she interacted so casually with the most powerful man on the continent.

Hadrian soon came to stand next to them, but saying nothing.

Jorrin tried not to be intimidated when his lover brought the king to them.

Neither Jorrin nor Braedon were small men, but he soon learned just how much he had to look *up* at King Nathal. Had he not been so nervous, he might've been amused.

Cera smiled, and he looked deep into her eyes, willing her to feel his love. Her gaze lingered and from the softness in her expression, she'd caught his thought.

He took a breath and relaxed.

"Jorrin Aldern, and his father Braedon, your Majesty. They are of Aramour."

Jorrin suppressed a wince at her almost regal formal tone. Hastily bowing, he followed his father's lead.

"Hadrian Rowlin, also of Aramour, though of Berat for the last twenty turns or so," Cera said.

Dragon's Tail
Mountains of Aramour
Elfin River
Terraquist
Greenwald
North Ascova
Netian Valley
Tarvis
Hadrian's Place
Berat
Islands
South Ascova
Dalunas
Southern Strait
Penal Territory

King Nathal looked them over, and Jorrin felt almost naked. Then finally, the king smiled and placed his hand out to shake each of theirs.

He stifled a laugh at the sight of Hadrian's barely four-foot-tall slight frame next to the big man. King Nathal had very kind eyes.

In the three turns he'd spent in the human world, Jorrin had heard nothing but good things about the king, but it was different being close to such a legend. A place not even his wildest dreams had ever taken him.

"I am indebted to them, your Majesty. In a way that can never be repaid." She looked directly at him.

Jorrin reached for her hand, stomach fluttering when Cera took it and came to his side, entwining her fingers with his. He was not comfortable, however, when the king looked him up and down.

The large man's gaze locked onto their clasped hands and lingered before he studied her, then him again. For a man who possessed no magic, there was nothing wrong with King Nathal's intuition.

Jorrin had inadvertently made a statement when he'd reached for her. He had to force himself not to squirm.

"I will see adequate rewards are given." The king's voice sounded sincere, but he didn't break eye contact with Jorrin.

"It was my duty, your Majesty," Braedon said. "I do not seek a reward."

"Nor do I," Hadrian said.

The king looked away from him finally, glancing at his father and the elf wizard. His smile took ten turns off his bearded face. "Regardless, you will all accompany me back to Terraquist." Tone pleasant, it was still a command, not a request.

No one objected.

"But first, I'd like to assist my aunt and uncle in restoring order to Tarvis," Cera said.

"Aye, lass," King Nathal said. "I've no intention of leaving until we see to that."

"Thank you, Majesty." She flashed a smile that had Jorrin's heart tripping. She was different, lighter than she'd been before.

He liked what he was seeing.

"We shall not linger, though. We have much to discuss, you and I, Ceralda Ryhan." Again, his voice was even, but his eyes bored into Jorrin's.

His love merely nodded.

Jorrin gulped.

Chapter Twenty-Five

CERA SANK ONTO the bench, and had to convince her eyes to stay open a bit longer.

The king had kept true to his word; they were all staying in Tarvis until the Province was back in order, but the work was back-breaking. King Nathal himself was directing most of it, despite her uncle's protests.

He was trying to help the duke by insisting he rest, but her uncle had never been a gracious patient. Uncle Everett had insisted multiple times that Tristan had healed him adequately and he had no need of rest.

When things had calmed that horrible day, she'd retrieved her father's sword from the kitchens. She smiled at the memory of everyone's astonished looks when she'd revealed where Neomi had helped her to hide it, but the sword was safe now.

Lucan had broken the spell on it.

Anyone could handle it, but she'd always be overprotective of it. Cera never had it far from her side.

Watching the boy take down something so powerful Hadrian had been afraid to try was amazing. It'd been effortless for him, too.

What a relief to have Lucan fighting for the right side. Using his magic whenever asked, he was also a tremendous help at repairing Tarvis. Everyone, no matter their station, pitched in. But with the king leading the charge, and performing work that was very much below *his* station, no one else complained.

King Nathal really was a great man. He'd summoned additional knights from Terraquist, replaced all the servants at Castle Lenore, as well as the duke's personal guard.

Most of her aunt and uncle's staff had come back with the rest of the people of the Province when they'd come out of hiding, but quite a few had been killed by Varthan.

Cera grimaced.

So many deaths.

King Nathal had immediately sent some men to hunt down all the other shades and anyone loyal to Varthan, vowing they'd be dealt with.

Tristan played an intricate part in identifying them all, but it pained him. He was a healer, and he didn't want more death, however justified; but they had to keep Varthan's army from trying to avenge him. When word of who'd killed him got out, they'd come after Lucan.

"Cera, love?"

She smiled at Aunt Em, pushing away pain at the reminder of her mother. It wasn't her aunt's fault she resembled her mother so much. They'd been identical twins. "Yes?"

Aunt Em reached for her hand. "I want you to go to your chamber and rest."

"I will in a bit." She fought a yawn, studying her aunt. She had to be exhausted. They'd been straightening and cleaning the great hall, clearing it of all signs of Varthan and his shades. Her aunt had been scrubbing floors next to the maids. "You should rest as well, Auntie."

Aunt Em gave a brilliant smile that reminded her so much of her mother and her sister, Kait, she couldn't blink the tears away fast enough.

"You admonish me?" Her tone was amused.

Cera pushed away her sadness, not wanting her aunt to sense it. "Avery tells me I'm bossy." She forced a smile.

"My son is still lacking in manners, then." Aunt Em winked.

"Lady Lenore." Gamel's father, Bannet, came rushing to them, two obviously worried maids on his heels.

"Yes, Bannet?" Aunt Em asked.

"I'm sorry, but we have need of you, milady." The head steward shot an apologetic glance to Cera, but she smiled.

"All right, what is it?" Aunt Em's voice was calm, causing the flustered steward to relax his shoulders and stand still—at least for a moment.

They left then, heading out of the great hall, his arms gesturing wildly as he told her aunt the problem.

Cera shook her head and let out a low laugh. Whatever it was, it'd be fine.

Bannet had always been good at overreacting.

"Here, love." Jorrin's voice took her from the scene and she looked up at him in appreciation of the flask he pressed into her palm.

Taking a sip of sweet wine, she closed her eyes as it quenched her dry throat. The warmth hit her belly pleasantly and loosened her tight limbs. "Thank you." Cera leaned into him when he slid onto the bench next to her.

"Anytime." He kissed her cheek and threw his arm around her shoulders.

When would they have time alone? She wanted his arms around her and his lips somewhere other than her cheek. She'd like his lips *everywhere* other than her cheek, like when they made love by the ruins. Her body heated, and she shifted against him.

Jorrin quirked an eyebrow, but said nothing.

She'd been transparent enough. Cera wanted him.

"His energy is exhausting." Her lover gestured to the king, whose head was bent in discussion with Lords Dagget, Gallard and her uncle, at the opposite end of the great hall. "No wonder he's so widely feared in battle."

She laughed. "But look at it this way; we'll be headed out soon."

"I know." He sighed.

Cera shot him a sharp look. "Don't you want to go to Terraquist?" When he hesitated, her heart pounded.

Is he going to leave me?

"The king said we'll go," he said finally.

"But you don't want to."

Jorrin smiled and shook his head. "Not what I meant, love. We'll go to Terraquist when we're finished helping your aunt and uncle."

She gave him a long look and swallowed hard to keep tears at bay.

What if he doesn't want to stay with me?

"I think I'm going to head to my room." Her gut when hard, chasing away her desire.

"I'll walk you to it." He rose and offered his hand. He met her eyes and smiled again, kissing her quickly.

She leaned into him when he pulled her into his side as they walked.

"Where's Trikser?" Jorrin looked around.

"Hunting, I think. I let him outside. He needed to run," Cera said, but her mind raced.

What if Jorrin left her? Did he want to?

He loves me, doesn't he?

They'd never discussed a future.

She had to get back to Greenwald; she was the only one who could run her Province. It was hers to care for, like its people, but could she ask Jorrin to be by her side? She wanted nothing more.

They didn't speak as they headed to the room she'd always occupied when staying with her aunt and uncle.

Jorrin opened the door, pausing so she could enter.

Turning to face him when she was just inside the doorway, Cera tried not to stare. She reached for his hand, heart cantering so hard there was no doubt he could hear it. "Don't go," she whispered. His eyes widened, so she tugged for effect. She stepped back, pulling him into the room.

"Are you sure, love? The others . . ."

"Shut the door," she ordered. She wanted to be with him again. Needed him.

Didn't want Jorrin to leave her . . . ever.

As soon as he'd latched and locked the door, Cera wrapped her arms around him and pressed her lips to his. His kiss tasted like the wine they'd shared in the great hall.

Jorrin groaned and plastered her to his chest.

She melted into him, sinking her hands into his hair, their tongues dancing in their joined mouths.

He tugged at the ties on her jerkin as his kisses covered her face and trailed down her neck. Warmth unfurled in her belly and settled between her legs, leaving her throbbing. Heat consumed her, firing her for more. A pleasant heaviness settled over her, and she had to clutch his tunic to stay upright.

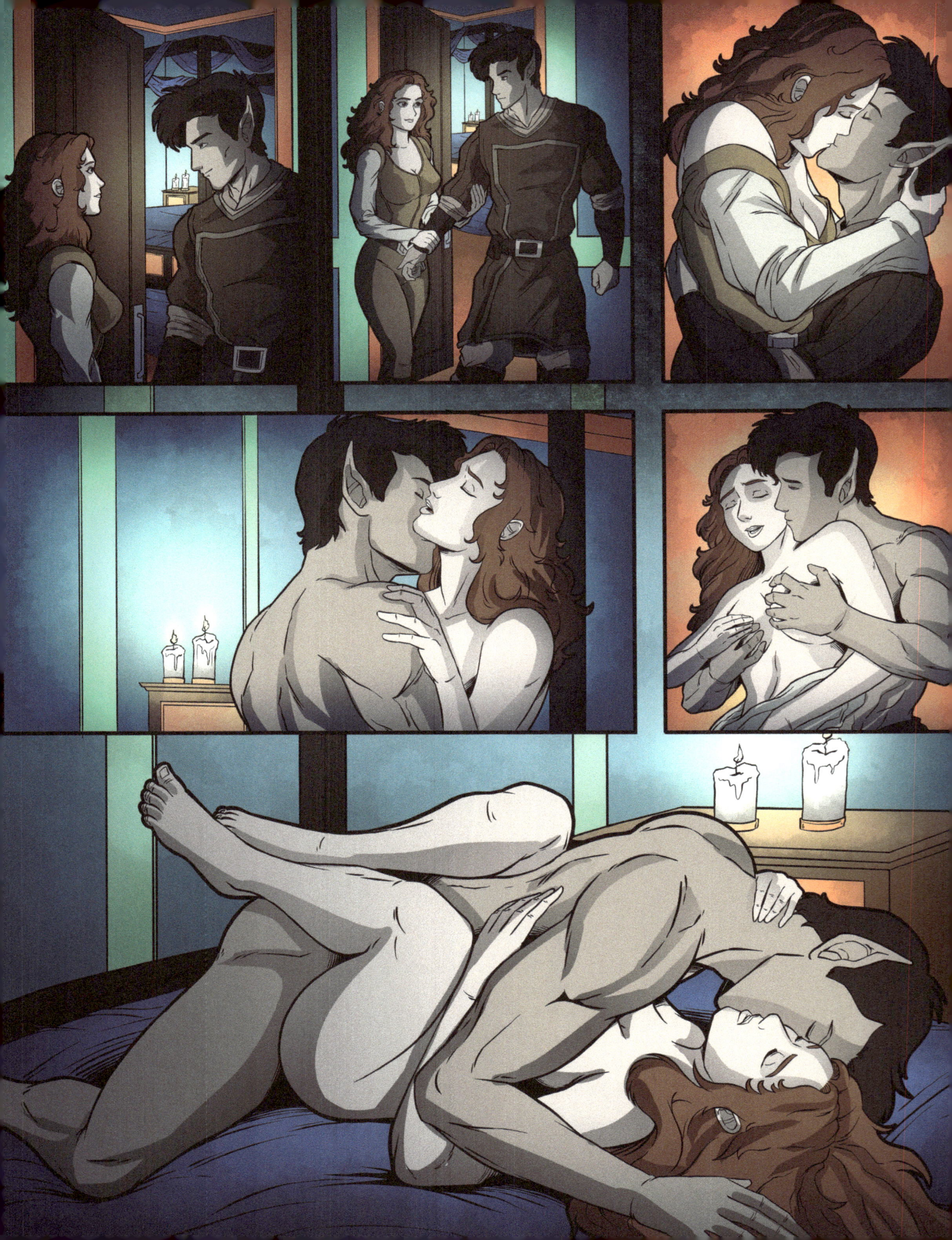

Cera shrugged out of her jerkin, trying not to stumble when he released her. Panting, she managed to smile as he slipped his tunic off and threw it down.

His nakedness beckoned, and she stared. She needed to touch him.

"I want to touch you, too," Jorrin whispered, pulling her back into his arms.

Had she spoken aloud, or was he responding to her thought?

She buried her face against his neck, shivering at the feel of him, as well as anticipating his words. She smiled as he pushed her upright with gentle hands and reached for her tunic. He helped her out of it, and soon they were both naked from the waist up.

Jorrin stared, too.

Courage faltering, she tried to rush back into his arms.

"No." He gripped her shoulder. "Let me look at you. There wasn't enough light at the ruins."

She nodded, but her cheeks burned.

"You're so beautiful." He took a step toward her and tilted her face up to meet his gaze, claiming her mouth in a tender kiss that made her quiver all over.

Cera sank back against his chest, and he made a noise when their skin met, trembling against her.

So warm and so right. Better than the first time.

Her breasts pressed into him and he held her, standing very still. "I need a minute, love. I want you so much."

They swayed in place, melded to each other. He kissed her slowly, tenderly, moving downward after a moment. Jorrin spread hot wet kisses along her jaw line and the hollow of her throat on the way to her collarbone.

She moaned and buried her hands in his dark hair, tipping her head back to allow him better access. She absently traced an outline up his tapered ear with her fingertip.

He shivered again, tightening his arms around her. Jorrin nipped and kissed his way across her shoulders. The trail of fire he left in the wake of his lips made her sear.

Cera leaned into him, crying out softly when his mouth went lower, and he cupped her breasts gently before enclosing a nipple. He added his tongue to the kisses and she liquefied, legs wobbling. Need threatened to consume her.

She crushed her mouth into his when he came back to her face. The kiss was demanding, and she met the thrusts of his tongue with her own, exploring his mouth as he plundered hers. It left them both shaking as their eyes met. She ran her hands over his chest and back, but nothing was *enough*.

"When you touch me, I can't think," he said.

"Good." She smiled and tugged at his belt.

Jorrin gasped as her hand dipped below his waistband, her fingertips brushing his erection. She opened his breeches and started to tug them down.

"I want to see you, Jorrin. I didn't get a good enough look, either."

"The feeling is mutual, love." He pushed hers off her hips after stepping out of his own.

Undergarments slid to the floor. They were both naked; they stood back, openly staring at each other.

Cera licked her lips, and he chuckled. Her cheeks blazed.

What's wrong with me?

She'd already been with him. Why was her stomach jumping, her heart skipping? While making love once didn't make her an expert, Jorrin loved her, wanted her. He'd been open about it, and they made each other feel good. The embarrassment was annoying.

Jorrin's beautiful defined muscles flexed as if they appreciated her scrutiny, and her eyes traveled down to the tight bands of muscle covering his stomach.

Cera ached to trace every line with her fingers, like she had before, to drag her tongue along every muscle like he had done to her.

His proudly jutting erection was gorgeous, like the rest of him.

The room was lit by the pleasant glow of many candles, and he looked even larger than he had the night by the ruins, but he hadn't hurt her when she'd given him her innocence.

Jorrin wouldn't hurt her now.

Her eyes landed on his muscular thighs and she shuddered as she remembered their legs entwined.

"Like what you see, love?" he teased. "I know I do." His blue eyes darkened with desire, and she flushed from head to toe.

Jorrin's heart thundered. He wanted her so badly he shook with it, and he hadn't even touched her yet. Just because he'd taken her once didn't mean she needed him rough and raw. He needed to take it slow until her body was used to making love.

Candles were worth ten times their weight in gold. He'd tasted her, felt her, and seen her, but not like *this*. Light made him appreciate the woman he'd fallen in love with even more.

Cera was perfect, from the size of her breasts to her slender waist, subtly curved hips and long legs. His gaze fell below her waist and he shivered as he saw the dark red curls at the juncture of her thighs.

He wanted to get his hands there. Hell, he wanted to get his lips and tongue there again. He remembered her taste and craved her. He opened his arms and she came back to him. Jorrin groaned as her skin seared him from head to toe.

Her hips rubbed his, breasts flattened against his chest, and his arousal pressed into her, cradled flush at her pelvis. She brushed caresses down his back; he shuddered and could've come undone right then and there.

Sweeping her up into his arms, he laid her on the large bed. He kissed her deeply as he followed her down, hands roaming her all over.

Cera opened her thighs when his fingertips passed over her sex, playing in the soft curls there. After few gentle caresses, she whimpered, lifting with a demand for more.

He slipped a finger inside, biting back a grunt—or another unmanly noise. She was already wet for him. It fired his blood to know no one else had ever touched her like this.

No one else ever will, either.

Her hand grazed his erection, and he moaned. Couldn't help it.

She yanked it back. "Did I hurt you?"

"Not at all, love." Jorrin lay on his side next to her. "But if you do that again, I won't last without you much longer."

"Then don't." She boldly encircled him with warm fingers, her gray eyes enticing.

He groaned, pushing her down into the bed, kissing her hard. She was right there with him, their tongues dueling. He knocked her legs apart and Cera lifted her hips, begging for his touch.

Jorrin trailed kisses down her neck, heading to her breasts. Paying special attention to them, he encircled each nipple with his tongue before suckling.

The pleasure he made her feel rolled over his magic, threatening to blow the top off his erection.

She was bolder than their first time, moving into his mouth and caress, letting her body tell him where she wanted to be touched.

He followed her every wish, his blood singing. When he kissed her inner thighs, she writhed, screaming his name. He brought her close with his mouth, sucking her most sensitive spot and laving it with his tongue.

Cera buried her hands in his hair and arched her back. The tugging tingled before it hurt, but he didn't care if she yanked it out by the root.

She was gorgeous with her head thrown back in passion, her skin flushed pink and her gray eyes heavy-lidded. Her red curls were spread wide, covering the entire pillow.

His manhood throbbed even more, and he swallowed hard.

When her thighs shook and her hips lifted of their own accord, he pulled away. His love cried out in frustration and glared, but Jorrin had impeded her orgasm because he needed to feel her clench around him when she came. He shot up and took her mouth, filling her sex with a full stroke that made her whimper against his kiss.

She gasped, panting into his chest, as her pleasure broke, rolling over his magic with his first thrust.

Jorrin paused as her contractions squeezed his arousal. She was wet, hot and tight, and if he moved, it'd be over.

Cera met his eyes, shifting her hips. Tilting up, she took him deeper and wrapped her legs around his waist.

"I need a minute, love," he breathed.

She nodded and pulled his face down, spreading tender kisses all over his mouth.

"Did I hurt you?" His chest brushed her dusky peaked nipples as they breathed together. "I joined us roughly."

"No, but I need you to move." She pushed against him for effect.

Claiming her mouth, he groaned her name into their kiss, pulling back to propel forward hard. They fell into a frantic rhythm. He tried to go slow, but Cera wasn't having it. Nails sinking into his lower back and rear end, she urged him even faster. Jorrin gave her what she wanted, taking them higher and higher.

Sweat covered them both as they moved together, and his spine tingled. He was close, but he wanted her to fall over the edge with him.

He didn't have to wait long. He pulled back and drove forward, with her gripping his arms and throwing her head back on a moan. She stiffened, crying his name.

Jorrin held her, watching her shatter completely, a wave of pleasure washing over them both that he felt, both physically and magically.

Overwhelming in its intensity, but it was different than before.

He felt Cera *absolutely.*

Her whole form contracted.

Pleasure assailed him.

Her thighs shook around his waist and he held her close as he thrust forward one last time. He jolted and squeezed her against him, burying his face in her neck as his erection jerked inside her, spurting his release.

She tremored in his arms as the ecstasy slid over them both.

He collapsed in her arms, pressing a tender kiss to her lips. "I love you." Jorrin wanted to explain what'd happened with his magic. Making love had never been so intense . . . *more* than just the love they shared, but no words would form to explain properly. He rolled onto his back and tugged her into his arms. He needed her as close as he could get her.

"I love you, too, Jorrin." Cera snuggled into his side, resting her head on his chest.

Letting his eyes slip closed, he reveled in the thrumming of her heartbeat as it slowed from its frantic pace. He absently stroked her back and tucked his other arm behind his head.

"Jorrin?"

"Hmmm?" he returned, not opening his eyes.

"It is always like this?" She blushed prettily when he finally met her gaze.

"What, love?"

"You know, making love . . . is it always . . ."

"Always what, love?" he asked, amused.

"So wonderful . . ."

His pulse quickened. "No one has ever made me feel like you do. The night at the ruins, as well as this time."

"Have there been . . . a lot of . . . others?" Her brows were drawn tight; a frown marred her beautiful face.

Jorrin chuckled and she glared. "No, love. A few." *No one but her matters.*

She harrumphed.

Cupping her face, he looked deep into her eyes. "I've never told another woman I loved her, Cera. Just you. Only you. *Always.* And I tell you truly that I've been with others, but you and I made love in the true sense of it."

She flashed a brilliant smile that took his breath away. Cera leaned up and pressed her lips to his.

Jorrin groaned as his body responded to her quickly and desperately, as though he was starved for her. His erection was instantly taut and throbbing, trapped pleasantly between their bodies.

The intensity of his need for *her* jolted him, prickling his magic to alertness.

His form warmed to Cera's desire as well. She wanted him just as badly as he needed her.

Love wrapped them both like an aura, and he shook as she held him tighter.

I love you. Blessed Spirit, I love you so damned much, he thought-sent. Kissing her deeply, Jorrin pressed her into the bed. He parted her thighs and settled on top of her, quivering from head to foot.

Her hands slid down his back, landing on his rear end and pulling him flush against her sex. She broke the kiss, and their gazes collided. "Again?" Cera whispered against his lips.

"If you're not too sore."

She answered by lifting her hips in an invitation Jorrin didn't refuse.

Chapter Twenty-Six

RIDING WITH A small army was different from what Jorrin was used to. Riding with the *king's* small army was something he'd never even fathomed.

Cera rode next to him on Ash. Her expression was pensive; he relaxed in his saddle.

They'd left Tarvis the previous morning, and although their pace wasn't exhausting, he'd be glad when they arrived at Terraquist. He'd never been to court, and definitely wasn't looking forward to it. Nerves flipped his stomach.

The large group rode until sunset, setting up camp in a sizable clearing for the second night. Jorrin groaned. A second night of no privacy, sleeping in a large tent with a group of other men. A second night with no chance to be alone with Cera.

He ached to hold her and take her again. A few stolen kisses behind the tents the previous evening was all they'd managed. He wanted to fall asleep with her in his arms, like the night at the ruins, like they'd gotten used to in Tarvis.

If nothing else, he'd learned how to be an excellent sneak.

After they'd endured the evening meal under the scrutiny of her family and the king in the great hall, Jorrin had snuck into her room, made love to her again and held her all night long. The first of the best nights of his life.

The three following had been the same. Making love and sleeping in each other's arms.

Cera would be in the same tent she'd been in the previous night with the few women traveling to Terraquist, her aunt and several maids.

He looked up from his seat on a log when someone called his name.

Tristan Dagget smiled as he strode over. No longer dressed in the black garments of a shade, the young lord wore the colors of his Province, browns and greens. He handed Jorrin a skin of water.

"Thanks." He took a deep drink and flashed a smile. "How much longer do you think it'll be until we get there?"

"Another day or two, I'd imagine. In a hurry?" Tristan arched a dark eyebrow.

His amusement made Jorrin's magic tingle as the lord followed his gaze to Cera.

She was talking to Braedon and Lucan, not far from them.

All around the camp, soldiers were starting fires and caring for horses. Everyone had worked together to pitch the large tents and, the last having gone up only moments ago.

He quirked a half-smile when he met Tristan's hazel eyes. "Privacy wouldn't be something I'd complain about."

"I'm also missing someone at the moment, though I haven't seen her in months." His expression sobered.

Guilt rushed Jorrin. He couldn't imagine being away from Cera for *months*. "Is she in Terraquist?"

"Aye."

"So, you're as eager as I am to get there?"

Tristan chuckled.

"Hopefully you'll be with her soon," he added.

"It'll be good to get back. I tend to spend more time in Terraquist than I do Berat, honestly."

Jorrin felt eyes burn him, and looked to his right.

Rory Leodin watched him, curiosity etched in his expression. The other half-elf's sister was now with Cera, Lucan, and Braedon.

The lord once again followed his gaze. "They mean no harm. They're curious because you're like them, not something they see often, if ever. I've known them for several turns, good mages and loyal to a fault."

He stood and stretched. "Oh, it doesn't bother me. I'm probably just as curious about them."

Tristan cocked his head to the side and nodded. The lord's demeanor was generally pensive and observant, but Jorrin liked the young man.

Does he ever loosen up?

What type of girl could've captured the stoic young man's heart? Then again, Jorrin could imagine long months with Varthan would traumatize anyone. Hopefully, Tristan wasn't damaged from the experience.

Their conversation was cut short by the king's bellow for a hunt.

Cera jogged over, bow in hand and her cheeks flushed pink with excitement. "Are you coming?" she asked, and hastily bid Tristan a hello.

He inclined his head and smiled.

"You're much better with a bow than I, love. I think I'll sit this one out," Jorrin said.

"But your father's going," she said, crestfallen. "You said he hunts with magic."

"Oh."

So Cera wanted to see what Braedon could do.

He took one of her hands and smiled. "You can go with him. It's all right, love. What do you think, Lord Dagget?"

Dragon's Tail

Mountains of Aramour

Terraquist

Elfin River

Greenwald

Pettian Valley

North Ascova

Hadrian's Place

Tarvis

Berat

South Ascova

Dalunas

Islands

Southern Strait

Penal Territory

"Just Tristan," he told Jorrin. "Hunting with magic is a sight to see, for sure."

Lady Ryhan grinned.

He said something that made her laugh, but Tristan's mind slipped away.

Aimil's dark eyes and her smiling face took command, and his companions' voices faded, giving his heart a pang. He hadn't seen her in so long. He missed his love more than he could put into words.

During his time with Varthan, he'd suppressed his feelings and memories in order to protect her. If Tristan closed his eyes, he could *see* her telling him she loved him and would wait for him, the night of the spring ball that felt like turns ago.

The night before he'd joined Varthan's shade compound.

Tristan had held her close, wishing he didn't have to rush into danger, at the time not knowing if he'd see her again, or see the day she'd finally become his wife.

He'd had to do the same with his family and the king, blocking his affection for them. Couldn't let Varthan have any suspicions about him.

Using memory charms and spells on the mages Varthan had in his service, he'd been able to convince them his alias, Dagonet, had been training as a shade for a number of turns. He'd had them report to Varthan how he'd steadily risen through the ranks. Soon, after only a matter of sevendays really, Tristan had been considered one of Varthan's elite.

Now it was over.

King Nathal had promised Tristan as soon as the rest of Varthan's followers were apprehended and dealt with, he'd be free of it all. He could get on with his life.

He'd been in the personal service of the king for the better part of the last turn, from the time Lord Ryhan had first suspected Varthan was really after the throne. He'd done several secret missions.

Right now, he wanted to go home.

Home was his rooms in Castle Rowan in Terraquist, not with his family in Berat. And *home* was Aimil, who also resided in Terraquist. She was a Senior King's Rider, like Lady Ryhan.

Being the third son, he wasn't the heir, so Berat held little for him. His father had always provided well for him, and he loved his family very much, but Tristan had been away from Berat more than he'd been at Castle Dagget, at least since he was about nine turns old.

He'd started honing his magic in Terraquist then, and a few turns after that, in Greenwald with Lord Falor Ryhan.

Lord Dugald Dagget had provided well for all five of his sons and daughters, and Tristan would always be grateful for his father. He'd made good marriage arrangements for them all, even for his two youngest sisters, who were only eight and ten currently.

Tristan had no qualms about marrying Aimil, and he thanked his father and the Blessed Spirit for her every day. He'd been told from the time he was very young that she would be his wife. He'd always accepted it as his duty as a son of Berat. He'd never thought much about love, but spending time with her was more than just pleasant. Even when they were small, he'd liked her, but he hadn't seen much of her until he'd settled in Terraquist, and made it a point to speak with her. Soon after, they spent as much time together as either of them could spare.

Exactly when he'd fallen in love with her was a mystery, but loving Aimil was as natural as breathing. Tristan couldn't wait to hold her again. It was safe to think about her, safe to love her, talk about her.

Jorrin had lifted his spirits.

"Lord Dagget?" Lady Ryhan called. From the concern in her tone, it likely wasn't the first time.

"Tristan," he corrected again.

She nodded, flashing a smile. "All right . . .Tristan. Are you coming?"

"No. I'll stay here as well."

Lady Ryhan frowned and looked back at Jorrin.

Was she going to pout? Tristan hid a grin.

"Suit yourselves, I suppose." She held up her bow. "I'll put this to use, then."

"Cera, stay close to my father, all right? I won't worry about you so much then."

She cocked her head to the side. "You're worried about me?"

"Not if you stay close to Braedon." Jorrin winked.

Tristan chuckled.

Jorrin glanced at him, wearing a lopsided grin.

"I can take care of myself," she said, taking step toward him.

"That's what I am afraid of," the half-elf said, tweaking her nose.

Tristan grinned as he watched a blush flare on her cheeks, up to her ears.

"Go catch me something to eat," Jorrin said.

She glared, and Tristan let out another laugh. "If you're going to be that way, I won't share with you."

Jorrin laughed and shook his head. "Did you hear that, Tristan? She said she wouldn't share her catch with us."

"Oh, no. Don't drag me down with you." He raised his palms in surrender.

"Coward," the man muttered.

Freezing, he stared at the half-elf, contentment washing over him, as if he'd known Jorrin Aldern for turns. Since when had Tristan felt that level of comfort with someone he'd just met?

"I never said I wouldn't share with *him*. Just *you*." Lady Ryhan winked at Tristan.

"Come on, love. That's not nice."

She shook her head. "Who said I was nice?"

Jorrin laughed again.

Tristan hadn't laughed in more months than he could count. More weight lifted from his shoulders. "Thank you, Lady Ryhan," he whispered.

She glanced at him, her brows drawing tight. "Call me Cera, Tristan. What're you thanking me for?"

He smiled and shook his head. Heat crept up his neck.

Jorrin shot him a meaningful look before turning back to Cera. "Have a good hunt, love." He kissed her knuckles and pulled her into his arms.

Tristan turned away when their mouths came together, but he didn't miss Jorrin whispering something in her ear afterward, or her answering nod.

"See you later, Jorrin, Tristan." Cera jogged over to where she'd left Jorrin's father when the king had made his call.

"Are you all right?" Jorrin asked.

Tristan looked into his blue eyes. The man's father was an empath; it'd make sense that Jorrin's magic was the same. He'd have to remember to build walls in his mind. "Aye. Thanks for asking."

"Anytime." He flashed a smile, but soon his eyes tracked Cera as she readied her horse, alongside the other gathering hunters.

"She's lovely."

"Yes, she is," Jorrin said, his eyes shining.

Tristan smiled, thinking of Aimil again.

Chapter Twenty-Seven

CERA DIDN'T WITHHOLD her gasp of pleasure as she sank into the large tub of hot water in the luxurious sleeping room. King Nathal's steward had put her in the vast guest wing at Castle Rowan, his palace in the capital city of Terraquist. The rooms were twice the size of her suite at home in Greenwald.

The scent of sweet flowers tickled her nose and she closed her eyes, resting her head against the edge of the tub.

"Is there anything else you need, Lady Ryhan?" the young maid asked.

Cera smiled as she looked up at her.

Petite, with dark hair and eyes, the girl was very pretty, and couldn't have been a day over fifteen turns. In a way, she reminded her of Kait, but she didn't let that sadden her.

It's over.

Varthan was dead, and her family could rest in peace.

"No, thank you . . ."

"Petra, my lady."

"Thank you, Petra, I'm fine."

"Shall I wash your hair?"

"No, I'll do it. You can go."

Trikser gave a soft wuff from where he lay by the hearth. A friendly fire warmed the room.

"If you insist, Lady Ryhan," Petra said, eyeing her bond warily.

Cera stifled a chuckle, lest she hurt Petra's feelings. "He won't hurt you."

The girl looked back, cheeks pink as she nodded. "The queen has given you a gown for the feast. I will leave it on your bed."

"Thank you. I'll call you when I'm through."

She maid curtsied, her striped uniform skirt billowing.

Desperation settled over Cera. She wanted to be alone. Half-wished for sleeping furs, a brisk night, and even the hard ground. Sleeping under the stars . . . Jorrin's arms around her.

Sighing as Petra finally took her leave, she could breathe again when the chamber shut door quietly.

Jorrin.

She wanted to remain with him, marry him and have him come back to Greenwald with her. The seriousness of that idea smacked her and a gasp fell from her lips.

Marriage?

She'd never given it much thought; it was the event that would happen *someday*, but now . . . Jorrin was the only man she wanted to call husband. Would he marry her?

Cera hadn't missed his expression of unease even before they had entered Castle Rowan. People had cheered the king's return as their group had ridden through the main courtyard. Her lover had sunk into his saddle even before they'd made it inside.

Hadn't he said he had no use for nobles? Did he love her enough to stay with her, now that she was back in her station? Before they'd defeated Varthan, she would've answered *yes*, but what now?

Had coming to the capital changed that? What if their time together faded into memories?

Cera's heart galloped and her eyes stung.

I can't lose Jorrin.

Trikser caught her painful thoughts and wuffed. He left the warmth of the hearth and came to the edge of the tub, hitting her hand with his long muzzle; a demand of comfort and affection.

Despite her thoughts, she laughed. "Well, Trik, I'll always have you, huh?"

Her wolf licked her hand, as if answering in the affirmative and she scratched behind his ear.

"Wretch," she teased when he groaned in pleasure and leaned into her touch.

Begging her bondmate's forgiveness with a final pat and scratch, she reached for the rose-scented soap Petra had left her, scrubbing her hair vigorously and smiling as she inhaled the pleasant aroma. It was good to feel clean again, and even *somewhat* all right to feel like a lady again. She'd never admit it aloud, though.

She exited her bath shortly, wrapping herself in the soft bathing sheet and padding over to the oversized four poster bed in the chamber.

Cera frowned at the gorgeous rust colored gown lying on the wide bed. She'd never been fond of lavish gowns or spending time at court. Even though she had grown up in a rich environment like Castle Rowan, she wasn't comfortable most of the time.

It was no surprise someone like Jorrin felt like a fish out of water in the palace.

Although her parents had been quite wealthy, she'd never had a gown quite as splendid as what lay before her now. Low-corseted bodice, intricate silver flowers stitched at every edge as well as along the hem. It was long, billowy and would flow when she walked. Made of the softest fabric she'd ever come into contact with.

Beautiful, but she didn't want to wear it.

Perhaps she should don her worn black breeches and torn brown leather jerkin for the feast. She'd have to find a new tunic to wear under it; hers was ruined. Cera had borrowed one from Avery for the ride to Terraquist, but Petra had taken it for laundering.

She touched the fabric of the dress, shaking her head. After a heavy sigh, she resigned herself to it. "Petra!" As much as she hated it, she'd need assistance to get dressed. She couldn't get into the petticoats or tighten the corset by herself. Groaning at the thought of tight lacings, Cera scrunched her nose. She hadn't worn a corset in turns.

"Yes, milady?"

"I'm ready to be trussed up," she muttered after pulling on undergarments. She donned the sheer chemise that'd been folded next to the gown.

"What was that? I didn't hear you, milady." The maid wore a frown.

"Oh, it was nothing. Will you help me dress?"

"Of course, milady." She hurried to her side.

Only *just* back in the world of the highborn, and she was already tired of *'Lady Ryhan,' 'my lady,'* and especially, *'milady'*.

"Where was Master Aldern placed?" Cera needed a distraction from the miseries of formality.

"The older or younger?"

"Well, both, I suppose."

"Young Lord Aldern is directly across the hall from you." Petra helped her into the restricting corset.

"Lord Aldern?" She threw the maid a look.

Does Petra know something I don't?

The girl averted her gaze, smile fading. She studied her shoes. "*Master* Aldern, I mean, milady. I was mistaken." But she still wouldn't meet her eyes, and Cera's instincts flared.

Is the king up to something?

"His father is in a chamber next to the elf wizard, down the hall from here, milady." Petra's words were rushed.

She stared, but the girl looked down again. She'd get nothing out of Petra. Cera would have to get to the bottom of things some other way. Making the young maid uncomfortable wasn't her aim, so she dropped it—for now. "Am I to be escorted into the hall?"

"I wasn't told, milady." Her slim shoulders relaxed, and she lifted her head, meeting Cera's eyes again.

"I can find my way down, I suppose." Glancing at Trikser, she frowned. He'd have to stay in her rooms. Sleeping by the fire should keep him content for a while, but her wolf would want to hunt later.

Swallowing a sigh, she mentally listed and relisted all the reasons she hated court. Even when she'd lived in Terraquist, at Rider Barracks, she'd avoided the castle as much as possible.

Unless summoned.

Or Aimil and Ansley—her two Senior Rider best friends—had forced her to some stupid ball.

"How shall I do your hair, milady?"

"I want it down."

Jorrin likes my hair down.

"I'll place flowers in the front, if you like," Petra said, smiling.

Cera nodded, wincing as the girl tugged the corset tighter. "Let's get it over with." Regret punched her the moment she saw her crestfallen expression. "Oh, it's not you. I promise. I don't like being a lady."

The young maid grinned. "But you look like one. Beautiful."

She glanced over herself in the mirror and gave a slight smile. The bodice was cut lower than she was used to, but the gown *was* gorgeous, highlighting her dark auburn hair and skin tone. Her breasts were high, but her cleavage was still modest enough. The corset hugged her sides and hinted at her hips more than a jerkin did. Even with legs hidden, her body looked fantastic.

Cera admired the silver embroidery. Roses had always been her favorite flower, but she was already uncomfortable.

Stifled.

"Thank you, Petra. I appreciate it. How about my hair?"

The girl nodded and she slipped into a chair in front of the guest room's oversized, gilded vanity.

With a sigh she couldn't quite hide, Cera handed her hairbrush over.

Overwhelmed.

Intimidated.

Out of place.

Just a few words of the words that popped into Jorrin's mind as he looked around.

How is this even happening?

He didn't belong here. How could he remain in this world? He'd never be comfortable. *Nothing* he'd ever wanted. Even standing in the corridor, the richness of his surroundings was daunting.

"Jorrin?"

Cera.

Something he wanted more than *anything.*

When he saw her, his breath caught. "You look beautiful." Heat engulfed his neck, searing its way up and across his face. He tried to convince himself to relax.

She blushed and smiled. Cera was wearing a rust-colored gown with prominent silver stitching that made her hair seem a richer shade of red. Her tresses fell in soft waves past her shoulders, free of all confines, save some small flowers woven in the front, framing her pretty face.

The corset hugged her torso, hinting at her delectable hips and pushing her breasts up just enough to make him growl.

She was still fashionably appropriate, but Jorrin would rip out the eyes of any man who decided to appreciate her body.

Cera is mine.

Gorgeous . . . more beautiful than he'd ever seen her before. A true lady.

Another reminder of her belonging here, where he didn't.

He sighed and tugged at the embroidered kit he'd been gifted to wear. He'd never in his life worn anything so finely made. The elaborate decorative stitching on the soft silver doublet was rust colored—he and Cera matched.

"Are you all right? I know this is overwhelming . . . Even for me . . ." Her gray eyes were full of concern. "I've not been to court often." She gestured helplessly to her gown.

"I'm fine." He smiled. Her worry for him washed over his magic, and he swallowed.

"You don't have to do this. I don't want you to feel uncomfortable." She looked down.

Stepping to her, Jorrin tilted her chin up so she'd meet his eyes. "You're here, are you not?"

Confusion clouded her expression. "Yes . . ."

"Then I am staying." He quieted any further protests by covering her mouth with a gentle kiss. "I love you."

"I love you, too."

"Besides, King Nathal summoned us."

She smiled. "I believe he *invited* us, as guests for a feast in *our* honor."

"I don't believe we really had a choice."

"Perhaps not." Cera shrugged. "As you know, he said he needs to speak to me."

"About Greenwald?"

"I guess so." She averted her gaze. "I don't think he'll force me to marry."

Panic, then jealousy, hit Jorrin squarely in the chest. He had to plant his feet so his powers wouldn't bowl him over. Since she had no male blood relatives, it was the king's place to decide such things for Cera, but he would *not* give her up, no matter what he had to do.

He wanted to marry her.

She'd given herself to him, given him her innocence. She was *his*. Nothing and no one could change that. But did she feel the same?

Cera loved him, but did she want to marry him?

He had no idea how to ask. He had nothing—no land, no title, and no coin. Just love for her. Would the king even consider a landless nobody of mixed blood for the daughter of one of his closest friends?

"Lady Ryhan? Master Aldern?" a male voice called.

Jorrin recognized the young knight who'd been at the king's side for the ride back to Terraquist.

"Sir Tegran, good evening," Cera said, taking his attention as she curtsied.

He shouldn't have been surprised at her show of manners. This was her world, after all. He bit back a groan.

"Leargan, my lady," the young knight corrected, smiling. "Good evening to you both."

Jealousy flared again, as she nodded and smiled sweetly at Sir Tegran.

"The king has asked me to escort you into the great hall, Lady Ryhan."

Cera threw a nervous glance at Jorrin and shook her head. "I assumed Master Aldern would do so, Leargan."

He looked smug, and Jorrin wanted to punch the look off his face.

"His Majesty would like to have a word with Master Aldern, milady." Leargan offered his arm.

"With me?" he croaked, then grimaced at his rough voice.

Leargan nodded.

Another knight appeared out of the shadows of the corridor. "I'll escort you, Master Aldern." The knight gestured for Jorrin to follow him.

He nodded, but looked at Cera. "See you in a while?"

She looked good on the arm of the handsome Leargan and Jorrin growled, unable to rid himself of the envy. He leaned in and kissed her cheek.

Cera smiled tenderly, and his heart flipped.

Leargan had the nerve to look amused, and he started to glare, but caught himself, repeating the order to mind his manners.

She loved *him*, not some stupid knight.

"Yes, see you in a bit." Cera nodded and squeezed his hand.

"This way," the other knight said as they fell into step together.

Jorrin didn't speak. He was sorely out of place, and had no idea how to make conversation with a knight, though the man didn't look much older than him.

He rapped lightly on a door about halfway down the wide corridor.

The king bellowed for them to enter.

"Master Aldern as requested, my liege." The knight bowed.

The king's personal ledger room. Butterflies stormed in the pit of his stomach.

"Aye, thank you, Willum," King Nathal said. The king was seated in an oversized, gold-inlaid, carved chair with a golden lion perched on the raised seatback.

Jorrin could've laughed at the irony of not noticing before. A lion was exactly what King Nathal reminded him of.

His desk was equally imposing and oversized. The furniture took up much of the small room, but perhaps considering the king's stature, the chair and desk really weren't all that oversized.

The knight named Willum bowed again, and slipped from the room, leaving Jorrin alone with the king.

He swallowed back a gulp, feeling like an errant child about to accept a harsh admonition.

"Come, come, Jorrin . . . may I call you Jorrin?"

Like I can say no to the king.

"Of course." He cringed. His voice had been little more than a squawk. He'd just given away his nervousness.

Dammit.

The king looked amused. "Have a seat, lad."

Lowering his frame into one of the two chairs in front of the king's desk, he forced a breath. Heat settled in his cheeks. Jorrin looked around the room, needing a distraction.

A large framed map of the Provinces dominated one wall, and the king's seal, also depicting a lion was on another. The seal was three dimensional, surrounded by a sword and shield and the blue flag of Terraquist. The lion looked like it might hop off the wall and devour him at any moment.

He skimmed bookshelves—most full to the brim—lining all four walls in the room. The king obviously liked to read. A learned man couldn't be all that bad, could he? He chided himself for being a coward and met the king's pale blue eyes.

It was obvious the man was waiting for him to acclimate before he began their conversation.

"You wanted to see me?" Jorrin grimaced at his wavering tone.

"Aye, lad." King Nathal intertwined his fingers and rested his hands on top of his desk. "I need to discuss a few things with you."

"Cera?"

One corner of the king's mouth lifted. "Aye, among others."

"I want to marry her," he blurted. His cheeks burned; his face had to be bright red.

"I thought, or I should say, I hoped as much."

"You did?" Jorrin croaked.

"Aye. I see how the lass looks at you. I wasn't going to force anything on her, but if she wishes to marry you, you have my blessing. Greenwald is hers, no matter what."

Blinking, he bit his lip to keep from gasping. Emotion rolled over him. No way could he have imagined King Nathal would approve of him for Cera. His temples throbbed with his storming pulse.

The king's smile was gentle. A smile like Braedon would flash, fatherly, and full of encouragement. Actually, the king's accent also reminded Jorrin of his father.

"I don't know what to say . . ."

"Well, for your bravery and assistance with the cause, I'm knighting you," King Nathal said.

He gasped, but the king didn't react.

"Your father, as well, young Lord Lenore, and Master Rowlin. Young Lucan, too, the bravest one of all of us. Last, but not least, young Lord Dagget, though honestly, I should've done so a turn or two ago with all he's done for me."

Jorrin sputtered.

The king chuckled and shook his head. "I've shocked you. If Cera agrees to marry you—and I'm sure she will—you'll be a duke, lad. The Duke of Greenwald."

"I couldn't . . . I don't . . . it's hers . . ."

His eyes softened considerably and once again he was reminded of his father. "Do you want the lass?"

"Aye, very much."

"Then that's what you focus on. After all, you have to get her to agree to marry you. She can be headstrong, you know." King Nathal winked.

Jorrin stared into his lap; his fingers laced together, knuckles white. He hadn't been born for running a Province. Had no idea what it entailed.

He wanted to marry Cera, *yes*. He loved her, but he wasn't a lord, a politician, or experienced in anything relevant to what the king was suggesting.

"Look, lad. If you marry Lady Ryhan, it's a win-win situation for me. I declared her the heir of Greenwald; no one will dispute that, no matter how the pompous old lords will complain. She loves you, so I don't feel bad about giving her to you. She'll be married, and you get a title. I'm going to give you the title regardless, Jorrin. You'll be 'Lord Aldern.' I'd rather award you Greenwald by marriage than some far-off tiny holding not worthy of being called a dukedom."

"I don't know what to say," he whispered.

"You're both young, so you'll not go back to Greenwald on your own. I'll send someone who knows how to run a Province." The king winked again. "And replace all of the staff Varthan killed."

Jorrin winced.

"Aye, I know it, lad," King Nathal whispered.

"That'll be a sad reminder of what she lost."

"She'll have you, lad," the king said. "*You* and your children are her future."

He managed a nod.

"I'm sad to see him go, but I'll send Leargan, too. To train your men and captain your personal guard." The king quirked an eyebrow when Jorrin growled aloud.

He composed himself, but when he made eye contact with the king, the big man chuckled.

Great. He can see right through me.

Jorrin cleared his throat. Squared his shoulders.

"Also, Lord Tristan Dagget has expressed the wish to accompany you to Greenwald and act as your second-in-command," King Nathal said.

"All of this has been decided? I'm the last one to know?" Should he be upset he was left in the dark?

The king gave him a long look. "It is what I wish for Greenwald. And you are not the *last* to know. Cera is. Blessed Spirit, I hope she forgives me." King Nathal looked chagrined.

Jorrin grinned. King or not, the man would be in hot water with his beloved.

"I needed to speak to you, before I announced your betrothal."

"Announce it? I haven't asked her yet." His stomach fluttered.

"Tonight, in the great hall." King Nathal's pale eyes bored into him.

Jorrin squirmed, the hard back of the chair biting into his shoulders. "Tonight . . ."

Will Cera say yes? What if she says no?

"If you announce it before I ask her, she'll be furious for not being consulted," he whispered.

"Aye, I know it," King Nathal said, laughter wrapped in his words.

His stomach did a back flip. "What if she thinks it's only for Greenwald . . . that I don't want her, but I want the Province . . . the wealth?" As soon as he voiced the thought, he pushed it away.

Cera knew him. She knew he'd never do such a thing, didn't she?

"Then I'll explain things to the stubborn lass," King Nathal said.

Jorrin looked him in the eye. "How long do I have?"

"About twenty minutes." The king laughed again.

"Twenty minutes?" He popped out of the chair so fast it screeched on the tile floor.

King Nathal laughed harder, but Jorrin didn't slow his retreat. He ran out of the king's ledger room, not pausing to worry about his lack of manners, either.

Jorrin had to get to Cera.

Now.

Chapter Twenty-eight

J ORRIN RACED THROUGH the corridors, not contrite at the looks of surprise and disapproval he received from several courtiers as he ran by them.

Twenty minutes? How could he convince Cera he wanted her to marry him in twenty minutes? He'd never kept his distaste for the noble class a secret, but would she think a knighthood and a title had changed his mind?

Not to mention the wealth of Greenwald.

Slowing, he forced a breath; didn't want to burst into the great hall of the king's palace. The giant double doors leading inside were open, a guard on either side.

They didn't react to his hasty stop as Jorrin entered the hall.

His heart pounded, and it wasn't from his run. He forced a few more breaths and surveyed the huge room.

The meal was not yet being served, as it was customary to wait for the king, but pleasant music drifted from the raised stage in the corner of the room. Four bards concentrated on their instruments while a fifth—the only woman of the group—added words to the melody with her sweet voice.

At the head table, on a dais higher than any he'd ever seen, the queen was already seated. Against tradition, the king and queen's two children were also at the table.

Prince Roblin was perhaps twelve or thirteen, and young Princess Mallyn was no older than nine or ten turns. Another testament to the fact that King Nathal was a good man. He adored his family.

Jorrin swallowed a gasp.

Cera was seated at the table with the queen, as were Avery and his parents, Tristan and his father, Lucan, and an obviously very uncomfortable Hadrian.

He didn't see his own father, but didn't expect Braedon to be very far behind. The empty seat next to the elf wizard was no doubt for him.

The queen herself caught his eye as he jogged up the several steps onto the dais. He fell into a polite bow as she smiled and inclined her head.

She was a very beautiful woman, hair done in an elaborate fashion, woven in and out of the golden jewel-encrusted crown atop her head. It was about the whitest blonde color he'd ever seen. Her eyes were a very dark brown, and rather stunning. He'd half expected them to be blue. She was definitely King Nathal's lioness. And *she* knew who he was.

Nerves fluttered in Jorrin's stomach.

"Good evening, Lord Aldern," Queen Morghyn said, with a wide smile.

Cera looked at him sharply, as did Avery.

Neither Lord and Lady Lenore, nor Tristan and his father, looked surprised. As a matter of fact, the elder Lord Dagget looked rather pleased. Avery's parents smiled at Jorrin.

That should be flattering, shouldn't it? Cera's family approved of him, at least.

Hadrian didn't look up; he appeared to be brooding.

Lucan didn't show a reaction, either. Eyes as wide as saucers, he looked stunned to be where he was, a sentiment Jorrin was quite familiar with.

"Good evening, your Grace." Jorrin flashed a tight smile, wanting desperately to grab Cera's hand and drag her from the dais. He needed to speak to her *now*, especially since the queen had inadvertently spoiled a part of the king's surprise announcement.

She'd know the queen would never make the mistake of calling him by the wrong honorific.

"Lady Ryhan," He begged her with his eyes. "Will you accompany me for a moment?"

"Of course, *Lord* Aldern," Cera said through clenched teeth. She rose from her chair with grace, but clutched his outstretched arm with a bit too much force.

He winced as her nails bit his skin.

When they reached an empty sitting room in the nearest corridor, she whirled on him. "What did the king want to tell you, Jorrin?"

Neither of them sank into the lavish chairs. Or the couch. Or the padded seat up against the bay windows.

"Nothing bad, love." He had to speak fast. "Why are you angry?"

"I think King Nathal is playing games." Cera tapped her foot. "I don't like to be the butt of his jests."

"There are no jests." Jorrin wanted to ask her to marry him before he told her about Greenwald . . . or should he do it the other way around? "I love you, Ceralda Ryhan," he blurted.

Her face softened and she took a breath. "I love you, too, but . . ."

He stopped her from finishing her statement by tugging her into his arms and kissing her. It was probably the coward's way out, but she'd respond to his kiss and touch.

"Somehow, I don't think this is what the king wanted to discuss with you," Cera whispered against his lips, placing a hand on his chest and gently pushing him away just when he was getting lost in the movement of their lips.

Drat.

She wouldn't be distracted so easily.

He quirked a half-smile. "Actually . . ."

Cera gave him a long look.

Sighing, Jorrin dragged a hand through his hair.

"What are you so nervous about?"

"Nervous?" He met her eyes. "I'm not nervous . . ."

Her expression shouted that she'd seen the lie for what it was. "Just tell me what's going on. Why did the queen call you, 'lord'?"

"That's the proper way to address a duke." Jorrin cringed. *Dammit*, he'd wanted to explain things to her.

Why did you blurt it out?

"Duke?" Cera asked, her eyes wide, but he took a deep breath when his magic sensed curiosity, not disgust or anger. "He made you a duke?"

He couldn't find his voice, so he nodded.

"Of what lands?"

He looked down, needing a moment to grasp for words. Jorrin had to say it the right way, but he'd taken too much time to compose himself.

Color drained from Cera's face. "Greenwald . . ."

His stomach roiled, heart pounding so hard it threatened to exit his chest. "Cera . . ."

She couldn't really be looking at him that way, could she? As if he had betrayed her.

No.

"No." Her denial was whispered.

Was it for him or what his silence had confirmed? *Probably both.*

Jorrin stepped forward, intending to pull her into his arms, but she placed her palm up, glaring. He froze in place. "Will you listen to me?"

"I can't believe he's doing this to me," she ranted, pacing. She ignored his urgent plea. "After everything . . . he'd give it away? My home . . . *my* Province . . ."

He winced.

Cera hadn't even considered him, she just wanted Greenwald.

His heart sank. He took a step back when he felt her rage. His limbs tingled and burned from it. "He's going to announce our betrothal tonight."

Great, blurting the wrong words seems to be my only talent this evening.

"Betrothal?"

"Yes, Cera. The king wants us to wed." Jorrin cringed. *That* had come out all wrong.

Her expression didn't soften at all. She stared, wide-eyed.

"No, that's not it. *I* want us to get married. I love you, will you marry me?"

Cera scowled.

Jorrin's heart ripped in two. He'd screwed everything up. Nothing was going as planned.

The *king's* plan. This was all King Nathal's fault.

He growled. The man had put him on the spot, but *he* wasn't there to see it through. Jorrin was doing a horrible job of it.

"So, I'm supposed to get *married* to retain something that should have been *mine* in the first place?"

He blanched. "No . . ." He couldn't tell her Greenwald was hers either way. If she knew, she'd never marry him. And *that* hurt.

"I thought you were different, Jorrin." Her voice was thick with hurt.

"What's that supposed to mean?" Jorrin barked, suddenly angry. His magic throbbed, making his head spin. They were both surrounded by angry red auras.

Cera gaped as the color drained from her face, and her shoulders slumped. Horror flashed across her gorgeous steel eyes. "Is that why you made love to me?"

Jorrin blinked and his stomach tightened. Bile rose in his throat.

"Did you tell him? So he would make us get married?" She appeared to recover, and made tight fists. Glared. Her chest heaved, as if she'd sucked in a great gulp of air. Cera broke their eye contact.

"Dammit, Cera. What do you think of me?" He clenched his fists at his sides, his blunt fingernails biting into his palms. He stared, but she wouldn't look at him. Jorrin wanted to grab her by the arms and shake her until she'd listen to him. Wanted to take it all back and tell her when he could get the words straight in his head. Hold her and wipe the hurt look off of her face.

She was wrong, *all wrong,* but he couldn't find his voice to tell her so. She'd accused him of using her in a way Jorrin couldn't even fathom. Cera ruined the memory of what'd happened between them. Their lovemaking had been pure and sweet and so *right.*

Now she'd tarnished it with her words.

Jorrin hurt more than he'd ever hurt before.

"I don't know *what* to think of you," she bit out.

Air rushed from his lungs, and he spread his arms wide. "This came out all wrong. It isn't at all what I wanted to say to you." He met her eyes and his heart clenched when he saw the tears on her cheeks. He stepped forward again, and tried to take her into his arms, but she put both hands on his chest and shoved him hard. He blinked and looked away, barely warding off his own threatening tears.

"Don't touch me," Cera ordered. So severe, as if silently reminding him of her station. As if touching her was a crime because he was not nobility.

The blood drained from Jorrin's face. Jaw clenched, he reached for anger to cover some hurt. "The king will announce his intentions, even if you refuse me. He won't allow you to do so. He said it's what he wants for Greenwald." His tone was every bit as harsh as hers had been.

King Nathal had told him he wouldn't force her, but Cera didn't need to know that.

She stared, silent and wide-eyed.

"I hate you," Cera said. She didn't pause when his expression was more crestfallen than it had been when she'd told him not to touch her. Her chest constricted so tightly every breath was a dagger cutting into her. Her heart had been torn out and stomped on.

How could Jorrin betray her?

I…need to…go.

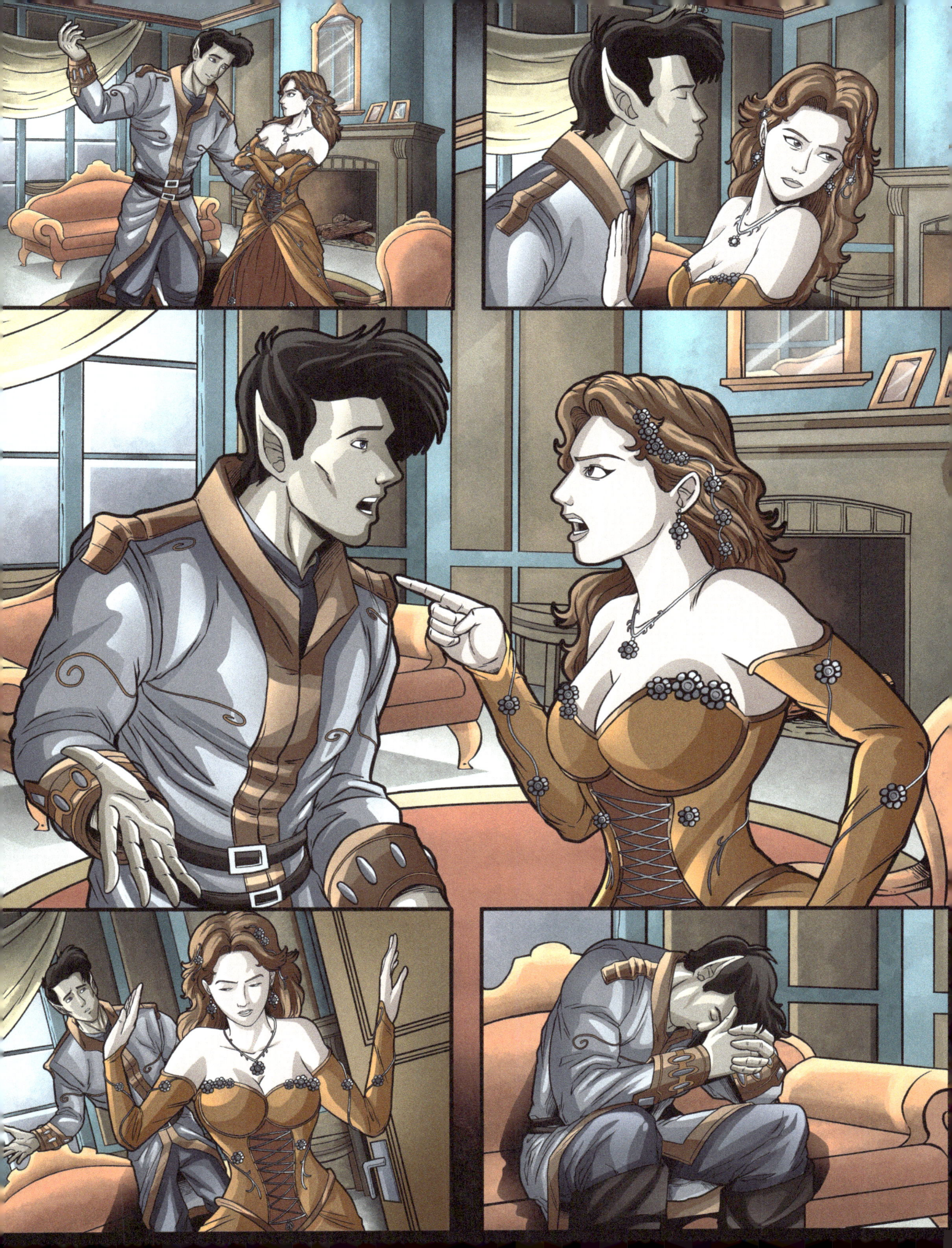

She fled, running back into the great hall, wiping tears away.

He'd never liked the noble class, but now Jorrin was a duke? And the Duke of Greenwald? *Her* Greenwald. The Province her parents died for. Guilt and pain hit her in waves.

Crushing her eyes shut, Cera regretted the words she'd flung at him. She didn't hate him, she could *never* hate him.

She loved him so much it hurt.

She'd shared more with him than anyone else, ever. Given herself to him. She'd wanted to throw her arms around him and comfort him from the words she'd inflicted the moment they'd exited her mouth. Cera sucked in a breath, clenching her fists at her sides. She was disgusted with her lack of control; he'd betrayed her, for Blessed Spirit's sake.

Ordering her heart to stop pounding, she smoothed her hands down her gown. She'd had many compliments on it since Leargan had brought her into the great hall, including one from Queen Morghyn herself.

Leargan rose when she neared the table designated for the royal family's personal guard, just below the dais.

The other knights at the table hastily did the same, and Cera forced a smile and inclined her head. Her cheeks warmed.

"My lady." Leargan bowed. His dark eyes locked onto her face, his expression obviously worried.

She made her smile wider and suppressed the urge to wipe her cheeks again. *Dammit. He can tell I was crying.* Cera turned away after inclining her head, and went back to the dais. She took several deep breaths, mounting the stairs slowly.

Jorrin asked me to marry him.

Her heart should be elated. Why was she so hurt? She wanted to marry him, didn't she?

Having him made into the Duke of Greenwald made things easier for them, didn't it? She wouldn't have to worry about him being uncomfortable, out of place.

No.

Jorrin had betrayed her. He didn't even *want* to marry her; he'd only asked her while doing the king's bidding. King Nathal . . . he'd betrayed her as much as Jorrin had.

They'd teamed up to conspire against her. He wanted her to marry—no, was *ordering* her to marry without even asking her if she wanted Jorrin? That hurt.

It was his right, not even Uncle Everett could step in, but it wasn't fair. Her father would never have made her choose a man she didn't want. Grief threatened to bowl her over when she thought about her father.

He wouldn't have forced her, but wait—didn't she want Jorrin? Cera cursed the voice that screamed she wanted him very much.

"Are you all right?" Avery asked as she took the seat beside him.

The empty chair on her other side was meant for Jorrin, but she was in no hurry to have him join the table. She squeezed her eyes shut, not realizing she'd done so until her cousin's expression was even more concerned than it had been.

He was looking expectantly when their gazes met.

No, I'm not all right.

Avery blinked.

Had she accidentally thought-sent?

"Yes, I'm fine," Cera said finally.

He studied her for a moment, but said nothing.

Glancing down the table, Cera noticed her uncle deep in discussion with Lord Dagget. Seated next to him, Tristan caught her eye.

She trembled and fought tears.

He stared, his hazel eyes warm and concerned. Asking questions she wouldn't answer. Tristan Dagget could see right through her.

She averted her gaze, biting her lip as the great hall wavered, suddenly blurry. Refused to look back at Tristan, but she could still feel his eyes on her. Cera didn't bother trying to smile, he wouldn't believe it anyway.

"Something's wrong, Cera. Tell me," Avery urged.

She met his gray eyes and shook her head. "I'm fine, cousin." She offered a wobbly smile.

He said nothing. Finally, Avery nodded.

Cera thanked him silently for not pushing anymore.

What the hell am I supposed to do now?

She turned to Hadrian, seated on the other side of Jorrin's empty chair, and struck up a conversation.

The elf wizard flashed a grateful smile.

It would have to be enough to distract her from *him* and her torrid emotions.

Chapter Twenty-Nine

CERA HAD RUN away from him.
What a disaster.
Jorrin blinked when his eyes blurred with tears. "That went well," he whispered sarcastically. How could he convince her Greenwald had nothing to do with the reason he wanted her? Did she think he was lying about loving her?

She'd believed him all this time. Well, King Nathal had said he'd fix it if it went wrong. His heart lifted a little.
Perhaps all isn't lost.
However, the king would still announce the betrothal that evening, and it'd only serve to further infuriate Cera. King Nathal would have no idea she'd refused him . . . *and* basically accused him of being a power-hungry monster.

Jorrin squeezed his eyes shut against the pain and groaned.
The king would *have* to help him. Jorrin had told her part of the truth. King Nathal *did* want their marriage for Greenwald.
I can't lose her.
"Jorrin?" A lilting female voice with a distinct Aramourian accent pulled him from his tormented thoughts.

A very familiar voice that warmed his heart. *No . . . it can't be . . .*

He slowly turned.
His father approached with a very diminutive woman on his arm, and a brilliant smile on his face.

Jorrin had tears on his cheeks and wasn't ashamed one bit. "Mother!" Closing the distance between them, he swept her into his arms and swung her around.

His mother wrapped her arms around him and laughed.
He shut his eyes and set her to her feet.
She clung to him in a fierce hug.

After the interaction with Cera, he *needed* his mother. The concept hadn't crossed his mind since he'd considered himself grown, but it was true nonetheless. Jorrin squeezed her tight.

Braedon chuckled.

The ache in his chest eased a little, despite the fact he still burned for Cera. Unless things were righted, *that* wouldn't change. "But how . . . ?" he asked, looking from parent to parent.

"A gift from the king." His father's voice was thick.

Jorrin grinned and hugged his father.

Braedon's arms shot around him, and he felt his father's pleasure and shock that he'd reached out to him.

His magic tingled, and his heart skipped. Clearing his throat, he glanced down at his mother, taking her slender hand in his. "I'm so glad to see you. I've missed you." He looked into eyes that mirrored his own.

"Oh, love, I have missed you, too," Vanora said.

He made eye contact with his father, who looked close to tears. Jorrin smiled and gripped his father's forearm.

Braedon nodded his thanks.

He couldn't imagine how it truly was for his father with his extensive empathic magic. Every emotion would hit him full force, including Braedon's own feelings. Jorrin didn't think he could deal with intense emotions being thrown at him all the time, whether he wanted them or not. The amount of empathic magic he had was bad enough, and nowhere near as strong as Braedon's.

Seeing his parents standing side by side should have been a shock. Something he'd never seen, but it wasn't odd at all.

It was *right.*

His mother loved his father as she always had, as if no time had passed. From the look on Braedon's face—as well as what Jorrin's powers told him—the feeling was mutual. His heart didn't know whether to ache with envy or burst with pride.

His parents gazed at each other, and at that moment they were oblivious of his presence.

Cera. She looked at him like that, or she *used* to.

Jorrin's chest constricted. He crushed his eyes shut again, only to find his father staring at him when he met his amber gaze.

"What happened with Cera?"

He looked down. "Nothing, Da." When he glanced at his mother, she also looked concerned.

Vanora was a bit of an oddity among elves; she had no magic, but she had excellent intuition and could definitely tell when her only child wasn't being honest.

Recalling all the times he'd gotten a tanning as a child, Jorrin bit back a groan. He'd never been able to lie to his mother and get away with it.

"Love?" she prompted.

"Jorrin . . ." Braedon started at the same time, voice and expression concerned.

"We can discuss it later. Mother's here . . . it's cause for celebration." He plastered on a smile that didn't seem to fool either of his parents.

Braedon gripped his arm and squeezed in comfort, and Jorrin almost lost his control when he saw the emotion in his father's eyes. He genuinely hurt *for* him, and not only because of empathic magic.

"Let's go into the great hall. We're to be seated on the dais with the king and queen." His words quaked and he cursed them.

"Aye, I was informed," his father said.

He sighed, ordering his emotions to calm. His father was going to leave it alone for now, and he was grateful.

"I am very anxious to see Hadrian," Vanora admitted, fidgeting at Braedon's side.

"I'm sure he'll be glad to see you, Mother."

As they entered the great hall, all eyes were on Jorrin and his parents. A hush fell over the crowd as they neared the dais, most likely in reaction to his beautiful mother, who didn't look a turn over twenty, though she was actually closer to sixty.

Elves lived much longer than humans, and appeared to age more slowly. To everyone in the room, Vanora probably looked much too young to be his mother. She probably also looked too young to be on the arm of a man who was actually twenty turns her junior.

Aramour was about the only place they *didn't* get stares. Elfin/human pairings were quite common.

A distinct hush fell over the crowd of courtiers, knights, lords and ladies.

Cera looked up from her conversation with Hadrian, which had actually been successfully distracting her from Jorrin. She gasped.

The man she was trying to forget walked toward the dais, but he wasn't alone. His father was with him, as well as the most beautiful creature she'd ever seen.

The elf maiden had to be Jorrin's mother, but it was hard to believe. She didn't look much older than Cera herself.

"Vanora," Hadrian breathed, stumbling to his feet.

She tried not to stare. It was a wonder, seeing her stand between the two tall men when she was so diminutive. Jorrin's mother couldn't be much past four feet tall, but she was probably still taller than Hadrian. Perhaps the wizard was considered short—for an elf.

She held herself regally, her beauty ethereal. Her flaxen hair fell past her waist in long luxuriant waves, framing her face and small body like a glowing aura. Her tapered ears were long—much longer than her son's—and added to her elegance. Her intricate gown was a silvery blue color and as she walked, it flowed, making it seem like she was floating beside Braedon.

There was absolutely no surprise why she was inadvertently mesmerizing the lords and knights alike, even the courtiers of the King's Court.

Were all female elves as beautiful as Jorrin's mother, or was she unusual? If that kind of beauty was ordinary amongst their kind, why had he even looked at *her* in the first place?

Cera couldn't hold a candle to Vanora Aldern.

The way Braedon and Vanora were looking at each other made her heart ache. She and Jorrin had looked at each other that way—*before*. Before he'd decided to crush her. And now she'd have to endure sitting next to him all evening.

Jorrin and his parents bowed collectively to the queen, who smiled and bid them to be seated. Even Queen Morghyn looked entranced as she regarded at Vanora. Ironic, because the queen herself was widely renown for her beauty.

Hadrian and Vanora embraced and spoke fast in Aramourian.

Could Jorrin and Braedon even follow the conversation?

Braedon looked amused, and Jorrin appeared indifferent as he slipped onto the seat next to her, saying nothing. He didn't even look at her.

She clamped her eyes shut, berating herself for caring.

"Mother, this is Lady Ceralda Ryhan," he said, his expression implacable.

That expression hurt as well, but Cera tried to look unaffected and be appropriately polite as she met his mother.

"Lo—Lady Ryhan, this is my mother, Vanora Aldern." He'd been about to call her 'love,' but had stopped himself.

She wanted to close her eyes and keep them closed. Tears threatened. Was everything between them all gone? If so, who exactly was at fault?

Vanora was even more intimidating up close, her beauty completely exquisite. She smiled sweetly and took Cera's hands in hers. "It's so nice to meet you. My husband has told me much about you. I'm so glad you've found my Jorrin." Her accent was thick like Hadrian's, and heavenly, just as Cera imagined it would sound. The warm smile on her shapely lips made her eyes burn even more.

Decorum. Manners. You can do this, Cera. You were born a lady, after all. Blessed Spirit, her mother would laugh if she'd heard that. She'd tried to make Cera into a *proper* lady for turns.

"Yes, so am I." Still the truth, despite everything. She inadvertently glimpsed Jorrin and tried for a smile, but it hurt too much. She forced her lips into a curve she hoped was convincing enough when she met his mother's eyes. Eyes so startlingly like his; it was like looking at him.

Braedon gave her a sharp look. He'd not been fooled.

Another hush fell over the crowd as King Nathal entered the great hall, trailed by a few knights, and heading straight for the dais.

His arrival gave her the perfect excuse to turn away from Braedon's searching gaze.

The king kissed the queen and his daughter each on the cheek, then ruffled his son's hair before taking his seat.

Cera smiled at his tenderness, even though she was disgusted with him. She had to swallow back a glare.

King Nathal addressed everyone warmly, and servants started to pour into the great hall with well-laden trays.

What a night this was proving to be. How the hell was she going to get through it?

Jorrin didn't talk to her at all.

She was tense, perched on the edge of her chair the whole meal. Didn't have much of an appetite, though she forced food into her mouth without tasting it, despite her growling stomach. Breakfast had been very early that morning, so she couldn't forgo what was offered.

When most of the hall had finished eating, King Nathal stood and cleared his throat. He'd definitely announce their betrothal if he'd told Jorrin he was planning to.

She groaned. Couldn't stand and shout a denial, but she had every intention of seeing the king privately to give him her refusal.

He went through his announcements quickly, publicly knighting Braedon, Jorrin, Tristan, Lucan, Avery, and Hadrian—who looked so uncomfortable it was a wonder if the elf wizard even considered it an honor.

Cera was overjoyed for all of them, especially Lucan and Avery. Both had cheeks the brightest shade of red she'd ever seen, but she mustered a tease and a hug for each male, genuinely proud of her cousin and the boy who'd saved them all.

Congratulations were given freely by many other knights in the hall, and people started moving around, migrating to the dance floor.

King Nathal said nothing of Jorrin's new title or a betrothal.

Did Jorrin lie to me?

She turned to answer a question Vanora asked just as the dratted king cleared his throat again. Cera glanced up, and his height was even more impressive from her seated position. She found him looking directly at her. Shifting in the chair, she swallowed her nerves.

Cera inclined her head and tried to keep her face a mask of pleasantness, but she was furious. Anger was good; it covered some of the pain in her chest.

"Please stand, Lady Ryhan," King Nathal said.

Was that amusement in his tone?

She narrowed her eyes, couldn't help it. "Yes, your Majesty?"

The king gave her a look that told her he knew she was aware of *exactly* what.

Scrambling to her feet, she planted her arms at her sides.

Jorrin stood when asked, squaring his shoulders and tugging his sliver doublet in place.

Cera tried not to watch him out of the corner of her eye. She ordered her gaze forward, scanning the expectant people in the great hall and ignoring the fluttering of her stomach, and the part of her that was happy the king would declare them betrothed.

Jorrin had betrayed her.

I don't want this. She didn't bother answering the voice in the back of her head that called her a liar.

King Nathal announced Jorrin's new title first and had to wait until the resounding cheers died down so he could continue.

Jorrin shifted his weight from foot to foot, and she had to stop herself from grabbing his hand. Reaching out to comfort him.

When the king proclaimed their betrothal, there was a moment of silence in the vast room. Glances were exchanged. Questions were visible in eyes.

She wanted to demand if there was a problem, but bit her tongue and remembered the hurt hovering agreed with the people who thought this betrothal was unusual. At one time, just hours ago, she would've told them all to go to hell.

Heat crept up her neck, scorching her cheeks. When Cera glanced at Jorrin, his expression was once again hard; unreadable. Somehow that crushed her all over again.

Queen Morghyn clapped her hands, everyone cheered. The whole head table started to speak at once, everyone embracing her, including Lord Dagget, Tristan's father. It was an awkward side hug, which would've amused her at any other time.

Congratulations ran rampant, and she plastered on a smile. She only glanced at *him* a few times, but he was also in the midst of being hugged and saluted. She failed to catch his eye. Not that she wanted to, anyway.

"Your mother would be so proud of you," Aunt Em said as she held her.

Her aunt hugged her the longest, and Cera couldn't hold back tears. Tears that were misinterpreted.

Avery hugged her next, but by the look he'd given her, he'd figured out something wasn't quite right. For the time being, her cousin held his tongue and for that, she was grateful.

When Braedon enfolded her in an embrace, it was one of comfort, not congratulations, and Cera squeezed her eyes shut against his shoulder. She didn't want to find comfort in Jorrin's father's arms. She didn't want him to know what was wrong.

Stupid empathic magic.

"Whatever is wrong can be mended," he whispered in her ear.

She shook her head when their eyes met, but couldn't muster a denial.

His smile was gentle, an obvious disagreement, but Braedon said nothing further.

Cera had no desire to stay for the dancing, or any other lengthy celebration, even though getting drunk had some appeal. Unladylike, but tempting. She excused herself, feigning fatigue from the journey to Terraquist.

The king nodded, allowing her dismissal, but she had a feeling he'd seen right through her. She bid her family and friends goodnight and left the dais in search of Leargan.

Cera found him with a small group of other young knights and asked him to escort her back to her assigned chambers.

The knight raised a dark eyebrow, but didn't ask why she wasn't being escorted by her newly betrothed. Instead, he offered his arm and she took it, silently grateful.

A gaze burned, and she glanced instinctively toward Jorrin. He was staring; fists clenched at his sides, knuckles white, but made no move to come to her.

"Ready, my lady?" Leargan smiled.

She could tell he was curious, but he wouldn't ask. Cera was grateful for his decorum. "Oh yes, thank you."

They walked down the corridor in silence, and for that she was also appreciative. When they arrived outside her rooms, she gave Leargan a genuine smile.

"Thank you, Leargan. I appreciate it."

"My pleasure, my lady," the knight said, with a small bow. "I look forward to getting to know you, if it's not too bold of me to say, Lady Ryhan."

"Meaning?"

Sir Leargan Tegran was very handsome. Tall, dark shoulder length hair, eyes like pools of midnight and the natural golden skin of an Ascovan, but her heart was in no shape to be courted. Not to mention their difference in station.

Cera winced.

Jorrin.

"The king didn't tell you?" Leargan asked. "I'm to captain your personal guard and train your men."

"There are a *few* things the king neglected to tell me," she snapped, then flushed when the knight's eyes widened. She reached for her manners. "Wonderful news, Leargan. Thank you. I look forward to it. Greenwald needs a strong leader."

"I'm sure with Lords Aldern and Dagget, along with yourself, Greenwald will have all it needs." He flashed a smile.

Tears hovered, and Cera could only nod. "Thank you for escorting me. Goodnight," she croaked, slipping into her room and shutting the door just short of a slam.

She hadn't even waited for his answer.

Cera couldn't hold back her sobs. She ran to the bed and threw herself down, burying her face in the pillows.

Trikser leapt up beside her and whimpered, nudging her shoulder, then her side when she didn't respond.

Looking up at her wolf, she wrapped her arms around him as he lay down and cuddled against her.

"Oh, Trik, everything's ruined."

Her bondmate whimpered and licked her face.

She couldn't even smile.

Chapter Thirty

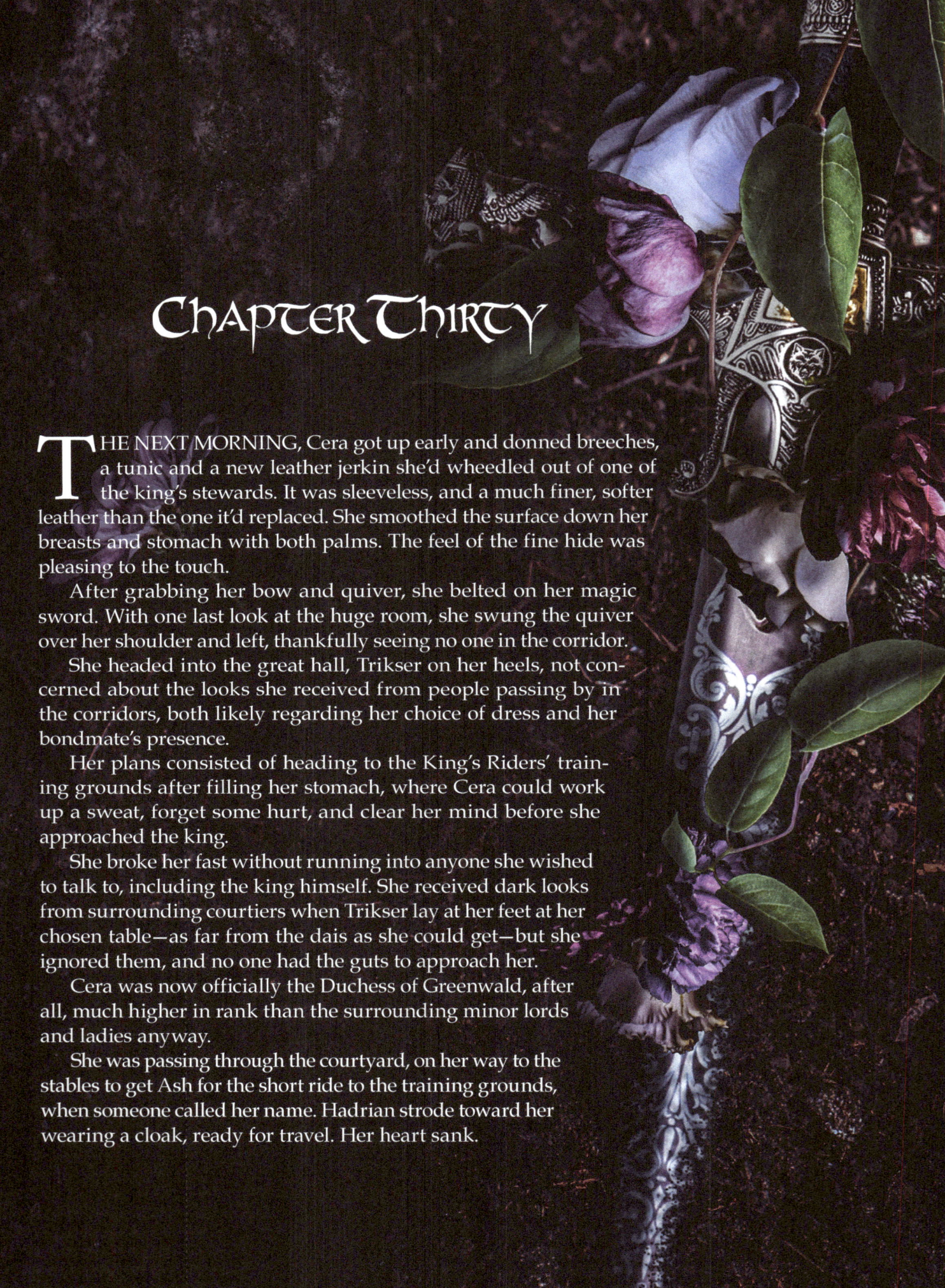

THE NEXT MORNING, Cera got up early and donned breeches, a tunic and a new leather jerkin she'd wheedled out of one of the king's stewards. It was sleeveless, and a much finer, softer leather than the one it'd replaced. She smoothed the surface down her breasts and stomach with both palms. The feel of the fine hide was pleasing to the touch.

After grabbing her bow and quiver, she belted on her magic sword. With one last look at the huge room, she swung the quiver over her shoulder and left, thankfully seeing no one in the corridor.

She headed into the great hall, Trikser on her heels, not concerned about the looks she received from people passing by in the corridors, both likely regarding her choice of dress and her bondmate's presence.

Her plans consisted of heading to the King's Riders' training grounds after filling her stomach, where Cera could work up a sweat, forget some hurt, and clear her mind before she approached the king.

She broke her fast without running into anyone she wished to talk to, including the king himself. She received dark looks from surrounding courtiers when Trikser lay at her feet at her chosen table—as far from the dais as she could get—but she ignored them, and no one had the guts to approach her.

Cera was now officially the Duchess of Greenwald, after all, much higher in rank than the surrounding minor lords and ladies anyway.

She was passing through the courtyard, on her way to the stables to get Ash for the short ride to the training grounds, when someone called her name. Hadrian strode toward her wearing a cloak, ready for travel. Her heart sank.

"Ah, lass. I've been looking for you all over." His pointed ebony hat was slammed over his unruly white hair, obscuring his face.

"Hadrian . . . you're leaving?" Her voice choked.

"Aye, lass. I don't belong here. Lord Dagget and his men are heading back to Berat, and they've said I can ride with them. It's time." The elf wizard smiled warmly and she met his crystal blue eyes.

A lump rose in her throat as his face started to blur. "Hadrian . . ."

"Hush, lass. It's for the best. You know where I live. Come visit me." His tone was gruff, but the corners of his mouth tugged upward.

Cera forced her mouth to echo the sentiment, since she was unable to form words. Before he could protest, she crushed him in a hug.

Hadrian returned her squeeze and chuckled when she released him.

Trikser wuffed and wagged his tail, insistent on getting the wizard's attention as well.

The elf gave her wolf a scratch behind the ears and a pat on the head that seemed to satisfy them both.

"Thank you . . . for all you've done for me." A single tear crept down her cheek.

Hadrian shifted in his boots, saying nothing, but gave her a curt nod.

"Have you seen Vanora and Braedon . . . and Jorrin?" It hurt to say his name.

"Aye, I've said my goodbyes, you were the last. I'm glad I found you."

The pounding of hooves echoed throughout the courtyard.

Tristan's father, Lord Dugald Dagget, and his men rode in, glancing in their direction. They waited for Hadrian, one of the knights holding Winthrop's reins.

Cera exchanged one last look with the elf wizard and swallowed against the lump in her throat.

"Looks like it's time. I don't want to keep them waiting," Hadrian said.

Forcing a nod, she walked the elf to Winthrop's side and watched him mount. Her stomach did a back flip, afraid she'd never see him again, but she pushed the feeling away.

Hadrian would be in his cottage any time she needed him. Like he'd said, she knew where he lived. She *would* visit.

"Good morning, Lady Ryhan," Lord Dagget said, bowing from his saddle.

Cera smiled at Tristan's father and inclined her head. "Lord Dagget. Safe travels," she said as pleasantly as she could manage.

The duke was dressed grandly, wearing crisp deep brown leathers with a bright green tunic and doublet made of shimmery fabric. No armor, but his saddle displayed the embroidered seal of Berat; a large brown bear surrounded by lush forests, depicting what his Province was known for. The finest lumber came from all over Berat.

"Thank you, my lady." He smiled warmly. His hazel eyes and sable hair were the exact shade of Tristan's—though his son's hair was much shorter. Despite the gray at the temples, he was a handsome man.

"Cera, take care of Jorrin, he's a good lad," Hadrian said, giving her a long look that told her he was aware all was not well.

Hearing his name made her wince, and she couldn't stop the tears on her cheeks, nor did she have the courage to speak. She nodded.

That seemed to satisfy the elf wizard.

She watched him ride away with the group of men, sadness threatening to overwhelm her not only because of her shattered heart. But sleeping on things hadn't changed her mind about Jorrin—he'd betrayed her—but that didn't mean it hurt any less.

Cera was fighting to function, instead of collapsing into a sobbing ball. Her body trembled and she wiped tears away, shaking her head.

I'm stronger than this.

Squaring her shoulders, she stood taller.

Trikser whimpered and nudged her hand. He wagged his tail, but all she could do was sigh.

Resuming her original course to the stables, she asked a young stable boy to ready Ash for her, pacing as she waited for him to be brought out.

"Your stallion, milady." The boy smiled as he held his hand out with Ash's reins.

He nodded before retreating into the stable after she'd thanked him.

She greeted her horse with a smile. Cera rested her forehead against his, closing her eyes, yearning for simplicity . . . to go back to a time when she was younger and free of responsibility.

Ash whinnied and lipped her hand.

Cera stroked his nose and gave him an affectionate rub along his strong jowls. "I've missed you, Ash." She smoothed her hand along his soft neck.

He nickered as if he agreed, and she climbed up in the saddle, kicking him into an easy trot.

Trikser wasn't far behind.

The King's Riders' Headquarters stood to the left of the open fields of the training grounds, not far from the main stables, and was bustling with normal activity that brought back memories.

Nostalgia hit as Cera rode in and remembered all the times she'd returned from a run. She'd spent most of the last seven turns in Terraquist here at the Riders' Barracks, and not in Greenwald with her family.

Swallowing hard, she ignored that line of thought. Regret wouldn't bring them back.

A group of Riders, their ranks announced by the three different colors they wore, was exiting the small dining hall in the center of the headquarters building. The newest Riders, who were equivalent to a page, wore a bright red cloak. The next ranking, like that of a squire, wore brown.

Each rank, including Senior Riders, had Tests they had to succeed in before they could move on. The ranks affectionately—or not so affectionate at times—were referred to as "Reds" and "Browns."

More memories of her time here came flooding back.

"Cera," one of them shouted.

She grinned, recognizing an old friend.

The group swarmed her and everyone demanded her attention at once.

Forcing out a breath, she greeted everyone she knew and met several she did not.

Normal.

She felt better than she had in days. Coming here had been a fantastic idea.

Here she wasn't *'Lady Ryhan'* or *'milady'*. Here she was Cera, Senior King's Rider. A leader, yes, but with some freedom. People didn't look to her because of who she was born to be; they looked to her because of her skills. And though many of the other riders were also children of the highborn, among the King's Riders titles didn't matter.

Rank was equally *earned.*

It was truly refreshing.

"I'd heard you were here," Simond said as Cera jumped down from Ash. He gave her an easy smile she was able to return.

He was around her age, and they'd joined at the same time. Simond was a pleasant-looking young man, with brown hair and light brown eyes. Tall, but on the lanky side, he wore his hunter green Senior Rider cloak with pride.

Cera grabbed her bow and gave Ash's reins over to the boy who had offered to take him for her.

Everyone surrounded her, all of them speaking at once. The chaos was welcome, and warmed her from the inside out.

"How are you?" someone asked.

"Are you staying long?"

"Have you come back?"

All the questions made her head spin, but she threw her head back and laughed.

Who do I answer first?

"Let her breathe, everyone," an amused female voice announced, parting the small group as she strode forward, with a distinct Ascovan accent.

Cera grinned. "Aimil!" She rushed forward and grabbed the other girl tight.

Aimil Gallard, daughter of Lord Paxton Gallard of the Province of Ascova, was one of her oldest and dearest friends. She'd joined the Riders because of Cera, something she'd always be proud of.

Her longtime friend was also bonded to a wolf, Isair. Large, with a coat mixed of red, brown and gray, the female was close on her mistress' heels, which was probably why the other Riders had scattered.

Although many a Rider was bonded, she didn't spot any other animals close by.

She felt a silly giggle bubble up.

"It's good to see you, Lady Ryhan," Aimil teased with a playful grin, curtsying with her hunter green Senior Rider cloak spread wide, since she wore breeches.

"You as well, Lady Gallard." Cera grinned back. She surveyed the crowd. A familiar redhead was missing. "Where's Ansley?"

Ansley Fraser, daughter of Captain Murdoch Fraser, knight and captain of the king's personal guard, was the third of Cera and Aimil's troika.

"Trouble comes in threes," their captain, Sir Artair Moray, would always jest.

When in Terraquist, they—and their wolves—were rarely apart. Ansley had a she-wolf named Ali, so even their bondmates were a threesome.

"She's on a long distance run to the Netian Valley. The lord there had some tragedy and she'll be running from holding to holding in the area. She'll be gone all sevenday, maybe next as well." Aimil frowned.

"Aww, I'd hoped to see her. I probably won't be here long." Cera pushed the disappointment away. She'd get to see Ansley another time.

"She'll be sad she missed you," Aimil said.

Trikser and Isair eyed each other for only a moment, followed by a thorough sniff, some tail wagging, then took off side-by-side into the nearby woods.

Cera and Aimil watched them fondly and then giggled at each other when their gazes met.

"What are you doing here, anyway?" her friend asked. "I don't see your cloak."

"No, I'm not back . . . just thought I might practice some." She lifted her bow.

"Oh . . . do I sense a challenge?" Aimil grinned, her dark brown eyes flashing.

Cera chuckled.

Her fellow lady was a petite girl, only about five feet tall, and had long raven hair that fell to her waist. It was plaited at the moment, as that made it easier to manage when making runs. Aimil was excellent with a bow, despite her size. Actually, she was one of the few real challengers to Cera's skill among the Senior Riders.

"You only beat me that one time." She smirked, crossing her arms over her breasts.

"Until today." Aimil winked. She took off at a jog toward the archery field.

Simond chuckled. "You gonna let her talk to you like that?" Head cocked to one side, he looked like he fought a smile.

"I'll make her pay when I defeat her."

He barked another laugh. "Come on, everyone. For those of you who don't know her, Cera's a legend around here." He gestured for the small group of Reds to follow them.

Her cheeks burned at his praise, her eyes raking over the members of the group, each clad in a red cloak. Her gaze rested on a small girl with light brown hair and big blue eyes, who couldn't have been more than three and ten.

The girl blushed scarlet, to match her mantel, when Cera smiled at her. "What's your name?"

"Isobel."

"Well, come on, Isobel, let me show you how to beat Aimil with a bow." She threw her arm around the girl's slender shoulders.

Fair brows arched, Simond grinned. "Confident, are we?"

"I never lose twice."

He gave another hearty laugh that lightened her spirits even more.

Visiting Rider Headquarters was a great idea.

Braedon looked down into the courtyard from the window of the room he and Vanora had been assigned to, observing Cera hugging Hadrian. He was saddened to see his old friend leaving so soon, but he'd known—and felt—Hadrian's unease at being immersed in the world of humans.

The elf wizard would return to his small parcel of land near Berat, and he was glad to know he'd be right there if and when Braedon needed him.

Hadrian had shot down Vanora's plea for him to return to Aramour with them; but despite that, Braedon was going to make sure it wouldn't be too long before he saw him again.

He'd been a fool for losing twenty turns of his life. Twenty turns away from his wife, his son, and all the loved ones he'd left in Aramour. He should've done a better job of investigation to see if it would've been safe to go home, but the running had become ingrained. Braedon sighed.

"Something wrong, love?" Vanora's voice pulled him from his thoughts.

He didn't have adequate words to describe how he felt about his wife. She'd accepted him back into her arms as if he'd never left. No blame for him, no malice, not very many questions. Vanora loved him as she always had. Reminded him so right away.

And making love to his wife was even better than he'd remembered. She was truly his life-mate, as the elves called them.

"Nay, nothing's wrong. Just thinking about Hadrian. I'll miss him . . . again."

She nodded, smiling.

His breath caught. He'd always been stunned by her beauty. Couldn't quite believe she was his. *Still his.* Braedon pulled her into his arms, smiling as he inhaled the floral scent of her hair. She didn't even come up to his chest, but no one could ever mistake Vanora for a child.

She looked up at him, her sapphire eyes shining and a loving smile shaping the curve of her full lips. "What are you worried about?" she whispered.

One corner of his mouth lifted. His love might not have any magic, but she had a keen sense of intuition. "I thought I was the empath . . ." He chuckled.

"You are, most of the time." She grinned and snuggled against him. "I just think I know you very well."

"Aye, love, that you do. Even after all this time."

Vanora held his gaze, a softness in her eyes that made his heart pound. "Time gone doesn't matter. Only time moving forward does."

Braedon nodded, feeling her love for him through his magic so strongly it could've knocked him over. "I love you, Vanora." He leaned down to claim her mouth in a tender kiss.

She smiled as they parted. "And I love you, Braedon." His lifemate sighed against him as he held her closer. "Are we to return to Aramour soon?"

"As soon as your son fixes his mess," he said, somewhat worried, somewhat amused.

Even after all they'd been through, Jorrin and Cera couldn't get it together. What exactly had happened was a mystery—neither of them had confided in him—but he'd gathered that the lady had refused his son despite the king's announcement of a formal betrothal.

What could've happened that Cera told Jorrin she wouldn't be his wife? They had to work out their differences so she would agree to wed. They belonged together, just as he and Vanora belonged together.

"I want to make sure they're all right before we depart, but I'm more than ready to get home."

Home. With my wife.

Braedon was actually *free.*

The king had confirmed the men who'd been after him—magic hunters that harvested people and magical creatures for power and gold—were either apprehended or dead. It made Braedon all the more the fool, though. He'd wasted turns.

You can't change the past.

He chided himself and focused on the woman in his arms.

"Jorrin has always been stubborn, but he loves that lass. I can see it plain as day," Vanora remarked.

"Aye, I know it, love." He caressed her cheek.

"I think they'll be fine," she said. "Will the twins accompany us?"

The Leodin twin mages had been even more fascinated with Vanora than they had been with Hadrian. Edana hadn't been far from his lifemate's side since they'd met.

She'd gathered the lass into her small arms and rocked her by the fire. She'd told her all about Aramour, holding her as if she was a child, and not a young woman in her early twenties.

Vanora had told him a lass needed a mother from time to time, no matter what age she reached. Rory had also clung to his wife's hand anytime she spoke.

To see the twins fascinated, content, and connected to their heritage had affected Braedon's emotions as much as it did theirs. And made him admire the woman he loved even more than he had before.

The mages had never seen Aramour. Had no knowledge of their parents, or even where they'd been born. Their mother was most likely their elfin parent, but of that they weren't even sure—although, Vanora and Hadrian both agreed it was probably the case.

Rory and Edana's earliest memories consisted of living in the human slums of Lower Terraquist, no adults to care for them. Jorrin was the first person they'd ever met like them; Hadrian was the first elf they'd ever seen.

Thank the Blessed Spirit the Leodins had found King Nathal.

"For a visit. They wish to return to King Nathal. They see him as a father in many ways."

"The king is a good man," Vanora said.

"Aye, he is, love. Our Jorrin is a duke," Braedon said, wonder washing over him. His son had never aspired to be such, but Jorrin loved Cera and he'd have to be strong for her.

"And you are my fine knight," she whispered, her smile proud.

He grinned. "Aye, but I thought I always was." He winked, and her smile widened to a grin.

"I don't know . . ." his lifemate teased, laughing and shaking her head.

Lifting her, Braedon swung her around much like Jorrin had when he'd seen her before the feast.

She laughed and hugged him tight when he set her to her feet. "Are you still worried about them, love?"

"I just hope love can conquer all for them."

Vanora nodded thoughtfully, saying nothing.

CHAPTER THIRTY-ONE

CERA KNOCKED ON the king's ledger room door. She waited for longer than customary before knocking again, but there was no answer.

"The king is not here, milady," a small boy—a page— informed her as he walked past.

She whirled on him and his eyes widened. He was a tiny thing, with bright copper hair, large brown eyes and freckles covering his face. "Where did he go?"

The boy shifted his slight weight from foot to foot, hands clasped tightly in front of him. "I . . . I was not told, milady."

Her fists clenched at her sides, Cera growled.

King Nathal's gone?

She looked down at the page and he flinched.

Did he have any magic? Her wild emotions seemed to be affecting him.

"Lady Ryhan, is there a problem with Padraig?" a voice with a southern accent asked, taking her attention from the young page.

Her gaze landed on the knight who'd escorted Jorrin to the king the night before. "No . . . not at all. He's been helpful," she said wryly when she noticed the pure relief on the boy's face as the knight approached.

Padraig excused himself, sprinting down the corridor. Had she not been so irritated at King Nathal, Cera would've probably been amused, but she took no pleasure in frightening a small boy.

"Can I help you with something?" He didn't miss a beat, but she read amusement in his hazel eyes.

"Well, I need to speak with the king, Sir . . ."

"Sir Willum Maron." He gave a small bow. His sandy hair was in need of a trim, and it fell forward. He shoved it out of his eyes and straightened to his full height. He was tall, and probably a few turns older than her. The smile he wore highlighted his handsome, beardless face.

He was clad in Terraquist-blue breeches; his tunic a steel gray. He wore no belt, sword or doublet, but she figured he'd already finished training for the day. His hair was damp, and the soothing scent of sandalwood tickled her nose, as if he'd just come from a bath.

Cera squared her shoulders. "I seek an audience with King Nathal, Sir Maron."

Maybe formality will help.

"I'm sorry, Lady Ryhan, but he's gone."

She almost stomped her foot, clearing her throat to stop the demand about to tumble out of her mouth. Taking a breath, Cera tried to smile.

Polite. Be. Polite.

"When will he be returning?"

"I'm not sure, my lady, but no more than a day or two."

"Great," she muttered.

"My lady?" Sir Willum asked, one fair eyebrow quirked.

"Thank you, Sir Maron." She gave a curt nod and spun away without another word, silently chiding herself for being rude. Her steps were jerky as she made it down the wide corridor.

Is the king avoiding me?

All the positive feelings and energy she'd worked up at the training grounds beating Aimil's arrows had faded away as she'd entered Castle Rowan, and once again her thoughts were of Jorrin and pain.

Cera would be unable to avoid him at evening meal—in less than an hour, to boot—they'd be seated together, unless she chose to stay in her room. That would probably be for the best. She couldn't look him in the eye.

Outside her assigned chambers, she stared at the closed door across the hall. She squeezed her eyes shut, refusing to think about him.

Yes, because that's working.

She ordered a bath for later in the evening, and smiled as Petra set out a light blue gown for her to wear to dinner. Cowardice set in and she asked the maid to order food so she could take her meal in her room.

The girl appeared curious, but didn't ask questions.

Cera looked at Trikser, who wagged his tail. "You're much better company anyway." She ran her hand down her bondmate's spine, savoring the soft feel of his white fur beneath her fingertips. He lay beside her on the large bed, leaning into her hand and licking her wrist.

She blew out a breath and settled against the plush pillows, smiling slightly as Trik cuddled closer, resting his large head on her thigh. She woke with a start at the gentle knock at the door.

Damn, she'd dozed off.

Cera hastily bid Petra to enter with her meal, smiling at the undisguised glare the young maid threw at her wolf for his location on the bed, but Petra said nothing.

"Will that be all, milady?" Her eyes were glued to Trikser.

She chuckled, and Petra blushed when they made eye contact. "Yes, thank you."

The maid curtsied, and her pink cheeks made her even more charming.

"Oh, Petra?"

"Yes, milady?"

"Can you please see that I'm informed as soon as the king returns?"

"Of course, my lady." She bowed again.

"Thank you."

"If you have need of me, please let me know. Your bath is still as scheduled?"

"Yes, after I eat. I don't plan on venturing from my room."

The girl excused herself, closing the door.

Cera sighed. Why didn't she feel better now that she was back in civilization? Her mind drifted to how it'd been when she'd been hiding from Varthan. Although she'd been on the run, being away from people had been nice.

It was still hard to believe he was gone.

Shaking her head, she ate, pushing the dark thoughts away, and tried to look forward to a good night's sleep after a warm bath. As with her last several meals, she didn't taste the food. She answered the demand of her body with no enjoyment.

Trikser whined and went to the door, wagging his tail hard.

Cera laid the fork on her tray, freezing. Her heart thundered at the footsteps in the corridor.

Jorrin's on the other side. . .

She steeled herself for the knock that never came. Biting her lip, she hovered on the brink of tears.

Should she be hurt or relieved the footsteps retreated?

When will this all stop?

"I'll not marry him!" Cera burst into the king's ledger room.

Sir Willum Maron had refused her entry. He rushed in behind her, immediately apologizing to King Nathal.

Tristan Dagget stood next to the big man as they studied a long piece of parchment.

Heat seared her cheeks as he looked up, exasperation evident in his pale gaze.

Tristan's hazel eyes were wide, his mouth half-agape.

She grimaced and glanced at Sir Maron in silent apology. He'd been telling the truth when he'd said King Nathal was busy.

It'd taken him two days to return to Castle Rowan.

Two days that only served to make her simmer. Two days of excruciating pain and devising clever ways to avoid Jorrin.

She'd convinced herself King Nathal was avoiding her, since she'd sent word to him seeking an audience first thing that morning. Cera had waited patiently all day for a call that never came, so she'd taken matters into her own hands.

"I'm sorry, your Majesty," the knight repeated, bowing.

Dragon's Tail
Mountains of Aramour
Terraquist
Elfin River
Greenwald
Netian Valley
North Ascova
Tarvis
Hadrian's Place
Berat
South Ascova
Islands
Dalunas
Southern Strait
Penal Territory

"It's all right, Willum. Obviously, you had no choice," King Nathal told him, but his eyes were locked onto hers.

Her cheeks burned even more; she looked down.

"Have a seat, Cera. Tristan, please excuse Lady Ryhan." The king looked at the lord, then back at her. "Although, this shouldn't take too long, I've already taken up too much of your day *working*. We will resume in the morning. Spend some time with your betrothed, if Lady Aimil's not on a message run."

She winced at his emphasis.

"Of course, Majesty." Tristan bowed and flashed a reassuring smile when their gazes brushed.

Cera averted her eyes from her friend's betrothed. Her cheeks were even hotter. "I'm sorry, Tristan."

He shook his head and left the room.

Sir Maron was not far behind, closing the door without a sound.

The king's massive arms were crossed over his imposing chest, and his head was cocked to one side. He stared. "Now, what is this nonsense, lass?" His tone was unyielding.

"I won't marry Jorrin." She sat taller in the chair.

"Blessed Spirit, you are Falor Ryhan's daughter." King Nathal threw his hands up. "I've never met such a stubborn lass in my entire life. Just like your da . . ." He shook his head. His tawny hair danced across his impossibly broad shoulders.

"I will *not* marry him," Cera repeated, crossing her arms, too.

"Why not, lass? I know you love him, and he loves you." The king's expression softened.

Cera blinked to clear her vision.

I can't cry here. I won't.

"I won't marry to gain something that should've been mine in the first place." She straightened her chin and looked him in the eye.

"What're you talking about?"

"Greenwald. It should've been mine. It was what my father wished."

"Didn't Jorrin tell you?" He sounded exasperated again.

"Tell me what?"

"Greenwald is yours—whether you marry him or not."

Cera stared.

No.

Her heart sank. Jorrin hadn't told her that. But had she really given him the chance? She hadn't listened, even when he'd begged her to do so.

Oh no.

She'd been so awful to him. Tears welled and started down her cheeks before she could stop them.

"Ah, lass, don't cry."

"I thought he wanted Greenwald, and not me . . ." Cera wiped her cheeks.

"The lad said you might think that."

"He did?" She sniffled, and swiped at her nose with the back of her hand.

The king flashed a half-smile and tried to hand her a white silk handkerchief he'd pulled from one of his desk drawers, but Cera shook her head and King Nathal set it down on his desk. "Aye, he worried about it." He sucked in a breath, his enormous chest rising. "I handled this wrong. I should've talked to you first, but the lad . . . I know how unfamiliar this is for him. I wanted him to know my reasons and plans, to give him a chance to get his bearings. Honestly, I didn't give him a chance to say nay to any of it. I didn't think you'd object to him. It's obvious you love him. I owe it to your father to see that you're happy. I thought I was doing that, lass. He's a good, decent lad. He'll make a fine duke."

She leaned across the oversized desk and reached for the king's hand. She touched his rough calloused skin and thought of her father. Cera smiled as he squeezed hers in comfort. "I'm the one who handled it wrong, your Majesty," she whispered. "I jumped to all the wrong conclusions. The things I said . . ." Her voice broke, and tears coursed down her cheeks again.

King Nathal wiped her cheek with one of his huge hands.

The corner of her mouth lifted; she was startled someone of his size could be so gentle. "I wouldn't be surprised if he never wanted to speak to me again, King Nathal."

"I doubt that, lass. He loves you."

"I said some awful things," she admitted. Shame heated her neck and cheeks. At this rate, her complexion would be permanently stained. Nothing less than she deserved, really.

"Apologize. I'm sure he'll listen to you."

She wiped the rest of her tears away and nodded, gaining her feet. Cera turned to go.

"Where are you off to, lass?"

"To go convince Jorrin he's the only one who can make me happy . . . under order of the king."

She flashed a smile at King Nathal's bark of laughter.

"And, to grovel." Cera winced.

"Then off with you."

"Thank you, King Nathal," she whispered.

He lifted his bushy eyebrows in silent question.

Her heart thundered as she reached for the elaborate door handle.

Chapter Thirty-Two

"GONE? WHAT DO you mean *gone?*" Cera's voice shot up an octave with each word.

The young maid shrank away from her.

She winced. Hadn't meant to intimidate the girl.

Trikser bristled at her side, growling, so that didn't help matters, but she wanted to know where Jorrin was. *Now.*

"I saw Lord Aldern leave." The maid studied her shoes.

No. I can't be too late.

She closed her eyes as her heart dropped to her stomach. Cera hadn't trusted Jorrin enough to listen to him.

This is all my fault.

Her chest constricted, and she swallowed back a sob. She ignored Trikser when he whimpered and nudged her hand.

Jorrin had left because of how awful she'd been to him.

Cera wouldn't get a chance to tell him what a fool she was . . . tell him she loved him and she'd be honored to be his wife . . . his Duchess of Greenwald.

How could he have left her? *Serves you right.*

"When did he leave?" she demanded. She'd been behaving abhorrently to all of King Nathal's servants. Wouldn't be surprised if they all thought she was becoming one of the bossy, shrewish ladies she despised. They were probably all whispering horrible things about her. Cera had never treated any servants this badly.

"Several hours ago, milady."

She'd been looking for him *everywhere.* When she'd left the king's ledger room, she'd gone to his room. Jorrin wasn't there, so she'd sought out anyone and everyone to ask if he'd been seen.

This maid was the first who had.

She snarled, and the maid's eyes widened.

Trikser, still standing behind her, also growled again, and the maid took an involuntary step back.

"I'm sorry," Cera said after forcing a deep breath.

Calm down. She chanted it, as well as thought-sent to her bondmate.

Trik's hackles were raised down the length of his spine.

She needed to control herself, for both their sakes.

The maid nodded, but her eyes didn't leave Cera's bondmate.

"Cera?" a female voice distracted her and she whirled away from the young maid.

Tears burned her eyes, threatening to spill over yet again.

Taking the chance to escape, the maid shirked away, but Cera made no to move to stop her.

Aimil strode toward her, dressed in a beautiful dark blue gown, simple yet elegant—the color usually representing South Ascova. She had a friendly smile on her face until she looked Cera up and down. "What's wrong?"

Her tears cascaded, and she wiped them away.

Trikser whined and bumped her hand with his nose.

"I'm fine," she muttered, patting the wolf's head and meeting her friend's concerned gaze.

"You don't look fine."

"I'll be fine." Cera's voice was shaky.

I have to be fine.

She'd have to find some way to get over Jorrin. Her heart throbbed as more tears welled and spilled.

"It doesn't seem so," Aimil whispered, stepping forward to hug her.

She wrapped her arms around her friend as a sob she couldn't swallow escaped. When Cera could compose herself, she pulled away and wiped the tears from her face. *Again.* "I've made a mess of things, and now it's too late to fix it."

"Tell me what happened." The words were a gentle order.

"Not here," Cera said. "We'll go to my room."

She wanted to plop on the large bed and sob until she couldn't anymore. She sat on the edge instead, and Trikser jumped up and lay at its center as if he owned it.

Aimil gave a small laugh.

Cera managed a half-smile at her bond. "Where's Isair?"

"I left her in my room. I only came up to the castle to see Tristan."

"Tristan Dagget?"

She nodded, a softness in her expression that made things click in Cera's mind. Her fellow Senior Rider had been betrothed since she was a baby. The two families had signed an agreement upon Aimil's birth. Her friend never really talked about the situation, or the man; it was another of those, '*someday*' things. She'd accepted her duty as the daughter of a duke, and still had two more turns until they would marry, when Aimil turned twenty.

Why hadn't she realized her friend's husband-to-be was someone she knew and liked? She had no idea Aimil had a fondness for him.

Cera liked the healer very much. He'd be good for her friend. They were both gentle souls. Sweet. "Are you happy?"

"Aye, I love him. I have for some time." Her face lit up, her dark eyes shining as she talked about her love. "I'm sorry I never told you and Ansley. I wasn't hiding him or anything. Things moved fast when we started spending time together, and you or Ansley were always gone, or I

Mountains of Aramour
Dragon's Tail
Elfin River
Terraquist
oire
sle
Greenwald
Netian Valley
North Ascova
Hadrian's Place
Tarvis
Berat
South Ascova
Dalunas
Southern Strait
Penal Territory

was. I wanted to tell you together, and then, well . . ." What she left unsaid was that Varthan had happened. Aimil winced.

She grabbed her hand and squeezed. "It's all right." She smiled, trying to ignore envy and heartache. Cera didn't want to think about Varthan or losing her family, but then again, she didn't want to think about Jorrin, either.

"Shouldn't you be happy, too? Tristan told me I missed quite a bit during the feast the other night. Aren't betrothed now, too? I was hoping to meet the new Lord Aldern today. I was on a run with two Browns who're almost ready to Test, or I would've been here the other night. I'm sorry I missed it—" she trailed off when Cera bit her bottom lip. "What did I say? What's wrong?"

"Everything's ruined, and it's all my fault." She sniffled and shook her head.

"What are you talking about? Tell me what happened."

She met her friend's eyes and nodded. The whole story tumbled out, her tears cascading when her friend cringed at what she'd said to Jorrin.

Aimil hugged her though, and Cera was glad she didn't offer any criticism or berate her for the awful things.

"I don't understand why it's too late to fix it," Aimil said.

"Because he left. I hurt him, and he left. He was never comfortable here, anyway." She slumped and crushed her eyes shut, forcing a breath.

"Cera, Lord Aldern didn't leave, at least not permanently."

"What d'you mean?"

"Tristan and Sir Leargan Tegran asked him to accompany them on a ride. If I know my Tristan, he wanted a chance to get to know both your Lord Aldern and Sir Tegran better."

"What? Are you sure?" Her heart stuttered.

"Yes. The stable boy told me when I arrived. I decided to wait up here for Tristan, since I have no message runs today. I was actually on my way to find you . . . then I ran into you in the hallway." Aimil shrugged, smiling.

"He's not gone," she whispered. "It's not too late . . ."

"You'd better hope he forgives you." Her friend's voice was stern.

Cera blinked.

"I'll not live with you at Greenwald if you're unhappy all the time." Aimil waggled a finger at her.

"What? Live at Greenwald?"

"Didn't the king tell you? Tristan will be Lord Aldern's Second. When we wed, I'll be coming to Greenwald. I want to see you happy with Lord Aldern, like I'll be with Tristan."

She smiled genuinely. Leargan had mentioned something about Tristan, but she hadn't asked him to clarify. "I'll be happy. I love him."

Her friend grinned.

Cera hugged Aimil again. "Thank you." Hopping up, she surprised both her wolf, and her friend.

"Where're you going?"

"To the stables. I have to talk to him as soon as they return. I've a lot of groveling to do." She made a face, but her heart lifted.

Maybe it really isn't too late . . .

"I'll go with you. I want to see Tristan first thing, too."

They exchanged another smile.

Chapter Thirty-Three

THE HARD RIDE felt good. Jorrin didn't need to think, didn't need to feel. The wind moved his hair, stung his cheeks and rushed in his ears. He didn't want to remember how Cera felt in his arms or how she tasted when he kissed her. What it was like when he touched her, and made love to her. Didn't want to remember the pain when she'd said she hated him. He growled.

No. Not again.

It'd been days. He needed to stop dwelling on it.

Lord Tristan Dagget was on his right, Sir Leargan Tegran on his left. They'd be his men. *His* men. It still baffled, and set butterflies spinning in his stomach. How could he run a Province? A small voice reminded him he'd need Cera at his side, but he silenced it. It hurt too badly.

Tristan had sought him out, asking if he wanted to go for a ride, along with the knight. The healer had just left a meeting with the king, but Jorrin hadn't asked for details. He'd accepted the invitation; he needed to get to know both men. Despite the petty jealousies he'd had about Leargan, Jorrin liked him. As a matter of fact, he liked what he saw in both so far.

They slowed, nearing the king's stables.

Grayna was much smaller than Tristan's dark brown stallion and even smaller than Leargan's buckskin-colored mare, but he didn't care. She was, and always would be, a companion to him.

Tristan caught his eye as he dismounted. Jorrin figured he was in for a good ribbing; they'd teased him that his mare was likely out of breath keeping up with their horses, but it wasn't true.

"You're a duke now, you know." He made a show of looking Grayna up and down.

Leargan laughed.

Jorrin shot them both a glare. "And?"

"You may want to get a more impressive horse . . . as in . . . larger?" Tristan grinned and hopped to the ground, giving his stallion an affectionate pat.

"Nay," Jorrin said, rubbing Grayna's neck and whispering to her. She neighed, as if answering, and he smiled. "She's been with me too long. We've been through hell together."

Like Cera.

"I suppose that's *one* acceptable reason to hold onto something." Tristan gave him a long look.

He groaned. No way the younger man was referring to Grayna.

"Aye, it is," Leargan remarked, dismounting his mare.

Jorrin swallowed a sigh. Did the whole castle know all was not well with Cera? Had Tristan asked him to accompany them to ambush him? He was so weary of intuitive people. "What was your meeting with the king regarding, if you don't mind my asking?" He went for a distraction with Tristan, as two stable boys came to take their horses.

The lord gave him another long look, but blew out a breath. "The proclamation dooming the last of Varthan's shades." Regret and hurt seeped from his aura.

Jorrin's magic tingled, telling him how hard it was for the healer to have a hand in their punishment and probable death. It was everything he stood against. Although, he'd not known the younger man for very long, it was apparent that Tristan's sense of justice was just as great as his aversion to death. He understood the necessity, but it would still cause him some suffering.

He clasped his forearm in comfort, surprising himself, as much as the healer. It was a casual gesture, and he didn't know Tristan well enough for such things, but instinct told him they'd be very close friends.

The man would show him a loyalty that equaled how he saw the king. It warmed Jorrin considerably.

His hazel eyes were soft when their gazes met, and he offered a small smile. "Thanks."

"Looks like you two have eager visitors, my lords." Leargan wore a big grin.

Jorrin and Tristan exchanged a glance before looking to where the knight had gestured.

Cera stood in front of the main stables, next to a petite girl wearing a dark blue dress, their hands entwined. The ebony-haired girl was beautiful, but his eyes locked onto his love.

Trikser sat next to his mistress.

Cera's companion released her hand and rushed to Tristan, who met her halfway and pulled her into his arms. Their mouths fused even before they'd stilled.

Jorrin looked away from the kissing the couple, his chest tight.

Cera rushed forward, but stopped about five feet away. She bit her plump bottom lip. Didn't speak.

His heart was about to pop out of his ribcage. He didn't read contempt in her eyes, but rather, regret and a hurt so strong it radiated off of her. His magic throbbed as he fought dizziness; the mixture of her agony and his own made his head spin. Jorrin wanted her in his arms, but he was afraid she'd reject him again.

Leargan, Tristan and the other girl slipped away, leaving him alone with Cera.

Should he be nervous or grateful? At least if she crushed him again, it'd be in privacy.

"Jorrin. . ." Her whisper was full of anguish.

Almost his undoing. He stared, unable to find his voice.

"Do you hate me?" she asked, so low he had to strain to hear it.

His gut clenched when he saw her tears. "No." Jorrin could never hate her.

Hope flared in her gray eyes, but she stood there, still crying quietly. Despite the redness in her face and puffiness under her eyes, she was still the most beautiful woman he'd ever seen. Her deep auburn curls were loose, wreaking havoc around her shoulders, windblown as if she'd been running. She was dressed as he'd seen her most often, in soft brown breeches and a white linen tunic, with a sleeveless buckskin jerkin over it.

Jorrin needed Cera like he needed to breathe.

She opened her mouth, but no words came. She glanced down, wringing her hands in front of her, still saying nothing.

And what could Jorrin say? Fear washed over him from Cera, shooting a tremor down his spine. *She's afraid.* Her body was shaking with fear that *he'd* reject *her.*

He could never turn her away. He wanted things right between them. Jorrin swallowed, fighting the tightness in his body as her emotions affected his. Relief warred with negative feelings. He begged his brain to connect with his speech.

The silence was finally broken by Trikser. The wolf wuffed and pawed at Cera's feet.

He sensed a thought-send, though he didn't catch the actual words.

The love of his life looked into her bondmate's amber eyes. "Go on, I'll see you later." She gave him an affectionate pat.

The wolf took off at a run. Didn't look back.

When Cera's gaze landed on his, Jorrin managed a small smile, holding his breath when she took a step toward him.

He didn't move away, but he didn't move closer, either. Yearned to throw his arms around her and pull her against him, but he didn't want to push her. He'd let her come the rest of the way to him when she was ready. "What's with him?" he whispered.

"My friend Aimil's bondmate. A she-wolf named Isair." Her words were rushed, as if wolves were the last thing she wanted to discuss.

"Oh . . ."

"Jorrin, is it too late?"

His *everything* surged. Tugging her into her arms, Jorrin took a risk that was well worth it.

She sobbed against his chest and wrapped her arms around him, almost too tight.

He smoothed her hair and whispered reassurances. Squeezed his eyes shut, inhaling her scent and holding her, molding her to him, basking in the rightness of it. He loved her so much.

No matter what he said or did, what she said or did, that would never change. Jorrin smiled against her hair.

"It won't be all right," Cera whispered, looking up at him, her gray eyes still misty.

"It won't?" He barely resisted the urge to kiss the look off her face.

"No, not until you forgive me, *if* you'll forgive me. I wouldn't blame you if you didn't want to. I was a fool, Jorrin. I didn't mean anything I said and I *am* sorry. I love you so much . . . and I . . ."

Her babbling was adorable, but he needed to assuage her worries.

Tears coursed down her cheeks as she trailed off, and he kissed them away, reveling in the feel of her moist skin beneath his lips. The salty tang only made him want her more.

"Shhh, love." Unable to resist her, he covered her mouth with his.

Cera clung to him, opening, deepening the kiss and pressing her tongue against his. He sensed her desperation.

Jorrin wanted to soothe her before he lost the ability to think, but his body was already responding to her taste and the light caresses she was spreading along the length of his back. It'd been too long and he'd missed her touch. He was desperate for her, too.

He gripped the back of her neck, burying his fingers in her soft curls. Her arms shot around his neck, and she rubbed her tongue against his. Taking control, he devoured her, kissing her until neither of them could breathe.

She moaned and he answered with a groan.

Jorrin needed her, and he needed her *now*. His erection strained against his breeches. Their bodies melded from hip to hip, breasts to chest, but he wanted her even closer.

Cera rubbed into him and he grunted, slanting harder into the kiss.

He stopped himself with the first tug on her jerkin. They were outside, for Blessed Spirit's sake. With willpower he didn't know he possessed, he broke the seal of their mouths, struggling for breath and coherent thought. He rested his forehead against hers, and flashed a smile.

Her breathing was uneven against his. Her cheeks were rosy, her eyes heavy-lidded.

Jorrin grunted and tore his eyes away from her kiss-swollen lips as his erection throbbed. He'd never get enough of her. "I love you, too."

She covered her mouth with one hand, crying out in relief, and closing her eyes. She gave him a hard fast kiss. "Do you still want me?"

His blood ran so hot he wanted to throw her down and make love to her right there. With his manhood poking into her, she had to ask? "I never stopped wanting you. I'm sorry I hurt you. I should've explained things better, but the king put me on the spot . . ."

Cera placed a finger to his lips. "I'm the one who was in the wrong. I should've listened to you. What I accused you of . . . it's so horrible. You never would've done that to me. I can't believe what I said. I meant *none* of it." Tears welled and spilled again, and she looked down.

"Shhh . . . I don't care what you said, as long as you realize it's not true. I love you." He guided her face back up to his, and Jorrin's heart danced when she smiled.

"You can forgive me, then?"

"You're already forgiven, love."

Her face lit up and she squeezed him.

Jorrin laughed. "Easy, love, I'm fond of breathing."

"Ask me again?" Cera whispered.

He smiled. Slowly, tenderly. "Lady Ceralda Ryhan, will you be my wife?"

"Yes, Lord Jorrin Aldern, I will."

His stomach did a somersault, although he'd known what her answer would be. He'd never been happier in his life. Jorrin could feel Cera's emotions, and his own echoed them.

They stared at each other.

"Aren't you going to seal my yes with a kiss?" She flashed a grin.

He grinned back.

Their spell had been broken with her question, but it helped Jorrin clear his head. "I'm afraid if I kiss you, we'll be naked in the dirt in a few minutes."

She giggled and caressed his cheek, her eyes darkening with desire. "How about naked in my chambers, instead?"

He shivered as she ran the pad of her thumb along his bottom lip. "That . . . would be . . . better," he stammered.

Cera grinned pure mischief and took his hand.

He nodded and let her lead the way. That was them, though wasn't it? She'd lead, he'd follow. But he was fine with that. No matter what happened, as long as they were together, they could do anything.

Being the Duke of Greenwald wouldn't be so bad after all.

Epilogue

"**M**Y LADY?"

"Yes?" Cera looked up from staring out of one of the many windows in the great hall down into the courtyard. She met Leargan's dark eyes, and tried to smile, but the handsome new Captain of Castle Ryhan's personal guard was too perceptive.

He looked worried. Leargan disguised his expression fast, and gave her a polite bow. "I wanted to give you a report."

"Oh?" They'd been back in Greenwald for over a month, after spending another fortnight in Terraquist, and things were going well. There was so much to be happy about. She should be overjoyed, and she was for the most part, but her emotions had been erratic lately.

"About the new men, training is going well."

"Oh, good," Cera said automatically. She shifted in the sky blue gown she was wearing, feeling restricted, as always. Other than several she'd worn at court, she couldn't remember the last time she'd donned a gown.

She suddenly missed the simplicity of breeches, a tunic, and a jerkin. Missed time to herself and long rides through the countryside on Ash, Trikser running with them.

"Is something wrong, my lady?" he asked, after hesitating. "I don't mean to overstep . . ."

"No, no. Nothing's wrong. Don't worry. You haven't overstepped. I'm fine, honestly." She forced a smile.

He'd seen it for what it was, but gave a curt nod. "I'll return to the fighting yard, then. We're going to start archery shortly."

"Archery?" Cera cocked her head to the side.

Amusement darted across face before he composed himself.

She gave a genuine smile.

"Aye, my lady. An interest of yours?" Leargan's voice was nonchalant, but he was obviously trying to hide his mirth.

"Somewhat." She grinned.

Her captain relaxed and gave a smile of his own. "Lords Aldern and Dagget thought you might want to know, milady."

Had Jorrin sent Leargan to her?

Cera nodded. "I'll change and be right out. Please have my horse readied."

"Of course, but I suggest you hurry, my lady. I think the new headwoman is coming this way." Leargan winked.

She groaned.

King Nathal was just trying to help by sending people to fill in all the missing positions, but the mother hen of a headwoman in charge of all the female staff, Morag, was enough to drive Cera to drink.

The woman was constantly reminding her of what was and wasn't the proper conduct of a young lady born of nobility. A *married* one, to boot, Morag would say, lecturing in her nasal voice. Unfortunately, Cera's day to day activity was usually placed in the *not proper* category by the older woman.

"I'll simply have to remind her who *exactly* is in charge around here." She ignored her captain's hearty chuckle. She raced past him out of the great hall, hurrying to her rooms. If Cera was seen, Morag would follow no matter what.

She'd brought Neomi from Tarvis to be her lady's maid, but the girl was too afraid of the new headwoman to actually lock her out of the duke and duchess suite. Neomi probably wouldn't do so even if Cera commanded her to.

Trikser caught up with her in the large corridor, wuffing curiously as he loped beside her.

Cera grinned, glad to see her bondmate. She'd let him out earlier to hunt. He didn't mind prepared meats of course, but like her, sometimes Trik needed be free to run on his own.

Passing a few shocked servants as she went down the corridor, she said nothing, and thankfully she didn't come across the headwoman. Running through Castle Ryhan was certainly *not* behavior becoming of a young married lady.

She didn't spot Neomi as she made it to the rooms she shared with Jorrin. Cera wrenched the door open and slipped inside, shutting it with a *thud*. She giggled and leaned on the thick panel to catch her breath.

Trikser leapt onto the large bed and lay down. She could hear Jorrin's usual growl in her mind. He wasn't any fonder of the wolf's place there than Morag was.

The headwoman of course, had been horrified the first time she'd seen Cera's bondmate in the middle of the place where nobility slept. Only the fact that he was a wolf, not a dog, had kept her from shooing him out of their home entirely. Morag did not approve of any beasts within the castle walls.

A wave of nausea hit, as Cera bent over her trunk to pull out a pair of breeches, but she took a deep breath and sat on the edge of the bed until it passed. She wouldn't let her stomach's objections change her plans, so she dressed quickly and grabbed her bow and quiver.

She was the best archer, even better than any of Leargan's selections for the personal guard, so she'd just have to convince Jorrin she was the one best qualified to teach them.

Cera wouldn't tell him her secret until he promised she could. It'd keep her busy and outside for a few months. She wouldn't be able to do it for very long. And if she was out on the training grounds, she could keep Morag at bay . . . at least until she came back inside the castle.

She smiled and called Trikser to follow her.

Ash would be waiting for her in the courtyard.

Jorrin grinned when he saw Ash racing toward them, Trikser close on the stallion's heels. He'd known Cera wouldn't be able to resist trying her bow against their new recruits. He glanced at Tristan when the lord chuckled.

Things were going well. He was settling in at Greenwald much better than he'd expected. Cera knew more about running a Province than he'd been aware of, and he wasn't embarrassed to have to learn things from his wife.

To her credit, she made it seem like *he* was in charge, and Jorrin admired her ability to do so with grace and humility. He didn't mind that it was for show for the most part, so everyone would not think him weak, but so far, knights and servants alike had treated him with the utmost respect. He didn't feel like a duke yet, but he'd be more comfortable with time.

"You were right, my lord," Leargan said in a low voice so only Jorrin and Tristan could hear. "I'd suspected you would be, so I suppose I was smart *not* to accept your wager."

Jorrin chuckled.

Tristan laughed, and the knight winked.

"Ah, Leargan, I wouldn't have taken your coin." He grinned at the disbelief in his captain's dark eyes.

In the short time they'd been in Greenwald, Jorrin, Tristan and Leargan had fallen into a comfortable rhythm. They were rarely apart, getting to know each other well, and he already considered them good friends. However, he'd never get used to '*my lord*' or '*Lord Aldern*'.

Hell, technically, Leargan had been higher born than Jorrin, yet he was calling him '*my lord*'? It still made him uncomfortable.

Jorrin had told Tristan; under no circumstances was *he* to call him anything but his given name, and the younger man had laughingly agreed, as long as the sentiment was mutual. He'd been uncomfortable with that at first, because after all, Tristan *was* a lord, but he'd gotten used to it when he'd observed even Lucan had no qualms about it.

Leargan was only a turn his junior, at two and twenty. He had a wicked sense of humor and was a great deal more easy going than Jorrin had originally assessed. The knight could swordfight better than anyone he'd ever met. His captain would protect Cera with his life if need be, and that made Jorrin feel better about being '*in charge*'.

Dragon's Tail

Mountains of Aramour

Terraquist

Elfin River

ire
le

Greenwald

Netian Valley

North Ascova

Hadrian's Place

Tarvis

Berat

South Ascova

Dalunas

Islands

Southern Strait

Penal Territory

He had good men at his side and more than adequate backup, if need be.

The captain had handpicked the eleven other men that made up the personal guard, and Jorrin was enjoying getting to know them as well.

Before they'd left Terraquist, they'd been scoffed at by some courtiers because the eldest man of the guard was not yet thirty, but all of Leargan's picks had been sanctioned and heartily approved by King Nathal. After all, he'd trained and knighted them all. Several had been raised at the palace as foster children, as Leargan had been, so he saw them as brothers. The kinship was something Jorrin was also starting to feel as time went on.

They were assisting in training the new recruits—Castle Ryhan guards and men-at-arms—and he appreciated it to no end. He'd never trained anyone in his life.

Lucan was also finding his place in Greenwald, although Jorrin's parents hadn't wanted to leave the boy with him and Cera. The young mage had become fast attached to both of his parents, and the feeling was mutual, but he was equally attached to Tristan, so he'd chosen Greenwald over Aramour when Braedon and Vanora had offered the boy a place with them.

And Lucan's budding attachment to Cera was already evident. Jorrin's wife missed her sister, and in a way, Lucan filled the place of a younger sibling—not a replacement for Kait, of course, but a younger brother she'd never had.

The boy was already fiercely loyal to Jorrin and King Nathal. Having someone with as much magic as Lucan was something to keep on one's side, though they didn't anticipate trouble.

Besides, he was reveling in being Sir Lucan, knight and head mage of Greenwald. At three and ten turns old, it was quite an accomplishment.

"She's probably the best qualified to teach the archers, Jorrin," Tristan said.

"Really?"

"No jest. Aimil says Cera can beat *anyone* with a bow. Even the captain of the King's Riders, Sir Artair Moray, who happens to be one of the king's best archers."

Leargan let out a slow, appreciative whistle. "I've seen him in action. There's none better."

"She's beaten Sir Moray more than once in competition, and not only Riders' Games . . . the king's open competitions as well," Tristan said.

Leargan's eyes widened, and the healer nodded for effect.

"It'd keep her busy for a while," Jorrin said thoughtfully.

The captain chuckled. "Out of trouble."

"Not touching that one." Tristan grinned.

Cera reined Ash in and dismounted.

One of the personal guard, a fair-haired man named Roduch, bowed to her and took the stallion's reins, leading him to the other horses.

Jorrin heard her thank him and saw the big man nod. When she met his eyes, she gave a brilliant smile that had his heart pounding.

"Husband." She inclined her head as she joined them at the fence surrounding the fighting yard. Cera grinned impishly at Leargan.

To his credit, the captain didn't react other than to nod back, but Jorrin chuckled.

"Lord Dagget," she said, bowing.

Jorrin fought a grin. It wasn't often he saw her so proper, even with Morag constantly hounding her.

Tristan also inclined his head and smirked.

"I have a proposition for you, wife," Jorrin said, trying to sound serious.

She looked curious, but said nothing.

"What are you doing for, oh, let's say the next several months?"

Cera cocked her head to one side and shrugged. "Training archers?"

Jorrin beamed.

Tristan and Leargan laughed out loud.

"I suspect that could be arranged," he said casually.

She threw herself into his arms.

He caught her up, half-expecting ribald remarks from his men. All of whom suddenly forgot that they were supposed to be training, having been paired off by Leargan's Second-in-command, Niall—to duel with swords and spears.

However, even Niall was looking in the direction of the Lady of Greenwald, no doubt wondering what she was doing on the training grounds.

Jorrin had confidence she could hold her own, but was worried about what they'd think of a woman training them. Most of the men-at-arms were locals with poor backgrounds. They'd come to Castle Ryhan for a steady job, as well a place to live. Not many of them would be used to seeing a woman do anything other than marrying and bearing children, especially a noblewoman.

He'd have no problems correcting any assumptions with challenges if necessary, though hopefully it wouldn't come to that. As soon as Cera fired off a few arrows, they'd see she was for real. Either way, she'd shatter their images of a highborn lady.

"Leargan, please have the first group of archers line up. I want to inspect their equipment," she ordered from the comfort of Jorrin's arms.

"Aye, my lady." The captain bowed and took his leave to organize the men.

Tristan was not far behind, stating he was going to further classify the men, separating those who claimed knowledge of the bow.

"Promise you won't change your mind?" Cera whispered.

"Why would I do that, love?" Jorrin looked into her gray eyes.

Uncertainty seeped into his magic from her. *Why is she playing shy?* He squeezed her against his chest, dropping a kiss on her mouth.

"I have a secret, but I won't tell you until you promise I can still teach the men. It won't interfere."

"A secret?" He quirked an eyebrow.

"Promise, Jorrin," Cera half-pleaded, half-commanded.

"Oh, all right, I promise, but I have a feeling I won't like it." Jorrin grimaced.

Should I brace myself?

"I'll train the men for a few months . . . then I'll be busy with something—someone—soon after." She blushed.

His heart went from canter to gallop. "What—who—will be keeping you busy, love?"

Cera smiled. It was slow and tender, and he couldn't help but return it. "Us . . . keeping *us* busy." Her voice was soft. "Our baby, Jorrin. We're going to have a baby."

He lifted her high and swung her around.

She laughed, hugging him tight.

Jorrin covered her mouth with his, forgetting their audience. He heard the laughter of his men and pulled away, but had to swallow against the sudden lump in his throat.

He was going to be a father. Cera was giving him a child.

"Are you happy?" she whispered, her voice shaky.

"More than happy. A baby, love? *A baby.* When?" Jorrin smiled at the wonder in her expression. No doubt, his own mirrored it. "I love you."

"I love you, too. About seven months, I'd guess."

Seven months? That likely meant—the ruins. Cera's first time.

"But this does change things, love."

She wiggled out of his arms and glared, hands on her hips. "No. You *promised*, Jorrin Aldern."

Trikser wuffed, as if he was speaking up for his mistress, but neither paid him any notice.

"But, love . . ."

She shook her head, grinned, and grabbed her bow and quiver. Cera jogged away, her wolf on her heels.

"Ceralda Aldern, come back here!"

She beamed over her shoulder and started to inspect the first archer's bow, ignoring his bellow.

Jorrin growled.

"Looks like you're on the losing end, today," Tristan said, his tone far too amused for Jorrin's liking as the lord appeared at his side.

"She tricked me into promising she can train them before telling me some news."

"She and the baby are very healthy, Jorrin."

"You knew? Before I was told?" He scowled at his friend.

"Only because she came to me as a patient. I *am* still a healer." Tristan's expression was apologetic.

"I suppose I have to forgive you, then, but not her . . . for tricking me." He gestured to his errant wife, trying to glare.

But as he watched her start the lesson, he had to admit Cera was her element, her glorious red hair dancing in the wind as she took aim.

Her arrow hit dead center.

The men gasped.

The rest of the guard stopped to watch.

Pride washed over Jorrin.

"I'll watch over them, I promise," Tristan said.

He nodded, meeting the younger man's warm hazel gaze. He trusted the healer completely. "At the first sign . . ."

"Aye, at the first sign." His friend's agreement was firm.

"I'm going to be a father," Jorrin whispered.

"You'd gathered that, did you?" Tristan chuckled.

He shot him a mock-glare, then grinned so wide his face hurt. "Let's hope the Blessed Spirit doesn't let him be as stubborn as his mother."

"Oh, aye, because his father isn't stubborn at all." The healer wore an unabashed grin.

Jorrin ignored him, thinking of a little boy with dark red curls, big gray eyes, tapered ears . . . and perhaps . . . a little magic.

THE END

About the Author

USA Today Bestselling, award winning author of romantic suspense, epic and historical fantasy romance, C.A. loves to dabble in different genres. If it's a good story, she'll write it, no matter where it seems to fit!

She's a hopeless romantic and always will be. Risking it all for Happily Ever After is what she lives by!

C.A. is originally from Ohio but got to Texas as soon as she could. She's happily married and has a bachelor's degree in criminal justice.

She's always writing, and helps small business owners by writing their websites, and she loves it!

WEBSITE: http://www.caszarek.com
EBOOK STORE: https://www.caszarek.com/ebook-store
PAPERBACK STORE: https://www.caszarek.com/paperback-store
AMAZON AUTHOR PAGE: https://www.amazon.com/stores/C.A.Szarek/author/B00BJY74BY
FACEBOOK: http://www.facebook.com/caszarek
INSTAGRAM: https://www.instagram.com/caszarek/
X: https://twitter.com/caszarek
BOOKBUB: https://www.bookbub.com/profile/c-a-szarek
GOODREADS: https://www.goodreads.com/author/show/5815085.C_A_Szarek
EMAIL: ca@caszarek.com

You can sign up for C.A.'s newsletter on her website, as well as buy all her books!

Milton Keynes UK
Ingram Content Group UK Ltd.
UKHW051931061124
450855UK00006B/48